SANDCASTLE
IN THE WIND

Kevin McGann

SANDCASTLE

IN THE WIND

Hometown Publishers

Hometown Publishers
www.hometownpublishers.com

First Published by Hometown Publishers September 2020.

ISBN: 978-1-7770337-8-1 (Paperback)
ISBN: 978-1-7770337-9-8 (E-book)

Library and Archives Canada (LAC) national library collection.

Cover Design by Kevin McGann.

Dedication

To Mathew, Jessica,

Daphne, and Brendan

To my parents,

Maria and Charles

Acknowledgements

All the wonderful people and establishments

in Madeira Beach, Treasure Island,

St. Pete Beach, and Clearwater,

Florida, USA.

Chapter 1

Brieanne knew she had lost him forever and the only person she could blame was herself. He was never coming back, and deep down she couldn't blame him; it was all her fault. The facts of what had happened, she would have to live with for the rest of her sad and lonely life, and the reasons why, would haunt her forever. It had been seven days since he had walked out of her life, and to this very second, sitting alone, waiting, her hope was quickly fading.

Since she could remember she loved coming down to the beach, almost every day around the same time, never once believing it could get any better than the day before. Until she met him, Aidan, how happy he made her feel; she had never smiled and laughed so much in her life. And how handsome, strong, gentle, and kind he was, her list could go on and on, if it wasn't for the pain of her heart slowly breaking apart, piece by piece; and the tormenting reality that he was the only person who could ever put it back together. Even the wine she sipped couldn't numb the aching she felt deep in her chest; instead, it only allowed tears of hopelessness, despair, and regret to fill her eyes, and slowly roll down her lonely face. Suddenly, the laughter of a young family sitting close by disrupted her harrowing thoughts. A most welcome distraction she hoped, as she listened to them talk about their sandcastle.

"This is Mom and Dad's room here," said the young girl, "and mine is right down the hall from them with my own bathroom."

"My room is over here," said the boy, "right next to the drawbridge so I can keep guard."

"This can be our family room," said the father pointing to it.

"And this is our dining room," added the mother, "and here, the kitchen."

Brieanne observed the family placing colorful seashells around its perimeter and couldn't help but notice the big smiles on the young girl and boy's faces; how happy they were. She thought about Jen and Ben in Jacksonville, and wondered if they were also happy and smiling, deep down she hoped so, and needed to believe they were.

All this was too much for her heart to take; she broke down letting the tears stream down her face as she whispered over and over again, "What have I done? What have I done?" But she found no comfort in asking that question, because she knew exactly what she had done, and had very little hope of being able to redeem herself.

Brieanne watched as the family eventually left their solitary sandcastle to the fate of the wind, and sadly looked beyond it to the sun slowly setting in the distance. And she knew, just as sure as the sun would set this evening, Aidan was never coming back to her.

Chapter 2

Seven Weeks Earlier: Wednesday, June 24

Aidan looked to his right and read the sign, 'Vegas Francisco's.'

"This is the best breakfast in town, in fact, the best restaurant in town," confirmed Larry with an English accent as he handed him his luggage, "make sure you tell Brie I said hello."

"Will do," replied Aidan as he watched the taximan jump in his car and drive away. He picked up his bags, headed for the entrance, and struggled through the first door.

"Here, let me help," said a female voice holding the second door open. "Leaving or just arriving?" she asked closing it behind him.

"Arriving," confirmed Aidan as he placed his two bags down and looked up at the voice. She was an attractive woman, with a cute smile, beautiful hazel eyes, and light brown hair pulled back in a ponytail.

"You can put those over there if you like," she suggested pointing to a spot in the corner. "They will be safe."

"Thank you," replied Aidan placing them in the vacant spot before returning.

"It's almost eleven, our patio is about to open if you want to sit outside," she said looking up at him from the seating chart. "Or maybe inside, with air conditioning?" she suggested, noticing the beads of sweat on his forehead.

Aidan noticed her looking above his eyes, wiped the sweat off with his sleeve, and confirmed, "inside is fine."

"I'm sorry, I didn't mean to—"

"It's okay, it's hot out there, and I'm not dressed for this weather yet," he confessed, as they both looked down at his long-sleeved shirt and jeans. "I could definitely use some cool air," he said reassuringly.

She grinned nervously at his thoughtful response. "Well, how about I give you a table not only close to the AC but with a great view," she said grabbing a menu.

"That would be nice," he replied. "Thank you."

"Please, follow me."

He watched her cute bum swaying in front of him under a short skirt.

"Lugging around those bags probably didn't help either?" she asked turning her head towards him, catching him off guard.

"Definitely not," he replied quickly diverting his eyes to hers.

Was he just checking me out? She wasn't a hundred percent sure, but it seemed that way. "Here is your table," she said pleasantly, as she watched him sit. "As promised, you not only have a beautiful view of the Gulf of Mexico," she confirmed looking out the window. "But your very own cool breeze," she said lifting her hand towards the AC vent residing high above the table. "Here's a menu, and your server Cathy with be with you shortly. Welcome to Vegas Francisco's, enjoy."

"Thank you," replied Aidan as he watched her walk away, before looking around the restaurant. He noticed the rows of tables in front and behind him, curved around the restaurant, and were the closest to the windows. To his right, and slightly up a level, were more rows of tables that also curved around the restaurant, then another level, then another. On the last level was the bar area. Looking back to his left, he realized the windows were floor to ceiling, giving everyone a hundred-and-eighty-degree view of the Gulf; it was a remarkable amphitheater design. Its overall décor was modern and elegant, yet with a friendly, cozy ambiance, and family-type atmosphere. He thought the place was magnificent.

Aidan looked outside and watched the children playing in the clear blue water, spotted adults lying on the white sandy beach, and groups of teenagers playing volleyball. Just below him, the staff were finishing putting up umbrellas on the large patio as a small group of women from the beach walked through the gate and were seated. As he watched one of the ladies speaking to the other, he realized she must have been talking about the restaurant because she pointed up in his direction. The woman who was listening glanced up to where her friend was pointing. Her face reminded Aidan of someone he knew back home, and he started wondering if he had done the right thing by abruptly leaving to come here without telling her why.

"Who is that?" asked Cathy arriving at the server station.

"I don't know, he just arrived from out of town," explained Brie looking over her shoulder, then back at Cathy. "But he has a lovely smile."

"He has a lot more than that," she stated. "If I wasn't a married woman I—"

"Well, you are," replied Brie tilting her head and giving her a quick smile.

"Excuse me," replied Cathy, backing off with her hands up. "I see he's caught your attention."

"Not at all," said Brie blushing and quickly changing the conversation. "Well, he needs your attention now, he's in your section."

"No, you should serve him," said Cathy animatedly, "get some small talk going."

"And what happens when he finds out I'm not a server?" she asked. "Then he will know I did it just to meet him."

"How is he going to find out?" queried Cathy. "Anyway, what if he does, he may find that cute."

"He may, but I would die from embarrassment," she confessed, although deep down, part of her wanted to. "Now get over there," she said pushing Cathy in his direction.

As Cathy walked to the table, she noticed he was looking outside. "Hello, my name is Cathy, I will be your server today."

Aidan was deep in thought. "Oh, I'm sorry," he replied looking up at her, "nice to meet you, Cathy."

"Beautiful view," she acknowledged. "I noticed you admiring it."

"It is," he replied, "must be nice coming to work and having this view?"

"Without a doubt, it's definitely one of the perks. It makes my day more enjoyable and the patrons happier."

"I can agree with you there."

Cathy noticed she was staring at him and looked down at the table. "Did you have a chance to look over the menu?"

"I haven't," he confessed opening it up. "Can you give me a few more minutes?"

"No problem, take your time," she replied. "Just to let you know we have several wonderful breakfast items available till two," she said pointing them out. "Appetizers are here, lunch items here, and the ones with the small umbrellas next to them, they are our most popular patio items."

"Thank you," he said surveying the wide selection.

"In the meantime, can I get you something to drink?"

"Coffee, please."

"Okay, I'll be right back."

Cathy walked over to the coffee pot, was pouring, when Brie, who was trying to look busy by wiping a clean counter, joined her. "What do you think?"

"He is absolutely gorgeous. Well-spoken, polite, and his voice makes me melt, and…no ring," said Cathy looking up at her friend's sheepish face. "You already looked?"

"Maybe," replied Brie, and as if being forced to admit something because of her friend's long stare, broke down. "Okay, I did! I looked!"

They both started to giggle.

Aidan heard them laughing, glanced over, smiled to himself then went back to the menu.

Cathy gave him his coffee and took his order. Aidan ate in silence, periodically looking outside at the beach, the busy patio, and the people filling the tables inside. When he finished, he paid his bill, and headed to the exit where he was met by Brie.

"How was your meal?" she asked.

"It was amazing. I had the eggs Benedict, and the hollandaise sauce was done to perfection, compliments to the chef."

"Thank you, I will pass it on to him," she said pleasantly.

"Oh, I almost forgot. Can you let a girl named Brie know that Larry the Taximan says hello? He's the one that recommended this place to me."

"You already have."

Aidan looked confused.

"That's me, I'm Brie."

"Oh," replied Aidan catching on.

"My friends call me Brie, but my name is Brieanne," she explained.

"Nice to meet you Brieanne, I'm Aidan."

"Likewise, Aidan," she said shaking his outreached hand. "Larry is always sending people are way, and eats here regularly, so dessert is always on us. Which, by the way, are also amazing."

"I will have to come back and try one."

"You should," she replied, "and I look forward to it." Oh no, did I just say that?

"Me too," he replied walking over to his luggage. Before picking them up, he stopped and looked over at her. "Larry said it was a twenty-minute walk to where I'm going. At the time I was thinking it was a good idea, but with this heat, these bags, I'm guessing probably not. He mentioned something about taking the Suncoast Beach Trolley that stops across the street from where I'm going. Where can I board that?"

"Where are you going?"

"Gulf Shore Condominiums."

"I can give you a lift, if you want to hold on for a few minutes?"

"I couldn't put you out like that," he said reaching down for his bags. "I will be fine taking the trolley."

"No, you're not putting me out at all, I have a meeting at one, and have to pass by there on the way," she explained. "Plus, I can point out some of the local attractions along the way," she said enthusiastically, "you won't get that on the trolley!"

"Okay," said Aidan shyly. "Thank you."

"I will be back in a couple of minutes I just need to pick up something from the office," she said walking backward, before turning, and going inside. She picked up her folder, her bag, and was about to leave when Cathy came in.

"So?" asked Cathy.

Brie pulled her away from the door. "I'm dropping him off," she said excitedly. "He is staying down the road from me at the Gulf Shore Condos."

"You, Ms. Cautious, offered him a ride?" said Cathy, a little surprised.

"Oh, you think I shouldn't have?" Brie asked, second-guessing herself.

"Of course, you should have!" said Cathy. "It's time you put yourself out there and take a risk; it's been way too long."

"I know," said Brie smiling. "How do I look?"

"As beautiful as ever," said Cathy happy for her best friend.

Brie walked out of the office, motioned one minute to Aidan, then went to tell the staff she was off to her appointment and would see them tomorrow.

Chapter 3

Aidan followed Brieanne to her Jeep and threw his bags in the back. "Do you like working in Madeira Beach?" asked Aidan as he closed the door.

"Actually, the restaurant is in Treasure Island, but I live in Madeira Beach."

"This is Treasure Island?"

"Yeah," she confirmed as she turned north onto Gulf Boulevard. "Up ahead is John's Pass once we cross the bridge, we are in Madeira Beach, or as the locals call it Mad Beach. Up to that point it's Treasure Island."

"Mad Beach," repeated Aidan curiously.

Brieanne pointed. "To your right is Gators Café & Saloon, an extremely popular place, especially on the weekends. It has lots of bars, four stages, live music, and patios on the waterfront. It even has a place you can dock your boat."

"Sounds like a lot of fun."

"It is," she confirmed, driving onto the bridge, and pointing to her right again. "Down there is the marina. You can rent boats, jet skis, kayaks, paddleboats, book a fishing charter, a sunset cruise, a dolphin cruise, or a pirate ship that sails around Boca Ciega Bay, you can even go parasailing in the Gulf," she explained as they crossed over the bridge. "Behind the boats you have over a hundred shops, restaurants, bars, and attractions. Far too many to describe or name. It's a wonderful place to walk around if you want to shop, eat, drink, and listen to live music…Down here at the very end is the Bamboo Beach Bar & Grill which has a tiki-style patio and live music, popular with locals and tourists." She placed her hand back on the wheel. "That whole area is called John's Pass Village and Boardwalk."

"Sounds like it has a lot of everything," stated Aidan impressed.

"It does, and it's a very popular place," she replied, happy with her descriptions. "Over here on the left is where I live. You can just see it through the parking lot. It's the teal house with the black roof," she said pointing toward it.

"Oh, yeah!" he said, spotting it. "Close to work."

"It is," she replied. "You're just down her on the left, even closer than my work," she blurted out before she could stop herself.

"I least I will know one person in the neighborhood," he said cheerfully.

Brieanne looked over and gave him an agreeable smile. She turned left, crossed over Gulf Lane, and drove towards the security gate. "Are you staying here on your own?"

"No, my parents, aunt, and uncle are here," he answered. "My aunt and uncle recently bought a unit and moved in a few months ago. My parents have been down here for several weeks visiting and they're trying to persuade my parents to buy one, too. They've been best friends since they were teenagers and are all retired now," he explained. "Me calling them, and showing up, is a last-minute thing."

"I'm sure they will be thrilled."

"I'm sure they will," he replied. "They've been asking me all spring to come visit them this summer. I told them I didn't have the time, but things happened, and now I do."

She wondered what he meant by that as she pulled up to the gate.

"Hey, Brie, what brings you in here?" asked the old security guard.

"Hi, Stan, just picked up this stray along the road. Said he was heading this way, thought I would show him some Madeira Beach hospitality, and drop him off," she joked.

Stan lowered his head to look in at Aidan. "Lucky you, to be picked up by such a beautiful woman."

"Can't argue with you there Stan."

Brieanne blushed at his response.

"This young lady is a fine catch," said Stan. "You wouldn't want to throw her back into the pond, no, sir, not our Brie."

"No, you wouldn't," replied Aidan politely.

Stan gave Brie a quick grin then went back into guard mode. "What's your name son and who are you staying with?"

"Aidan, staying with the Ritchie's, condo number 1604."

Stan looked down at his list. "Here you are! Ritchie's, new tenants, lovely couple," he said passing him a clipboard. "Now, if you can just sign your name here."

Aidan did and returned it.

Stan went inside and came back out and handed him two cards. "This one is for the condo and the other is to access the building and the grounds. Keep them on you at all times, otherwise you will be locked out."

"Will do."

"The day you depart, leave them with Bill and Amy, they will know what to do with them," he concluded. "Enjoy your stay."

"Thank you."

Stan went back inside, pressed a button, and then came outside as the barrier went up. "Nice to see you again, Brie. The wife and I will be in early Friday evening for the special dinner, say around five; I will call and make the reservation tonight."

"No need to, I'll put your names down for five, and save you your favorite table," she replied with a smile.

"Thanks, Brie," replied Stan waving, as she slowly drove away.

"Do you know a lot of people around here?" asked Aidan.

"I do. It's a small area, and most of the locals have been here all their lives, so you get to know them," she explained. "Stan and his wife were both born and raised here."

"Is she a catch?" he kidded.

Brieanne burst out laughing and gently touched his arm. "That's funny," she said looking over at him. "Many of the locals are fisherman so they tend to use a lot of fishing phrases from time to time."

"So, I better get used to it?"

"I'm afraid so," she said, slowly stopping. "Here you are."

"Thanks for the ride."

"You're welcome," she said watching him get out the Jeep, take his bags and place them on the sidewalk before walking over to her door.

"Maybe I will bump into you at the local bar, buy you a drink for the lift?"

"I would like that," she replied, "I'm usually around." You idiot why did you say that! Give him your number, a place, a time, a day, something, but it was too late.

"Well, I will see you around then."

"Okay," Brieanne replied as enthusiastically as possible. She watched him pick up his bags, go inside, and was waiting for something, anything, and then it happened. Aidan turned around, smiled, and waved goodbye. Brieanne did the same and felt all wasn't a loss. She said goodbye to Stan, went north on Gulf Boulevard, and arrived at the real estate office ten minutes later.

"Brie, how are you doing?" asked Joyce.

"I'm doing well."

"Come inside, have a seat. Do you want a coffee, tea, water?"

"No, I'm fine, thanks."

"I won't keep you long," said Joyce sitting. "As you know your payment went through, the paperwork is done, and they vacated the house yesterday. I went by and they've left it immaculate. I believe you letting them close a couple of days after the end of the children's school year probably had something to with that."

"They were such a nice couple and had lovely children; it was least I could do."

"Some people aren't so understanding," contested Joyce, "they would have wanted them out a month early to get the property ready for summer renters. Speaking of which, did you decide what you wanted to do with the place yet?"

"I think I'm going to take my time over the summer fixing it up. Painting, decorating, furnishing the rooms, working on the garden, that sort of thing. It's not a big place, so it's something I can work at on my own, and at my own pace," she explained. "Hopefully rent it out in September."

"That's your mother in you," noted Joyce, "she loved doing that sort of thing. How are they doing?"

"Both doing well," she confirmed, "and enjoying retirement."

"Let them know I was asking of them."

"I will."

Joyce put the papers into a folder and picked up the house keys. "I will get in touch with you at the beginning of August to see how you're making out with the new place, and we can talk about September some more then," explained Joyce standing, walking around the table, and handing her the keys. "Congratulations!"

"Thank you, Joyce," replied Brie standing and giving her a hug, "for everything."

"My pleasure dear," responded Joyce with a squeeze.

Aidan pressed the elevator button turned around and watched Brieanne drive away. He wished he had asked for her number, but he didn't want to seem too pushy, especially after accepting a ride from her. He got off on the sixteenth floor, walked down to the corner suite, and knocked on the door.

"Aidan! It's Aidan!" he shouted over his shoulder. "Come in!"

"Thanks, Uncle Bill," said Aidan putting down his bags, before giving him a hug, then his aunt Amy, and parents.

"We weren't expecting you for another hour," stated his dad.

"I was bumped up to an early flight and arrived here a few hours ago."

"What have you been doing since then?" queried his mom.

"I knew you guys were out till twelve, and since I didn't have time to eat at the airport, I went for breakfast at a restaurant down the road."

"You timed it perfectly, we just got back twenty minutes ago," said his mom. "Did you take a cab from the restaurant?"

"No, one of the employees is a local and had a meeting north of here; she dropped me off on the way."

"You see Paul, that's the kind of people you get around here," said Bill looking at Aidan's dad, "kind, friendly, and hospitable."

But his mom and Aunt Amy had picked up on something more important, the word 'she' had sparked their attention. "What is she like?" asked his mom.

"Tell us, is she pretty?" insisted Amy.

"Like Uncle Bill said, she was kind, friendly, hospitable" he teased, to their disapproving looks, "and yes, very pretty."

Which made the women glance at one another and smile, they were about to interrogate him further.

"Now, let the boy get settled in, you can ask him all the questions you want later," said Bill grabbing a bag and saving Aidan for now. "Come on let me show you to your room."

Aidan picked up the other, then followed his uncle down the hallway to a large bedroom on the right and placed it next to the one on the floor.

"You have a great view of the Gulf and beach from here," he said pulling aside the blinds.

"Wow! This is incredible!"

"You have satellite TV with all the channels. The dressers and closet are empty. Across the hall is a full bathroom, that's all yours. Our room and your parents both have an en suite, so we don't need to use it," he clarified then looked at him momentarily. "I'm so happy you are here…we all are. This is such a wonderful surprise."

"I'm sorry about me showing up last minute, I—"

"Hey, don't say another word, you are welcome here anytime. Family never needs an invitation," said Bill comfortingly. "You relax, enjoy yourself, and your summer."

"Thanks, Uncle Bill," replied Aidan feeling a lot less awkward.

"Why don't you unpack your stuff while we have some lunch?" suggested Bill. "Afterwards, we are heading outside to the pool. Are you up for a swim or do you want to take a nap?"

"A swim sounds great."

Chapter 4

"Mr. Ritchie, just to reconfirm, that's for tonight, Friday, at six?" asked Jess waiting for his response. "Thank you, we look forward to seeing you then, bye."

Brie darted over to her. "Did you say Ritchie?"

"Yes," she replied. "We are now booked solid for dinner inside, and outside on the patio, waiting list only," she replied proudly.

"Jess, you said Ritchie!" stated Brie in a panic looking over the guest list.

"Yes, I did," replied Jess thinking that she had done something terribly wrong. "Did I mess something up?" she asked nervously.

Brie realized her reaction had frightened Jess a little and looked up at her with a smile. "Of course not, you are doing a wonderful job, I'm a little excited. The Ritchie's are…" she said searching for the right words, "friends of mine, and it caught me off guard when you said their name. It will be good to see them again."

"Phew!" said Jesse relieved.

"Let's have a look at their reservation," said Brie. "How many are in the party?" Please be five, please be five, she thought.

"Five," replied Jess.

"Awesome!" expressed Brie with a big grin. "Let's see, where are you putting them?"

"They wanted to sit on the patio, which worked out well because that was our last table, which is table two," she confidently.

Although Brie knew all the tables had a wonderful view, some were better than others. "Table nine, was that requested by that party?" she asked. She could tell by the reservation it hadn't been.

"No, Brie they didn't, I marked it as such with a green tick. The red ticks are table requests."

"Yes, of course. What would I do without you?" she said complimenting her with a smile.

Jess blushed and smiled back.

"Here is what we will do," suggested Brie, "move the Ritchie's to table nine, and Brown's to table two."

Jess made the changes, placing a red tick next to the Ritchie's, then looked up at Brie. "They must be really good friends," stated Jess, feeling more relaxed now, "that's our best patio table."

"They are Jess," replied Brie, "and thank you for helping me out."

The phone rang and Jess picked it up while Brie went over to the server station and waited for Cathy to return.

"What's up with you?" asked Cathy noticing a big smile on her face.

"Aidan is coming in at six with his family for dinner, tonight, on the patio," she whispered excitedly.

"He is!" she said in a low voice. "What are you going to do?"

"I'm going to leave now, do some errands, get ready, and be back by five," she explained. "Are you here for the dinner rush?"

"Yeah, till eight," she confirmed. "Go, everything will be fine!"

Brie quickly grabbed the other servers then pulled the bartender over. "I'm leaving now but I will be back at five to host our Special Friday Night Dinner Event this evening."

You could have heard a pin drop.

Brie looked at their surprised faces. "Don't worry, Bev with still be the manager in charge, so any issues or questions you have go to her," she informed them. "I will only be hosting the event and doing PR with the customers."

Brie watched as the staff dispersed to their duties except Cathy who she held back. "What was that about?"

"Everyone is just surprised you are coming back; you always let Bev host the special evenings, that's all," Cathy rationalized. "Just make sure you are not too obvious tonight with you know who."

"Don't worry I won't be," she replied. "There are a lot of locals coming in this evening which is perfect. I will play it cool, calm, and collective."

Brie returned at five wearing a pretty knee-high blue floral summer dress, which was tasteful, yet appropriate, and fit her perfectly. Her hair was curled past her shoulders, makeup was light, and lips subtle with a soft shade of creamy lipstick.

"Brie, is that you?" asked Bev walking toward the entrance in amazement. "You look stunning!"

"Thank you," she replied nervously.

"You are absolutely glowing," continued Bev. "I heard you were coming back to do some schmoozing with the customers, which by the way, I think is a great idea."

"It's been a while," she revealed, "I thought why not."

"With this glow about you, you should do it more often," said Bev still admiring her. "Listen, I should get back to work. There are a few regulars already seated inside and out, I'm sure they will be so happy to see you, I know I am," she said, hugging her cousin before leaving.

A hand grabbed hers from behind pulling her into the staff office. "Brie, you look absolutely perfect," said Cathy dumfounded, "I hardly recognized you."

"Oh, thanks a lot," Brie replied lightheartedly.

Cathy laughed. "You know what I mean," she said. "You look gorgeous wearing shorts, tank top, and a baseball cap, but looking at you now, I realize you have been hiding yourself away for far too long."

"You don't think it's a little much?"

"No, not at all! The dress is beautiful. It's summery. It screams sophistication, elegance, sexy, and fun. It's perfect!" she said favorably.

"Thank you."

"Are you nervous?" she whispered.

"Butterflies," she revealed.

"Just be yourself and you will do fine. No, you will do better than fine," said Cathy boosting Brie's confidence.

"I'll try," confirmed Brie exhaling. "I guess I should get out there and mingle with the customers."

"Come to my section first, inside table number four, it's Stan and Mildred. They will be a perfect warm up for you."

"Good idea," Brie admitted, "I'll follow you."

"Look who came to give us a visit this evening," said Cathy to the seated couple.

"My, my, don't you look like a breath of fresh air?" praised Mildred.

"She most certainly does," agreed Stan. "Come have a seat with us and tell us what you've been up to."

Brie sat and talked with them for twenty minutes before moving on to chat with another older, local couple.

"We're a little early," Bill said apologetically, after giving his name.

"That's not a problem," replied Jess. "Would you like to have a drink at the bar while we finish setting up your table?"

"That will suit us just fine young lady," he replied, "lead the way."

They followed Jess to the bar where they sat around a cocktail table and ordered drinks. Cathy came out of the kitchen and noticed Aidan immediately. After dropping off the food she realized Brie hadn't spotted him yet and desperately tried to get her attention. Finally doing so, Brie followed Cathy's stare towards Aidan, then smiled happily back at her friend.

Fifteen minutes later Jess came to the bar and led the party down the stairs to a doorway near the front entrance. They followed her through the doors, down several steps, and outside onto the covered patio where they were seated on formal dining chairs around a table covered in white linen, which had a colorful, floral center piece, elegant crystal glasses, and shining silverware. The canopy's top shaded them from the hot sun, but the front and sides had been left open, revealing a spectacular view of the Gulf of Mexico, and allowing a light breeze to pass through at will. It was enchanting.

Jess came back, dropped off their drinks, and informed them that their server Kelly would be with them momentarily. While they waited the group talked about the restaurant and the view.

"Good evening, and welcome to Vegas Francisco's," said a soft, siren voice. "How are you all doing?"

Aidan recognized the voice immediately, "Brieanne," he said warmly as he turned around.

"Aidan, what a lovely surprise seeing you here again," she said, trying to sound professional and surprised, but deep down happy to see him. "How are you enjoying your stay at Madeira Beach?"

"I'm enjoying it immensely, thank you," he replied, and you look absolutely gorgeous, he thought.

"I'm glad to hear it."

"You two know each other?" asked his mom, as the two puzzled couples looked back and forth at them.

"This is the girl that dropped me off at the condo on Wednesday," he explained. "The one you grilled me about all afternoon at the pool."

Brieanne was pleased to hear that Aidan had spoken of her.

"This is the girl you called kind, friendly, hospitable?" queried Bill.

"And very pretty," finished his dad.

Brieanne was trying not to blush.

"That was definitely an understatement," said Amy.

"Most definitely," said his mom in agreement.

"Thank you, you are very kind," she said looking at each of them. "In Aidan's defense, I was a lot more casual on Wednesday than this evening," she said unpretentiously.

"Modest, too," stated his mom approvingly.

"Around here, she is quite the catch," said Aidan so matter-of-fact that it caught Brieanne totally off-guard and made her laugh out loud.

"Aidan!" said his mother disapprovingly.

"It's okay," said Brieanne containing her laughter, "it's an inside joke between us."

Woman's intuition made Theresa and Amy quickly glance over at one another, while Paul and Bill were too spellbound by Brieanne to notice what their partners were conjecturing.

"Well, my name is Brieanne," she announced.

"I apologize," declared Aidan standing up. "This is my mother, Theresa, her best friend Amy, my father, Paul and his best friend Bill."

To which they each replied hello and shook her hand.

"Just to let you know, I am doing PR for the restaurant tonight. So, I'm going from table to table welcoming new and local patrons to the restaurant, introducing myself if need be, and eliciting their feedback on the ambiance, atmosphere, food, and overall experience of their evening…as well as catching up with some old friends."

"Well, the table setting is impeccable, the view is breathtaking, and that breeze is lovely," said Theresa.

"It's absolutely beautiful," added Amy.

"Thank you, I'm glad to hear it," replied Brieanne. "Wait till you try the cuisine?"

"I'm sure we won't be disappointed," said Bill looking forward to it.

"I'm sure you won't," said Brieanne with a smile. "I should go visit some of the tables inside. A few of the customers arrived earlier and I would like to meet them before they depart," she explained. "It was nice meeting you all, enjoy your evening."

"Thank you," they replied.

As she walked away, she wondered if it would have been better to hang around until they offered her a seat, but realized she would have had to excuse herself shortly after to meet the earlier arrivals before they left. Besides, they still had to eat, which gave her a reason to go back to their table later. As she started to ascend the stairs deep in thought a voice called her name, it was Aidan's, and her face lit up. "Aidan," she said pleasantly.

"After you finish meeting people, my family and I were wondering if you would like to join us for a drink at our table?" he said hoping she would. "Unless you have other plans?"

"I don't," she said openly. "How about I save your table for last? We can have a drink while you and your family can tell me about the food and your experience here tonight." Oh no, did I just say that it sounded more work-oriented rather than wanting to have a drink with him and socialize. Then she remembered, don't look too obvious, one step at a time.

"Great, we will see you later."

She watched him walk back to his seat then hurried up the stairs to tell Cathy.

"Tonight, we have four specials to choose from: Mahi-mahi seared in lemon and garlic; filet mignon with grilled shrimp; prime rib au jus; and chicken fettuccine Alfredo. As well as the starters and entrées on the menu," explained Kelly.

After they finished their meal and dessert, the canopy cover was pulled back allowing them to watch the warm sun set in the distance. When dusk finally crept in, the patio lights were turned on and soft music gently played, while the stars quietly appeared one by one.

"Is it okay if I join you?" asked Brieanne as they turned to face her.

"Of course," replied Aidan standing and pulling over an empty chair.

"Thank you," she said sitting. "So, how was your meal?" she asked looking around the table.

"It was absolutely perfect," complimented Amy, "I had the chicken fettuccine Alfredo, the sauce was divine, chicken juicy; it was delicious."

"I'm glad you enjoyed it. Our Alfredo sauce is made from scratch," explained Brieanne looking at Amy, "and it's important to us that it has perfect texture and taste." She then turned her attention to Theresa.

"I had the Mahi-mahi on a bed of rice," she revealed, "it was so tender it melted in my mouth, and the flavor was out of this world; truly, a culinary delight."

"Our catch of the day is one of our most popular specials, so we take them very seriously here. Plus, we have a lot of locals who know how to cook fish at home, so we have to impress the toughest of our critics," she joked. "Let me guess," she said looking at Paul and Bill, "prime rib."

"She's good," said Paul looking over at Bill who nodded his head approvingly, then back at Brieanne. "I had medium-rare."

"Medium for me," responded Bill, "and it was cooked to perfection!"

"Mine too," added Paul, "soft, tender, and juicy."

"And I believe the perfect cut, one-and-a-half-inch thickness?" asked Bill looking over at Paul who nodded his agreement then back at Brieanne.

"I can see I am with a couple of prime rib connoisseurs here," she said playfully, "and you are right, while most place tend to give one-inch cuts we pride ourselves on the perfect cut."

"The perfect cut for the perfect meal," stated Paul.

"I like that," she said with a grin, "maybe we should use that in our marketing campaign?"

"Be my guest," replied Paul.

"Aidan," she said studying him. "I'm guessing you were the one having the most difficult time choosing, going back and forth, because they all sounded wonderful. You knew you wanted meat, but you also wanted seafood. So, you decided to have the best of both worlds and picked surf and turf," she suggested. "Filet mignon with grilled shrimp."

"That is him to a tee," verified Theresa, "he was going through that exact same discussion before he chose!"

Everyone broke into a laugh, except Aidan, who awkwardly grinned and went red-faced.

"What did you think?" asked Brieanne quickly, feeling she may have inadvertently embarrassed him.

Aidan thought momentarily. "The filet mignon was tender, juicy, flavorful, and cooked to perfection. The shrimp was plump, firm yet soft, and brushed with wonderful, succulent, garlic butter. It is one of the best meals I have ever had."

"Wow!" said Paul to Brieanne. "Trust me, coming from him that is quite the compliment."

"Thank you, Aidan," she said giving him a lovely smile.

"Excuse me, Brie," said Kelly from behind, holding a tray of drinks.

"Oh, I hope you don't mind?" said Brieanne apologetically, "Before I sat down, I bought us a round of drinks."

"No need to apologize when it comes to drinks," said Paul. "We were just about to order another round before you arrived."

Bill waited for Kelly to place the drinks on the table and leave before standing. "A toast to a delectable meal, Aidan for being here, and our beautiful, charming, guest Brieanne…Cheers!"

The rest stood, cheered, clinked glasses then sat. Paul and Bill talked about the stars, while Theresa and Amy spoke about nothing important, to give Aidan and Brieanne some space.

Brieanne seized the opportunity. "What have you been up to these last couple of days?" she whispered.

"After you dropped me off, I unpacked. Then we went to the pool for the afternoon. That evening we ate in, sat on the balcony, had a few drinks, and talked about Madeira Beach. Later we watched the sunset and the families walking up and down the shoreline. After they went to bed I stayed up, listened to the waves, and stargazed, it was incredible."

"That's what I love about Madeira Beach, in the day, you have the blue sky, white sand, and turquoise waters, and in the evening, you have the magnificent, awe-inspiring, sunset. Then at night, the waves, and the stars."

"Which one is your favorite?"

"Hmm, that's a tough one," she said with a nervous giggle. "They are all so different, unique, and wonderful."

"They are," he agreed.

"Although I say it's a tough one, I have to tell you honestly the decision is pretty easy for me, sunsets."

"Mine too."

"Really, why?" she asked happily.

"It's difficult to put in words," he confessed as he thought. "We can describe sunsets in many different ways but if I had to describe it with only one word it would be love."

"Love?" she asked, liking his response.

"As the sun sets, you see all the families and couples enjoying their time together, and it reminds me of love.

"I really like that," she said warmly. "Cheers to us both for picking sunsets."

"To sunsets," he replied, touching her glass, and taking a drink. "What have you been up to? How did your meeting go?"

"The meeting was with my real estate agent; it went really well. After that I did some grocery shopping then later that night I went for a walk on the beach."

"Maybe you were one of the people I saw?"

"Possibly, I walked by your condo around ten."

"Then I most definitely did," he said. "I remember seeing an alluring figure pass by around that time."

"Alluring," she said playfully. "You must have been the rowdy group I heard on the sixteenth floor?"

"Guilty," he replied, "I think we may end up getting tossed out of the condo."

"It will be all your fault, no doubt."

"Yep," he said nodding his head and taking a sip, "only two days there and I'm getting us all evicted."

She chuckled at his antics and realized it had been a while since someone had made her laugh.

"What did you do today?"

Today, she thought. "I came into the restaurant for a few hours, ran some errands, went home, and then back here for this evening."

"I was going to ask you—?"

"Okay, let's drink up, go listen to some live music, and do some dirty dancing," said Bill starting the party.

"I like the sound of that last bit," acknowledged his wife.

"Are you coming with us, dear?" asked Theresa looking over at Brieanne.

"Where are you going?"

"The Bamboo Beach Bar & Grill," Theresa replied.

"I wouldn't want to impose any more on your evening," she said, but really wanting to go.

"You're not imposing at all," reassured Amy.

Brieanne looked at the women then Aidan.

Aidan leaned over and whispered in her ear. "You would be saving me from my mom and Amy feeling sorry for me and dragging me up to dance."

"What happens if I ask you to dance?" she whispered mischievously.

"Well, if it's dirty dancing, baby! You got a partner!" he joked out loud.

Brieanne burst out laughing. "You are intolerable," she said squeezing his arm. She turned to Theresa and Amy who hadn't taken their eyes off them. "I would love to, thank you for asking," she said cheerfully and agreed to meet them outside before excusing herself.

"They invited me to the Bamboo," said Brie. "They are so nice."

"Especially, Aidan?" hinted Cathy.

"He is so wonderful," she cooed, "and dreamy."

"He is," admitted Cathy.

"I should get going, they're waiting for me outside. They were going to take a taxi, but I said I would drive them over." The look on Brie's face revealed there was more.

"What? What?" asked Cathy impatiently. "Spit it out!"

"I told Aidan I wanted to have a couple of drinks and didn't want to leave my car there," she said excitedly. "He is coming with me to drop it off at my place then walking me back."

"Then you better get going before they leave," said Cathy walking her quickly out of the office to the front doors.

Brie stopped. "Wait! What are you still doing here?"

Cathy gave her a 'Do you really have to ask that question?' look. "Did you think I was going to go home at eight and miss all this? This is better than anything on TV!"

Brie shook her head, smiled at her dear friend, gained her composure, and walked outside.

Chapter 5

"Here she comes," said Paul noticing her first.

"Sorry to keep you waiting," she said apologetically, "I had to get my bag and say bye. My car is over here."

Aidan and his dad sat in the front, while the other three jumped in the back.

"This is a lovely car," said Paul. "What is it?"

"It's a 2010 Cadillac DTS. It used to be my dad's."

"It's in mint condition," he stated.

"My father bought it new and only drove it locally," she explained. "It hardly has any miles on it."

"That would explain why, and it's a nice ride."

"I think so, too," replied Brieanne as she drove onto Gulf Boulevard, over the bridge, took a right onto 129th Avenue West, then a left onto Village Boulevard to the end, before pulling over. "The entrance is straight ahead on the right," she said as they got out of the car, "we will back in about ten minutes."

"Okay, we'll see you soon," acknowledged Paul before closing the door.

Aidan watched his family walk inside as Brieanne turned the car around and drove down Village Boulevard, then made a quick right onto 130th Avenue, another right onto Gulf Boulevard, before making a left onto 131st Avenue West, and another left onto Gulf Lane. She passed several houses before pulling into one of the driveways on the right and parked next to her Jeep.

"Wow! This is your place?" he asked as he walked around the front of the car to meet her. "Do you live her on your own?"

"Yeah, it's all mine," she replied timidly as he admired it. "I was thinking I should go change into something more casual?" she asked searching for a sign from him as to whether she should or not.

"No don't, I like what you're—" Aidan caught himself. "I mean you should if you want to be more comfortable."

She smiled at him. "Finish what you were going to say," she said in playful voice.

Aidan hesitated and thought about how to word it the right way. "I like what you are wearing, I think you look stunning, and I would like you to keep it on," he said hesitantly.

Yes, thought Brieanne. "Thank you, and for you, I will," she replied cheerfully. "We can cut through the parking lot across the street."

"You didn't drive your Jeep tonight?"

"The Jeep is good for running around in but not for when you are wearing a dress," she explained. "Plus, the Cadillac is roomier and more elegant."

"It did get six of us in there," he stated, "but I think you give the car most of its elegance."

Wow, did he just say that? She looked at him shyly then remembered something. "You never told me what you did today. Or did you actually get evicted?"

"No," said Aidan chuckling. "We spent the morning at the pool. Around lunchtime my dad and Uncle Bill went to get some beer and wine, while my mom and Aunt Amy went to get their nails done. I hung out at the beach. On their way back, my uncle Bill and dad were talking to Stan at the gate, he told them about this special dinner at a local restaurant tonight saying we should go. So, my uncle Bill called and booked it."

"Did they know you had been there?"

"I didn't know where we were going, all my uncle said, was that there was this restaurant having a special dinner tonight, and if we missed it, we would have to wait till September for the next one. It wasn't till he told the taxi driver our destination I realized where we were going and decided I would mention it to them when we sat down for dinner."

"Did you?"

"No, when we sat down you came over and said hello, so I didn't have to."

"Oops, sorry."

"Worked out better that way, if I would have told them prior, my mother and Aunt Amy would have been pestering me all night to point you out."

"And would you have?"

"I could have when we were sitting at the bar."

"You noticed, I mean, you saw me then?" she asked awkwardly.

"Actually, I noticed you as soon as I walked in," he said smiling at her.

Brieanne was beaming.

"What are these special dinner events all about?"

"Well, we have a special dinner every last Friday of the month, as well as special occasions throughout the year, like Thanksgiving," she elucidated, "But we don't have any in the summer, which is why Stan was saying the next one would be in September."

"I think it's a wonderful idea. I thoroughly enjoyed it."

"I'm happy you did," she said, pleased, "everyone seems to."

They arrived on Gulf Boulevard, went to the crosswalk, and sauntered over.

"The bar is right here," said Aidan surprised, "your place is close."

"I know, it's a perfect location," she admitted, as they walked toward the entrance, then she stopped. "You call Bill and Amy, aunt and uncle?" she asked curiously.

"They have known me since I was born so I call them aunt and uncle. Also, they have no family of their own so to me it lets them know they are part of ours."

"I understand," she said liking him more and more every minute. "That's really sweet."

They entered and looked around for Aidan's family. All the tables were full of people sitting and drinking under bamboo umbrellas.

Suddenly, Brieanne noticed Bill standing up waving his arm, and they walked in his direction. Brieanne and Aidan ordered beers from the server and joined in on the conversation as a guy with a guitar began to sing.

"That didn't take you very long," noted Teresa.

"I'm very close, I live two roads over," replied Brieanne, "Your condo is pretty close, too."

"Funny you mention that," said Amy. "We were saying that we can probably walk home from here tonight."

"Definitely," replied Brieanne.

A song played that the older couples liked and left to dance, leaving Brieanne and Aidan alone.

"What are you up to tomorrow?" he asked.

"No plans yet," she replied. "You?"

"Probably hang out at the beach," he said thinking out loud. "Tomorrow evening they're having a BBQ at the Shoreline Beach Bar, that's the condo's bar, its right next to the pool area. If you around you should come by?" he suggested, trying not to sound too forward.

"To the BBQ?"

"Yeah, or earlier."

"Maybe I will," she said, knowing it was a definite yes, but not wanting to come across too eager.

Aidan listened as Brieanne talked about John's Pass Village and the names of all the stores, restaurants, and bars it had. They talked about the songs the guy was playing and watched the couples dance. When the soloist finished his last song, he said goodnight, and was replaced by music playing from the surrounding speakers.

"Brieanne, I meant to ask you back at the restaurant about the desserts, specifically the pies, are they homemade?" asked Theresa.

"Yes, they are."

"I thought so," she replied looking for additional information.

"My mom and I made them," she revealed. "We only sell them at the restaurant."

"They were delightful," said Theresa with a snicker, "I'm not implying I had two. I ordered the apple, Amy had the cherry, and we tried one another's."

"They were divine," added Amy.

"Thank you," replied Brieanne.

"Does your mom live locally?" asked Theresa.

"No, my parents live in California, but she visits several times throughout the year and when she does, we make pies together. It's one of our favorite things to do."

"And then they bake them at the restaurant for the special evenings?" searched Amy.

"Yes, "every last Friday we have a dinner like tonight where we offer four specials, and for those nights only, homemade pies for dessert. Depending on the time of the year, it could be apple, cherry, blueberry, peach, pumpkin, and so on. As well as our regular desserts, which are also made from scratch," she explained. "Around here the special dinners have become somewhat of a tradition. We have a lot of locals and regulars come in, and it's a wonderful way to meet old friends, and make new ones. Although, as I explained to Aidan earlier, we don't do them in July or August because it's our busiest time of the year. So, the next one is September."

"I really think that it's wonderful that the restaurant does that," said Theresa with Amy nodding in agreement.

"I think so, too. It's good for the community, and people like yourself and Aidan, who are visiting," she said noticing he was quiet on the subject. "What kind of pie did you have?"

Aidan's face reddened. "I…eh…had the crème brûlée."

She giggled at his awkwardness. "That's okay," she said touching his arm, "that's one of my father's favorites and his very own secret recipe."

"He likes to bake also?" asked Aidan.

"Yes, well, he's actually a chef, well was. He's retired now with my mom in California," she clarified. "He worked in Las Vegas for a long time."

"That most of been something," said Aidan.

"When they lived there my dad and mom met Elvis a few times."

"Really!" said Aidan, Theresa, and Amy in harmony.

"They have a picture with him," she said proudly. "He's one of my dad's all-time favorites and still is. I've grown up listening to Elvis since the day I was born and I'm pretty sure I know all his songs."

"Which one is your favorite?" queried Aidan.

'Love Me Tender,' started playing through the speakers.

"I don't believe it!" said Brieanne excitedly. "It's this one!"

Aidan stood, reached out his hand. "What are we waiting for?"

She reached for it and walked with him to the dance floor as the older couples watched on. They put their arms around one another and started to gently sway in unison under the starry sky. Brieanne liked his arms being around her, his cheek touching hers, and being so close to him. Aidan liked how soft her skin felt, how sweet she smelt, and his arms around her. When the song ended, they separated and shyly looked at one another, then slowly walked back to the table and sat.

"That was so odd that we were talking about Elvis and my favorite song by him comes on," said Brieanne somewhat in disbelief.

"Coincidence?" asked Aidan.

"I don't believe in coincidences," said Theresa.

"Me neither," agreed Amy.

"No?" asked Brieanne wanting to hear if they were thinking the same thing she was.

"I believe everything happens for a reason," said Theresa.

"Me too," said Amy.

Brieanne was happy that they thought the same way as she did and smiled at them both.

"How are you guys doing down there?" questioned Paul looking at Brieanne and Aidan. "Why don't you two come talk with me and Bill for a while?"

They moved over and sat next to them. Paul mentioned he had overhead something about Elvis, Brieanne told him and Bill the story.

They talked about Elvis for a while, before moving on to the current song playing through the speakers.

After midnight they finished their drinks and left the bar. They used the crosswalk on Gulf Boulevard, said goodbye to Brieanne and Aidan then walked down the street. The younger couple watched the older couples for a few minutes before strolling across the parking lot to Brieanne's front door.

"That was such a fun night," said Brieanne cheerfully as she unlocked the front door. "Your family is great."

"Thank you, they are," agreed Aidan starting to go, turning around, and walking backwards. "Hopefully I will see you tomorrow?"

"I think there is a good chance you will," she said with a cute smile. "Maybe look out for me on the beach tomorrow morning," she suggested, wanting him to.

"I will," he replied, turning to leave, "I'll see you tomorrow."

"Tomorrow," she confirmed, then went inside, closed the door, and leaned on it. She had never felt this way about anyone before. "Tomorrow," she whispered to herself, it couldn't come soon enough.

Chapter 6

Brieanne put on sunscreen, a bikini, jean shorts, and a tank top. Then placed the sunscreen, along with a towel and bottle of water, inside her beach bag before going into the bathroom. Looking in the mirror, she brushed her hair, put it in a ponytail, applied lip balm then put it in her bag. Happy with the way she looked she walked downstairs out the back door and along the path to the beach. She guessed they would be on the beach around eleven, as she glanced down at the time on her phone, "ten minutes to, perfect," she whispered before throwing it into her bag and putting on her sunglasses. She strolled close to the shoreline saying good morning to people as they walked past her. When she got closer to the condo, she slowed her pace; the beach was busy. Her eyes darted everywhere looking for his group, but to no avail. She decided to continue a little further down the beach, turn around, and try again.

"Hey, are you ignoring us?" asked a recognizable voice from behind.

"Aidan," she said happily. "No, I didn't see you, I was looking around," she said motioning to the beach, "but it's so crowded."

"Yeah, it is."

"Where are you sitting?"

"Towards the back," he said pointing.

Brieanne looked over, noticed his family, and waved back.

"I was calling your name, but I guess with the noise of the kids splashing and running around you didn't hear me."

"No, I didn't, I'm glad you caught up to me."

"Me too," he said with a handsome grin. "Come and join us?"

"Thank you," she replied as he took her bag from her and followed him. He had a muscular build, light blond hair, and judging by his swimming shorts, a nice, tight bum.

"She couldn't hear me," explained Aidan as they joined his family, "it's noisy down by the water."

"I'm glad Aidan was watching out for you," said Theresa wanting Brieanne to know that he was.

Brieanne liked hearing that.

"Do you want to lay your towel next to mine?" suggested Aidan, "I'm not one for sitting on beach chairs."

"Me neither," she concurred taking her towel from her bag, and with his help, laying it down before removing her sunglasses, shorts, and top.

As she did, Aidan went to the cooler and slowly grabbed two bottles of water; he tried his best not to stare but was unsuccessful. She was wearing a sky-blue bikini that showed off her well-rounded breasts, thin waist, and shapely bum. Brieanne hoped he was watching and needlessly sprayed suntan lotion on her body making it glisten. Aidan thought she was gorgeous. Suddenly something hit his arm, it was a small seashell, and he looked over at the direction it came from.

"Can you grab me a water?" asked Bill. "That is, if you aren't too busy?" he continued, chuckling along with Paul.

Busted, he thought. Aidan gave Bill water, then one to Brieanne, before sitting on his towel.

"Have you been down her long?" she asked wondering if she had timed it right.

"About ten minutes," he answered. "You timed it right."

She smiled at his reply. "Or maybe you did?"

"You're good," he said letting out a nervous laugh. "I thought I may bump into you around eleven, so we came down a little earlier."

"Same here," she replied liking his honesty and looking around. "I like it when the beach is active with families, especially with children."

Aidan followed her gaze. "Their happy faces, that excitement in their voices—"

"It's like the best day ever."

"Yeah, the best day," he repeated in agreement looking back at her. "Do you want to take a walk down the beach? Maybe soak up some of their fun?"

"I'd like that."

They walked towards the water, then headed north on the beach pointing out the children playing in the water, throwing Frisbees, and building sandcastles. After a while the crowd thinned, the noise level dropped, and they walked quietly for a moment.

"Tell me about yourself?" asked Brieanne timidly.

"Okay, what would you like to know?"

"Where do you live?"

Aidan laughed a little.

Brieanne felt a little awkward by his laughter.

"I'm sorry," he replied, "I wasn't laughing at you, it never struck me until you just asked, but in a month or so, nowhere."

"Nowhere?" she asked unsure what he meant.

"Well last Monday I put my house up for sale," he explained, "and it will be sold by the time I get home, so I won't have a place to live."

Brieanne gave him an odd look which made Aidan laugh out loud.

"Okay, okay, let me clarify," he said realizing he couldn't leave it at that, besides for some reason, he wanted to tell her. Leisurely putting his arm around her he began, "let me give you the quick A to Z about me. I will leave out some private stuff, but overall, it will help you get to know me a little better and understand what I mean."

"Well, you do have my curiosity," she confessed, liking his arm around her, "and I would like to know more about you, but I don't want you to feel like you have to."

"I'm fine, besides I want to tell you, and you will be the first to know things about me that no one else does, not even my family."

Brieanne was intrigued and excited at the prospect of him taking her into his confidence. "Okay," she said eagerly.

He removed his arm and started to speak in a casual tone. "My parents, sister, and I—"

"You have a sister?"

"Yes, a couple years younger than me," he replied glancing over at her, "she would like you."

And what about her brother, wondered Brieanne.

"Unlike me of course, I just put up with you," he joked, quickly moving out of her reach, and jogging away.

"Why, you, I'll get you for that!" Brieanne warned as she gave chase. She caught up with him and tried to pull him into the water but couldn't. Aidan put her over his shoulder and ran into the Gulf. She shrieked as they both fell with a big splash. "I'm going to get you for that, too," she said laughing and wiping the salt water from her face.

"Oh, I'm so scared," he said with an exaggerated frightened face that made her laugh louder.

"Well, take that," she said splashing him before swimming away.

Aidan pursued her, caught her, and pulled her close to him.

"What are you going to do to me?" she asked playfully.

Aidan thought momentarily as he watched the water dripping down her pretty face. "I've decided that I will…"

"Yes?" she asked patiently.

"Continue with my story that will be torture enough for you,"

"Actually, I want to hear your A to Z," she confessed with a cheeky grin and moved closer to him.

Aidan smiled back at her. "Where was I…oh yes, my family. We grew up outside of Syracuse, NY. My dad was a corporate lawyer, my mom was a teacher, principal, and school superintendent. I went to Syracuse University, got my master's degree in English, and taught for five years at a high school in Syracuse before taking a position in Rochester, where I have been for seven years. My parents retired about five years ago and bought a property on Canandaigua Lake in the Finger Lakes Region. It's a beautiful lakefront place about thirty minutes from where I live," he explained then stopped momentarily. "Now, what I'm going to tell you next, only you will know, no one else."

"I understand," she replied, listening intently.

"The current Head of the English Department was offered a position at a university last fall, which she accepted it, and was leaving at the end of this school year. So, last November I applied for her position…In March, I was offered the job, which I refused, and instead handed in my resignation, which became effective last Friday. That Friday, my last day at work, I decided to sell my place. I met with my real estate agent on Saturday, we came up with a price, and I signed a contract with her that day. Over the next few days, I moved the items that I wanted into a storage facility along with my car, and told her whatever furniture was left she could sell with the house or do with as she pleased. The only request I had, was that she not list my house till Thursday, because I knew I would be leaving to come here Wednesday." Aidan stopped and dunked the back of his head in the water before looking at her.

Brieanne had a few questions, but didn't know which one to ask first, she decided on the most obvious. "Where you married or living with someone, and it ended?"

"No, I lived there on my own, it's all mine," he confirmed. "It's a lovely place on a big plot of land and I fixed it up myself. Today it's worth a lot more than what I originally paid for it."

"So, you sold it because the market is good?"

"No, I just wanted out of there."

"Is it because of a woman?"

"Yes and no," he said cautiously, "that's one of the private things."

"Oh, I'm sorry."

"Don't be. I'm just not ready to talk about that yet. Do you have any other questions?"

She thought for a moment. "I have two, if that's okay?"

"Go ahead," he said liking her inquisitiveness.

"Is the reason you refused the position and selling the house, the same reason?"

Aidan gave her a smile. "You are pretty good at this," he said complimenting her. "Yes, part of the private thing."

It had to be a woman, a relationship gone badly, maybe a work colleague. "Last one," she declared, "and it's a loaded one."

"Ask away CSI: Madeira Beach," he teased.

"Stop it!" said Brieanne, splashing him. "You showing up here unexpectedly, is that to do with you having no job, selling your house, and your family having no knowledge of it?"

He gave her a facial expression as if he was deeply thinking about her difficult question.

"Tough one, eh?" she said proud of herself.

"It is a toughie, all right," he lied. "Are you ready for my long, detailed answer?"

"I am," she concluded with a satisfied grin.

"Yes, yes…and yes," he replied, and with each yes, he comical moved his head from side to side.

"That's it, that's your answers!" she exclaimed jumping on his shoulders and pushing him under water before letting him up; her lips where inches away from his.

"Promise you won't tell anyone?" he asked putting his hands on her waist.

"I won't, I promise" she said putting her arms around his shoulders. "When are you going to tell them?"

"I'm not sure," he replied. "The four of them are driving tomorrow morning to Port Canaveral, staying overnight at a hotel close by, then taking a four-day cruise to the Bahamas. That will give me some time to think while they are gone. I don't want to say anything before hand and have them worrying about me while they're away."

"I think waiting till they return is a good idea." She then thought about him selling his place. "You know I have a real estate agent, her name is Joyce, and she is not only an excellent agent but a particularly good friend of mine. She could help you while you're here. Receiving and reviewing offers, that sort of thing."

"That would really help me out," he said appreciatively. "I think I'll take you up on that offer."

Brieanne was happy he had accepted her help and taken her into his confidence. Although the reasons behind why he had done what he did, was still a curious mystery to her.

"Maybe we can talk about Joyce more next week when they are away," he suggested.

"Okay, we will," she replied, happy with the fact they would be seeing each other again. "We should probably head back," she said looking in the direction of his family. "Your parents will think I've kidnapped you."

When they returned, they sat on their towels and were handed sandwiches, cut-up vegetables, and fruit. As they ate, Brieanne asked them about their cruise, which they explained in detail, revealing it was a birthday present for Amy from Theresa and Paul. The group spent the next few hours talking about last night and the local area. Taking breaks in between to cool off with a swim. It was getting late in the afternoon and the older couples packed up, said goodbye, and left to get changed for the BBQ.

"Thanks for walking me home, I had a wonderful time today," she said cheerfully.

"I did too," he said glancing over at her. "Are you coming back for the BBQ?"

"Is it okay? I mean, with your parents?"

"Yes, of course. My parents would have asked you themselves, but they didn't want to put you on the spot. Besides, I told them I wanted to ask you myself."

"You did, did you," she said looking at him mischievously. "After those comments you made about me earlier and throwing me in the water. Are you sure you can put up with me?"

Aidan snickered. "Guilty," he confessed. "But in my defense, you did splash me a couple of times and dunk me."

"Well, if this was a court pal your rebuttal would be rejected and thrown out because you have no witnesses to corroborate your accusations."

"Pal is it," he teased. "So, you are not only prosecutor, but judge—"

"And jury!"

He put his hands together as if cuffed and held them up to her. "Then I am the mercy of the jury. What is their verdict?" he asked lowering his head dramatically. "I beg for leniency."

She laughed at his escapades. "The jury says yes to your invite but on one condition," she said authoritatively.

"Anything, name it, please?"

"I will let you know, but not now, you will have to wait till the BBQ to find out," she said in an ominous voice.

"Hmm, I don't like the way you said that I'm a little scared."

She moved close to his ear whispering, "you should be." Then ran off the beach up the path towards her place, turned around, and shouted, "I'll see you in ninety minutes."

"See you then," replied Aidan happily waving back, before heading to the condo.

Chapter 7

"Good evening," said Aidan as Brieanne approached him on the beach.

"Where you waiting for me?" she asked as they turned onto the wooden path towards the condo.

"I was."

She liked that.

"You look amazing."

"Thank you," she said shyly, "just something I threw on, shorts and a blouse." Which was untrue, she had spent a good half an hour looking for something to wear before deciding on something comfortable, casual, cute, and appropriate.

"It's perfect for a summer evening BBQ on the deck," he said placing his card inside the reader, unlocking the gate, and walking through.

"I guess I'm lucky you waited for me on the beach. Otherwise, I would have had to climb over the fence."

"The thought had crossed my mind to stay on this side and watch you try scale it before calling security."

"That would be something you would do," she said. "I'm actually surprised you didn't! I can see you sitting over there sipping on your beer, watching me struggle, and having a good laugh."

"That would have been a sight to see," he replied. "But alas, I would have come to your rescue."

"My very own Prince Charming," she said trying to contain her happiness.

They walked over to the bar, ordered a drink, and then sat at a table. A couple of guys on guitars started to play and they listened to a couple of songs before Aidan's family joined them. Twenty minutes later the buffet was ready, so the duet took a break while people filled their plates and ate.

"Have you ever been up to Syracuse or around that area?" asked Paul looking over at Brieanne.

"A went to Syracuse once when I was younger to the New York State Fair and several years ago I went to Niagara Falls for my friend's wedding," she replied. "Aidan said that you live on Canandaigua Lake in the Finger Lakes Region and that it's really pretty there."

"Oh, it's picturesque, and there is so much to do!" said Theresa. "In the summer you can swim, boat, and fish; in autumn you can hike and watch the leaves change color; and in winter, snowmobile, and ski. It has it all."

"Where Aidan lives is quite a nice spot, too," said Paul. "A good piece of land close to the city but far enough out in the country."

"And he's only thirty minutes from where we live so he can visit us as often as he likes," added his mom.

Brieanne quickly glanced over at Aidan. He was looking at what he was eating so he didn't have to make eye contact with his parents, who were wondering why he wasn't joining in on their conversation. She felt bad for him. "I'm sure they are both wonderful places," said Brieanne then changed the subject. "Amy, how do you like living here?"

"Bill and I think it's wonderful. It has gorgeous weather, a beach, pool, bar, live music, and lovely people. What more could you ask for?" she replied happily. "We are trying to get these two to come live down here with us," she said, as her and Bill looked at Theresa and Paul.

Paul looked back at them, then at Theresa. "We are seriously thinking about it. We're not getting any younger and having warm weather year-round is a very, big plus."

"I will admit," said Theresa turning to Brieanne. "We love Canandaigua Lake, but here, things are a little more accessible for us, and like Paul mentioned, the weather is a big plus. So, we are giving it a great deal of thought."

Brieanne smiled at them, then thought of something to say in hopes of bringing Aidan back into the conversation, and potentially help him out. "Maybe Aidan will sell, too, move down here and be closer than he is in Rochester."

Aidan perked up. "I never really thought about that but it's not a bad idea."

"Really!" said his surprised parents in unison.

"You would consider moving here?" asked Theresa. "What about your house? Your job? The department head position?"

Aidan sat up in his chair. "Well, a house is just a house, I could easily sell mine and buy another one here. The job, well that's something I would need to look into, and see what's available."

"We have lots of high schools locally, and in Tampa," suggested Brieanne.

"In that case, it could just come down where I want to teach," he said, finishing off his food.

His mom looked at his dad, and they both looked at Amy and Bill.

After they ate, the live music returned, and Brieanne and Aidan watched the older couples dance.

Aidan leaned over. "Thanks," he whispered.

"You're welcome," she said with a kind smile. "By the way that makes two: this one and my condition for coming to the BBQ."

"So, now I owe you two?"

"Yep," she replied with a proud grin.

After watching the sun set, the older couples left the younger ones alone explaining they had to be up early to drive and would see Brieanne when they returned from their trip. Brieanne and Aidan went onto the beach, took off their shoes, and waded into the water.

"Did you mean what you said about maybe moving here?" she asked wondering how serious he was.

"I have no job…soon no house. I think it's a viable option worthy of consideration," he said honestly. "I would have to look at what positions are available, where they are located, house costs, and so on."

"Have you talked about moving already?"

"I mentioned it to my family about a month ago, and had already handed in my resignation at work, in the back of my mind I knew I wanted to sell my place."

"Where did you say you were thinking about moving to?"

"I only told them Boston, although I had thought about a couple of other cities like Albany or New York. I know my parents are seriously considering moving here and I thought if I planted it in their minds that I was going to move away it would make it easier for them to make their decision," he said looking at her. "But that's only part of the reason, mostly I just want to get out of there."

She wondered what had happened to him in Rochester, who this female was, and what had she done? Whatever the reasons, they must have been bad enough to make him want to run away from his home, his career, and his life. "You mentioned that you are here so your house can sell, is that the only reason?"

"One of them," he said with an uneasy laugh. "I also needed to get away, and with my family being here, I figured they would be a good distraction for me."

"They certainly are that," she confirmed, "they are so much fun and so nice."

He gave her a long look and grinned, like he knew something she didn't.

"What?" she asked anxiously.

"They all like you."

Brieanne bashfully looked down to hide her blushing face. "They do?" she asked quietly.

"They say, and I quote, 'that you're intelligent, always happy, fun, down-to-earth, and very attractive,' end of quote."

"That's very kind of them," she said graciously, contemplating if he thought the same as they did.

They quietly walked past her house to the bridge at John's Pass, turned around, and started back. Brieanne wanted to ask about his last relationship, but thought it was too soon, and probably best to let him tell her when he was ready to do so.

"Have you lived here all your life?"

"Yeah, I was born and raised here, and went to the University of Tampa for my Business degree," she replied. "I can't see me ever leaving here."

"How is that someone as pretty as you are still single?"

Damn, I wished I would have thought of a non-evasive question like that to ask him. "I've dated on and off, but none of them ever amounted to anything serious. My last relationship was eleven months ago, and it lasted less than a month."

"Oh, okay."

"You?"

He wasn't sure how to word it and thought momentarily. "I started dating someone in January and it ended in March. It started out well enough, and I guess, you could say it was kind of serious," he said glancing at her, "but after a while I realized she wasn't the one."

They walked in silence for a few minutes absorbing their information. When they reached her back gate, she stopped, and they looked at one another.

"Thanks for another great night."

"Thank you, you make them great," he replied.

"You too," she said beaming. "Goodnight."

"Goodnight," he replied watching her open her gate and walk in.

Then she remembered something. "I almost forgot, I never told you my one condition of coming to the BBQ," she said hastily turning around.

"No, you didn't. What is it?"

"Earlier today, you mentioned that while your family is away, you were going to use that time alone to do some thinking."

"That's right."

"Now, I won't be offended if you say no, because I know you need that time alone," she clarified. "So, I can pick another condition."

"Okay," said Aidan grinning at her awkwardness.

"My condition of going to the BBQ is that you let me take you out over the next four days so that I can show you around and give you some Madeira Beach hospitality" she said eagerly. Then realizing that may be too much time. "Or three days…two days…one day?" she offered waiting for an answer. Then whispered, "no days," her eagerness now turning to uncertainty.

Aidan gave her a concerned face. "Earlier today, you said you were prosecutor, judge, and jury, where you not?" he asked in a low tone.

"Yes," she answered apprehensively.

"Your final judgment was that you would go to the BBQ on one condition?"

"Yes."

"And that condition would be told to me at the BBQ."

"Oh-huh," she said understanding now that he was up to something.

"You arrived at the BBQ, we enjoyed the BBQ, and then went for a walk. We have already said our goodnights," he stated shaking his head regretfully. "Meaning that the BBQ and this night have already come to an end, and the condition was to be mentioned to me in the approved given time, at the BBQ. Unfortunately, you have run out of time, and the statute of limitations is in effect."

"Why you little," she said playfully shoving him away and closing the gate behind her. "I will find someone else to spend my time with over the next several days, goodnight, sir."

"Goodnight, ma'am," he replied.

They turned, started off in different directions, and went several feet before they both looked over their shoulders, laughed, and went back to the gate.

"What time tomorrow?" he asked.

"I will meet you at twelve at the crosswalk, you remember the one from last night," she said pointing in the direction of Gulf Boulevard.

"I do," he confirmed. "Tomorrow at twelve."

"At twelve," she repeated with a heavenly smile.

They slowly walked away. Aidan stopped, turned around, and called out, "four."

"Four?" she asked, unsure.

"Four days of sightseeing," he confirmed. "If that's still available?"

"Yes," she replied happily.

Chapter 8

"Did they get away okay this morning?" asked Brieanne as Aidan walked toward her.

"They did," he replied. "We had breakfast together and they left about an hour ago."

"That's good," she confirmed with a smile then turned her attention to their day. "This afternoon I thought we would walk around John's Pass Village and have something to eat. It will be busy with locals and tourists, and the atmosphere will be very friendly, you will love it."

"Sounds like fun," he said keenly.

They crossed the road, past the Bamboo Beach Bar & Grill, and went onto Village Boulevard. They walked south along its palm tree-lined sidewalk going in and out of the shops along the way. Brieanne bumped into a lot of her friends and locals whom she stopped to chat with and introduced them to her friend Aidan, who she explained was on vacation. After a couple hours, they strolled into the Mad Pub where they ordered two craft beers, took up two seats close to the sidewalk and watched the people walking by.

"Such a beautiful sunny day," observed Aidan.

Brieanne nodded in agreement. "But I must admit it's good to get inside under the shade where it's a little cooler, and have one of these," she confessed lifting up her glass of beer and taking a mouthful.

"Can't argue with you there," Aidan agreed taking a drink. "You do know a lot of people."

"I guess I do" she replied. "With living her all my life and it being a small community, anyone who isn't a tourist you know."

"I think it's great, and like you said earlier, it has a very friendly atmosphere."

"That's why I love it here," confessed Brieanne.

They finished their drinks, took a left out of the pub and crossed the street by DeLosa's Pizza & Italian Restaurant, then went under the 'John's Pass Boardwalk' sign. As they headed west, she pointed out the boats in the marina and restaurants as they passed them. "This is Pirates Pub N Grub, the Friendly Fisherman Restaurant, and here's Hooters, with the 'World's Largest Wing!' on display. It's a half-ton chicken wing, hanging from a fishing hook on a fourteen-foot-tall crossbeam, over buckets of mild, medium, and hot sauces," she said as they walked past it, "and at the end here, is the Bubba Gump Shrimp Co."

Brieanne then pointed to the bridge opening up to let the bigger boats in, and to the beach beyond it on the north side. "Last night when you walked me home, and we went by my place, that is where we stopped and turned around," she explained, and described how the beach started there, went north passed her place and Aidan's condo, and up the coast to Sand Key Park in Clearwater.

After they watched the bridge closing, they looped right onto Boardwalk Place East where she pointed out the charter and tour operators. "That's Hubbard's Marina, The Pirate Ship Royal Conquest, and the Dolphin Quest, if you decide you want to go fishing, be a pirate, or watch dolphins while you're here," she said, before crossing over Village Boulevard and continuing. "This is The Hut Bar and Grill street entrance, over there is Woody's Watersports, Fly-N-High Waverunners & Parasail, Gators Parasail, and across the street is Walt'z Fish Shak, and this is Don's Dock & Wild Seafood Market," she said before making a right U-turn onto the boardwalk. "That's The Boardwalk Grill, this is The Hut Bar & Grill boardwalk entrance, and over there is Sculley's Waterfront Restaurant, but around here we just call it Sculley's," she said with a smile, before taking his hand and leading him into The Hut.

They sat around the bar, had a drink, and noticing it was almost four, asked for menus and ordered. As they waited, Aidan talked about how casual and charming the tiki bar was and all the TVs it had, while Brieanne drew his attention to its large dockside patio filled with people eating and drinking.

"Here we are," said the bartender. "Buffalo Chicken Wrap for the lady, and the Grouper Sandwich for you sir, both with fries and coleslaw, enjoy."

"Thank you," they replied, admiring one another's choices, and deciding to share.

"That was delicious," said Aidan as they walked out into the hot sun.

"It was. I am so full!"

"I'm not sure who's was the best?"

"I see it's a tie; both meals were amazing!"

"What's next?" he asked.

"We have one more store to visit," she replied. "The owners are very close friends of the family. Then after that, I think we can safely say we've done enough walking around for one afternoon, don't you think?" she asked, wanting to spend some time with him alone.

"Yeah," he agreed, "after we visit your friends why don't we go somewhere and enjoy the sunshine, relax, and take it easy."

"Definitely," she replied.

"Do you want to come to the condo? We can hang around the pool and go for a swim."

"Yeah, I would love to," she replied, pleased with his suggestion.

Arriving at the store, Aidan opened the door, and they walked inside. He noticed it was one of those retailers that sold a little bit of everything: from T-shirts, hoodies, beach apparel, to jewelry, coffee cups, and fridge magnets. You could even order one of those burnt wood signs that you see hanging outside a home with their family's name on it.

"I could use a couple more swimming shorts," professed Aidan noticing the men's swim apparel.

"Follow me," said Brieanne grabbing his hand and leading him there. She darted through the selection of styles, before picking out one, and then went to another rack before picking out a second. Aidan smiled as he watched her. "I'm guessing you're a thirty-four-inch—" she stopped and looked up at him. "I am so sorry," she said embarrassed. "I'll put them back," she said lifting up the surfer shorts.

"No, wait," said Aidan, "I'll take them," as he reached for her hand, gently touching it before removing the two hangers from it.

"You really don't have to, I'm sorry," reiterated Brieanne, still uncomfortable, and now red-faced.

"There's no need to be," said Aidan reassuringly.

"It's just that I don't get to shop for men, and I love swimwear, and I—"

"I was going to ask you for your help anyway," he said truthfully. "I haven't bought swimwear in a while and I have no idea what is hip for a dude like me," which he said in a righteous, surfer's voice making Brieanne laugh. "So, I really appreciate you doing this," he said moving closer to her, "and to be honest, I was a little unsure how to ask you for your help, thank you for taking the initiative." He whispered softly, "but keep this on the low-done between you and me, you know what I mean, I don't want this getting out that you chose my surfer shorts," as his eyes shifted comically around the store.

She laughed out loud. "You're crazy!" she joked, as she grabbed his free hand, hopefully about me, she thought, because she knew she was about him.

"That I am!" he admitted, then waited momentarily for his punchline. "Especially if I'm hanging out with someone like you!"

"Why you stinker!" said Brieanne letting go to tickle his stomach, which made him jerk backward, and almost crash into the rack. She quickly grabbed his free hand to balance him. They broke into a boisterous laugh that made people in the store look over. She kept hold of his hand. "This way," she instructed her embarrassment from picking out his swimwear completely gone. Brieanne stopped at the bikinis and started rifling through them. "You don't think I'm leaving this store empty handed, do you?" she said quickly glancing up at him before returning to her quest.

"I'm just glad I don't have to pick out yours."

"Don't think for a second you are getting off that easy, mister!" she said picking out the last one and turning to Aidan. "I have four bikinis, but I only need two, one from each set," she said lifting each set up. "One from the solid colors," she said motioning her head to the right, then to the left, "and one from the floral." Then gave him an innocent smile. "You have to choose."

Aidan gave her a look of uncertainty.

"Please," she pleaded, "I would like you to pick something you want to see me in."

"Okay, let me see the solids first."

"Yay," said Brieanne as she put the florals down, then lifted the yellow bikini in her right hand, and indigo in her left.

He looked at each, then decided. "Yellow."

"Yellow it is," she said giving it to him to hold while she put the blue away. Then she picked up the other two, "white or peach floral?" she asked moving each hand up and down.

"This is a little tougher," said Aidan, who would like to see her in both. "Peach!"

"Good choices," she said putting the white away and taking the yellow one from him. "Before we pay, let me show you the jewelry they make here, it is absolutely gorgeous." Brieanne led him to the counter and pointed out the earrings, necklaces, and rings.

"Brie, how are you doing darling?" said a voice walking down the counter and hugging her.

"I'm doing well, Harriett," she replied. "And you?"

"Doing fine dear, just fine," she said looking past her at Aidan.

"This is my friend Aidan," she said turning towards him. "Aidan, Harriett."

"Please to meet you, Harriett," he said politely.

"Likewise, Aidan," she replied kindly then looked at Brie. "I noticed you two earlier," she admitted, "it's nice to see a young couple laughing and enjoying one another's company," then noticed the swimsuits in their hands. "Did you find everything you were looking for?"

"Yes, thank you," said Brie. "I was just showing him the jewelry you make."

"It's very beautiful," complimented Aidan.

"Thank you," said Harriett graciously then suddenly remembered something. "Oh Brie! Did you want to show him your favorite?" she asked excitedly.

"If you don't mind?"

"Of course not," she said as they followed her into the backroom. "Besides, George is back here, and he wouldn't forgive me if I let you leave without saying hello."

"George, look who paid a visit," said Harriett walking over to the safe.

George looked up from his desk. "Brie!" he said cheerfully standing up. "Come over here and give me a hug." As George pulled away, he held her hands, and admired her. "You are getting more and more beautiful each and every day."

"Thank you, George," said Brie blushing. "This is my friend Aidan, Aidan this is George, Harriett's husband."

"Nice to meet you," said George enthusiastically shaking Aidan's hand.

"You too," replied Aidan.

"Here you go dear," said Harriett passing a small box, then looking over at Aidan. "This is Brie's favorite. She's been in love with it since she was a young girl. I can still remember her running into the store ahead of her mother asking me to show it to her from behind the counter. It's one of a kind and very special, just like Brie."

"Here take these seats," offered George moving out of the way.

"Let me have those," said Harriett reaching for their swimwear, "and I'll take them to the register for you. Come on George, I need your help moving some items off the store floor." Which she didn't, she wanted to give Brie and Aidan some privacy.

Brieanne and Aidan watched them leave. Sitting close to one another she opened the box and her face lit up. "Isn't it beautiful!" she cooed taking it out to give Aidan a closer look.

"It is."

"The ring is platinum and has three lines running side by side around a third of its length. The first line is half the width of the band, and is covered in exceptionally fine, crushed, granular, white sand from Madeira Beach. The middle line, which is a quarter of the band width, is crushed dark sand, also from Madeira Beach. The last line, the final quarter width, is tiny pieces of compressed, blue aquamarine…. Look here, see how the three lines slowly curve around each side of the ring, then gradually fade…Feel how smooth and soft they are to the touch." Which Aidan did. "Do you see those glittering pieces mixed throughout the lines of the band? Those are clear, crushed diamonds, embedded into each line. Do you notice how they glitter when I move the ring?" she asked.

"Yes," whispered Aidan mesmerized.

"The setting is a round, yellow diamond. If you look closely, you will notice it's slightly lower, off-center, and in between the dark sand, and aquamarine," she said looking up at him with a smile, satisfied with her assessment. "So, now that you know what the ring is made up of independently, what do you see when look at the ring as a whole?" she asked inquisitively.

Aidan wasn't sure, knowing it was special to Brieanne, he decided to let her tell him. "Why don't you tell me what you see, then I will always see it as you do?"

She was taken by his response. "Okay, I will," said Brieanne looking down at the ring. "The ring is called, 'Sunset for Two Lovers,'" she revealed. "If you look at it simply: the white sand is the beach, the dark sand is the wet sand, and the blue aquamarine is the water. The yellow diamond is the setting sun, and the sparkling diamonds are the reflection of the sun's rays off the sand and water." She glanced up at him. "But if you look at it closer, deeper, you see it is much more than just a sunset," she eluded looking back at the ring. "There are also two lovers sitting on the white sand beach and they are talking and laughing. The two lovers rise, and holding hands they walk down to the wet sand and talk of their love for one another as the waves softly caress their feet. The two lovers now arm in arm, quietly look out at the blue aquamarine water knowing they will be together forever and soulmates for life. And with the yellow diamond sun slowly setting they turn to one another saying, I love you, then gently kiss as the final sun's rays' shimmer on the ground around them, like diamonds." She stopped, looked up at him and smiled. "That is what I see."

Aidan had goosebumps. "Brieanne, thank you for sharing that with me," he whispered, "I will always see it that way, too," then kissed her tenderly on the cheek.

Brieanne looked deeply into his eyes, their mouths slowly moved closer, closer.

"Beautiful ring, eh Aidan?" interrupted George unaware of what was going on.

The two quickly moved apart.

"It is," replied Aidan as he watched Brieanne put the ring back in the box.

Harriett, who had been casually watching the pair from a distance, had seen them moving closer but didn't notice George in time to stop him from barging in. Instead, she walked in after him. Grinning at both of them she took the ring from Brie, and with her back to them, gave her husband a disapproving look. By his wife's expression, George knew he had done something wrong, and would find out about it soon enough.

Harriett was about to lock the ring in the safe but turned to Aidan asking, "Brie told you all about the ring?"

"Yes, what it was made of, and what it meant to her."

Harriett hid her happiness at what Brie had done and decided she would like to tell Aidan her part of the story. "Would you like to know the whole story, that is, my missing part?" she asked looking at him.

"I would love to," replied Aidan enthusiastically and offered Harriett his seat.

Brie and George looked at one another in dismay, to this point only three people in that room, plus Brie's parents, knew the story she was about to tell.

"Where do I begin...Let me start with the ring," she stated. "I had a plain platinum ring that had an empty, off-center setting. Now in the past I had used different types of jewelry together, you know costume jewelry with real jewelry, and such. So, I wanted to do something similar with this one, but I wanted it to be quite unique; one of a kind. One evening, I was out walking along the beach, and I was looking at the white sand, the wet sand, and the blue water. Then and there it came to me; I decided that I would use the platinum ring to represent Earth, using those three distinct colors. So, I picked up some white and dark sand, went home, and added the sand lines, and then the aquamarine for the blue. But I still had a problem, an empty setting. I looked down at my ring and thought what my Earth needs is some divine light to give it life. At first, I used a clear diamond, but it didn't look right, although somehow, I felt a diamond is what it needed. Then I remembered the round yellow diamond I had and placed it in the setting. It looked perfect, and it now had its energy. But something was still wrong, something was still missing, it needed something else, but what? Then I thought about my walk along the beach and the shimmering lights, then it hit me, the colors needed illumination. So, I added exceedingly small, clear, crushed diamonds to the lines of sand and aquamarine. The ring was complete. But now I had the biggest problem of all," she said theatrically. "Do you know what that problem was?" she asked Aidan.

Aidan shook his head no.

"Well, I had my Earth, my places on it, my shimmering lights, and my energy...But I couldn't describe my ring in a few precise words to give it a worthy name and I needed a name to capture the spirit and the soul of the ring," she said sadly. "If a ring is especially important to you, it must have a description, a history, and most importantly, a name. I was at a loss." She looked over at Brie and smiled. "A couple of days after finishing the ring Brie and her mom came into the shop to see me." Harriett looked back at Aidan. "The shop was much smaller back then, as was this room, but still this is the very room in which we sat. I opened the box and showed Brie's mom the ring and told her my problem. We were now, both at a loss. Brie was quietly sitting there watching us, she was almost twelve. So, I turned to her, showed her the ring, and asked, 'What do you see?' She asked if she could remove the ring, which I said she may. She studied it for a minute or so, looking at it from side to side, and top to bottom, then she glanced over at me. I asked her again, 'what do you see?'" she said looking over at Brie affectionately. "She replied, 'Sunset for Two Lovers.' My face lit up, I looked at her, this young child, and asked how she saw that. Then she explained it to me just as she had to you." Harriett looked up at Aidan. "You see, others who have looked at the ring, and still do today, only saw it as a beautiful, unique, ring," she said glancing back at Brie, "were Brie has always seen it as much more than that. To her it's a reflection of love: no more, no less." She paused momentarily. "I see it as a beautiful, unique ring, and I also see it as love, too, only mine is a labor of love, not a reflection of love, like Brie."

Everyone was quiet momentarily as Harriett stood and placed the ring back inside the safe.

"Thank you for sharing your story with me," said Aidan.

"You're very welcome," she said walking towards him and uncharacteristically hugging a stranger, then hugged Brie.

They said goodbye to George and followed Harriett to the cash register where she handed them each a bag and refused to take money from them. They thanked her, said goodbye, and left the store. Once they had, Harriett went to the back office to have a word with George then made a call.

"They're a really nice couple," said Aidan.

"Yeah, I like them a lot. They have been friends with my parents for an awfully long time and are very close to them. They still call one another quite frequently, especially Harriett and my mom, mostly with latest town gossip," said Brieanne with a snicker. "That's the reason why Harriett and George never ask me how my parents are doing, they probably know better than I do."

Aidan stopped suddenly, pretending to look concerned. "Will your mom find out about me?"

Brieanne walked back to him. "Are you kidding, she is probably on the phone with her right now, as we speak."

They both laughed.

"Well, we have bathing suits. I have sunscreen, towels, beer, wine, and food at the condo, unless you need something else from home?"

Brieanne thought for a moment and couldn't think of anything. "No, I'm good," she replied.

Chapter 9

"They have a corner, penthouse suite," said Brieanne standing in the foyer.

"Yeah, let me show you around," replied Aidan as he took her plastic bag, placed it on a small table next to his, and led the way. "Down here on the left is the master bedroom, this is my aunt and uncle's," he said, opening the door, and walking in. "They have a walk-in closet, en suite, and sliding doors out to a private balcony with a view of the gulf." They walked out of the room. "Back here these doors open up for the washer and dryer, this door here is a small storage area, and this one is the powder room." They went back past the foyer and down the hallway. "This is another master bedroom, where my parents sleep, it's the exact same as the other one except their private balcony has a view to the east." Brieanne followed him out to the hallway as he continued. "Behind this door is a full bathroom," he said opening it up. "This door next to it is a bedroom with two single beds, a closet, and view of east and south." She followed him across the hallway. "Inside here is a larger bedroom with a king-size bed and a view of the west and south. This is where I sleep." They went back to the foyer where Aidan pointed out the remainder of the condo. "Over here is the dining room, the kitchen and kitchen area, and the living room. These doors between the living room and kitchen slide open," he said as they walked out, "onto the balcony, which extends the length of the living room and kitchen."

"Wow, this place is lovely, and I love the view!" she said turning to him. "I very rarely get to see the beach from up here," she confessed, "especially this high up, it's breathtaking."

"If you look down you can see the pool area and bar," he said as they looked over. "The pool looks busy."

"But there are some loungers available," she noted.

"Well, let's get them before they go," suggested Aidan. "Come with me." She followed Aidan, who picked up her bag along the way, into his room. "You can change her and leave your stuff on the bed. If you need the bathroom, it's right across the hall. I'm going to change in my parent's room, grab some towels, suntan lotion, and meet you at the front door."

"Okay," she said watching him close the door behind him. Brieanne undressed, put on the yellow bikini, then her shorts and top. She went into the bathroom, put her hair in a ponytail, and went to the front door where Aidan was waiting. They went to the pool, grabbed two lounges, undressed to their swimsuits, and put on sunscreen, before lying down on them. Within minutes they were soaking up the hot sun.

"This feels amazing," sighed Brieanne. "After all that walking this is exactly what we needed."

"I can't agree with you more."

As they lay there Aidan asked Brieanne about the local restaurants, bars, and the best nights to go. She told him about the happy hours, which ones had nightly entertainment, and when.

"Thanks for showing me around today."

"My pleasure, it was nice to have someone to walk around with that's male, usually I'm with my girlfriends."

"I guess people will be talking," he teased.

"Don't joke, I'm sure someone spotted us, I'm just surprised no one has texted me yet."

"Well, you made it quite clear we were friends, so you are safe."

Safe, she thought, what did he mean by that.

"Do you want to go for a swim?"

"I would love to," she replied.

Aidan stood up and jumped in the pool. When he surfaced, he looked over at Brieanne walking slowly towards him down the steps and into the water. The yellow bikini complimented her tanned skin and fit her perfectly. Aidan guessed she was a thirty-six, twenty-four, thirty-six. The only reason he thought that is because he read an article in a health magazine that someone had left on the airplane, which stated that they were the perfect female body measurements, and Brieanne's body was perfect.

She quickly swam over to him, undid her ponytail, put the elastic around her wrist, and leaned her head back to soak her hair. "This feels so refreshing," she sighed lifting her hair out of the water and moving remarkably close to Aidan who took a step back. "I don't bite," she said with a grin and put her arms around his shoulders. After he placed his arms around her lower back, she wrapped her legs around his waist. "I've been meaning to ask you something," she said curiously.

"Do you want to know if I bite?"

She giggled. "No."

"Okay, what?"

"Why did you kiss me today?"

"You had just told me something very personal. I said thank you and wanted to show you I appreciated your openness. I thought giving you a kiss would be a nice way of doing that."

"It was, thank you," she said, it was a nice gesture, but it wasn't the answer she was hoping to hear. "That's the only reason?"

"Yes."

"But, not on the lips?" she probed.

"No."

"You don't like my lips?" she said playfully.

"Hmm, they're okay," he said nonchalantly.

Brieanne splashed him. "You filthy…Scallywag!"

Aidan laughed. "Not only do you speak using fishing terms but pirate ones, also."

Brieanne laughed with him.

"Time to throw ye overboard."

"No," she screamed as she was lifted in the air, thrown, and landed with a splash. When she came up, she deliberately left her hair draped over her face, and pointed to him saying in a foreboding voice, "I'm going to get you for that!"

"Can we help, miss?" asked a young boy from behind.

"How many are there of you?" she asked looking back at him.

"Me and my two brothers," he replied, desperately wanting to be part of their fun.

"Come over here and join me," she said, then turned to Aidan who was now slowly backing away.

"On three," she whispered to them. "One, two, three!"

"Get him" screamed the boys as they followed Brieanne around the pool chasing Aidan until they eventually cornered him.

"He's all yours, boys," said Brieanne.

The children proceeded to dunk him without showing any mercy.

After they finished, Brieanne high fived them as they swam past her, then slowly made her way to Aidan who was wiping his wet face and catching his breath. She put her arms around his shoulders, her legs around his waist as he put his hands around hers, awfully close to her bum, she noted. "I think that was a mutiny, captain."

"I believe so," he said between breaths, "I think I swallowed half the pool." He looked into her pretty eyes, smiled at her, and said, "you got me…you got me good!"

"Yep! I sure did!" she said gleefully. "Try topping that!"

"I'm not sure I can."

"You can't and you know it," she said proud of herself.

"Do you want a victory beer?"

"Yeah, I'm kind of thirsty from kicking your butt," she gloated with a cheeky grin.

"I'll meet you by the loungers," he said starting away, then turned around, and called her back. "To be totally honest with you," he whispered," in that storeroom I wanted to kiss you passionately, lift you up from that chair, and lay you on that desk. Remove your top, shorts, panties, and have my way with you over, and over, and over again."

Brieanne could feel his breath on her ear. His words excited her and by the time he had finished she was completely turned on. "Really?" she asked in a gasping voice, moving closer to him, wanting to kiss him full on the mouth.

"Nah!" said Aidan removing his hand and swimming away.

He had got her; he had got her good. She swam backwards yelling, "You filthy—"

"Scallywag!" he called back.

Suddenly out of the blue the three boys jumped into the water shouting, "get him!" and dunked him some more.

"Serves you right!" she said as she turned around and swam to the steps. Climbing them, she thought, their playfulness was a good sign.

Brieanne stood by the edge of the lounger drying herself, as she watched Aidan get out of the pool with the three boys and walk over with them to talk to a man and woman. Aidan turned, pointed, as the couple looked over at her. Then, with the three boys in tow, Aidan headed to the bar. Several minutes later he was walking toward her, as the three boys holding their drinks went toward the man and woman.

"Here you go," he said placing the beers down under the shaded table.

Brieanne grabbed a towel, passed it to him, and took a seat while she watched him dry off and sit next to her.

"Cheers," he said as their plastic cups touched and took a sip.

"Are the man and woman the boys' parents?"

"Yeah," he confirmed, "three brothers, six, seven, and nine. Nice boys."

"They are, and good to have watching your back."

"I wouldn't know about that," he replied, "all I know is that they like jumping on mine."

Brieanne laughed, spilling her beer, wiped it off then looked at him grinning. "What were you talking about?" she asked, although she kind of knew the answer.

"When I got out the pool, I asked the boys if they wanted a drink, they said yeah. I said we better check with their parents first, so we did, I got two of them chocolate milkshakes and the other one vanilla," he explained.

Brieanne reached over, squeezed his hand affectionately, before taking a drink of her beer. Aidan didn't ask her why she did that, and she didn't have to tell him, they both knew the reason. She glanced over at the parents and wanted to discuss why he pointed at her, but since he never brought it up, she decided not to. Instead, they sipped on their beers, watched people passing by on the beach, and tried to guess whether they were locals, retirees, or on vacation.

Chapter 10

In the condo Aidan threw the towels in the hamper put the sunscreen away and joined Brieanne on the balcony.

"I think it's going to be a very warm night," she speculated.

"I don't know about you, but I wouldn't mind getting a shower," said Aidan.

Brieanne gave him a startled look.

"I'm sorry, that didn't come out right, I didn't mean it that way," he fumbled. "Not together, I meant on our own, get cleaned up. I smell of chlorine and suntan lotion."

"Are you sure that's what you meant?" she asked mischievously, walking towards him.

Aidan was flush. "Of course," he mumbled. "Did you want to take one too, on your own?"

"How about we take one together?" she asked, stopping inches from him. "You could lather me up and help me wash those, hard to reach spots."

Aidan was aroused but wasn't sure if she was serious or not.

"Ha! Got you!" she yelled. "Got you! Got you! Got you!"

"Why you filthy—"

"Scallywag!" she said laughing, then kissed him on the cheek, and ran inside.

Aidan followed her into his room where she had flung herself onto his bed and sat down next to her lying body.

"I have so much fun with you," she admitted as her finger ran down his arm, "I can't remember the last time I've laughed so much."

"Same here," he said truthfully.

"I would love to take a shower, on my own, although I would have to put these shorts and shirt back on," she said smelling them. "Maybe I should run home quickly, shower, and come back." Which she preferred not to, but she did need clean clothes.

Aidan walked over to his chest of drawers and pulled out a gray oversized T-shirt. "You can change into this," he suggested passing it to her, "it will probably fit you like a dress." He opened up another drawer, saying, "I may have some drawstring shorts, but I think they may be a little big for you. You can try them on if you want?"

She jumped off the bed and read the T-shirt out loud, "New York State Fair."

He turned to her. "I went last year with my sister and her family, I bought one for my niece and nephew, and they told me I had to have one, too."

Brieanne placed the shirt against her body, it went a few inches past her bum, and she looked over at him. "No, this will be fine with just my underwear, and it's going to be a warm night so this will be perfect," she said. "I will be nice and comfortable" Did I just say this will be fine with just my underwear.

"As long as you're comfortable," said Aidan. "You can have the bathroom across the hallway to yourself. There are towels in the cupboard, shampoo and soap containers on the ledge, a hairbrush on the counter, and a hairdryer hanging next to the mirror. Is there anything else you will need?"

"No, I think that's everything."

"Well, I'm going to use my parent's room. I just need a couple of things from here," he said rummaging through a drawer and pulling out a couple of articles of clothes. "I will meet you on the balcony when you're done, there's no rush, so take your time."

The door closed, she mouthed yes excitedly and threw herself on the bed, then jumped up and down on it.

The door opened again. "Before I—" he stopped as he watched her slowly become stationary.

"I was…just checking out how springy your bed is, that's how we do it in Madeira Beach. If you go to a mattress store around here, that's what you will see, people jumping up and down on them. We don't lie on a bed here to test it, no, sir, and by the way this one is excellent," she said awkwardly.

"Good to know," he said nodding his head slowly up and down.

Quick, change the subject, she thought. "Before I," she repeated.

He gave her a blank look.

"When you came in, you started saying, before I."

"Oh yes, I did. Before I go, do you prefer red or white wine?"

"White, please," she said in a calm voice, trying her best to sound in control.

"White it is," he confirmed, "see you on the balcony."

"See you soon," she said managing a grin. When the door closed, she crumbled onto the bed, "that's how we do it in Madeira Beach. If you go to a mattress store around here, that's what you will see, people jumping up and down on them. We don't lie on a bed here to test it, no, sir, and by the way this one is excellent," she repeated to herself, mortified.

Forty minutes later she joined Aidan on the balcony. He was wearing cotton, plaid boxers, with a white T-shirt that showed off his fit body. He looked incredibly cute and sexy.

"Did you find everything okay?" he asked passing her a glass of wine.

"I did, thank you," she replied taking it.

Aidan watched her as she took a sip. Her blow-dried hair hung captivatingly on her shoulders, the tan on her face made her eyes sparkle, and her body was seductively stunning. "You look, amazing."

"Thank you," she softly said. "It's just a T-shirt." Just a T-shirt, she thought, who are you kidding? Before you left the room, you gave yourself a final once over, and knew the T-shirt made you look cute and seductive. You couldn't have planned a more perfect look for this evening. "But you're right, it fits like a dress, and I'm very comfortable."

"I took your advice and dressed comfortable, too."

Brieanne looked into his eyes, steely blue, yet gentle and kind. She realized she was staring at him and distracted herself by walking to the edge of the balcony and gazing out at the horizon. "The sun will be setting within the hour," she predicted.

"It should be another beautiful sunset," he said standing next to her. The word sunset reminded him of something. "I wanted to ask you about that ring?"

"Sure."

"Why does Harriett keep it locked up in a safe?"

"She doesn't always," replied Brieanne, noticing his confused look, she elaborated on her answer. "The day after she showed it to my mother and me, she had it on display all the time. People were always asking to look at it and telling her how beautiful it was. Overtime, she was getting so many requests that she decided to limit the time she put it out. Plus, people always wanted to hold it or try it on, and she was worried it would get damaged. The majority of the time it sits in the safe, except for a couple of hours each day, where she will put it out on display."

"Doesn't she want to sell it?"

"Originally that was the plan," explained Brieanne. "You see Harriett is a well-known jeweler in these parts and her main passion is costume jewelry. But as she said, once in a while she would dabble by mixing costume with real gems. Not only is her costume and mixed jewelry unique, but they are also reasonably priced and affordable for the people shopping in her store. But the 'Sunset for Two Lovers' ring is the exception; it's platinum, has a one and a half carat yellow diamond, crushed clear diamonds, and is very expensive. So, the average person walking off the street into her store wouldn't be able to afford to buy it."

"Did anyone ever offer to buy it?"

"One month after she put it on display there was one wealthy woman from New York City who came into the store offering her twice what it was worth, Harriett refused. The lady offered her three times, Harriett refused again."

"Why?"

"A few years ago, I asked my mom that same question. She told me that when the woman made an offer for the ring, Harriett asked her why she wanted it, the woman replied because I will be the envy of Manhattan. Harriett wasn't impressed. She asked her when you look closely at the ring, what do you see? The woman replied it's unique, like me. My mother said the woman could have offered any amount of money to Harriett but would never have sold it to someone like her. From that day on, when she displayed the ring, it had a small sign in front of it, not for sale."

"Really," said Aidan interestedly. "Why do you think she holds onto it?"

"I believe there are a couple of reasons, obviously money isn't one of them. I think she wants whoever wears it to truly appreciate it, and for it to a have a real meaning to them, not just to show off and flaunt." She looked over at Aidan, "compare it to an artist who has painted her finest picture, a one-of-a-kind painting. Would she not want the person who purchased that picture to appreciate it, to be able to envision the story it is conveying, and have a lifelong connection with it? Not just be hung on a wall for show."

"I can see her point."

"Now, with that being said, deep down I think she just doesn't want to let it go. What her reason is behind that, I don't know, that's her secret."

"She never wears the ring?"

"Oh no, never!" said Brieanne emphatically. "Harriett would never do such a thing. She would look upon that as being conceited and vain."

"That makes sense," replied Aidan turning his body toward her. "I can see how a twelve-year-old girl can come up with the ring being a beach and a sunset, but how did you come up with the two lovers?"

"When you say it like that it sounds odd but it's really quite simple. As you know I have lived here all my life, and when I was very young, almost every day my parents would take me for a walk along the beach at sunset. There were always other families out strolling so all the children used to run ahead and play together while the parents chatted. When I was around ten, I said to my mom and dad I felt sad that some of the parents had no children. My parents told me that those couples were two lovers who came out to share their love with the sunset. After that, when we walked along the beach at sunset, I would look out for the two lovers. I would notice them sitting on the sand, walking along the shoreline, or holding one another as they looked out at the horizon. From that point on I always associated the sunset with two lovers."

"That's incredible," said Aidan amazed.

Brieanne blushed. "It's really not that incredible, it's right in front of you, you just have to look for it."

"How so?" he asked.

"Come closer," she suggested. "Look down along the beach."

Aidan moved his cheek close to hers to see what she was pointing at.

Brieanne could feel his skin touching hers and liked it. "Look there, a couple sitting on a blanket cuddling…and over there, a couple on beach chairs holding hands…there, a couple sitting on the sand with their arms around each other." She then motioned along the shoreline. "Look at the couples walking in the wet sand, some are even holding their shoes and walking in the water…and right down there, a couple is standing ankle deep in the water holding one another looking out at the horizon." She stopped, turned around as did he, their lips inches apart.

"And a couple on the balcony," he said.

"Yes," she whispered.

He kissed her softly on the lips, smiled, and then moved away. Was that another thank you kiss? she thought, as she watched Aidan go inside and come out with his cell phone.

"A selfie of us, on the balcony, with the sunset behind us?" he offered.

"Yes, yes, hurry!"

Aidan took the picture and showed it to her.

"That is an amazing photo. The sunset behind us is perfect. Will you text it to me?"

"I will. Here, put in your number," he said handing her his cell, which she did and handed it back. "I will send it now" he said typing the message, "there, sent."

"Oh, my phone is in the bedroom, one second," she said excitedly leaving.

Aidan noticed her slowly walking back looking at her phone. "Is everything okay?"

"Yeah, I missed a call from my mom, and a text. She wants me to call her tomorrow. It just so happens she sent them thirty minutes after we left Harriett," she said shaking her head and smiling. "I just got yours," she said looking at it. It was the picture he had just taken with the caption, 'Quite the Catch!' She looked up at him, "I am, am I," she said happily.

"Actually, I was talking about me."

"Why you filthy—"

"Don't say it!"

"Scallywag!" she cried, then went on her phone, and did something. She smiled, looked up at him, and put it on the table. Then picked up her glass and swallowed the last mouthful of wine.

Aidan's phone dinged and he looked at her reply. Brieanne had sent the same picture back but with the caption, 'Quite the Bait!' He walked slowly to her. "Am I the bait?" he asked.

"Yes," she whispered as he came closer.

"Then you must be the catch of a lifetime," he suggested.

"Maybe."

He was silent for a moment then whispered, "can I fill you up?"

What? Fill me up, she thought, with what? "Umm, I guess."

"Okay," he said slowly reaching his hand out towards her.

Am I trembling? I am.

"Another half a glass?" he asked loudly.

"What?" As she snapped back into reality and watched him walk away with her empty wine glass. You filthy—

"Scallywag," he said as if reading her mind.

"Better make it a full glass!" she shouted over her shoulder then looked down at the children playing in the pool.

Aidan handed her the wine and looked at what had her attention. "You like children."

"I do, I think they're great," she said sipping her wine. "I can tell you do."

"What gave it away, the pool today?"

"You told me you were a teacher. I assumed to be in a profession like that you must like kids, and seeing you in the pool today, confirmed it for me," she said turning to him, and realized this was as good a time as any to ask. "What were you talking about with their parents to make you point at me?"

"I asked if could buy the boys a drink. They asked if the kids had been bothering me. I said no, quite the opposite that we had a lot of fun, and…"

"And what?" she asked impatiently.

"I pointed you out, told them you started the whole thing, and if the boys were naughty, you were to blame."

"You didn't?"

"I sure did!"

"What did they say?"

"They laughed, they knew I was joking, but the wife did say that my girlfriend was a very attractive troublemaker."

Girlfriend, she thought. She wondered if everyone at the pool thought the same or just her. It made her happy to think so. "What did you say?"

"I told them you were my older sister!"

"You did not," she said looking at him unsure. "Did you?"

He snickered at the look on her face. "No, I said she is very attractive, is a lot of fun, and loves kids."

"But you just asked if I like children?" she said puzzled.

"No, I said 'you like children,' it was a statement," he said smiling at her. "Anyone who lets her hair hang in front of her face, then turns around to invite three boys join in on the fun, has to like children."

Brieanne knew Aidan was spot on and she adored the way he seen her for who she really was. "You didn't tell them I wasn't your girlfriend?"

"If I told them, then I would have to tell everyone at the pool," he said matter-of-fact.

He also thinks everyone thought we were a couple.

Aidan laughed a little.

"What's so funny?"

"The boys thought we were married. After I bought them their drinks, they asked me to say thank you to my wife."

"And?"

"They had walked away, and I didn't want to shout out across the deck that you weren't."

"Does it bother you what the parents and boys said?"

He looked at her for a moment before answering. "No."

"No?"

"The way I look at it, if the parents and kids see us having a fun time in the pool and want to assume we are either a couple or married, I don't see any harm in that. Even if they knew we were only friends they would still see us acting in the same way," he explained.

Brieanne realized what Aidan was implying. "So, what you are saying, it's more important for people to see us for who we are; not what we are."

"That's a perfect summation."

Brieanne liked the way they communicated it was like they were in sync with one another.

"I like the way we both see things the same way," said Aidan, "it's like we are—"

"In sync with one another," she said laughing.

"You see, that's the phrase I was going to say."

"I was just thinking the same thing," she admitted.

They chuckled then both went silent.

"You must be hungry?"

"I am a little."

"I'll be back in a minute." A few minutes later she returned with three plates and placed them on the table. "We have a selection of cheeses and crackers, veggies and dip, and fresh fruit."

"These look delicious. Did you make them?"

"I did, while you were getting ready."

They sat down, and as they ate, pointed out the stars as they appeared one by one, then the constellations. After Aidan poured them another glass of wine, they talked about their day at John's Pass Village.

"What are the plans for tomorrow?"

"I'm glad you reminded me. I have to be at work in the morning around ten and I should be done no later than two. I thought you could come over to my place and hang out, I will make us dinner, and we can just chill. Because Tuesday I'm off and I have something planned for the whole day and night," she revealed. "Does that sound okay?"

"Of course, it sounds great."

"The only thing is, I'm not sure the exact time I will be off tomorrow, it maybe earlier or later," she said, knowing where she was going with it, but not wanting to directly ask him.

"Text me," he suggested. "You have my number."

"I will," she replied happily and finishing her wine. "It's late; I should get going home and go to bed."

"What time did you say you needed to be at work?"

"Around ten."

"Why don't you stay here?" he suggested. "You can take my room and I will take my parents. It would save us from having to change, walk to your place, and me walking back."

"You don't mind?"

"Not at all, you're more than welcome to stay, and we can have breakfast together before you leave."

"Okay," she said standing. "First, let me help you tidy up."

"No, I got this." He stood, walked her to the bathroom, and reached into the cabinet. "Here is a new toothbrush, wrapper still on, and I will come by in a few minutes and say goodnight."

Brieanne brushed her teeth, washed her face, and went into the bedroom and got under the sheets. In the distance she could hear Aidan cleaning up in the kitchen, then stop, and him walking to her room. There was a knock on her door. "Come in," she said.

Leaving the door slightly ajar to let some light in from the hallway, Aidan walked over to her bed, and lay on his side next to her. "I'm so glad," he said quietly to her.

"Glad about what?" she whispered.

"That you tested the bed out earlier rather than having to do it now."

Brieanne burst out laughing and put her hands over her face. "Please don't, I am still mortified about that."

"We don't lie on a bed here to test it, no, sir, and by the way this one is excellent," he said mimicking her.

She laughed again. "Please stop!" she begged.

"Okay, I will…But I am glad I met you, and I want you to know that I really like being with."

"I like being with you, too," she said turning to him.

"Goodnight," said Aidan kissing her delicately on the lips. "I'll see you in the morning."

"Goodnight," she replied softly, kissing him back.

Aidan closed the door behind him, the room went dark, and in the silence, she could hear her heart racing.

Chapter 11

The following morning Brieanne stirred, looked at the time on her phone and read 8 a.m. She stretched, got out of bed, fixed her T-shirt, and opened the door. As she did, she could hear faint noises coming from the kitchen and followed them to Aidan.

"I hope I didn't wake you?"

"No," she replied groggily.

"Good, I'm almost done," he said putting the last items on a tray, "follow me."

Brieanne followed him down the hallway, into his parents' room and out on the balcony. The sun was shining brightly, in the distance. To her left she could see Crystal Island, straight ahead Little Bird Key, and to her right Jack's Boat Basin and John's Pass Village. "This is quite a view, too," she sighed, sitting down.

"Yeah, my parents love it. They say if they move here, they will have the best of both worlds, watching the sunrise and the sunset."

"Why didn't your aunt and uncle take this one?"

"I'm not sure, could be because they are more evening people and know my parents would appreciate the sunrise more than they would or maybe they're trying to bribe them to move down by giving them accessibility to sunrises and sunsets."

"Maybe a little bit of both."

"Probably."

"If your parents move here, are they are going to live in this condo?"

"That's the plan," said Aidan taking the items off the tray and placing them in front of her. "Cheese omelet, fresh cut cantaloupe, toast, orange juice, and coffee."

"Oh, this looks divine," she said as she cut through the omelet and took a bite. "Hmmm, this is so fluffy and cheesy."

Aidan talked while they ate. "If my parents move here, they will keep the house on Canandaigua Lake, that way they can all go there for a vacation."

"They are going to leave it empty?"

"Probably not, my sister's place is getting too small for her family, and her and her husband are talking about moving to a bigger place. So, I think my parents are going to tell them to move into theirs."

"Give it to them?"

"Yeah," he said. "That way the house won't be empty, and my sister's family will have a nice big place on the lake. Also, when my parents visit, they can stay with them, there's more than enough room. Or at my aunt and uncle's, it's literally the next house over."

"What is your aunt and uncle going to do with theirs?"

"They're going to rent it out by the week or the month, and when they want to go there, they won't rent it off for that period. If my sister moves into my parent's place, her and my brother-in-law will keep an eye on it for them and take care of it."

"I see."

"Of course, it all depends on my parents moving here."

"Do you think they will?"

"I don't know," he said, frankly. "I know they love it here, but I get the feeling that something is holding them back."

"You?" she asked cautiously.

"Yeah, I think so," he said regrettably. "As I mentioned to you, I told them I was thinking of moving, but I don't know if I sold them on that."

"Your parents seemed pretty happy with the idea of you moving here?"

"They sure did."

She was about to ask him why he just doesn't but didn't have to.

"I need to sell my place first before I can make any major decisions. I really can't plan my next step till that happens."

"That makes sense," she said, and decided to leave it at that, but in her heart, she hoped his house would be sold sooner than later.

"All done?" asked Aidan reaching for her empty plate.

"I am," she replied, "that was delicious, thank you."

"You're welcome," he said, putting the empty dishes on the tray. "Now we have room to enjoy our coffee."

"I will text you later on and let you know what time to come over," she said taking a sip.

"That's fine."

"What are you going to do till then?"

"Hang around the condo, tidy up, and catch up on the news. Maybe go for a walk, have a swim, grab some lunch," he said with uncertainty. "I'm at a loss on my own."

"That's for sure," she said candidly. "What would you do without me?"

"I don't know," he said honestly, "these last few days have been great and I'm looking forward to this afternoon."

"So am I," she said eagerly then looked at the time. "Oh no, I have to go."

"Do you want me to walk you home?"

"No, that's fine I have to hurry, you can watch me from balcony," she suggested standing and heading for the bedroom. She quickly changed, put everything in her plastic bag including his T-shirt, and went looking for him. He wasn't in his parents' room. "Aidan," she called.

"I'm here," he replied as he came inside from the balcony. "Can I have one more minute of your time? I promise it will only be one minute."

She smiled and walked over to him. "All right, you have one more minute."

He held her hand and led her outside as the sun's rays crept slowly onto the beach.

"Oh my, this is beautiful!" she cooed. "From up here you get such a different perspective. Look at all these early risers, walking and jogging, and the families with their toddlers, how cute." Brieanne looked over at him. "Thank you for showing me this, in fact, thank you for last night, this morning, everything." She gave him a big hug and didn't want to let go.

Aidan walked her to the elevator, gave her a smile, and said goodbye. Once inside he went onto the balcony to watch her. "On the ride down Brieanne was a little sad to be leaving him, but only a little, because she knew she would be seeing him in several hours. She walked onto the sand, looked up at Aidan and waved, as he waved back. Then quickly walked down the beach, onto her path, and to her gate; knowing in her heart that he was watching her walk all the way home.

Brie walked into work a minute passed ten, where she was immediately met by an excited Cathy.

"Tell me, tell me, tell me!" she pleaded.

Brie grabbed her hand, pulled her into the office, closed the door, and sat next to her. Brie was about to speak when there was a knock on the door.

"Come in," said Brie.

The door opened and Bev walked in closing it behind her.

"Bev! What are you doing here?" asked Brie surprised. "You don't start till four."

"I was in the neighborhood, thought I would drop in," said Bev walking around the office, lifting up pieces of paper like you see a detective do in a TV show.

"What are you doing?" asked Brie laughing along with Cathy.

"Okay, Cousin, what's going on?" asked Bev suspiciously.

"What do you mean?" replied Brie, acting innocently.

"No, no, no, don't you try that innocent routine on me Brie," said Bev giving Brie the once over before taking a seat next to them. "Let's start with Friday night, shall we. I thought it was a little peculiar you showing up for the dinner, but it was a special night, so I let it go. How stunning you looked in your dress—"

"Why, thank you," interrupted Brie.

"You're welcome," replied Bev with a grin, and then got serious again. "I thought, what's the big deal, she wants to dress up and get out of the house, so I let that slide too. Throughout the night you were mingling and talking with all the customers, I thought okay, maybe it's legit."

Brie and Cathy were amused by her detective role playing.

"But!" she said loudly startling Brie and Cathy. "Around sunset you sit with that group, you know the ones I'm talking about, with the two older couples and a very handsome man. Not only that, but you sit next to said man."

"Said man!" said Brie and Cathy in unison and burst out laughing, Bev joined in.

"I heard it on CSI," she explained between her giggles, then went serious again. "Yes, said man. Not only did you sit next to him but also left with them."

"She just dropped them off," said Cathy, playing along.

"This is true," confirmed Bev.

"It is?" asked Cathy looking at Brie, trying not to laugh.

"When I left here on Friday night, I drove up Gulf Boulevard glanced over at your place and spotted your car parked in the driveway," revealed Bev. "I thought to myself my instincts were off, my favorite cousin Brie was being straight with me, and I felt bad for doubting here."

"Oh, don't be too hard on yourself, and your instincts," blurted out Brie which made them laugh again.

Suddenly Bev stopped. "But my instincts weren't off, were they Brie?" she said standing and pacing back and forth in front of her.

"They weren't?" asked Brie.

Cathy took the light from the desk, turned it around, and shone it in Brie's face.

"Thank you," said Bev to Cathy while trying to keep a straight face. "Where were you Sunday afternoon around four?"

Brie knew exactly where she was but said nothing.

"And who where you with?"

Brie knew that, too, and was silent.

"I think you were with that same man from Friday night walking north on Gulf Boulevard," stated Bev.

"I think you have me confused with someone else," replied Brie.

Bev reached for her phone, fidgeted with it, and then put it inches from Brie's eyes. "Does this look like I have you confused with someone else?"

"Let me see," said Cathy as Bev showed her the photo, then put it back in front of Brie's face.

"Wait, you were across the street, in the—"

"Bamboo, having a drink with my friends," she confirmed. "By chance I glance up to witness my hot cousin with her hunky man-friend crossing the street."

Brie thought for a moment. "He was lost, and I was pointing him in the right direction."

"Uh-huh," said Bev shaking her head in disbelief. "Look at this picture you both have the same plastic bag from Harriett's store."

"You went shopping with him?" asked Cathy impatiently, wanting the interrogation to stop so she could hear the details.

"How could you lie to me, your own cousin, your own blood?" asked Bev, very dramatically.

"Okay, you got me CSI: Bev," said Brie. "I'm guilty, but I did say to Cathy before I left Friday night, that I would tell you as soon as I saw you."

"I know," said the old Bev sitting down.

"You know?" asked Brie confused.

"Cathy told me everything after you left Friday night," confessed Bev. "I was going to text you the picture Sunday, but I preferred to see you squirm for a bit."

"Sorry Brie, you know I'm not a good liar, and I was so happy for you," said Cathy in her defense, "and Bev is very persuasive."

"Thank you," said Bev.

"That wasn't a compliment," kidded Cathy, who turned her attention to Brie. "Tell us!"

"Everything!" added Bev.

Brie gave them all the details from Friday night up until this morning.

"You haven't slept together?" asked Bev.

"No," replied Brie, "but there have been sexual undertones."

Bev and Cathy were all ears as she explained each of them.

"Oh, you guys definitely need to get it on," said Bev bluntly.

"Maybe, but right now we are just enjoying our time together. We talk, we laugh, and we think and see things the same way," she explained. "We're still getting to know one another and it's nice."

"Are you in love with him?" whispered Cathy, who was the romantic of the two.

"I don't know," replied Brie hesitantly. "I think about him a lot, I wonder what he is doing, and it's difficult leaving his side."

Cathy and Bev quickly glanced over at one another.

"When are you seeing him again?" asked Bev.

"This afternoon, he is coming over to my place. I'm cooking him dinner."

"Dinner!" said Cathy. "How romantic!"

"Not that kind of dinner, BBQ and beer," contradicted Brie.

"It's not about the food," suggested Bev.

"It's about the company," added Cathy.

"Will you two please, stop!" said Brie smiling at them "Oh, I almost forgot." She searched on her phone then showed them the photo.

"Oh, you guys look so happy," sighed Cathy.

"You look like such a couple," said Bev.

"You think?" asked Brie looking at the picture and totally thinking they did too. Suddenly her phone rang. "It's my mom I have to take it."

The three stood up and did a group hug.

"We are both happy for you," said Cathy.

"You deserve this," said Bev.

"Thank you, love you both." Brie waited till the door closed behind them, then answered. "Hello, Mom."

"Brieanne honey, how are you doing?"

"Fine, I'm just at work."

"How was your weekend?"

"Busy," replied Brieanne knowing her mom was slowly circling into the reason for her call.

"What did you do yesterday?" asked her mom trying to be nonchalant.

"I walked around John's Pass Village, had a late lunch, and shopped."

"Oh," she replied trying to sound casual. "Did you go on your own?"

"No, I went with someone."

"Bev?"

"Mom, I know you know," said Brieanne laughing, "so cut out the act."

"Okay, honey, I didn't want to sound like I was intruding, and will cut to the chase. Tell me about him, Harriett said he is quite the—"

"Were you going to say catch?"

"Well—"

"Mom, you're not even a fisherman."

"Actually, I was going to say…" she said stalling to find another word, "that he is quite handsome, polite, kind, and…adorable. That's the word, adorable."

"That's only the tip of the iceberg Mom," said Brieanne with a sigh.

"I'm listening," said her mom, as Brieanne told her about him. "He sounds wonderful; I can hear the happiness, and excitement in your voice."

"He is wonderful and makes me feel that way whenever I am with him."

"I'm happy for you, honey. Promise me you will call in a couple of days and let me know how you are doing."

"I promise," she replied.

"Oh, I almost forgot to tell you. We are thinking of coming to visit next month for several weeks, probably fly in on the twenty-seventh. We haven't booked yet, when we do, we'll let you know."

"That's great Mom! Let me know as soon as you do," replied Brieanne. "How is Dad?"

"He's fine, he is on a fishing trip this morning with some friends and should be back in a few hours."

"Tell him I said hello and that I love him."

"Will do honey. Love you."

"Love you too, Mom," she replied. "Oh Mom, before I forget."

"Yes, dear."

Brieanne couldn't resist. "Harriett gave Aidan a hug."

"What?" screamed her mom in disbelief. "No, she didn't? Did she? Tell me!"

"She did, I saw it with my own eyes, George too."

"Brieanne I have to go, love you, bye," said her mom quickly hanging up.

Brieanne knew exactly who her mom was calling next. She looked at her phone, and wondered why not, and sent a text to Aidan: "At work, was a minute late but that minute was worth it, hope you are having a nice morning." She looked at her phone, waiting for a response, and then realized she needed to get some work done if she wanted to be out by two. Before she could start Aidan replied.

Aidan: "Not bad, just finished tidying up, watched the news, going for a swim around 11.

She read his message a little disappointed, there was no question to reply to.

Aidan: "Sorry, how is your morning so far?"

Brieanne: "Busy." Well busy, in so far as being interrogated by Bev and talking about him to her mom.

Aidan: "Okay, I should let you get back.

Brieanne realized she had made a blunder by saying she was busy.

Aidan: "If you get some down time feel free to text me."

Brieanne replied happily: "Will do."

She worked for ninety minutes, took a lunch break with Cathy, during which she texted Aidan: "How is the pool?"

Aidan: "Crowded. Lots of families, lots of kids. How is work?"

"Aidan?" asked Cathy.

"Yeah, he is at the pool," she said then replied to Aidan: "On a lunch break with Cathy."

"I bet he looks hot in a bathing suit?" queried Cathy.

"Superhot!" replied Brie.

Aidan: "Tell her I said hi. Those three boys found two more friends to add to their group, been playing with them, I'm taking a breather now."

"He said to say hi," said Brie to Cathy.

Cathy blushed. "Say hi, back."

Brieanne: "Cathy says hi. Did you have lunch?"

"He's been playing with the kids in the pool," said Brie.

Aidan: "Walking over to the bar now, probably something healthy, like a burger, fries, and milkshake."

"He's ordering lunch," said Brie with a sad face.

"What's wrong?" asked Cathy.

"I don't know, it's kind of silly," she replied. "It's just that he will be eating on his own."

Cathy shook her head. "Oh Brie, you are in trouble!"

Aidan: "I'm now with those five kids, they have checked with their parents, and I'm buying them lunch. We are going to sit together."

Brieanne let out an, "Aw!"

"What?" asked Cathy.

Brie told her.

"That is so sweet," said Cathy. "Like I said, if I wasn't married—"

"But you are, and good looking, with a nice set of boobs, so back off," snapped Brie comically.

"Girls, Brie is in the house and in love! Look out or she will put a hurt on you if you go near her man, Aidan!" said Cathy, making some of the people on the patio look over. Brie laughed hysterically at her friend's unconventional antics.

Aidan: "Going to eat lunch now. Hope you are enjoying yours?"

Brieanne: "I am, you, too."

After another ninety minutes of work Brieanne was finished. It was almost two, and she still had a couple of stops to make on the way home and decided to text Aidan first. "Finished, have to make a few stops, do you want to come over in forty minutes?"

Aidan: "Okay."

Brieanne: "Leave by the security gate entrance, make a right on Gulf Lane till you see my house, knock on the front door."

Aidan: "Will do. Do I need to bring anything with me?"

Brieanne: "Just your bathing suit."

Aidan: "Ok."

Brieanne: "Since we are up and out early tomorrow, did you want to sleep here? I have a spare room. It will save us some time in the morning." She waited five minutes but there was no response. She wondered if she was being too forward with him and contemplated letting him know it was okay if he didn't want to. She decided to wait and left to run her errands. Fifteen minutes later she received a text from Aidan, anxiously she read it out loud: "Apologies, I had to take a call, that's a great idea, will bring change of clothes." Her anxiety now gone she cheerfully finished her tasks.

Chapter 12

Brieanne heard a knock on the front door and opened it. "Aidan, come in," she said warmly.

"I can't believe how beautiful this place is from the outside," he said walking into the foyer.

"Thank you," she replied shyly, "let me do you the honor of showing you around the inside."

"I'd like that," he said following her.

"To your left, through these French doors is the dining room," she said opening them.

"Wow, this is a big room."

"If you follow me through these doors here, we walk into the kitchen, with a nice, big island."

"This is incredible."

"This is one of my favorite rooms," she confessed, "my mom and I spend a lot of time in here when she visits. On the other side of the island is a breakfast bar, and if we walk past that, there is a breakfast area with large windows looking out onto the Gulf. If we cross over here, this is the family room, again with a large window. This is where I usually read or listen to music."

Aidan was now speechless.

"If we head back towards the foyer, in here is the laundry room," she said opening the door. "The door next to it is the powder room and then the stairs to the bedrooms. But first, let me show you the living room."

Afterwards, he followed her up the spiral stairs to a bedroom on the right. "This is my room," she said walking inside, "it has en suite, walk-in closet, and a balcony." As they walked over, she opened the balcony doors to reveal the view, and it was spectacular. They left her room going into the one next to hers. "This is your room," she said glancing at him. "This room has a walk-in closet, and these doors here also open out to the same balcony. Through this door, is a full Jack and Jill bathroom, and if we walk across and open this door on the other side, we are now inside the third bedroom. The only differences between this bedroom and yours, is that this one has its own balcony, and it faces the street."

They left the third bedroom and went into the hallway. "In case you're wondering about this door, it also goes into the bathroom. That way visitors have direct access to it and don't have to go in through one of the spare bedrooms," she explained. "Behind this last door is a closet that has towels, blankets and pillows."

Brieanne took him down the stairs to the kitchen, opened two patio doors situated between the kitchen area and the family room, and took him outside to a large deck. She stopped at a cooler, grabbed two beers gave him one, and then proceeded to show him the swimming pool and ten-person hot tub. They walked past the pool to the back, down several steps, and onto a smaller deck that had several chairs and loungers. Beyond that there were several steps leading down to a locked gate that opened up to the path leading to the beach.

"Brieanne this is beautiful, I mean looking at it from the street you can see that it is, but from the beach you see a good size house, but you wouldn't believe it was this magnificent," he caught himself. "I'm sorry, I didn't mean that the way it sounded, it's not that is doesn't look nice from the beach."

"I know what you mean," she said reassuringly.

Aidan attempted to explain himself better. "I guess what I mean is that from the beach, even walking up the path, you would never suspect this amazing place was here. Does that make sense?"

"Perfect sense," she said. "One of the features I love about this place is for that reason, it's hidden from the beach. In other words, when you look at it from the beach everything is above eye level, so all you can really see is the deck, so it's deceiving and very private."

"Yeah, that's the word, deceiving."

Brieanne wondered whether he was still talking about the house or about her not sharing this with him sooner. "Let's go back to the upper deck," she said leading the way and offering him a seat.

"I see what you mean by seeing the beach from different perspectives," said Aidan sipping on his beer. "I think this view is one of my favorites."

"It's one of my favorites, too," she admitted smiling at him. "I love sitting out here."

"Thanks for inviting me over."

"You're, welcome," she replied as she touched her beer can with his and took a sip.

"Is this the house you grew up in?"

"No," she replied taking him down by the pool and pointing to the house next door. "I grew up there, it's quite a bit smaller, but it has many fond memories. I lived there with my parents from the time I was born till I was twenty-three. While I was attending university, I told them that after I graduated, I needed to move out and have a place of my own. Before I graduated this place came up for sale and my parents bought it. They told me they were going to fix it up, rent it to vacationers, and asked me to decorate it in the way I would if I owned it. They said since I was younger, I would have a much better idea knowing what singles, couples and families would want in a house. So, I did. When I graduated this was my graduation present."

"Your parents live next door?"

"No, not anymore, for a while they did. After they told me the house was mine, they also said that within a year they were moving to a place on the causeway once the kitchen renovations were completed. Eight months later they moved," she explained. "As much as my parents loved the house and the beach, my dad loved fishing and boating more, and my mom, baking. So, they got a place where my dad could dock his boat and my mom got a big, brand-new, kitchen."

"That makes sense," said Aidan. "Did they sell the house when they moved to their new one?"

"No, they kept it and rent it out to vacationers. There is an older couple renting it for the summer and they'll be arriving after the Fourth of July weekend." She wasn't too sure how much to tell him but decided he might as well know some of it now. Grabbing his hand, she led him to the deck swing and sat with him. "There is something I want to tell you," she said nervously.

Aidan sensed her anxiety. "Hey, it's okay, you can tell me anything."

That made her feel a little better and she started slowly. "As you know I own this place, and my parents live in California."

Aidan nodded his head.

"Several years ago, just before my parents moved to California, they also gave me the house next door."

"You're talking about your old house?"

"Yes," she replied quietly. "They had lost interest in it and asked me if I wanted to take over it. I said of course, assuming they meant taking care of it, renting it out, that sort of thing, which they did. But they also told me that it was mine. My parents said if I owned it, I would be responsible for it and take better care of it."

"And they had already said they were moving to California?"

"Yes, there were planning on moving within a couple of years."

"That makes perfect sense," said Aidan, "better to let you do it for a few years before they go, rather than having it thrust on you last minute. Or worse, you saying you're not interested."

Brieanne was perplexed; she thought he would have reacted differently.

"Do you like taking care of it? Working with a real estate agent to rent it? Keeping it in tiptop shape and whatever else you need to do?" asked Aidan with a dubious look on his face. "I'm spit-balling here because I have no idea what it entails," he said laughing.

She giggled with him; he always made her feel better. "I love it!"

"I don't understand, what's the problem?"

"I just wanted you to know more about me," she admitted, "that's all."

"Is there anything else?"

"Actually, there is," she said standing happily, "and this is my pride and joy because it's all me."

"I'm ready," he said wondering what it was.

"Do you remember the first day we met? I had to go to a meeting, and I told you later it was with my real estate agent?"

"I do."

Brieanne grabbed his hand, walked him to the other side of the deck, and pointed to a small two-story house on the other side. "I bought that on my own," she said jubilantly, "with my own money."

"That's wonderful," said Aidan happy for her. "You must be excited about it."

"I am over the moon," she confessed.

"Are you going to the same as your old house, you know rent it out?"

"I am, but not until September, I want to take my time and fix it up. It's mostly cosmetic; I'm not renovating or tearing down walls. I just want it to look like I house I would want to live in."

"Can you show it to me?'

"Really, you want to see it?" she said cheerfully.

"Of course, I do!"

"Okay," she said eagerly, "I haven't even been in it myself, I've been so busy," she admitted. "How about tomorrow morning before we go sightseeing?"

"Perfect."

"I can make some notes and having a second pair of eyes will be extremely helpful."

"I'll help you as best as I can."

"Thank you, it will be nice us doing it together, rather than me on my own," she said beaming. "Until then, let's take it easy, and have some fun." Brieanne reached into the cooler for two more beers.

"I'm up for that," said Aidan taking one from her.

"I'm hot and sticky," she said as she took a sip. "Do you want to go for a swim?"

"Yeah, I would love to."

"Looks like you already have your swimsuit on," she acknowledged looking down at the second swimsuit she picked out for him. "Throw your shirt on the lounger and jump in. I'll be back in a few minutes." Ten minutes later Brieanne came out onto the deck wearing the peach floral bikini. Diving in she swam under water surfacing in front of him. "I am going to assume my favorite pool position with you," she said in a sensual way, as she put her arms and legs around him.

"How do you feel now?" asked Aidan placing his arms around her waist.

"Much better," she replied, "the water is cool and refreshing." She looked at him carefully, then asked, "how come you never got married?"

"Quick answer, I haven't met the right girl."

"I guessed that," she said with a grin. "What would be the long answer?"

"University, job, house, then career, they all took up a lot of my time, the latter one more so."

"Do you mean becoming a department head?"

"Yeah, I worked hard for that."

Brieanne wanted to ask why he refused the position but didn't want to push him. "What happens after you become a department head?"

"I don't know, never thought about it much, maybe balance it with marriage and a family."

"Seems pretty straightforward," she said, making Aidan laugh. "Why are you laughing?"

"Because as of today I have no job and by the end of summer I will be homeless," he said laughing again.

She laughed with him. "I guess it's not that straightforward."

"Life will always throw you curves."

"My mom always said to me, and I quote, 'everything happens for a reason; but those reasons are yours to decide.'"

Aidan thought about what she had just said it had hit close to home with him.

Brieanne noticed the distant look on his face. "Are you okay?" she asked snapping him back.

"Yeah, I was thinking about what you were saying," he said, "it's so true."

"I know it's one of the sayings I live by."

"Do you mind if I use that, too?"

"Of course not," she replied, and wondered what it was that happened to him.

"What about you?"

"Me?' she asked, puzzled.

"Marriage?"

"Same short answer as you, haven't met that special somebody, and same long answer, university, work, rentals units. But I would have to say with me, it's more that special somebody."

"You said you took business in university?"

"That was my major."

"And that is why you work at the restaurant?"

"Yeah," she replied quickly. "As well as taking on the rentals," she added to move the conversation away from her job.

"So, what do you do at the restaurant?" he asked curiously.

Oh no, she thought, she had to tell him but not now, later. "How about after dinner we go for a walk along the beach, and I will tell you then."

"Okay," he replied, realizing she had already opened up a lot about herself. "I guess it's time to throw ye overboard," said Aidan lifting her up and tossing her high into the air.

Brieanne wasn't expecting it and came down with a big splash. She had this look of bewilderment on her face when she surfaced. "Why…you…you filthy Scallywag!" she said as she slowly came towards him. "You are going to pay for that!"

"Well, you have no crew to back you up this time," said Aidan taunting her to bring it on with his hands.

"Oh, trust me," she warned, "I don't need one."

Aidan fled, Brieanne chased. She caught up to him and dunked him several times. He lifted her up tossing her high again. The battle continued back and forth for some time until Aidan conceded defeat in the shallow end. Brieanne assumed her position around him, as she bragged about her victory.

"What is my reward for winning?" she asked.

"I didn't even know we had a bet."

"As soon as you challenge someone, and they accept that challenge, and they defeat you in that challenge, they are rewarded."

"I challenged you?"

She nodded her head. "As soon as you said, time to throw ye overboard and threw me," she clarified.

"And you want to know what your reward is for winning?"

"Uh-huh."

"I get to choose the reward?" he asked playing along.

"Yes, you do, and trust me, I'm being generous."

"Generous," said Aidan smiling. "How so?"

"Since you didn't state what the reward would be prior to challenging me, I could actually select any prize I see fit. In my generosity, I am giving you a break in allowing you to decide my reward instead."

"Whose rules are these?"

"I believe this is called a stalling tactic on your part," she said trying not to giggle, "but if you must know, these are 'Brieanne's Rules of Engagement.'"

Aidan gave her an unconvinced look. "You just made that up?"

Brieanne chuckled. "Yes, I did." Then spoke sternly, "enough stalling, what is my reward?"

Aidan thought quickly. "My lady, I believe a kiss would be a fair and just reward, do you concur?"

A kiss, thought Brieanne, better than she had anticipated. "I concur."

"Then close your eyes, do not open them, hold my hands and receive your reward."

Brieanne did as he asked wetting her waiting lips in anticipation. Delicately Aidan lifted up her right hand, brought it to his lips saying my lady, and kissed it.

Brieanne opened her eyes unimpressed. "That's it."

"That is your reward," he replied swimming backward with a wide grin. "If I were you, I would have picked my own reward."

Brieanne realized he was right, he had tricked her yet again, and muttered something under her breath.

"Yes, I am," agreed Aidan, with his back now resting against the side of the pool.

"You have very good hearing," she noted swimming in front of him.

Without warning he kissed her delicately on the lips for several moments before pulling away.

"What was that for?"

"Two reasons," he replied.

"Two?"

"I owed you from the other day when we were at the BBQ with my family, I said thank you for helping me out, and you said I owed you one."

"You did," she said, suddenly remembering. "I'd forgotten all about that."

"The second reason is you," he said putting his arms around her waist.

"Me?" she asked with a puzzled look.

"Yes," he replied, "for you being amazing."

Brieanne smiled, as she put hers around him, and rested her head on his broad shoulder. She looked out at the Gulf of Mexico thinking how perfect he was. "I really like you Aidan," she whispered.

"I really like you, too, Brieanne" he said, gently kissing the top of her head.

Brieanne cheerfully looked up at him. "I want to make you something to eat," she said. She realized that after dinner she would still have to tell him everything, the only difference now, is that she wanted to.

They got out of the pool and dried off. Brieanne passed Aidan a beer as he sat on the deck swing while she turned on the BBQ. She went inside, picked up the dinner items, and placed them on the patio table. Then sat next to Aidan, sipped on her beer, and waited for the BBQ to warm up. Once it had, she threw items wrapped in tinfoil on first, then sat down again.

"It will be about thirty minutes," she informed him.

"Anything I can do to help?"

"No, it's my turn to spoil you," she said, looking into his eyes, then out at the water. She always thought the blue water was the nicest shade she had ever seen now she realized she was mistaken.

"What are you thinking about?" he queried.

"The color blue," she replied, returning her gaze upon him.

Over the next thirty minutes they talked while Brieanne cooked, then sat down to eat.

"This is prime rib, medium-rare, with my father's famous peppercorn sauce, potato au gratin, again our secret recipe, and grilled asparagus. On the table there is extra sauce in the bowl, in front of you is a glass of white wine, and the rest of the bottle is chilling over here," she said motioning to the ice bucket.

"This looks delicious."

"Thank you," said Brieanne lifting up her glass, "bon appétit."

"Bon appétit," he replied as they ate their dinner.

Aidan put his knife and fork on the empty plate. "That was delectable. The prime rib was cooked to perfection; the sauce was unbelievable—"

"I noticed you had two more helpings."

"Guilty, but you can't blame me?"

She gaily shook her head no.

Aidan continued. "The potato au gratin was rich, creamy, flavorful, and the asparagus was tender and fresh." He lifted up his glass. "To the chef, not only is she beautiful, but also an amazing cook."

"Thank you," she said blushing, "I do have dessert, but it will take an hour once I put it in the oven which just so happens to give up enough time for a leisurely walk along the beach."

"Perfect," said Aidan standing up to help her.

"You relax and drink your wine," she said, my turn to clean up. She took the dirty dishes inside, put the dessert in the oven, and several minutes later joined him.

They finished their wine and left barefoot for the shoreline.

Chapter 13

"There are a lot of people out walking," said Brieanne.

"Can't blame them, it's a lovely evening for it."

Brieanne looked down at the wet sand. She wanted to talk to him about her job but was struggling to find the right words to begin the conversation. Aidan unexpectedly held her hand and all at once she felt at ease. "You wanted to know what I did at the restaurant?" she asked slowly.

"If you don't mind?"

"I don't," she said honestly. "Can I ask you first what you think I do?"

"Sure," said Aidan stopping, letting go of her hand putting it on his chain, and made a face as if sizing her up.

"Will you stop that!" she said playfully tapping his arm with a chuckle.

"First time I was in there you didn't serve anyone or the second time, but you did walk around, mingle with customer and ask how everything was, so I'm thinking…" he said trying to decide.

"Yes?" she asked anxiously. He won't guess it, she thought.

"Restaurant manager?"

She shook her head no.

"Assistant manager!"

"No."

Aidan was trying to think of what position was below that. "I have it!"

"You do?" she said knowing he was going to crack a funny.

"You are the head busgirl!"

"I was at one time," she said shaking her head, but not now. "I own the place."

"You own the place," stumbled Aidan, caught off guard.

"I do now. My dad originally owned it, well my parents, and they still have a twenty percent interest in it, I own the remainder," she explained. "Now please, don't go thinking it was handed over to me like the houses, I worked my butt off to get to where I am today."

"I believe you," he said giving her a curious smile. "I'm guessing you are now going to tell me how much you worked your cute butt off to get where you are?"

"Yes, I am" she replied proudly.

"Wait, so your dad owned it?"

"Yes," she said wondering where he was going with it.

"So, your name is Brieanne Francisco."

"What?" she asked bursting out laughing. "Why would you think that?"

"If your dad owned the restaurant and his name is Vegas Francisco then—"

Brieanne burst into a laughter that made her double over.

Aidan watched her with uncertainty wondering what he had said that was so funny.

Brieanne composed herself. "That is not my dad's name, it's fictitious, and something he made up. My last name is Byrne." Brieanne couldn't stop thinking about what he said. "Brieanne Francisco, and my dad Vegas," she repeated as she chuckled again and looked over at Aidan's red-face. "You must admit it's pretty funny?" she asked moving close to him.

"It is and if I were you, I would be laughing hysterically too. But damn it, it's not me!" he said good-naturedly.

"You know what I like most about you?" Brieanne whispered as she moved inches from his lips, "you." She suddenly kissed him on the mouth, her tongue touching his for a brief second, before pulling away. She gave him a seductive smile, held his hand, and started to walk.

Aidan wished she had kissed him a little longer.

"I must admit, Brieanne Francisco, it's a catchy name."

Aidan wasn't sure if she was teasing him.

She noticed the uncertainty in his eyes. "No, I'm serious I like it, it's catchy."

"It is," agreed Aidan realizing she meant it.

They walked for a while in silence until Brieanne broke it.

"Would you like to hear the story on how my father picked the restaurant's name?"

"With a name like Francisco Vegas, how could you not!"

Brieanne walked for a moment, gained her composure, and began. "My grandfather and grandmother moved from Boston to San Francisco with a newborn, my dad. They went there because my grandfather's brother had moved there earlier, spotted a diner for sale, and convinced them to buy a fifty percent share in it. The plan being the two brothers would own it and run it. At the time, my grandfather's brother was single, so he moved out of his rental unit in San Francisco and lived with my grandparents who had bought their own place. Anyway, over the next few months they fixed up the diner, eventually opened up for business, and called it, 'Two Brothers' Diner.' It was a typical dinner: round seats along the counter, booths, an opening where you could see the cooks. They even had one of those round things where the waitress puts the orders on; the cook twirls it and plucks it off. Oh, what's it called?" she said looking at Aidan for help.

Aidan gave her a blank look, he knew what she was talking about, but didn't even know it had a name.

"Ticket holder, that's what it's called!" said Brieanne happy with herself. "Now one of the best features of this diner was the view. It was situated high on top of a hill, and when you looked outside its windows, you could see the San Francisco Bay, the Golden Gate Bridge, and Alcatraz."

"That would be some view."

"I know," she said in agreement. "Now my grandfather had a lot of experience cooking while his brother, not so much. But what he lacked in my grandfather's culinary skills he made up as a savvy businessman; together, the two of them made a great team. Besides the view and their teamwork, the diner had another great outstanding feature, my grandfather's culinary expertise; he became legendary in San Francisco. My grandfather only used fresh ingredients, made his own sauces and gravies, and created spectacular special entrées. Because it was a diner, they kept the traditional diner meals; they just made them taste much better and added several special of the day entrées." She looked over at Aidan who was listening attentively to her. "Fast forward, my dad is not doing too good in high school but graduates, and during his teenage years has been spending a lot of time working with his father at the diner, which has now become a gold mine."

Aidan chuckled. "San Francisco, gold mine, pretty funny Brieanne Francisco," he said liking her joke.

"I thought you would appreciate that, and it was off the top of my head, too," she said with a smile. "During those years, and over the next several, my father would learn the culinary expertise of his father, along with the business savvy of his uncle. Soon my dad began experimenting with his own recipes, sauces, and meals; and before long they added them to the menu. Now my dad's uncle, that's my grandfather's brother who lived with them, had gotten married a year after the diner opened, moved out, and had two sons. The elder one went to college and took a Hospitality Program, I believe it was Hotel and Restaurant Management, while the younger left high school and worked at the diner. Everything was going well until my grandfather had a heart attack; he didn't die but was strongly advised to do something less stressful. So, reluctantly my grandfather sold his half of the business to his brother, with the guarantee that my dad always had a job there. After selling their house, my grandparents moved back to Boston."

"Your father didn't move back with them?"

"No, my father had no interest in going back to Boston. He stayed and lived with his aunt and uncle."

"Why didn't your grandfather leave him a percentage of the diner?"

"My grandparents offered that to him, he refused, he said he didn't want to but tied down to the diner for the rest of his life. He also told me the one thing he enjoyed most about the diner was working with his dad, after he left, it was never the same."

"That makes sense."

"Do you remember I told you my dad's uncle had two sons?"

"One worked in the diner, the other went to college, Hospitality Program."

"Yes, the one who went to college is my uncle Patrick. Well, when he graduated his father thought he would help manage the diner, instead, my uncle Patrick said he wasn't interested, and took off to work in Las Vegas. At the time, his dad wasn't too thrilled about it, but he got over it. One weekend my uncle Patrick came to visit, noticing my dad wasn't happy he asked him what was wrong. My dad told him he didn't like working at the diner anymore, that his brother was now working as a cook and he wasn't particularly good, and that he had no desire to go back to Boston to live with his parents. My uncle Patrick told him he could get him a job as a waiter at this upscale restaurant in Vegas. My dad was hesitant because he had never waited before, my uncle convinced him that he worked with customers every day and knew all he needed to know. That weekend my dad flew back to Vegas with my uncle Patrick, lived with him, and started a new job as a waiter."

"How did he make out?"

Before she answered Brieanne looked at how far they had walked. "We should turn around," she said, and glanced over at him as they did. "Are you always this good of a listener?"

"Sorry, what did you say?"

"Are you—?" she caught onto his little joke. "Ha! Ha!"

"I'm pretty good," he said truthfully, "more so because this is such an interesting story."

"It must be the English teacher in you. Are you going to grade me when I finish?"

"Do you want me to?"

"I do," she replied, hoping to get a better reward from him this time around.

"Then I will. Now continue French teacher."

"French teacher?" she repeated. What is that supposed to mean? She was about to ask what he meant before realizing. "Aren't you the funny guy? You're referring to my kiss?"

"French kiss," he said, correcting her.

"It must have been quite memorable for you to bring it up?" she asked searchingly.

"Eh," he said making it sound average, which he knew it wasn't.

"You're in big trouble when we get back, mister!" she said in a serious voice as an older couple walked by giving her a disapproving look. "I'm joking, we're joking" she shouted to them, "we are just playing around." She turned to Aidan for some support; he was too busy laughing. "Thanks very much for your help," she said embarrassed.

"Come here," he said comforting her by putting his arm around her shoulder.

She quickly placed her arm around his waist and with her free hand grabbed the one hanging over her shoulder.

"Feel better now?" he asked. "Do I get a smile?"

Brieanne felt much better and gave him a beautiful smile.

"Good, now let's back to your story."

"Where was I?" she asked herself out loud. "Oh yes, you asked how he made out as a waiter. At first not too good but it didn't take him long to get a handle on it. You see my dad was exceptionally good at talking with people, remembering orders, and could tell when someone was complaining about their meal whether it was genuine or not, just by looking at it. After being there for a few months, there was a panic in the kitchen, the grill chef had called and said he had to leave immediately for an out-of-town family emergency and wouldn't be able to make his evening shift. The restaurant manager remembered when he hired my dad that he had experience as a cook, so they pulled him off his waiter shift and put him in the kitchen. The manager told him it would just be for one night and tomorrow they would find a temporary replacement. To make matters worse it was one of their busiest nights, Friday. My father realizing this was the opportunity of a lifetime seized the moment."

"Everything happens for a reason; but those reasons are yours to decide," quoted Aidan.

"Exactly," said Brieanne coming to a stop, turning to him, and smiling. She put her arms around him, and he pulled her as close as he could. They stayed like that for a few minutes before Brieanne French kissed him.

"That's much better young lady," said an old woman walking by with her husband.

"Is that that the older couple that heard me before?" whispered Brieanne.

"I'm afraid so," confirmed Aidan, as they both giggled and started to walk slowly.

"How did your father make out?"

"My dad excelled that night! After the shift, the head chef hired him, took him under his wing, and my dad never looked back. They became good friends, and he learnt as much as he could from him as well as the people around him." Brieanne stopped and looked over at Aidan. "My dad has this incredible memory for retaining orders, how long food has been cooking, elapsed time, and if someone showed him something once, he would remember it. The head chef knew my dad had no formal training, but my dad would listen and do whatever he said without question, which he respected. But most of all," said Brieanne, "the head chef knew my father was an extraordinary cook."

"He must have been, to be hired on the spot, and have the head chef take to him like that" said Aidan as they started to walk again. "Did he meet your mom in Las Vegas?"

"He did. At the hotel my uncle Patrick worked at, he met a family. The father's job had been relocated from San Francisco, and they were staying there for a couple of days till their furniture arrived. He started talking to them about San Francisco and during the conversation it was mentioned that one of his daughters had waitress experience and was looking for work. My uncle Patrick got her a job as a waitress at the same restaurant my dad worked at, and they hit it off immediately. My parents both worked in the same place, had the same shifts, and the same time off; it was perfect. They dated, then after a couple years, got married.

"It must have been fun for them to work together and have the same time off."

"I don't think they were ever apart," she said smiling at the thought and continued. "Just after they were married the head chef noticed that the baked pies were coming back half eaten. He thought maybe people were full, so he told the waiter staff to ask the customer why they didn't finish their pies. The responses were: people didn't like them. Now you have to remember this was an American style restaurant: steaks, prime rib, chicken, and ribs were their biggest sellers. They made chocolate cakes and pastries for dessert, but the pies were by far their biggest seller. Unfortunately, they didn't have the staff to make them, so they had to order them in. One evening my father overhead the head chef saying that he didn't want to order factory pies anymore, he wanted fresh, farm-type pies. Now, my mom grew up in San Francisco, but her mother was raised on a farm in the Midwest and loved to bake. My grandmother and her mother, my great-grandma, taught my mom all their secret pie recipes. My dad, after not only dating and marrying my mom, had had his fair share of pies, and always told her that she should sell them. She never did. So, the next morning my father comes into work early and bakes three of them. The head chef is sitting at one of the restaurant tables writing up the specials of the day when my dad approaches him with a slice from each pie and a coffee. He asked my dad what was going on. He told the head chef that he had tried these fresh, farm pies, and thought they were quite good. My father had enough manners never to say they were the best he ever tasted; he left that decision to the head chef. The head chef tasted all three, sipped his coffee, and said one word, excellent. He told my father to cut up the rest of the pies, bring them out, and have the staff try them. The staff thought they were delicious. The head chef asked who had baked them and my dad told him. The staff knew my mom, and she was very well liked, so they cheered when they heard it was her. When she came in for her shift, she was swamped by staff telling her how delicious her pies were and congratulating her. She was confused until my father explained what had happened."

"What was her reaction when your father told her?"

"She was thrilled, it what she loved to do. She never dreamed they would have such an appeal, and she could actually make a living from them."

"A dream job," stated Aidan.

"It would be," said Brieanne cautiously, "she had to pass the test first."

"Test?" asked Aidan wanting to know.

"That same evening, the head chef who was also a shrewd businessman, spoke with my parents saying he would give my mom the pie orders for the next two weeks and see how they sold. That was the test."

"What happened," he asked anxiously.

"They sold out within the first week! My mom was given a contract for the year! So, she started her own business, 'Anne's Homemade Farm Pies.' The terms of the contract stated that she was only allowed to sell in bulk to that restaurant, apparently the restaurant kept her busy enough, but any extras she could sell on the side, which became steady traffic."

"Did she keep working at the restaurant?"

"Only a shift or two on the weekend, just to be around my dad at the restaurant," she explained. "Over the next couple of years, my grandfather, the one who had the heart attack passed away, then six months later my grandmother. They say she died of a broken heart."

"That's sad," said Aidan, "especially losing them so close together."

"I know, luckily my dad had my mom," declared Brieanne, and went silent for a moment. "When my grandfather died, in his will he had put some money aside for my dad, so my dad used that to buy a house. My grandmother was a single child, and her parents were loaded. When they died, she inherited their fortune, and then that fortune passed onto my dad who invested it carefully. His plan was to one day open his own restaurant. A few years passed and everything was going well, my father had been promoted to sous chef, and my mother's business was very profitable. But the one thing they didn't have and wanted dearly was children. They had tried unsuccessfully for a couple of years and were concerned that it wasn't meant to be, until one day they got good news, my mom was pregnant."

"With you?" asked Aidan.

"Adorable me," she replied with a cute look. "My parents had always agreed that if they had a family, they would leave Las Vegas and move here. That time had come."

"Why here?"

"My mom's sister lives in Clearwater, that's my cousin Bev's mom, and they came to visit a couple of times and fell in love with Madeira Beach.

"So, they just packed up and left."

"It wasn't quite that simple. My parents flew out here and the house I grew up in was for sale, so they bought it. My mom stayed while my dad went back to help the restaurant to oversee the transition of his replacement. During which time he put the house up for sale, arranged for movers to ship their stuff, and was back here three weeks later."

"What about your mom's business?"

"Luckily, her contract was expiring at the end of that month and had a two-month supply of pies. She gave them all to the restaurant to help them out till they could find a replacement," said Brieanne as they walked down the path towards her house.

"What happened next?"

"I've got you hooked," stated Brieanne. "I'm guessing a good grade is coming my way."

"I'll admit it's a fascinating story."

"Shall I continue?"

"Please, do."

"My father spotted a restaurant that was up for sale that had an incredible view. Back then the patio was a separate business, it had a different owner and wasn't for sale. Neither place was in decent shape. My father made an offer on the restaurant first, the owner accepted. Then he made a generous offer to the owner of the patio, which he also accepted. He tore down the building and built a restaurant with a Las Vegas amphitheater design. He also wanted to capture the feeling of the diner that his father had in San Francisco and give all his customers access to an amazing view of the Gulf, which he did, as well as its warmth and friendliness. My father took all his culinary expertise from Las Vegas and San Francisco and came up with his own unique menu, and the name, 'Vegas Francisco's.'"

"That is brilliant," exclaimed Aidan thoroughly impressed with her story so far.

"Thank you," replied Brieanne opening the gate and leading him to the upper deck. "It's really my parent's story."

"I know, it's incredible, and I think you're telling it really well."

She blushed and handed him a beer. "I will be back in a minute," she said and went inside. A few minutes later she popped her head out. "Do you mind if we have dessert at the breakfast bar?"

"No, we can eat wherever you want?"

"Okay, come on then," she said, then stopped him at the door. "Be honest, what is your favorite type of pie?"

"Blueberry," he said without hesitation.

"Do you like it with or without vanilla ice cream?"

"With," he replied, following her in.

Sitting on the counter were two slices of hot blueberry pie each with a large scoop of vanilla ice cream.

"How did you know?" he asked sitting next to her.

"It's my favorite, too," she revealed. "I know we have many things in common, I guessed this would be another one," she said happily, "and I was right."

Aidan took a bite of his pie and made a yummy sound. "This is so delicious."

"Thank you."

"Did you make this?"

"I did," she said proudly watching him enjoying it. "I only have a few more blueberry pies left. I keep them here for my own personal stash so the restaurant's out of luck till I make more," she confessed. "When my mom visits, we bake here a lot. After we finish, we sit right here, eat, and talk. Just like us."

Aidan now understood why she wanted them to eat the pie inside. "Do you miss them?"

"I do," she said, "although, I can't complain, they do visit me quite frequently. But it would be nice if they lived here though. Which reminds me, they may be coming next month on the twenty-seventh for a few weeks."

"That will be nice," said Aidan watching her take the empty dishes and put them in the dishwasher before following her outside. She grabbed a beer and sat, while he picked up his half-empty can from the table and sat next to her. "Is this where you tell me how much you worked your cute butt off?"

"Yes," said Brieanne chuckling and looking over at him. "Since I was a teenager, I worked at my parents' restaurant. I started off bussing tables, moved to hostess, then server. After I went off to university and got my business degree I came back and worked for my father. I helped him out with the business operations of the restaurant, learning mostly the financial and accounting aspects, during which time I still had to work in the restaurant as a server, I may add. Then I got shifts as night manager, day manager, tended bar, and on some weekends managed the patio. But most importantly to my father was that I learned how to run the kitchen. He showed me how fresh ingredients were selected, how meals were prepared; everything from order to table."

"He wanted you to know his restaurant inside and out?"

"He wanted me to know it as well as he did, and I did, I do," she said correcting herself. "Once my father was convinced, I knew all that I needed to, he made me the restaurant manager."

"My guess," suggested Aidan.

"It was a good one," she said tongue-in-cheek and looked away from him. "But still wrong," she whispered.

"I heard that," he said giving her a slight push.

"I'm kidding it was a good one," said Brieanne standing up and casually sitting on his lap." I was restaurant manager for many years, then a few years before my dad retired my parents made me the majority owner and gave me the restaurant. My dad helped me with the transition up until they moved."

"You're right you did work your butt off," he said tapping it at the same time.

She giggled at his playfulness. "I sure did."

"Do you still work it off today?"

"No, not even close. With all the staff I have - head chef, day and night managers, head bartender, senior staff, accountants, and the list goes on and on - it practically runs itself."

"Is that why you only have to go in for a few hours a day, special events, that sort of thing?"

"Pretty much, unless I'm covering for someone," she clarified.

"Not only was that a great story," expressed Aidan. "You also shared your family history with me, and I feel extremely honored that you did, thank you," he said sincerely.

"Aidan, you are the only person I have ever told that story to," she said, wanting him to know how special he was.

"That makes it all the more special," he said giving her a gentle squeeze. She responded by putting her head on his shoulder.

Brieanne suddenly remembered something and sat up. "What is the grade for my story?"

Aidan pretended as if he didn't know what she was talking about.

"Stop it!" she said, knowing what he was doing. "My grade?"

"A, plus, plus," he replied. "I suppose you will want a prize or what did you call it?"

"A reward," she said enthusiastically. "And this time I get to choose," she said, remembering what happened the last time.

"Okay, you choose."

"Can I think about it and let you know?"

"You can, and you have till midnight for me to fulfill it," he said impishly.

"Oh yeah, I forgot, I'm with 'Mr. Statute of Limitations,'" she said laughing.

Chapter 14

Brieanne noticed the sun was starting to set and jumped off Aidan's lap. She ran inside, grabbed a blanket, led him to the beach, and placed it on the sand. She lay down on her stomach and he did likewise. "I very rarely miss a sunset," she confessed looking out at the horizon.

Aidan watched as the sun's rays fell on her face; she was a vision of beauty. He stared at her for a few moments before turning to watch the sun setting. Putting his arm around, she snuggled close to him, and quietly they followed the sun as it slowly slipped out of sight. Brieanne turned onto her back and looked up at him, he had such a handsome face, and she reached up and gently touched his cheek. Aidan bent down tenderly kissing her on the lips. He went to move away but she placed her hand behind his head, pulling him back, and kissed him with a partially opened mouth. To Brieanne, that would always be their first kiss. She removed her hand and Aidan turned onto his back. They looked up as the night crept in, and the stars' game of hide and seek came to an end, as they appeared one by one. Aidan reached for her hand, and she held it tightly. They lay in silence for quite some time, no words were needed, they both knew what was happening. They eventually stood, smiled at each other, and then walked back hand in hand.

"Did you have any questions about my family story?" she whispered.

Aidan looked at her thinking. "Your mom's name is Anne, what is your dad's?

"Oh, let me tell you this first, okay?" she said excitedly.

"Okay," replied Aidan grinning at her childlike excitement.

"My parents had said that when they had their first child if it was a girl, it would be named after my mom, and if it was a boy, after my dad.

Now, when they talked about this, they were under the assumption they were going to a have a few children."

"That must have been difficult wanting a family, talking about names, and then faced with the uncertainty of never having even one," said Aidan sympathetically.

"It must have been awful," agreed Brieanne sadly. "But they had me, so not so bad!" she said happily.

"I'm sure they were overjoyed."

"They were," replied Brieanne. "After they found out my mom was pregnant, they decided to stick to the same agreement they had made years before. My mom, realizing this may be the only child they have, wasn't too happy with it. Not because it may be a boy, but because I may be a girl, and my father would never get the chance to name a child. When she was in labor, she said to my dad that if it was a girl, she wanted to talk to about it with him before they named me. So my dad, whose hand was in the strong grip of a woman in labor, readily agreed. And as you know they had me, a cute, little girl," she said with a smile. "When my dad asked my mom about my name, my mom said she wanted to name me after both of them. My father replied that he didn't like the idea of a hyphened name, and more so, one of those names being a boy's name. My mom said it took her a while to stop laughing before she explained to him what she meant. She told him that they should use the first four letters of his name plus her name," said Brieanne looking over at Aidan who looked confused. "My dad's name is Brien, and is spelt, B-r-i-e-n. So, they took the first four letters of his name, and added my mom's name Anne…B-r-i-e-a-n-n-e…Brieanne."

"That is so cool," said Aidan, "so, both your parents got to name you."

"Yep," she said as they walked through the gate. "Do you have an interesting story about your name?"

"Actually, I do," said Aidan stopping on the lower deck and facing her.

"Tell me! Tell me!" she pleaded.

"Okay, here it is," he said, pausing momentarily. "My mother was home alone when her water broke and she tried getting in touch with my dad at work, to no avail. The contractions weren't far apart but she knew she couldn't drive so she called a taxi, jumped in the back with a towel, and told the driver her situation. The taximan was straight off the boat from Ireland and had a thick Belfast accent. So, he tells her not to worry, love, everything will be fine, you just stay calm and zooms off. With my dad's work being on the way to the hospital, he pulls up to the front doors, takes off inside and runs around like a madman shouting my dad's name. He finds him in no time. They run outside, my dad jumps into the back seat, and he tells my mom to lie down while the taximan floors it. The Irishman is coaching them from the front; remember your Lamaze, slow steady deep breaths. All of a sudden, my mom shouts out the baby is coming! The baby is coming! My dad screams, I can see the baby's crown! The taximan looks in the back telling them that they won't make it to the hospital and pulls off to the shoulder. He tells my dad to go up by my mom's head and comfort her, which he does, as the Irishman is rolling up his sleeves. My dad asks him, what are you doing? He replies I'm delivering this baby. My dad asks him if he has ever done this before, to which he replies, of course, I'm Irish—"

"Wait!" said Brieanne giggling and loving his story. "What does that even mean?"

"Trust me, to this day my parents still don't know," replied Aidan with a chuckle as they continued slowly past the side of the pool.

Brieanne put her arm through his whispering, "go on."

"After ten minutes of pushing, the baby is delivered, me, an adorable, little boy. The Irishman smacks my bum and I cry. He wraps me in the towel, tells them they have a healthy boy, ten fingers, ten toes, and passes me to my mom. My dad asks him, don't we have to cut the umbilical cord? To which the Irishman replies, don't be daft man they will do that at the hospital. The taximan jumps in the front, drives them to the hospital, and runs inside. Moments later he comes out with nurses and a stretcher. And as they are taking my mom inside, my dad said he remembers looking back at this Irishman waving to them, completely covered in blood."

"The back of his taxi couldn't have looked too good either," said Brieanne making a ghastly face.

"No, probably not," replied Aidan. "A few hours later the Irishman shows up all cleaned up with a coffee for him and my dad, and flowers and chocolates for my mom."

"That is sweet," cooed Brieanne, "this is such a great story."

"Before the Irishman leaves the hospital, they ask him to pick them up in a few days and drive them home, which he did. As he walks with them to the front door, my mom turns around to him saying I never got your name, to which he replies, Aidan."

"You were named after him!"

"Yep!"

"That is such a great—" she stopped, noticing Aidan laughing. "Wait, you made that up, didn't you?"

Aidan laughed louder.

"You filthy," she screamed, as she pushed him into the pool.

"Scallywag!" finished Aidan as he was falling in, making Brieanne burst into hysterics.

"You know I'm never going to believe anything you say to me ever again."

"What if I said jump in and I'll make it up to you with a kiss?"

"Do you mean it?" she asked knowing his tomfoolery all too well.

"There's only one way to find out."

Brieanne jumped in. Aidan swam to her and kissed her tenderly on the lips.

"I'm guessing you studied creative storytelling at university," she joked.

"Did you like it?"

"I really did," she said, as they swam to the end of the pool and got out. "Is there any story around your name?"

"Unfortunately, not, they just liked the name Aidan."

"I like it too. What's your last name?"

"Jones," he replied.

"Aidan Jones," she repeated to herself then thought Brieanne Jones that sounds nice, too, and smiled. "Let's get out of these wet things, put on our pajamas, have a bottle of wine, and stargaze."

"That sounds wonderful," he replied.

Aidan followed Brieanne upstairs, walked into his room, and into the bathroom. He took off his wet clothes and started to dry himself when there was a knock on the door.

"Do you want to pass me your wet clothes?"

"One second," replied Aidan trying to wrap a towel around his waist.

"There is a white robe hanging on the door, it's for you to use."

Aidan put it on, opened the door and looked out at Brieanne, who was also wearing one.

"Give me your clothes and I will hang them up," she said as he passed them to her. "I'm going to get a quick shower if you want to take one. I will meet you out on the balcony in about fifteen minutes. Just hang up your wet towel on one of the door hooks."

Aidan showered, put on his pajama bottoms and a T-shirt, and went out onto the balcony. Noticing two glasses of wine on the table he picked one up and leaned over the railing. He could hear the shower in Brieanne's room turn off and imagined what she looked like naked.

Brieanne got out of the shower, dried herself, and put on a long, gray T-shirt. She quickly blow-dried her hair, put it in a ponytail, and went outside to join him. "I hope you don't mind?" she asked shyly looking down at his 'New York State Fair' T-shirt. "I was going to wash it, but I haven't had a chance and thought I could wear it again."

"I think you look cute in it; you should keep it."

"No, I will give it back as soon as I wash it," she promised.

"I would like you to have it, I really would. That way it's yours, you can wear it as often as you like, and don't have to worry about returning it."

"Thank you," replied Brieanne. She was glad he said that because she really did want to keep it, and would wear it often, it reminded her of him. She took the glass of wine from the table and stood next to him. "Look at all the stars in the sky, so pretty."

"You can see all the constellations."

Brieanne turned to him. "Did you just make that story up about your name or was it one you have told before?"

"I made it up."

"Just like that," she said snapping her fingers.

Aidan nodded yes.

"I enjoyed it immensely," she said. "You had me hanging on every word."

"More than pushing me in the pool?"

"Hmm, that's a tough one, but yes. You know I was joking when I said you took creative storytelling at university, but you must have taken creative writing?"

"I did," he replied. "It was one of my favorite subjects."

"Why didn't you purse it, you obviously have a talent for it?"

"My big plan, along with teaching in the school year, was to start writing a novel in my spare time, then knuckle down when I was off in the summer and finish it."

"Why didn't you?"

"I never seemed to find the time, and year after year, it fell down my list of priorities."

"Job, house, and career?" she repeated recalling what he had told her.

"In a nutshell," he said a little melancholy.

"Sometimes things happen—" she stopped herself.

"For a reason, I know."

"Maybe when you sell your place, figure out your next steps, you should move writing up your list of priorities, or better still, make it a top priority on your list," she said positively.

He went quiet and thought about what she had said. "You know, that's not a bad idea, I should include that as a priority."

"Really?" she asked, happy to have been so influential. "Maybe you could write over the summer?"

"I have the time, and work isn't an issue, maybe I will," he said thinking out loud.

"I think you should," said Brieanne encouraging him.

"Maybe I'll write about you."

"Me?" she asked animatedly.

"You're right, too dull."

Brieanne slapped his arm.

"I'm joking, I'm joking. I think you would make a beautiful, wonderful, sexy story."

"You're forgiven" she said with a grin.

"Can I ask you a question?"

"Yes," she replied, noticing his apprehension.

"When you were talking about your parents giving you this house and your old house, I got the feeling you were anxious. Were you?"

Brieanne looked away from him at the horizon wondering if she had been that obvious. "A little," she replied.

"You don't have to tell me why if you don't want to?"

She looked over at him nervously. "I didn't want you to think I was some spoilt, rich girl that had everything handed to me on a silver platter."

"I would never think that of you," said Aidan moving closer. "The person I know and adore is the person I met before I knew about all this, and that is still the same person I see is standing in front of me."

His words went straight to her heart.

"I want to be with who you are; not what you are."

"Who you are; not what you are?" she asked, puzzled.

"Who you are: is kind, fun, down-to-earth, easy to talk with, intelligent, open, and honest…and trust me I could go on and on."

Her heart was pounding.

"What you are: is a friend, a daughter, a graduate, a landlady, a restaurant owner…and a French teacher."

"Hey," she said giggling.

"Okay, I will be serious."

She gave him a doubtful look.

"During our relationship I have gotten to know who you are, and today, what you are. And I must say, both are incredible and amazing."

Did he just say relationship, incredible, amazing? Her heart was melting. She thought of something her dad once said. "When my parents first met and got married, they didn't have much and worked extremely hard for what they got. My dad told me this, many times, and still does to this day, 'you will know a person truly loves you, when all you have to offer is yourself, and that is good enough for them.'"

"I like that, I like that a lot."

"Doesn't it tie into everything we are talking about?"

"It definitely does."

"Having this conversation has just made me come up with my reward."

Aidan shook his head. "Let's hear it."

"Don't worry, I'm letting you off easy, this time," she said grinning. "What is the one thing you like most about me?"

Aidan looked at her curiously. "I have a clarification question?"

"Yes, what?" she asked impatiently wanting to know his answer.

"Do you want me to give you a physical or character attribute?"

Good question she thought, she was really looking for character, but she wouldn't mind knowing a physical one also. "Slight change," she instructed. "What are—?"

Aidan interrupted her. "Can you hold that thought while I use the bathroom?"

"Of course," said Brieanne watching him leave and taking a sip of her wine. She noticed he was gone for a while and was out of breath when he returned. "Did you run back?"

"Yeah, I didn't want to keep you waiting," he fibbed, not noticing what he had in his pajama pocket. "So, this is a brand-new reward, you are starting over?"

"That's right," she responded, curious as to why he would ask that.

"Ask away?"

Brieanne started over. "What is the one thing you like about me physically and the one thing you like about me characteristically? And it can't be general such as pretty or nice personality," she advised, excited to hear his answers.

Aidan gave the impression he was deep in thought as he rubbed his chin and eyeballed her. He opened his mouth as if to answer her then said, "I can't.'

"What do you mean, you can't?" asked Brieanne confused. "It's my reward pay up buddy!"

"Buddy is it!" he replied with a chuckle. "I can't Cinderella!"

"Cinderella, what?" she asked, then it dawned on her. "No!" she screamed.

Aidan pulled his phone out of his pocket and read the time, "one-minute past twelve."

"I only had till midnight for me to fulfill it," repeated Brieanne.

"You're right, you do have a good memory," said Aidan walking slowly back, he knew what was coming next.

"You filthy Scallywag!" she yelled.

Aidan took off into his room, out the door, down the hall into her room. Brieanne chased him. He went out of her room, onto the balcony then back into his room, down the hall into Brieanne's room and stopped after noticing the balcony door was now closed, he turned to make a hasty retreat, but it was too late. Brieanne closed her bedroom door. He was trapped.

"You may want to remember that intelligent compliment you gave me, catching you was way too easy," she suggested leisurely walking toward him. "You didn't go to the bathroom, did you? You went downstairs to get your phone, didn't you? You waited downstairs till it was almost twelve, didn't you? You asked me if this was a brand-new reward to stall me, didn't you?"

"Uh-mm, did I?" mumbled Aidan slowly walking backwards. As she got closer, he felt the balcony door at his back, and stopped. "Is another one of your finer characteristics, leniency?"

"Not tonight," she cautioned. "I want my answer or else?"

"Or else, what?"

"You don't want to know," she warned him.

Aidan unexpectedly picked her up, carried her to the bed, and gently placed her down before lying next to her.

Brieanne moved onto her side to face him. "I'm waiting."

"I want you to understand that this is very difficult because you have so many great qualities," he said, thinking. "Okay, physical feature, I would have to say your smile, your smile lights me up inside…Character attribute, how down-to-earth and open you are."

"I think that last one counts as two," she said quietly.

"When it comes to you, they go hand in hand."

Brieanne blushed.

"And because I played that rotten trick on you, I will give a third attribute."

"A bonus!" she said cheerfully.

"It's your lucky night," he said playing along. "I'm not sure where this one sits, it's not a physical feature or a character attribute. I guess it's more of a physical interaction."

"Physical interaction," she repeated, wanting to know more.

"The kiss you gave me on the beach."

"You mean like this," she said, kissing him the exact same way.

Aidan rolled onto his back and put his hands behind his head. "With a kiss like that on my lips I can now die a happy man."

She laughed at him. "Is that something corny you are going to write in your novel?"

"If it's going to be a non-fiction story about you, then yes, it will be."

Brieanne realized he wasn't teasing her and tenderly snuggled into him.

Chapter 15

Brieanne woke up the next morning under the sheets to the sound of splashing. She got up, opened her balcony door, and went outside to look.

"Good morning sleepy head," shouted Aidan from the pool.

"Good morning," she replied. "When did you wake up?"

"About thirty minutes ago."

"Do you want some coffee?"

"Love some."

"Join me in the kitchen in ten minutes," she said and went inside to the bathroom. She brushed her teeth, put on her robe, and looked at her hair; it was all over the place. Brieanne brushed it, put it in a ponytail, then headed downstairs into the kitchen and put on a pot of coffee. A few minutes later Aidan walked in, she chuckled at him. "I see you are taking full advantage of the robe."

"I sure am," he replied lifting out his arms and admiring it, "it's sweet."

Brieanne shook her head. "I take it you found your swimsuit?"

"I did," he replied, as he went to sit down.

"Hey, you may want to take it off and put something dry on before you sit on your sweet robe, or it will get wet."

"Already have," he revealed, "they're hanging outside to dry as we speak."

Brieanne looked at him a little confused. "But you just came in and I didn't see you go upstairs?"

Aidan gave her a look as if to say, yep, that's right.

The penny dropped. "You aren't wearing anything under the robe?"

"The only thing that separates my nakedness from you, is this robe," he said pulling on its collar.

"What am I going to do with?" she asked as she poured the coffees, although in her mind she knew what she would like to do to him.

"You fixed your hair this morning?" asked Aidan matter-of-fact.

"What do you mean by that?"

"At the condo you were less worried about it," he said drinking his coffee.

Brieanne's mind quickly ran back to that morning: I woke up, looked at the time on my phone, stretched, got out of bed, fixed my T-shirt, opened the door, and went to the bathroom. No, I didn't, I heard faint noises coming from the kitchen and followed them to Aidan. "Ah!" she screamed, went around the counter, and slapped his arm, "and you didn't mention it to me."

"No," he replied. "I thought you were one of those free-spirited girls letting me know this is how you look in the morning."

"I was groggy, not free-spirited," she said explaining the difference, before slapping his arm again. "Was I like that the whole time I was there?"

"Yes," he snickered, "but you looked cute."

"Oh no," she said, with a sad face.

Aidan stood up and put his arms around her. "You look beautiful, and perfect, all the time."

With those words her embarrassment evaporated. "But you let me walk home that way," she said in slow, exaggerated, sad voice.

Aidan let go of her and took his seat. "Actually, I didn't."

Brieanne sat next to him. "Yes, you did. After breakfast I quickly changed, put everything in my bag, including your T-shirt, and went looking for you. You grabbed my hand, led me to the balcony, I hugged you, said thanks, and you walked me to the elevator," she said looking at him. "You let me walk home looking like I had a wild night of sex."

"You wish?" he teased.

"I do," she said with sexy smile as she thought about it. "Wait a second! You're getting me off topic," she contested and looked at him waiting for some sort of explanation.

"Do you remember after you hugged me on the balcony?"

"Yes."

"We walked to the front door on the table I said you forgot this and handed you—"

"My hair elastic. You said you don't want to forget this; you may want to put it in your hair, so you don't lose it, and I did," she said remembering. At the time, the gesture didn't seem like much but now it spoke volumes. "Will you always lookout for me?"

"Always," he promised, "and I will always be there for you."

Brieanne liked the way that sounded. "I'll make us some breakfast."

"Let me help," offered Aidan, which was met with a refusal.

Brieanne talked as she cooked. "I fell asleep on you, didn't I?"

"Yeah, you snuggled into me and within minutes you were sound asleep."

"I had the sheets and duvet over me this morning?" she queried.

"I pulled them from under your body then covered you with them."

"I didn't wake up?"

"You moved a little."

"How did you sleep?"

"I slept great.

"Good," she replied. "After breakfast I will show you the house and then we'll go sightseeing down the coast."

After breakfast, they got ready, and met in the foyer. Brieanne grabbed a notepad and pencil from the desk drawer and went next door to her new house. She stopped on the driveway, looked up at it, then over at Aidan. "The people I bought it from were a husband and wife, with two young children. Because they were selling it, they fixed it up to get a better price; it's in excellent shape. I just want to make it look more like something I would live in," she explained. "From the outside you can tell it's small. I'm thinking of a family of four, maybe a couple, or a professional like a writer or an artist," explained Brieanne walking with him to the front door. "Before I forget, they also left some of their furniture that they didn't need, which if it's in good condition saves me replacing it." Before she turned the key, she looked at him. "Besides Joyce, you are the person who knows I bought this place."

"I'm flattered," he said with a smile.

She opened the door, and they walked inside. "Wow! They left a lot of furniture," said Brieanne happily. "You will probably notice it's very similar to my place."

Aidan couldn't help but laugh, it was a lot smaller than Brieanne's place.

She gave him a light shove as she chuckled. "You know what I mean, similar as in setup, not size," she said walking to her left. "This is the dining room."

"The table and chairs are in really great condition."

"They are," she said sliding her hand over it, "this is staying."

They moved to the back to the kitchen area. It was open concept, with all the appliances, a microwave, a kitchen bar with stools, kitchen table and chairs. Adjacent, was a small family room that had a couch, armchair, and coffee table. It was perfect for reading a book or playing board games. Both the kitchen and family room had nice-sized windows and a pretty view of the Gulf.

"I would like to paint the kitchen and this family room, brighten it up a little," she said making notes. "I like the furniture so far."

Aidan nodded his head in agreement. "You're renting so you probably wouldn't want to buy new furniture, anyway, would you?"

"Definitely not, if it was tattered, I would replace it, but only with good secondhand stuff," she answered, then thought for a moment. "The only exception being electronics, TV, DVD player, they are cheap enough to buy new."

In the hallway she opened up the first door, behind it was a laundry room with a washer and dryer. The next door was the powder room, then the stairs, and the living room. Which was a nice size, and had a sofa, chair, and coffee table. Aidan walked over, moved the table out the way, felt underneath the sofa, removed the cushions, and pulled it out into a sofa bed.

"Look at that, it's never been used, it still has the plastic protection on the mattress," said Brieanne as she watched Aidan change it back into a sofa. "I will need a TV stand, TV, and DVD player in here," she noted.

They walked up the stairs into the first room, which was originally the parents' room. It had a queen-size bed frame with a headboard, a chest of drawers, two end tables, and a closet.

"It will need a mattress. A TV and DVD player, they can go on the chest of drawers. I don't like the blinds, I prefer sheer white curtains, and thick drapes," she said, before motioning Aidan over. Brieanne gently pulled the blinds to one side revealing two big windows with a beautiful view. She opened the door in between them, and they walked onto a small balcony.

"Wow, I really love this!" said Aidan. "Look at the view."

"This is one of my favorite features about this place."

They went inside, out to the hallway, and into the children's room. It had no furniture, a closet, and a decent size window with the same breathtaking view. The door opposite the kid's room was a closet, and the door opposite the parents was the bathroom, and was in excellent condition.

"I want to paint the parent's room, kid's room, bathroom, and hallway, all bright colors. I'm not sure what to do with the kid's room. Maybe bunk beds, pull out sofa bed, small desk, and chair?"

"They all sound good," replied Aidan. "But you don't have to decide today."

"True, I have all summer to think about it."

They went downstairs, opened the patio doors, and walked onto a large deck that took up half the yard.

"The deck is in fantastic condition," said Aidan.

"It is and I like it because it is so big, you can put a BBQ and furniture on it, "she said looking around. "I want to do something with the other half of the yard, clean it up somehow, and some of the fence over there is broken, that will need to be fixed."

Aidan walked over to her. "You have got a great place here, and once you get it done to your liking, it will be a gem."

"Thank you, I know," she said smiling at him, then looking down at her notes. "A lot of work needs to be done first, but fun work," she admitted.

Brieanne locked the front door, and they walked onto the driveway. She stopped again, turned around, and looked at it once more. She had done it; all on her own. It was hers and no one could ever take that away from her. She smiled and put her arm through Aidan's as they walked away.

"You should be very proud."

"I am," replied Brieanne, "and I'm happy I'm sharing this moment with you."

Chapter 16

Brieanne ran quickly into her house, dropped off the note pad and pencil, grabbed her beach bag, and led Aidan to Gulf Boulevard.

"We are taking the Suncoast Beach Trolley it goes up the coast to Clearwater and down the coast to Pass-a-Grille, the latter is the direction we will be going today, and with a pass we can hop on and off as much as we like. It's been quite a while since I have been on it, so I'm looking forward to it," she said excitedly looking down the boulevard.

Ten minutes later the trolley came, they paid for their passes walked towards the middle, and took a seat on the left side.

"Our first stop is Treasure Island," she said as the trolley started to move, "it's no more than a ten-minute ride."

After they crossed over the bridge at John's Pass, Brieanne pointed out Vegas Francisco's, the streets where some of her friends lived, and the motels, and cottages. "There's the Shake Shop; I love the ice cream there. We will have to go one day, sit on their deck, and get a sundae." As the trolley continued through Treasure Island, Brieanne pointed out all the restaurants and resorts, before arriving at their stop. They exited onto 104th Avenue, walked to the boardwalk, and took a right. "You can park your car here in the public lot and access Treasure Island Beach," she explained. "This boardwalk will take us right back close to the Shake Shop, but we won't be going that far today."

Although it was only nine thirty, Aidan noticed that the boardwalk was busy with families, couples, and kids on their bicycles. On his left was the wide beach, and to his right were the back of the resorts with their swimming pools and sundecks. "Treasure Island is a tourist hotspot."

"Yeah, it has everything you need. Resorts, swimming pools, access to a wide beach, the Gulf, the boardwalk, restaurants, bars, McDonald's,

Walgreens, and a Publix Super Market. You really don't have to wander too far, and because we are so close, Vegas Francisco's and John's Pass Village get a ton of business from this area."

"After being here, and looking around, I think your restaurant is in a perfect spot."

"Thank my dad for that, he knew what he was doing," said Brieanne. "Coming up is one of my all-time favorite resorts. Do you remember when I pointed out Treasure Island Beach Resort from the street?"

"I do."

"Well, this is it from the back."

"Wow, I can see why this would be one of your favorites."

"Isn't it gorgeous," she said. "The palm trees, pool, view, pretty light blue loungers and matching umbrellas."

"That it is," said Aidan slowly.

"Can I let you in on a little secret?"

"Sure," replied Aidan, curious.

"When I get married, this is the place where I want to spend my wedding night."

"Any particular reason why?"

"Because it is so beautiful," she said looking away from him and at the resort. She wasn't sure whether to tell him the main reason, then decided why not. "When I was younger, I always looked at this place, the way we are looking at it right now, and thought it was magical. Like something out of a modern-day fairytale. My dream ending to a perfect wedding day," she said glancing over at him and feeling slightly embarrassed. "Corny, right?"

"When your Prince Charming marries you and brings you here on your wedding night, you won't be thinking you were corny then, only thrilled that your dream came true."

"You're right," she said with a smile. Brieanne suddenly realized she could share anything with him, and he would never mock her, or her dreams.

They walked past the resort and took a right down a path that brought them to Gulf Boulevard across from the Middle Grounds Grill. They waited several minutes for a trolley and hopped on. Along the way they passed rows of houses scattered between resorts, condos, motels, and cottages. Brieanne named the restaurants as they passed them.

"You're really enjoying this?"

"I am," she replied. "I haven't done it for such a long time and…"

"And?"

"I don't know, somehow being with you makes it that more special," she confessed, putting her arm through his.

"I think this is great, I would have done this, definitely not on my own," he admitted and looked at her, "it's special for me, too."

They talked for a while before the trolley stopped at 75th Avenue and Gulf Boulevard, close to the Corey Avenue Shopping District, where they disembarked and jumped onto another trolley heading to St. Pete Beach. At first, they passed neighborhoods, but as they got closer to the beach area, the resorts and restaurants started to pop up. They got off the trolley in front of the Dolphin Beach Resort, went through the beach parking lot, down a path and onto St. Pete Beach. Brieanne grabbed his hand as they took a right, heading north up the beach, before she stopped.

"Here's a good spot," she said taking the beach bag from Aidan.

With his help she laid out the two towels, then took off her shorts and top and sprayed her body with sunscreen, before passing it to a shirtless Aidan who did the same. Then they lay on their backs and soaked up the hot sun. Twenty minutes later Brieanne woke up, sat up, and looked over at Aidan's handsome face and fit body as he slept. She grabbed a bottle of water, looked around as she drank, and noticed a restaurant behind her.

"Did you have a good sleep?"

"Yeah, I guess I needed that power nap."

"Same here, I woke up ten minutes ago," she said passing him a water.

"How long was I asleep?"

"About thirty minutes."

"Did you want to go for a dip in the Gulf, then get some lunch?" she asked. "There's a restaurant called Crabby Bill's back there," she said motioning behind her.

"That sounds good," he replied.

They waded into the water till it was deep enough for them to swim, then swam further out. Brieanne stopped, turned around, and looked toward the beach. "Look how scenic it is from here."

Aidan stood next to her. "It's beautiful."

Brieanne turned toward him.

"Assuming the position?" he asked.

"As a matter of fact, I am," she said placing her arms and legs around him. "It doesn't get any better than this."

"No, it doesn't," said Aidan softly kissing her lips. "I couldn't let a moment like this slip away."

Brieanne responded with a passionate open mouth kiss. "I think you will remember this moment a little better now."

"I definitely will," said Aidan with a smile. "I love the way you kiss."

"Well, if you are nice to me maybe you will get more."

"Well, if you are nice, maybe I will let you kiss me," he countered.

"Then I will make sure I am extremely nice to you, and the nicer you are to me, the more I will give you," she said in a low, sexy voice.

Aidan playfully let his jaw drop.

Brieanne laughed and with her finger pushed it up. "Are you ready for some lunch?"

They dried off, packed up their stuff, and walked to Crabby Bill's where they sat on the rooftop tiki deck facing the Gulf.

"I bet this place has a lovely view of the sunset," said Brieanne.

"It sure does," replied the middle-aged server, "especially for two lovers like you."

Brieanne gave her a blank look.

"A couple of locals at the bar and I were talking about how it's going to be a busy season. We looked out at all the people on the beach and noticed you two in the water," she said, glancing over her right shoulder to the two old men at the bar who raised their glasses and smiled. "My name is Dee," she said, putting two menus on the table.

Brieanne went silent, although a little embarrassed, she was happy they had noticed them and called them lovers.

"Dee, you should see what we are like at home in our swimming pool," stated Aidan straight-faced, as he picked up a menu.

Brieanne had a stunned look on her face.

"I bet," replied Dee with a chuckle and a grin. "What would you like to drink?"

"Do you have any specialty drinks?" he asked.

"We have The Original Crab Trap," she suggested, "our house specialty."

"What's that?" asked Aidan.

"It's a sixteen-ounce drink with four tropical flavored rums and fruit juices."

"That's sounds good," said Aidan. "What you think baby?" he asked, playing the role of a lover as he squeezed her hand.

"Yeah, it does, I'll have one, too," she said, still trying to get over what Aidan had said.

"Two of those," confirmed Dee.

"And can you get a drink for the two guys at the bar, on me," added Aidan.

"Sure, thing sweetie," she said then looked over at Brieanne. "He's quite the charmer."

"He sure is," replied Brieanne as she watched Dee walk away. "You are impossible," she said laughing.

"Impossible is one of my better traits," said Aidan in his defense.

A few minutes later Dee came back with their drinks. "You two need some time with the menu?"

Brieanne spoke up. "We decided to share some appetizers, can you suggest a few?"

"My favorites are the calamari, crab cakes, and buffalo shrimp."

"We'll take those," said Brieanne.

They talked about the restaurant and beach while they waited for their food to arrive, when it did, it was devoured in no time.

"How was it?" asked Dee picking up the empty dishes.

"That was delicious," replied Brieanne. "All of it was amazing."

"It truly was," added Aidan.

After they finished their drinks, Dee walked over with two more. "They would like to repay your kindness," she said placing them on the table.

"Thank you," said Aidan as he watched Dee walk away. "Let's go over and talk to them."

"No," said Brieanne nervously, "I'm sure they want to be left alone."

"I'm sure they don't."

Brieanne wasn't convinced and felt awkward.

"We can leave your bag here, if we are intruding, we will come back, okay?"

"Okay," she replied.

They went over to the two old locals and talked for thirty minutes about St. Pete, Madeira Beach, and Rochester, before returning to the table. Aidan paid their bill, then motioned Dee down to speak in her ear, and handed her rolled up twenties. Dee acknowledged him and looked over at Brieanne. "That's a fine man you have there."

Brieanne and Aidan said goodbye to Dee, the two older gentlemen, and left the restaurant, then walked across the parking lot towards Gulf Boulevard.

"What was that about?" asked Brieanne.

"Nothing," he replied trying to make it seem unimportant.

She stopped. "Why won't you tell me?"

"It's not that I don't want to tell you, it's just not that big of a deal," he replied looking at her. By the look on her face, he could see she was unhappy with his response.

Brieanne decided she wasn't going to press him and started to walk.

Aidan grabbed her hand, pulled her back, and looked into her eyes. "Those two men reminded me of a couple of old-timers back home I knew who drank at the local bar I went to. Their wives had both died so they went to the bar to get out of their lonely homes. I remember one day going over and striking up a conversation with them and how happy they were that someone had talked to them. From that moment on, I always made a point of having a chat with them, and every so often I would pay their bill."

"Is that what you did, paid their bill?"

"Yeah, I told Dee that this money was to cover their drinks and any food they had, whatever was left over she could keep."

"That is so kind and thoughtful of you," she said putting her arm through his. "Why didn't you want to tell me?"

"I don't know," he said shyly.

"It's because you're modest," she revealed with a smile, "I like that." She tenderly kissed his lips, then took his hand, and walked with him to Gulf Boulevard where they took a left. "Here it is, the Freaky Tiki Surf Shack" said Brieanne. "I just need some lip balm."

Across the street Aidan noticed Norman's Liquors. "I want to see if that liquor store has something, I will meet you back here."

"Okay," replied Brieanne letting go of his hand and going inside.

Aidan crossed the street and went into the liquor store. He quickly found what he was looking for, paid the man, put the item in her beach bag, and covered it up with a towel. He walked outside, spotted Brieanne waiting across the street, and joined her. They doubled back to 51st Avenue and waited for the trolley.

"Did you find what you were looking for?"

"No," he fibbed.

"Did you get your lip balm?"

"I did," she replied. "That's a lovely store. It has really nice shirts, shorts, hats, and sunglasses. We will have to come back here one day when we have more time."

They rode the trolley south for twenty minutes, along the way they passed The Don CeSar. "After my wedding night, I want to spend a few nights there before I go on my honeymoon. It's so beautiful, elegant, and charming. It would be so romantic. It's known as the Pink Palace and has such a history," she said and told him all about it.

They jumped off at 9th Avenue and Pass a Grille Way, walked down to 8th Avenue and entered the town's main shopping district. They spent a few hours looking in the stores before going onto 10th Avenue and touring the Gulf Beaches Historical Museum. It was getting late, and they decided to start their journey back. They took the trolley back to 75th Avenue and transferred onto the one passing by Madeira Beach.

"That was a lovely area," said Aidan. "I thought museum was great it was packed with information."

"I've never been in it before I'm glad we went in," she said looking at him, "I bet you could write several novels down here."

"No kidding."

"What do you feel like for dinner?" she asked.

"I kind of know what I want, but I want you to tell me yours first."

"I do, too. Let's see if we both pick the same thing," she said excitedly. "On three…One, two, three."

"Pizza," they said simultaneously.

"Pizza it is," she said giggling, "I know the perfect place."

At 106th Avenue in Treasure Island the pair disembarked from the trolley, crossed the street into Ricky T's Bar & Grille, and were seated at a table on the outdoor patio. Aidan sipped on his beer while Brieanne looked at the menu for the pizzas. "I'm thinking pizza loaded with meat."

"You read my mind."

She glanced up at him. "I know you better than you know yourself," she said with a grin, before returning to the menu. "Here we go, supreme pizza: pepperoni, ham, sausage, green pepper, onion, and mushroom. How does that grab you?" she asked putting the menu to one side and sipping her beer.

"Like a chubby kid holding onto a chocolate bar," he replied instantly.

Brieanne uncontrollably spit out her beer in laughter.

Aidan couldn't help but laugh out loud, too.

Brieanne reached for a napkin and wiped the beer off her chin, leg, and table. "That's twice today you've embarrassed me, in two different restaurants," she attested. "No French lessons for you."

"Are you learning French?" asked the server looking at Aidan.

"Me, no," said Aidan gesturing to Brieanne.

The server looked over at Brieanne confused.

Brieanne's face went red, she realized that Aidan was about to tell this pretty twentysomething year old, what French lessons he was referring to.

"Parlez-vous français?" asked Aidan.

"Je parle un peu mais je fais beaucoup d'erreurs."

"Apprends-tu le français?"

"Oui."

"Pourquoi?"

"Je vais à paris en vacances."

"C'est gentil…tu es français c'est assez bon."

"Merci beaucoup."

"Brieanne ne parle pas français et voudrait commander une pizza en anglais."

"Ok, je comprends."

"Merci."

"What kind of pizza would you like?" asked the server turning her attention to Brieanne.

Brieanne was a little overwhelmed. "Umm…twelve-inch supreme, please."

"Okay," replied the server. "Voudriez-vous deux autres bières?" she asked turning to Aidan.

"Oui s'il vous plait."

"Ok, je serai de retour avec eux dans une minute."

"Merci," replied Aidan as she walked away.

"I didn't know you spoke French," she said a little surprised, and impressed.

"I know a few phrases to help me get by."

"What did you two talk about?"

"I asked her, do you speak French? She said, I speak a little, but I make a lot of mistakes. I asked her, are you learning French? She said, yes. I asked, why? She said I'm going to Paris on vacation. I said, that's nice…your French is quite good. She replied, thank you very much. I said, Brieanne doesn't speak French and would like to order a pizza in English. She said, okay, I understand. I replied, thank you. Then she asked you in English what kind of pizza you wanted. Then asked me, would you like two more beers? I said, yes, please. She replied, okay, I will be back with them in a minute." Aidan noticed her heading their way. "When she drops them off say, 'merci beaucoup,' that means thank you very much."

"Merci beaucoup?" repeated Brieanne.

"That's it," said Aidan encouraging her.

"Here you go," said the server.

"Merci beaucoup," replied Brieanne.

"C'est très gentil de votre part vous êtes les bienvenus," she responded. "That means, that's very kind of you, you are welcome," she said giving her smile before leaving.

"When people are trying to learn a language, they appreciate anyone who knows it to speak to them in it, no matter how little they know, because it helps them practice."

"I was horrified, I thought you were going to tell her about my French lessons," she whispered.

Aidan leaned over, and whispering too, said, "maybe I did, but just decided to leave that part out when I told you what we talked about."

"You didn't tell her," said Brieanne, unsure. "Did you?"

"No," said Aidan, "you think I'm foolish. I'm not going to go around and tell everyone anyone about my French lessons or my sexy teacher," he revealed. "I want her all to myself."

"Well, Mr. Flirty Pants, sorry, Mr. Flirty Shorts, you better keep your eyes forward," she warned. "Or else I may have to take on additional students," she teased.

"Were you jealous?"

"What, of a stunning twentysomething year old with a tight body having a conversation in French with my man, no," she said. The 'my man' slipped out and she knew he was going to pick up on it straight away.

"Your man?" Aidan asked teasing her.

I knew he would, she thought. "It was just a figure of speech."

"That's too bad," he said looking around nonchalantly.

"Why is it that too bad?' she asked.

"It doesn't matter," said Aidan sounding uninterested.

"Well, say I did mean it?" she probed.

"Then I would have to say you are absolutely right, because sitting across from me is the only girl I'm interested in, which doe make me your man."

Brieanne blushed, leaned over, and kissed him.

They listened to the live music, ate their pizza, and had a few more beers. As Aidan was paying, he instructed Brieanne on how to ask the server for her name in French, to which she replied, Kim. Then they told Kim that the service, food, and live music were excellent. She thanked them, said goodnight, and twenty minutes later Brieanne and Aidan were swimming in Brieanne's pool.

Chapter 17

"How long do we have?" asked Aidan.

"We should get out in five minutes, shower, and change into our pajamas."

Thirty minutes later Brieanne went out onto the balcony to sit with Aidan, but he was nowhere in sight. She looked in his empty room and started for the stairs calling out his name.

"I'm in the kitchen."

"What are you doing?"

He showed her the ice bucket filled with two cans of beer on top."

"What's this?"

"I thought we would watch the sunset from your new place," he explained. "Christen it, so to speak."

She loved the idea. "But we are in our pajamas."

"So what, grab the key and let's go."

Brieanne picked up the key, walked with him to the foyer, and noticed he was also carrying a towel.

"What's the towel for?"

"Well, the balcony has no chairs, in case we want to sit."

"Okay," she replied not giving it a second thought.

They went inside the house, upstairs to the bedroom then outside onto the balcony. Aidan put down the ice bucket and threw the towel to one side revealing a bag.

"What's this?" asked Brieanne curiously.

"It's sort of a housewarming present, slash, congratulations gift," he said. "I didn't have a chance to wrap it, here you go."

Brieanne took the bag from him. "You didn't have to do this she said." But was excited he had.

"It's not much."

She took the box out of the bag and looked at its contents: it was a bottle of Moët & Chandon, with two champagne flutes on either side.

"This is perfect," she said, beaming.

"I didn't want to take it out of the box," he explained, "and it will probably need to be chilled."

"That's why you brought the ice bucket with the beer," she said realizing his attentive gesture, "I thought it was just one of your silly antics." She opened up the box and took out the champagne, while Aidan removed the beers from the bucket, and placed it deep in the ice. "We will give it fifteen to twenty minutes," she said leaving momentarily to rinse the champagne flutes. When she returned, she spread out the towel in the corner, placing the ice bucket on top, along with the two champagne flutes upside down allowing them to drip-dry. Brieanne was thrilled. "Thank you," she said kissing him on the cheek, "that is so thoughtful."

Twenty minutes later they poured the champagne and Aidan made a toast. "Congratulations to you, Brieanne, on your lovely new house."

"Thank you," she replied joyfully and touched glasses.

They sipped their champagne and quietly watched the sun gently dissolve into the horizon as the night snuck in behind it.

Brieanne suddenly realized something. "Wait," she said looking at him. "Is this what you bought in the liquor store today?"

"Yeah."

"You hid it in my beach bag and carried it around all day?"

Aidan nodded his head.

The gift itself was special, the fact that he done all that to surprise her, made it even more so. Brieanne moved close to him, gave him a kiss, and put her arms around him. She rested her head on his shoulder, looked out at the horizon, and thought about how wonderful and romantic he was. She pulled away and looked up at him tentatively. "Will you lie with me like last night till I fall asleep?"

"Yes," he whispered.

"Yay!" said Brieanne receptively clapping her hands.

They talked for a bit longer, finished off the champagne, then went back to Brieanne's place and got ready for bed. Lying next to him, Brieanne rested her head on Aidan's shoulder as he held her. Within minutes they were sound asleep.

Chapter 18

Six Weeks Earlier: Wednesday, July 1

Brieanne woke up alone. She couldn't hear anyone in the pool but went out onto the balcony to check. It was empty. She peaked into Aidan's room; he was asleep in bed, so she quietly lay next to him. Aidan roused, noticing her he told her to come under the sheets; his body was nice and warm. She put her back to him and he put his arm around her; they quickly fell asleep.

Aidan woke up to the smell of bacon as he sauntered downstairs into the kitchen. "Good morning beautiful," he said to her.

"Morning handsome," she said turning around. "What time did you leave my room this morning?"

"About ten minutes before you came into my bed," he replied. "What time was that?"

"Six," she answered. "Breakfast will be ready in fifteen minutes. Do you want some coffee?"

"Please," he said. "What's on the agenda for today?"

"I thought we would take the trolley north, purely a beach day, we could do with some rest and relaxation."

"I couldn't agree more," said Aidan. "I need some clean clothes so we will need to stop by the condo first."

"That fine," she said handing him a cup of coffee.

"My parents with be back in a couple of days, I was going to suggest we hang out at the condo this evening, probably be one of the last nights we will have it to ourselves."

"Okay," she said with a smile. "I will get some things together and leave them at your place when we stop by. I have chicken pot pie I can bring over; we can have it for dinner tonight with some salad, unless you have something else in mind."

"No, that sounds great, and after tasting your blueberry pie, I know I am in for a treat."

They ate breakfast, stopped by his condo, then walked to the security gate where they stopped and talked to Stan. Brie told him where they were going, and Stan told Aidan that it was a beautiful spot and gave him some history of the area. They said goodbye, crossed over Gulf Boulevard, waited a few minutes, and boarded the trolley.

"Up this way is very residential, houses and condos, there are still plenty of beaches and restaurants, just not as many resorts. It should take us about thirty minutes," explained Brieanne. "I've been meaning to ask, where did you learn to speak French?"

Aidan reflected for a moment and decided she may as well know. "My last girlfriend taught languages, mostly Spanish, and some French classes. At first, I learned some practical conversations; ones I could use at a restaurant, a bar, or at a tourist destination, and then some useful everyday conversations. I guess I picked it up pretty quickly. I knew a little Spanish so that helped."

"Seems like you guys got along?"

"There're were some qualities I liked about her—"

"And some you didn't?"

"It's not so much that I didn't like them," clarified Aidan. "They were not ones I was looking for."

Brieanne had a perplexed look on her face. "I'm not sure what you mean?"

Aidan didn't want to go into specifics about his relationship with his ex. "Let's look at us as an example. I like to laugh, joke around, and have fun. Brieanne number one, you, likes to be with someone like that. Now say, hypothetically, Brieanne number two was a little more serious, and enjoyed having profound, intellectual, conversations. She may find me, Aidan number one, annoying, and somewhat childish. It's not that my qualities are bad, they're just not suited for what she is looking for. Instead,

Aidan number two, who is very intellectual and can stimulate her mind, is much more to her liking. So, I don't necessarily think they're bad qualities, they're just not the rights ones."

"Are you are saying that individuals are looking for qualities in a person that meet their needs and vice versa?"

"You just explained it simpler and better than me," complimented Aidan.

"What about opposites attract?"

"They can, they do," said Aidan. "Take Brieanne number two, the intellect. Maybe she hangs out with intellectuals all day and wants to be with the Aidan who makes her laugh, jokes around, and has fun; rather than the intellectual Aidan."

"That makes sense, but it's impossible to match up perfectly. We all have our niches."

"I agree. What do you do then?"

"Accept them," she replied. "We probably end up loving those differences more than the similarities. Besides, who wants to be with someone exactly like you?"

Aidan grinned at her. "I don't think I will be taking the intelligent compliment back from you ever."

Brieanne smiled back at him she loved having these talks with him.

"What happened to you and your last boyfriend? That's if you want to tell me. I don't want to encroach on your past or put you on the spot."

"Trust me you aren't, and you won't be," she said reassuringly. "It started off well, in the beginning he was very charming and charismatic, but it went south fast when his true colors started to show. He was always talking about himself, what he had, those kinds of things. He was definitely, 'a what' guy, rather than 'a who' guy, and he treated me like I was his trophy. I soon realized the reason he bragged so much about what he had was because he had no personality. Eventually I had enough of his arrogance and chauvinism and ended it." Brieanne looked over at Aidan, "he was nothing like you at all," she said putting her arm through his. "The house you are selling is it the first one you bought, or did you hopscotch from a smaller one up to this one?"

"It's the first one."

"You've lived there for a long time?"

"I have."

"You must be sad to see to it go?"

"Yes and no," he replied not wanting to elaborate. "Do you want to know how I came about buying it?"

She gave him a doubtful look. "Does it have something to do with an Irish real estate agent?"

Aidan laughed. "No, but it does have to do with a California surfer dude."

"Right there, I know it's another one of your tales. Why would a surfer dude be in Rochester?"

"I swear it's true. If at the end of the story you think I made it up I will do any one thing you want, deal?"

"Deal," she said already knowing that she had won.

Aidan began. "After I got my position at the high school, I was looking for a place to buy. So, I would drive around different neighborhoods in the outskirts of Rochester looking to see if any houses were for sale. There was a particular neighborhood that I really liked but there never seemed to be anything available. Early one morning, I was driving around this neighborhood, and I noticed a real estate agent's car in one of the driveways, so I pulled over. Shortly after, a man walks out the house, jumps into the car, and leaves. I'm thinking the owner must be selling the place. I get out my car and go up to the front window to look inside to see if its vacant or some sign indicating they were moving—"

"Some sign?" interrupted Brieanne with a giggle. "Like what?"

"I know, when I think back to it, I wonder what the heck I was doing."

"You're lucky no one called the police," she said still laughing.

"Tell me about it. So, here I am snooping around when all of a sudden, the door opens and out walks this straggly, shoulder length, blond haired, tanned guy with no shirt on wearing surfer shorts. He goes hey dude, what's your problem? I explain to him that I saw the real estate agent's car, thought maybe the house was empty, and coming up for sale. He tells me it is and that he was thinking about listing it with the agent that just left. He must have been about twenty, if that, and tells me his nickname is Rip."

"Rip," said Brieanne laughing, "because he slept a lot like Rip Van Winkle!"

"No, Rip, as in ripped body," corrected Aidan laughing with her, "and he was."

"Oh," she said imagining him.

"You're drooling Brieanne," teased Aidan.

"You have Kim, I have my Rip," she said playfully.

"Next minute this stunner walks out next to Rip asking him what the situation was, he introduces me to his girlfriend, Misty."

"A stunner named, Misty? Sounds like a stripper!"

"Close, she owns a boutique that sells beach apparel," clarified Aidan.

"You're joking?" she asked laughing.

"I'm not, it's the honest truth," he declared and continued. "Rip invites me in and shows me around the place. It's absolutely beautiful and has a huge plot of land. He informs me that he lived here with his great-aunt, before taking off to California at sixteen, and that she passed away several months ago. Because he was the only family she had left, her inheritance and the house, were left to him. Rip then continues to tell me that he wants to get rid of it quickly, so he can get back to California, and really doesn't want to go through the hassle of listing it. And will take a cut in the price, if necessary."

"Seriously?"

"Oh yeah," replied Aidan. "I turn around to him, ask him what he told the real estate agent he wants for it, subtract the agent's fee, add a little more to the price and give him an offer. Rip shows Misty then turns around and says sold my man."

"Just like that? Sold my man!"

"Exactly like that. He had some of his great-aunt's personal items boxed up as well as some things with yellow sticky notes attached to them around the house that needed to be packed. The only thing he asked of me, is if I would ship them to him, and I said I would. He told me whatever was left, mostly furniture, I could keep, donate, or throw out. That same day we get all the documents signed, he asks for twenty thousand in cash, and the rest in a certified check; the deal is done. Rip tells me him and Misty will be gone by noon tomorrow."

"That is incredible," said Brieanne.

"To be honest with you I think his great-aunt had left him a great deal of money and the house was just pennies to his dollars. At the end of the day, we both got what we wanted and were happy. That night Rip and Misty took me out for dinner and to party. The following day I showed up at the house at one, as promised he is gone, and in the mailbox is his address to send his stuff to, the extra house key, and an envelope with two thousand dollars inside to pay for the shipping costs."

"Wow, that is amazing!" said Brieanne. "I've never heard a story like that before."

"It's completely true; Rip the Californian surfer dude and his girlfriend Misty. To this day I still keep in touch with them from time to time. They eventually got married, have a couple of kids, and are always saying I should go visit."

"What did you do with his aunt's furniture?"

"My plan was to get rid of it all, but as I started looking at some of the items, there were some really nice antiques. I realized I could make it work with the vision I had for my place. Plus, it had sentimental value attached to it and I hated to see it just thrown on a dump pile. I could understand Rip not wanting it, so I treated like…"

"She had left it for you."

"Something like that." admitted Aidan. "There were other pieces of furniture that were just bought from a department store that had no history, those things I donated."

"Did you tell Rip what you did?"

"I did; I wanted to make sure he was okay with it."

"I'm taking it he was?"

"He was, and his exact words were," said Aidan, putting on his surfer accent, "Bro, I've been tossing and turning worrying about that, missing all my waves because my heart was saddened. I'm happy that you told me. I think my great-aunt would approve a gnarly and righteous dude like you, has not only found a place in your home for them but also in your heart, we love you man, Rip and Misty."

Brieanne laughed hysterically. "That was so kind of him to say."

"It was. So, I kept all the sentimental pieces and still have them today."

They jumped off the trolley, crossed the road, and went into Sand Key Park. As they strolled along the path Brieanne pointed out the nature trail, outdoor showers, restrooms, and playground. At the beach they found a spot, spread out their towels, and lay on their stomachs facing the Gulf.

"There're a lot of families," noticed Aidan looking around, "and couples, too."

"It's a very popular spot," stated Brieanne.

"I can understand why," said Aidan. "Stan's right, it's beautiful."

Brieanne watched a group of children for a while building a sandcastle in front of them. "I think relationships are like sandcastles," she revealed. "Some like my parents, your parents, your aunt and uncle, have stood the test of time over years, and fought off the destructive winds that can harm them or even end them. Other relationships aren't so lucky, those winds cause irreparable harm and damage, especially a strong gust like infidelity," she said glancing at Aidan. "My mother told me that to love someone is very important in a relationship, but just as important, is that you have to like them. That love is the emotion you feel for that special someone; liking them is what you do with that special someone every day."

"I can agree with that," said Aidan looking at her. "Loving and liking someone, are those the two foundations of your strong, sandcastle, relationship?"

"Two of them," she replied looking back at the children. "What do you see when you look at a sandcastle?"

Aidan hesitated for a moment. "I see a bunch of kids having fun, playing with the sand."

"You jerk!" said Brieanne playfully giving him a shove. "Don't make me sound like I'm a weirdo."

"I was just teasing you. I can see your analogy of a sandcastle in the wind in regard to relationships and the challenges they can face. I just have never really thought about like that, it's very insightful."

"Thank you," she said happily. "My sandcastle in the wind analogy is one I believe in, and I guess I always will, until someone comes up with a more insightful one."

"I think that may be tough, yours is pretty good."

They swam in the water for a while, sunbathed, and talked. A few hours later they packed up their stuff, walked to Gulf Boulevard, and jumped on the trolley. It took them north onto a bridge that went over Clearwater Pass, then took a left onto South Gulfview Boulevard, and stayed on it for several minutes before disembarking. They walked to Frenchy's Rockaway Grill and were seated on the colorful outdoor patio that had an incredible view of the beach and Gulf. They each ordered a cup of Frenchy's She Crab Soup to start, then Brieanne ordered the grilled grouper sandwich while Aidan ordered the Caribbean grouper sandwich.

"The soup is delicious," said Brieanne having another spoonful.

"It is so good," commented Aidan finishing up his.

"What time is your family back on Friday?"

"They're going to have an early breakfast on the ship then drive home. I'm guessing they will be at the condo around ten or eleven."

"It will be interesting to find out how their cruise was?"

"I'm sure they will have many stories and pictures," confirmed Aidan.

"I can't wait to hear them." said Brieanne, feeling close to them.

"My sister and her family arrive Friday afternoon," slipped in Aidan.

"They do," said Brieanne surprised. "How come you never mentioned anything sooner?"

Aidan was silent.

Brieanne noticed something was wrong." What is it?"

The server dropped off their sandwiches and took away their empty soup cups.

Aidan waited till she left. "When I booked my flight here, I left my return ticket open. As you know, I showed up unexpected, but my sister planned this trip over a month ago."

"You feel like you are infringing on their holiday because you are here?"

"I guess. My family told me we would work some sleeping arrangements out when my sister arrived."

"They are family," said Brieanne, "I'm sure you can all work something out."

"I know."

Brieanne remembered something he said earlier. "What's this have to do with the open ticket?"

"The reason I purchased an open ticket was so I could tell them I was heading to Boston."

"What?" asked Brieanne, not sure she was hearing him correctly. "You are planning on going to Boston?"

"My original plan was to sleep on the couch, stay there till Monday, then tell them I had booked a trip to Boston and go. That way I've spent the Fourth of July weekend with them, and they wouldn't feel like they had forced me to leave."

"I'm sure your sister and her family would love for you to vacation with them for the summer, rather than go to Boston," she stated, trying to convince him to reconsider.

"They would, and I would like to spend more time with them also. It's just they need space, and more importantly, so do I."

Brieanne realized that was the real issue. With everything going on in his life, being around his family nonstop wouldn't give him the luxury of time or space to figure out what he was going to do. "So, you're not going to Boston?"

"No, I thought when I left on Monday I would move into a hotel, one that is close to them, and close to you," he said looking at her. "I can see them as often as I want, use the amenities at the condo, and even have the occasional dinners with them. It also gives me the option of coming and going at my leisure. This way I have my own place, my own space, and it also gives them more room to breathe."

Brieanne finally understood what he was saying, and her anxiety dissipated.

"I noticed there was a place called Madeira Bay Resort which is very close."

"That place is beautiful. They have fully equipped condo suites, pool, spa, fitness room, and balconies with a view of the Gulf or causeway."

"That sounds perfect!" said Aidan cheerfully. "On Monday, I will drop in and see what they have available."

She wondered how much of his decision to stay had to do with her. "How long are you going to book it for?"

"Do they offer long term?"

"They do."

"Six weeks for now, take it from there," said Aidan biting into his sandwich.

Brieanne bit into hers and before long they were trying one another's. "These are both so delicious," she said taking another bite.

"I don't know which one I like better," said Aidan.

"I say we agree, both are amazing," replied Brieanne, "and call it a draw."

"Agreed," said Aidan as they finished up, paid, and left the restaurant.

They walked onto the beach set up their blanket and sunbathed.

"Sometime next week I was going to begin fixing up the new house," she said, "and this is only if you want to, I was wondering if you may want to help me out? You've seen what needs to be done, it's not a lot of work, I could use an extra set of hands."

"When do you want to start?"

"Really!" she said excitedly sitting up. "I was thinking Tuesday we can make up a list of things we need to buy, decide what rooms to do first, and start Wednesday."

"Okay," replied Aidan, "Tuesday it is."

Brieanne was ecstatic at the thought of them working on it together. She jumped on him kissing his face all over. "Thank you, thank you, thank you."

They spent the afternoon on the beach, then took an early evening walk down to Pier 60 and strolled out along the one-thousand-and-eighty-foot fishing pier to its furthest point. When they got to the end Brieanne informed Aidan that couples and families come out here every night to enjoy the sunset. They slowly sauntered back to the park and watched the children in the playground, listened to the musicians, were entertained by performers, and viewed the vendor's crafts, before taking the trolley home.

When they arrived at the condo, they took showers, while Brieanne's chicken pot pie warmed in the oven. Together they made a salad, cut up the pie, and ate on the balcony. After they finished, Aidan picked up the dirty dishes and was heading through the doors when his phone suddenly rang. Brieanne took the dishes from him and put them in the dishwasher while he answered it. Fifteen minutes later, he came out onto the balcony holding a bottle of wine and two glasses. He gave the glasses to Brieanne, opened the bottle, and filled them. Then put the bottle down, took a glass, and stood beside her.

"Everything okay?" she asked as he stared out at the horizon.

"Yeah, that was my real estate agent, Liz."

"Good news."

"She told me that quite a few people have been through the house, four of them want to make offers."

"That's great news," said Brieanne enthusiastically.

"It is," he said glancing over at her. "Liz told them that she wasn't accepting any offers till Monday because of the holiday weekend, and she's leaving on Friday afternoon to visit her family and won't be around."

"So, you will be getting four offers on Monday?" Brieanne clarified.

"No, one of couples gave her an offer today and gave me to Tuesday midnight to accept. Liz then went to the other three potential buyers, told them what had happened; now they want to do the same. She gave them till five tomorrow afternoon to get the offers to her; otherwise, they would have to wait till Monday."

"That's exciting," said Brieanne favorably.

"Liz asked if there was a way to get documents to me, I told her about your real estate agent Joyce, and that she could help me from this end. She said that was perfect and if I could send her Joyce's information tomorrow," explained Aidan looking at her. "I would prefer to meet with Joyce first and make sure she is fine with it before I send anything to Liz."

"You should," said Brieanne, "I will call her tomorrow morning and see what her availability is. I'm really happy for you."

"Thanks," he said forcing a smile. "I just need to figure out where I'm going to live."

Brieanne was silent for a moment. "Have you given any more thought to living here in Madeira Beach?"

"To be honest with you I have, and I'm finding the more time I spend here, the more I like it."

"Maybe once you sell your house you can concentrate on your next task, seeing what jobs are available in the area," she suggested.

"Maybe," he replied moving closer to her. "I'm glad we met."

"So am I," she said putting down her wine and wrapping her arms around him.

Aidan kissed her softly on the lips and grinned. Brieanne pulled him close and seductively kissed him open mouth before stopping and smiling at him. They turned arm in arm to watch the sun's final rays fade out of sight. Then talked for a while, finished their wine, and went to bed.

The last two nights at her place, Brieanne had slept with him till she fell asleep, and wanted the same tonight. But she wasn't about to go into his parents' bedroom and lie next to him in their bed. Before they said goodnight, she had thought about asking him to lie with her, then realized it may make him uncomfortable having to tell her it wasn't a good idea.

Just as she was coming to terms with the fact that she would be sleeping alone, Aidan came in and slid under the blankets, Brieanne snuggled into him and fell asleep.

Chapter 19

At nine Brieanne came out of the bathroom went into the kitchen and watched Aidan put the eggs on the plate next to the bacon and toast before handing it to her. She waited for him to do his then followed him out on his parents' balcony. Aidan left briefly, when he returned, he put orange juice and coffee on the table before sitting.

"I'm glad you came and slept with me last night," she said sipping on her juice.

"Me too," he replied.

"I was having a difficult time falling asleep, and then as soon as I cuddled into you, I was out like a light," she said snickering. "You're like a warm glass of milk."

Aidan smiled at her. "I love you snuggling into me, which is the reason why I crept in last night."

And left with my heart, she thought.

After breakfast Brieanne called Joyce then informed Aidan she would meet him at one. At ten they walked over to Brieanne's, where Aidan waited, while she went upstairs to drop off her bag.

"Aidan," she shouted, "come here quickly."

Aidan went into her room and out onto the balcony.

"Look," she said motioning to the water, "a pod of dolphins."

"That's incredible!" said Aidan putting his arm around her as they watched them swim out of sight.

Brieanne grabbed his hand and led him into the bedroom where she stopped and looked deeply into his eyes. Aidan put his arms around her, pulled her close, and kissed her passionately. She responded vehemently. Aidan's hands roamed up and down her body. He gently lifted her up and she straddled him. Feeling his hardness through his shorts, she put her

155

wetness closer to it, and moved up and down over it. Aidan sat her on the edge of the bed, lifting up her arms; he removed her top and bra. He went on his knees, took her hard nipple in his mouth, and gently sucked on it while his fingers tenderly pulled on the other. Brieanne moaned and played with his hair as he moved his mouth from one nipple to the other.

Aidan stood and lightly pushed Brieanne onto the bed motioning her to lift up her bum as he removed her shorts and underwear. Spreading her legs, he kissed her toes, foot, calf, inside her thigh, up to her wet and wanting vulva. Hs tongue gently massaged her clitoris, slowly at first, before applying more pressure, and quickening his pace. Brieanne moaned loudly as she lifted her pelvis up to his fervid tongue. Aidan moved his tongue deep inside her folds, then back over her clitoris, then back inside her. She moaned loudly as she covered Aidan face with her juices. Aidan continued to move feverishly between her folds and clitoris till she gave out a loud moan and came. As she lay, he moved slowly up her body, kissing her stomach, nipples, neck, and mouth.

Brieanne lustfully looked at him. She told him to stand up as she removed his shirt then dropped to her knees to remove his shorts and boxers. She took his hardness as deep as she could, letting it slide in and out of her mouth, before taking it out and licking his shaft. As she rubbed and licked him, she could feel her juices flowing once again, and wanted him inside her. Brieanne stood, grabbed his hand, and led him to the bed, then pulled him on top of her open legs.

Aidan teased her with let the tip of his manhood as it slowly brushed against her labia. She was about to beg him to put it inside her, but there was no need, slowly his hardness entered her slippery folds. He started slowly, gently, at first, slowly sliding in and out, allowing his shaft to rub against her clitoris. Brieanne responded receptively by moving her pelvis to his rhythm. Aidan could feel her wetness soaking his manhood as she moaned his name in his ear. Brieanne couldn't take it anymore. She kissed him hotly on the mouth, grabbed his bum, and pleaded with him to go faster, which he did. Brieanne moaned loudly as the tempo increased. Aidan's manhood slid deep inside, spreading her folds, and messaging her clitoris, again and again and again; faster and faster. Brieanne cried, "don't stop...I'm cumming, I'm cumming, I'm cumming!" and let out a loud moan. Aidan continued the pace and with one final thrust, moaned, and came deep inside her. He slowly moved his manhood inside and out for a few more minutes, kissing her tenderly in between, before rolling off and onto his side. Brieanne put her head on his chest while Aidan held her tightly.

Brieanne looked up at him. "I love you," she whispered.

"I love you," he whispered, looking down at her.

Brieanne gently kissed him, then his chest, before resting her head on it.

"Brie, how do you like the new place?" asked Joyce taking a seat behind her desk.

"I love it!" replied Brie. "We looked around it a couple of days ago and made notes of the changes I want to make. Next week we are going to make a list, prioritize, and start fixing it up."

"I'm glad to hear," replied Joyce looking at Brie peculiarly. "I must admit Brie you have a certain glow about you today."

Brie blushed. "I've had some time off work this week and been showing Aidan the sights," she replied.

"That must be it," said Joyce, "time away from work."

Brie agreed as she glanced at Aidan trying not to giggle.

"Aidan, Brie has explained to me what you need my help in, and that's fine, "she said looking at him. "Here is my card with all my information, you can pass that on to Liz, and she can call me anytime this afternoon," she explained passing it to him. "I understand that Liz will be sending me up to four offers, sometime after five tonight?"

"That's correct," answered Aidan.

"What I will do," Joyce said slowly looking for a pen, "is give you a call once I receive them, then we can schedule a time for you to come in, and we can review them."

"Perfect," said Aidan.

Joyce then asked him for some personal information which he gave. "What I will be doing won't take up too much of my time, and as you are a friend of Brie's, there will be no charge," she stated.

"All the same, I prefer if you billed me for your time and any expenses you incur," he said openly, "I wouldn't feel uncomfortable otherwise."

Joyce looked at Brie's blank look then back at him. "How about a compromise?" she asked. "I will charge you in full for my time and expenses I incur but will give you a twenty-five percent discount on your final bill. Does that sound fair?"

"That's fair," agreed Aidan.

"Good," she said with a smile. "I will call you when I receive the offers from Liz."

Joyce came around the desk, shook Aidan's hand, and gave Brie a hug. Then showed them to the front door, watched them climb into the Jeep, and returned to her office.

"That's taking care of," said Brieanne. "Now, what shall we do for the remainder of the afternoon?"

"Yesterday on the trolley we passed a miniature golf course," mentioned Aidan.

"I haven't played for ages," she said enthusiastically, "but I have to tell you I'm pretty good."

"Then let's make a wager," suggested Aidan as they pulled onto Gulf Boulevard and headed north.

"How about," said Brieanne thinking, "the loser buys ice creams at the Shake Shop?"

"Deal," agreed Aidan.

A few minutes later Brieanne and Aidan arrived at Smugglers Cove Adventure Golf. They paid the admission, bought some alligator food, and walked over to the pond enclosure. Inside there was a congregation of about two dozen young American alligators.

"Each Smugglers Cove has an 'Educational American Alligator Exhibit,'" she informed Aidan. "Just grab one of those cane fishing poles, put the food on, place the pole over the fence and feed them."

Aidan did what she said and watched as the alligators swam over and took the food. Brieanne joined in. With the food gone, they started their round of golf. They played eighteen holes on a multilevel design which took them behind a waterfall, inside a cave, and onto a pirate ship. After finishing the last hole, they sat on the bench while Brieanne tallied their scores.

"Read it and weep," she said, standing up and doing her happy dance.

"You beat me by four," he said looking at her dancing. "At least you're a good winner."

She leaned over and gave him an affectionate kiss saying, "that's your prize for coming in second."

Aidan pulled her onto his lap and kissed her passionately. "I guess you will be wanting your victory ice cream?"

"I do," she admitted with a smile.

Arriving at the Shake Shop Aidan ordered Brieanne a strawberry sundae then asked for a chocolate sundae for him. They walked onto the deck, sat on a bench, and ate.

"This is so good," said Brieanne spooning down her sundae. "I have been craving this ice cream since we passed here a couple of days ago."

"I'm glad you brought me here, it's delicious," he said glancing over at her. "Yesterday, when you were talking about your sandcastle, you said that loving and liking someone were two of the foundations of a relationship, what would the others be?"

Brieanne was pleased he brought it up, it showed he was interested in what she thought, and gave her a good feeling inside. "Honesty, trust, kindness, compassion, affectionate, supportive, physical love—"

"Love making?"

"Definitely that," she said with a big grin as she recalled their morning vividly. "Plus, other types of physical contact: like holding hands, cuddling, caressing, and kissing." She looked up from her ice cream.

"Overall, I guess all the attributes that would be positive to a relationship that help you grow as a couple."

"And those winds of destruction?" asked Aidan, sounding foreboding, and making her laugh.

"Simply, those negative attributes which are the opposite of the positive ones."

After they finished their ice creams they drove to Publix. Brieanne picked out a potato salad, along with items to make a garden salad, and then went to her place. After putting the items in the fridge and changing, she went outside, and lay on a lounger next to Aidan.

"I wish I had brought my bathing suit," he said looking at Brieanne in her bikini. "I wouldn't mind going for a dip."

"Swim in your boxers, it's the same as a swimsuit, and no one is going to see you."

Aidan took off his shorts and dove in, Brieanne jumped in after him. They swam to the shallow end and sat on the steps.

"This feels much better, I needed to cool off," he said looking out at the beach then over at her. "Tell me, what are your friends are like?"

"Well, I have two incredibly good friends. One is Cathy, who you have met. She is sweet, kind, and thoughtful, a romantic at heart. She is extremely low key but has her moments when she tries to act out of character and is very funny." Brieanne explained further by telling him about the lunchtime conversation they had. "And she is married to a really nice guy. While Bev, on the other hand, is more outgoing and very personable. She is somewhat of a romantic, but a lot more of a party girl, but in a fun way not in a slutty way. She is naturally funny, last week she was pretending to be a detective from CSI interrogating me," she said telling him the story.

"They seem like good friends," said Aidan.

"The best," declared Brieanne. "I did have another best friend, her name was April, but she died about thirteen months ago in a car accident."

"Oh, I'm sorry to hear about that."

"Thank you," she said sadly as she thought about her. "She lived in the house next to the one I just bought. Her son Ben, he's nine, and her daughter Jen, she's eleven, live there now with their grandmother. They've been away in Orlando visiting family and will be back tomorrow." Brieanne was getting a little upset, calmed herself down, and continued. "You will meet them, probably tomorrow," she said managing a grin, "because they are always over here." Brieanne went quiet.

Aidan decided to change the subject. "What do Cathy and Bev do at the restaurant?"

Brieanne was grateful for the redirection. "Cathy is the daytime manager and started off green like me. She has a fantastic work ethic, is intelligent, and picked it up very quickly. Bev graduated from university with a degree in Hospitality Management. She worked for me part-time during the school year and full-time in the summers. Now she is the full-time night manager and is amazing. She knows just as much as I do and she has been working with me for many years; actually, they both have."

"Do the three of you always get along?"

"For the most part," she replied. "We have had our differences socially, never work related, what friends don't?"

"True."

"I have been thinking of something these last several weeks to do with my restaurant, do you mind if I bounce it off you to get your thoughts?"

"Yes, of course, but I'm not sure how much help I can give you in regard to your restaurant," he claimed.

"Actually, it's more to do with people," she clarified.

"Okay," he said, "ask away."

"With Bev having her degree in Hospitality Management, as well as her experience and knowledge, I was considering promoting her to Restaurant Manager at the end of the summer, and promoting Cathy to senior manager under Bev, who will fill in for Bev when she is away. Bev and Cathy can hire the nighttime manager to replace her since they will be reporting to them anyway," she explained. "Bev is very career minded and I know she would love the challenge. Cathy is happy with being a daytime manager and I know she will gladly accept being a senior manager, but she wouldn't want to progress any further like Bev. Although, I'm think her filling in for Bev once in a while she would enjoy."

Aidan wasn't sure what she was asking him. "They seem like next logical steps, evolving your restaurant, and promoting staff from within."

"I totally agree," she said, looking at him thoughtfully. "Remember when I told you I owned eighty percent and my dad twenty."

"I do," said Aidan.

"My parents wanted me to own it outright. I told my father that I wanted an eighty-twenty split or no deal. He asked me why? I told him I had two reasons: first, if he continues to have a stake in the restaurant, he will want to continue to see it succeed; second, his name exemplifies excellence, and by keeping his name on as owner and promoting it, means that him, we, the restaurant, are committed to that value."

"What did he say?"

"He turned to my mother, I think his eyes were watery, and said that his little girl had grown up into a fine, strong, intelligent woman, and was now owner of eighty percent of their restaurant."

He was still unsure where Brieanne was going with this.

"If I do promote Bev and Cathy, they will get a significant salary increase. My dilemma is whether I should give them a percentage of the restaurant, making them partial owners?"

"You're thinking they will work more diligently to make the restaurant successful, if they have a share in it."

"I'm hoping more successful. Plus, it will keep them from leaving, I can never see Cathy going, Bev is more the concern. Yet, I want to treat them equally in my decision making."

"Are you going to give them a percentage out of your ownership?"

"No," said Brieanne shaking her head. "I will give it to them from my father's. My father is always going to be an owner, even if it's only one percent. Although I'm not talking about giving Bev and Cathy the remaining nineteen percent, it will be much less."

"Let me see if I understand?" said Aidan.

"Okay," said Brieanne happy about being able to talk so freely with him.

"You're thinking about promoting Bev to Restaurant Manager, Cathy to Senior Manager, both with a significant salary increase. You know they will both accept, but you are also thinking if you give them a small, ownership percentage in the restaurant, they will be more likely to stay and make it more successful because it will affect them directly."

"Exactly," she said, "I couldn't have summarized it any better." She moved close to him. "What do you think?"

"I don't own a business, and I wouldn't want to say what you should do with your restaurant and your money," he said tentatively.

"Please," she begged, "as an outsider looking in. I only want to hear you take is on it, that's all."

He looked at her carefully. "If you decide to promote them, I would give them a small percentage."

"Hmm, that simple," she said. "May I ask why?"

"You convinced me that they are both outstanding candidates for promotion based on the qualities they possess. You and your dad have an ethic that is one of the foundations of running a successful business, simply put: if you own a piece of the place you work at, you will work diligently to make it more of a success."

"You're right. I guess I knew that all along," said Brieanne smiling at him. "It's nice to have someone to talk it through with and see if they noticed anything I may have missed."

"I'm glad to be of some help."

"You most definitely were," she confirmed. "I really like talking with you."

"And I like talking with you," he said as they kissed.

"Are you hungry?"

"A little."

"I should start dinner," said Brieanne standing up and walking out of the pool.

Aidan watched as she dried herself, turned on the BBQ and went inside. He got out of the pool, wrapped a towel around his waist, changed out of his wet boxers into his shorts and hung them over a chair to dry. Brieanne came outside wearing shorts and a top, lifted up the BBQ lid placed two chicken breasts on the grill, and a small bowl containing BBQ sauce on the side table.

"Come inside while I make the salad," she said as he followed her in. She grabbed the vegetables from the fridge and a bottle of white wine. "Can you open this? Glasses are in here," she said pointing to a cupboard.

Aidan poured two glasses handing her one. "Do you need any help?"

"No, have a seat."

Aidan sat watching her slicing the vegetables. "You're working tomorrow morning?" he reconfirmed.

"Till about two, then I have errands to run, be home around five," she replied. "Will you be hanging out with your family tomorrow?"

"Yes, unless I receive a call from Joyce. If I do, I'm hoping I can meet with her early in the morning prior to them getting home."

"Are you going to say anything to your parents?"

"No, there is nothing much to tell them right now."

"If it sells?"

"I don't know," he said unsure. "I'll worry about that when it happens."

She looked over at him. "Where are you going to say you're going if Joyce does call when they're home?"

"That's why I'm hoping it's early, so I can slip out and be back, before they get home," he replied as he watched her finish the salad.

"I need to keep an eye on the chicken," she indicated grabbing his hand and leading him outside. Brieanne lifted the lid, turned the chicken over, and closed it.

"Do you think I'm wrong keeping it from them?"

"I don't believe there is a right or wrong to what you are doing. You need time to figure everything out, why complicate it at this time," she said supportively. "Although at some point, you will have to tell them."

"I know," he said. "That's inevitability for you; you can't escape it."

"True, but remember you are in control, and you get to decide when it's the right time to tell them."

"Unless they find out from someone other than me," he said half-joking.

"Is there a chance that could happen?"

"No," he said candidly, "I can't see that happening."

"Then you have nothing to worry about," she said with a grin. Brieanne opened the lid, picked up the small bowl, and spread the BBQ sauce liberally over the chicken. "My dad's secret BBQ sauce from the diner in San Francisco."

"Smells divine!"

"Tastes even better."

Brieanne turned the chicken once more, applying another liberal coating, before going inside to get a plate. She lifted the chicken off the grill and onto it. "Let's eat at the counter inside," she said as he followed her. She separated the chicken breasts onto two plates, placed the bowl of tossed salad and containers of salad dressing in between them, along with the potato salad. As she loaded their plates Aidan filled up their wine glasses. "Cheers," she said.

"Cheers to the amazing and beautiful chef," replied Aidan touching her glass

"Thank you," she replied approvingly, and then watched for his reaction as cut off a piece of chicken and placed it in his mouth.

"Oh my! This sauce is incredible!"

"Isn't it," she said starting to eat, "it's one of my favorites."

"One of them?" asked Aidan.

"He has eight different types of BBQ sauce, and it looks like you may be here long enough to try them all," she suggested and happy at the thought.

After dinner they walked down the beach towards John's Pass, arriving at the end, they stepped onto the boardwalk and walked towards its furthest western point. The bridge opened to let a boat out; they leaned on the railing, and watched it sail out into the Gulf.

"That's the sunset cruise," explained Brieanne pointing to another boat in the distance. "It departs at seven and cruises for an hour and a half. On board, you get free beer or wine, listen to music, and watch the sunset."

"I wouldn't mind trying that one evening," said Aidan keenly, "sounds like fun."

"I will have to mark it down on our to-do list," she said cheerfully.

Aidan put his arm around her as she rested her head on his shoulder. As they watched the sun slowly melt into the horizon Brieanne wondered if it could ever get any better than this. Holding hands, they slowly strolled back.

"If you do go through with the promotions at the end of summer, will you still need to go to the restaurant as much?"

"I don't know," she replied. Brieanne wanted to tell him more about her plans, but it was too soon, and she was unsure of them herself. "I will probably still need to go in," was all she told him. Arriving back at her place, she looked into his eyes, and thought about how much in love she was with him. "Do you need to get going?"

"No," he whispered.

"Will you lie with me till I fall sleep?"

"Yes."

She led him to the room, opened her balcony doors, and let the breeze gently blow the sheer curtains. Brieanne moved to the side of the bed, undressed, and slid in between the sheets. Aidan did the same. He held her quietly in his arms listening to the waves lap against the shoreline.

"Make love to me, slowly," she whispered.

Aidan did.

Brieanne cuddled into him, smiling contentedly, she fell asleep.

Chapter 20

Brieanne: "Good morning, loved last night, getting ready for work."

Aidan: "Same, just out of the shower, received a call from Joyce, meeting her at ten."

Brieanne: "Let me know how it goes, miss you."

Aidan: "Will do, thinking of you, always."

"I received the four offers last night around six. I also spoke with Liz around six thirty to get some additional information from her," she elucidated, before looking up at him. "Is this amount here, correct? Is this what you originally paid?" she questioned thinking she may have heard Liz wrong as she pointed to a figure written on a notepad.

"That's the price I paid."

"Can I ask how you managed that?" she said leaning back in her chair.

Aidan told her a summarized story about the great-aunt, Rip, and Misty.

Joyce laughed. "Talk about being in the right place at the right time," she said shaking her head, "that's remarkable." She looked back at her notes. "The house is paid for?"

"It is."

"Okay, let's get down to business and review these offers," she said. "All the offers are the same, in as much as the wording. There are only two differences between all four: the price they have offered and the closing date. If you are interested in making the most money, offer number two is the highest bid; it's nine percent higher than what you listed it for, and over four times the original price you paid. The next best offer is number one, at eight percent. Two and four, are seven percent. If you are looking to sell quickly, are you?" she asked glancing up at him.

"I am. I've already moved out."

"Then, offer number one wants a thirty-day close. Number four wants forty-five days. Two and three want a sixty-day close," she stopped and looked up at him. "When I spoke to Liz about offer number one, it seems that they were looking for a house immediately. So, they may have put in a thirty-day closing on the assumption that would be the earliest you would vacate. How soon would you like to sell it?"

"As soon as possible," replied Aidan.

"Then what I would suggest, and this is only my suggestion, because I will advise you to talk to Liz to get her input also," she said clarifying. "I would refuse all offers; stipulate you want to close immediately, and that you want more money for this inconvenience, and see what comes back," she said staring at him intensely. "And if I'm right, and I believe I am, I think offer number one is going to bite. They will give you an immediate closing and hike the price up, to at least…ten percent over your asking price…I would even be so bold as to predict somewhere close to twelve to fifteen percent. If they don't come back with a better offer, you can decide from the offers you receive, which one you like best." She sat back in her chair. "I'm guessing you were probably planning on taking offer number one anyway, because of the earlier closing?"

"Yes," replied Aidan extremely impressed with Joyce.

"You talk to Liz, call me on Monday, and let me know what you've decided. Then we will take it from there. Oh, by the way, if you go with my suggestion and decide to refuse all four, don't let them know that till Monday, even Tuesday, let them sweat it out."

Aidan admired this woman.

"Do you have any questions?"

"One," he stated. "When you say immediately, and one of them agrees to that, how soon would that be till it is sold?"

"Taking everything into account, I would say by next Friday. Friday afternoon you will have your check," she said convincingly.

Aidan thanked her, left her office, and called Liz. Liz agreed with Joyce and said she would let the prospective buyers know Tuesday morning that their offers had been refused. He hung up, called Joyce, and told her. Then texted Brieanne: "Met with Joyce everything went well."

Brieanne: "Good to hear. Where are you now?"

Aidan: "Sitting on the patio at Lisa's Cafe, drinking coffee, and eating a scrumptious breakfast."

Brieanne: "Let me guess…cheese omelet, home fries, toast, coffee, and orange juice."

Aidan: "We definitely hang out too much!"

Brieanne: "Wait, I'll call you."

Aidan's phone rang. "Hello, who's this?"

"Aren't you funny," she replied. "What happened with Joyce?"

Aidan told her.

"So, you are probably going to get some offers, Tuesday, Wednesday?"

"Hopefully," he replied, "Liz and Joyce believe I will."

"I'm sure you will, too," she said confidently. "Where did you tell your parents, you were going?"

"They're not home yet. I left them a note saying I'd gone out for a walk and breakfast."

"Oh okay, what are your plans for this afternoon?"

"I'm heading back to condo. Talk with my parents about their trip. Wait for my sister."

"What time is your sister arriving at the condo?"

"I'm guessing around two thirty. Do you still have errands to do this afternoon?"

"Yeah, I should be finished no later than five." Brieanne went silent, she wanted to see him tonight, but he had his family, and she didn't want to invite herself.

"Do you have any plans after?"

"Not really," she replied. Damn, she thought, she should have been honest and just said no.

"After dinner, we are going to hang out at the pool for the night. They're having live music. If you're free, you're more than welcome to join us. You can meet my sister and her family."

Meet his sister, she thought. "I'd love to, what time?"

"Why don't I come to your place around six thirty and walk back with you?"

"Okay," she said excitedly.

"I miss you," he said.

"Miss you," she replied, "I'll see you then, bye." Brieanne let out a loud cheerful, "yes!"

A minute later Cathy ran into her office. "I could hear you from the patio," she gasped, out of breath. "Good news?"

"Great news," she said telling her about tonight.

Brieanne finished up at work, ran her errands, ate, and got ready. "Six thirty, right on time," she noted letting Aidan in the front door. "I need to grab my bag from upstairs, only be a minute," she said walking away. "We'll leave by the back."

Aidan walked to the back doors, went outside, and waited.

Brieanne joined him, put her bag down, and threw her arms around him. "I've been thinking about doing this all day," she said, giving him a long kiss.

Aidan held her tightly.

Brieanne stopped and looked at him. "I guess we should go?"

Aidan kissed her passionately as his hands freely roamed down her back and gently clasped her bum.

Or not, she thought, as she responded wholeheartedly, wanting him.

Aidan slowed down, stopped, and pulled away. "You're right, we should get going," he said picking up her bag, handing it to her, and walking away.

What just happened, she thought. Realizing, she hurried off after him. "You filthy Scallywag! That is so cruel!" she cried looking at Aidan's mischievous smile. "Now I have to sit with your family with that thought in my head all night!"

"I know," said Aidan laughing as they walked onto the path.

Suddenly something made her stop and look up at him alarmingly.

"What's the matter?"

Brieanne was trying to think of the right way to put it, there was none, and blurted it out. "No one knows about us; everyone believes we're just friends."

"They don't need to?" he replied. "Not yet anyway."

"I'm not worried about that," she confessed, "more so on how we behave in front of your family, my family, and friends?"

Aidan understood where she was going with this. "Okay. What would make you most comfortable?"

Brieanne considered the options. "In front of people we know, we act like friends, close friends, no physical contact," she clarified, as she slowly moved closer to him. "But when we are alone, we can do whatever we want," she said with a sexy grin and giving him an erotic kiss.

"Okay," said Aidan, extremely turned and wanting more.

And she knew it. "Time to go," she said impishly and started to walk.

"Brie!" cried two voices in the distance running in her direction.

"Jen! Ben!" she yelled as they ran into her arms.

"We missed you," they said.

"When did you get back?"

"An hour ago," replied Jen. "We came over to visit you and see if you wanted to play with us in your pool?"

"Where is your grandmother?" asked Brie looking past them.

"I'm coming," said a voice closing her back gate.

"Who's this?" asked Ben looking at Aidan.

"This is my friend Aidan," she said introducing him to the two children, and their grandmother, "Isabella."

"Everyone calls me Bella," she said shaking his hand.

"Unfortunately, I am going with Aidan to meet his family," she told them.

The children's smiles disappeared.

"You can still use the pool, though."

Brieanne and Aidan looked down at their sad faces.

"Do you see that condo over there?" asked Aidan looking at the children then pointing in its direction.

"Yes," they both said.

"That's where we are going," explained Aidan. "That condo has a big swimming pool; my niece and nephew are playing in it right now with a bunch of other children. And when they stop for a break, they get ice cream," described Aidan looking at their adorable faces transfixed on him. "Does that sound like something you would like to do, too?"

"Yes," they replied eagerly.

"If your grandmother says it's okay, you can all come with us?" he asked looking at her.

"Please Grandma," begged the children.

"Ben, Jen, we shouldn't be imposing on Aidan and Brie's night with his family," said Bella looking at the children then Aidan, "but thank you for the offer."

"You won't be imposing at all. My parents, sister, her husband, my aunt, and uncle, are also there," said Aidan reassuringly.

"They're great company, there's a bar, and live music," added Brie.

"I'm inviting you as my personal guests, please come," implored Aidan.

"As long as we are welcome guests," said Bella. "Thank you, we would love to join you."

The kids ran joyfully down the path as Brie, Bella and Aidan leisurely walked behind them. When they arrived at the pool area, Aidan called his niece and nephew out of the pool and walked with them to his family's table.

"This is Brieanne, her neighbor Bella, and her two grandchildren Jen and Ben," said Aidan. "Over here are my sister Jane, her husband Steven, and their children Madison, who likes being called Maddy, and Ethan. And next to them are my parents Paul and Theresa, and my uncle Bill and my aunt Amy."

With the introductions done the four kids dashed off into the pool.

Bella sat with the older couples while Brieanne sat next to Jane. When Aidan and Steven returned with drinks, Aidan sat between Brieanne and Steven.

"Have you lived here all your life?" asked Jane looking at Brieanne.

"Yes," she answered.

"Do you live close?"

"It's a ten-minute walk from here. My place backs onto the beach."

"That must be nice looking at the Gulf every day?" said Steven.

"I love it!" replied Brieanne.

"How did you two, meet?" asked Jane inquisitively.

Aidan told them about the day he arrived, then the Friday night dinner, and everything they had done since. Steven took it as nothing more than sightseeing; Jane intuitions knew better.

"Seems like you two have become good friends?" asked Jane looking at both of them, wondering who would respond.

"We have," replied Brieanne, "I would actually say close friends. Not only have we done quite a bit together, but we also talk a lot, too." She was about to grab Aidan's hand but caught herself in time, and nervously said, "as a friend, he's quite the catch." *Oh no, did I really say that?*

It made Aidan laugh as he explained to his sister and Steven how some of the locals use fishing terms in their dialogue.

"And pirate ones," added Brieanne.

"Yes," agreed Aidan, explaining further.

"Brieanne hopefully you can give us a list of places to go visit, and perhaps, even join us on some excursions," suggested Jane. "We have never been here before and it would be a great help to us."

"It would be my pleasure," said Brieanne liking Jane immensely.

The group listened on as the two older couples talked off their cruise, showed pictures, and said how they would do it again. The kids stopped for a break, had ice cream, and watched the sunset with the adults before jumping back into the water.

Brieanne whispered to Aidan, "Bella is having a wonderful time talking with your parents, aunt, and uncle."

"Fourth of July tomorrow," said Paul out loud as the group looked at him.

"What are you doing to celebrate?" asked Bella, talking as if she had known them for years.

"We have always had a backyard party on Canandaigua Lake," admitted Theresa. "They are doing something down here for a few hours, so we may do that."

"We're also considering going to a restaurant for a meal," added Amy.

Brieanne had wanted to mention it to Aidan before but with his family being here she thought they would be busy with plans of their own. "I'm actually having a BBQ at my place tomorrow," she said looking around at them, "you are more than welcome to come."

"What time shall we be there?" asked Bill.

"Bill!" said Amy giving him an unfavorable look. "Dear, we couldn't inconvenience you like that?"

"I have more than enough food, beer, wine, and liquor, and I'm having a large canopy set up on the beach with seats and tables. Lunch is going to be hors d'oeuvres, cold cuts, salads, vegetables, and fresh-cut fruits. And in the evening, I'm having a BBQ, with hot dogs, hamburgers, chicken, steak, corn-on-the-cob, grilled vegetables, and apple pie for dessert."

"Are you sure you have enough, there are nine of us?" asked Theresa. "That's nine more mouths to feed?"

"Trust me, it's not an issue," she said glancing around at them. "The kids can play on the beach, swim in the pool—"

"You have a pool at your place?" interrupted Jane.

"A big one," said Aidan looking at Jane, then Steven, "and a hot tub."

"Hot tub," whispered Steven.

"Are you sure?" asked Aidan. "Mom's right, there is nine of us and it is very last minute."

Brieanne looked at Aidan. "I was going to ask you earlier, I thought you and your family may have already made plans, so I didn't," she said to him, then looked at his family. "I will have so much food you will each be taking a doggie bag home," she said, nervously giggling.

The group laughed with her.

"I would like you to come," Brieanne said sincerely. "It will give you a chance to meet some of my family and friends, and me the opportunity to return the friendship and hospitality, you have shown me."

"It would be our pleasure," said Jane. "What time would you like us to come over?"

"Around twelve," replied Brieanne.

"Then it's settled," said Jane. "We will see you at twelve."

At ten thirty Brieanne and Bella rose, saying it was time for them to go, and gathered Jen and Ben. Aidan offered to escort them back, with Jane and Steven saying they would join them for the walk. Jen and Ben ran ahead, in front of Brieanne and Aidan, while Bella, Jane, and Steven walked slowly behind them.

"I think you sister suspects something?" whispered Brieanne.

"Suspects something between me and you?"

"Yes."

"Why do you think that?"

"The way she looks at us, it's like she knows."

"Maybe you're being a little paranoid?"

"Maybe," she replied unsure.

"What do you think of her?"

"I truly like her," Brieanne said candidly. "I think she is amazing."

"Thanks for inviting us tomorrow."

"I wanted to ask you sooner, I wasn't sure if you had made plans already," she reiterated. "I'm glad you are coming."

Aidan chuckled.

"And your family," she said correcting herself. "You know I'm happy they're coming, too?"

"I know."

Jen and Ben were waiting by the path for the rest to catch up.

"I'm just going to walk them to their gates," said Aidan to Jane and Steven. "Are you guys going to wait for me?"

"We will," replied Jane.

Aidan and Brieanne walked to Bella's gate first, they said goodbye to Aidan, while Bella hugged Brieanne, followed by the children who said they loved her. They watched them walk to their back door, go inside, before Aidan walked Brieanne to her back gate.

"Jen and Ben really like you," said Aidan, "actually, I should say love you."

"They do," confirmed Brieanne, "I am very close to them."

Aidan stopped with her at the gate.

Brieanne looked at Aidan, then over his shoulder at his sister and Steven. "I want to kiss you, goodnight," she revealed, "only Jane and Steven are looking at us."

Aidan glanced around at them and started snickering.

"What?" she asked, shoving him.

"It's so dark, how could you tell if they are looking at us?"

"I can't," she said laughing, too. "I just have this feeling they are facing this way."

"How about a hug?" he suggested.

"Fine," replied Brieanne, taking what she could get but really wanting to kiss him.

Aidan gave her a long hug, watched her go inside then joined Jane and Steven.

"Brieanne is really sweet," said Jane as they headed back to the condo.

"I like her. She's fun, down-to-earth, and friendly," said Aidan.

"She's very beautiful and sexy," she said looking for a response.

"I guess," said Aidan acting uninterested.

"What do you think Steven?" asked Jane putting him on the spot.

Steven thought quickly. "I think she's a terrific catch!"

They all laughed.

Brieanne waited thirty minutes before texting Aidan: "Where are you?"

Aidan: "On the balcony with the adults."

Brieanne: "I wanted to kiss you so bad. Now I won't be able to sleep, especially without you holding me."

Aidan: "When I left you, I walked to Jane and Steven, they were facing the water."

Brieanne: 'Ugh! You mean I could have sneaked a kiss?"

Aidan: "Yep."

Brieanne: "Darn!"

Aidan: "Do you need any help tomorrow?"

"Who is that your texting big brother?" whispered Jane teasing him as she took a sip of her wine and hovered over him.

"Brieanne," he said so everyone could hear him and making it look like he had nothing to hide. "I was asking her if she needed any help tomorrow."

"What did she say?" asked his dad.

Brieanne: "No, I'm good tomorrow…but not tonight, I want you!"

"She said no, all is good."

"Good of you to ask," replied Bill.

Aidan: "Jane's asking who I'm texting."

Brieanne: "What did you say?"

Aidan told her.

Brieanne: "I told you she knows."

Aidan: "Maybe."

Brieanne: "I will let you get back to your family, thinking of you, goodnight."

Aidan: "Thinking of you, too, sweet dreams." Aidan turned off his phone, placed it on the table, and looked up catching his sister's curious stare.

"Just friends?" she asked him quietly.

"No." he replied openly.

"No," she repeated taken by surprise with is answer. "More than just friend?" she probed.

"Yes."

"Do tell?" she requested, not realizing she was being baited as she leaned in.

"I will be honest with you, Brieanne and I, we are…"

"Yes?" asked Jane who was now hooked.

"We are good, close, friends…that's it."

Jane suddenly realized her brother had baited, hooked, and reeled her in. "Why you…you," she said loudly, searching for the words to finish her sentence, as everyone stopped to look at her.

Chapter 21

Brie kept a watchful eye on the condo as guests started to arrive. She checked the time, "twelve," she said to herself. They should be on their way she thought.

"Brie," said voices walking towards her.

"Eric, Stacy," she said happily and gave them a hug. "It's been a while. How are you guys doing?"

"Good," replied Stacy, "busy working."

"And you parents?"

"They're both doing well."

"How are things with you Eric?"

"Busy too, looks like we are going to have a stellar summer."

"He's so busy he's had to refuse bookings," added Stacy.

"That's great news," said Brie pleased for him.

"Who is this new guy I heard about and seen you with?" asked Stacy interestedly.

"Seen me with?" asked Brie wondering what she saw.

"I was working…" she said, thinking. "Let's see…on Sunday. You two were on the boardwalk and walked right passed Hooters."

"We were," confirmed Brie. "His name is Aidan, he's a friend, and I was giving him a tour of the area."

Stacy gave her a strange look. "Bev seems to think it may be a little bit more than friends," she said revealing her source.

"You know Bev and her vivid imagination," said Brie passing it off as Bev's overactive imagination.

"True," agreed Stacy leaving it at that. "I'm going to grab us some beers."

"There are some in the cooler, next to the table," said Brie pointing and watching her walk away.

"On vacation?" asked Eric curiously.

"What?' asked Brie, not understanding him.

"This guy, he's on vacation?"

"Yeah, just for the summer."

"Just for the summer," repeated Eric emphasizing the word 'just.'

"Eric, don't get started with that tourist versus local crap with me again."

"Really," said Eric looking at her a little bewildered. "Did you forget what happened last time?"

Brie went silent. "I remember, and I'm truly thankful for your help, this guy is different."

"Isn't that what you said about the last guy?" warned Eric.

"No, I didn't!" said Brie firmly, her guard now up. "Don't you stir anything up with him?"

Eric went silent.

"You will like him, he's a really nice guy," Brie gloated in a friendlier tone to an unconvinced Eric. "At least wait till you meet him before you judge him, please, for me."

Eric managed to smile. "Okay," he replied, "for you."

"Meet who?" asked Stacy returning and handing them each a beer.

"Mr. Perfect," said Eric sarcastically.

Brie gave him a displeased look.

"Is this guy tall, handsome, sexy?" asked Stacy.

Brie wasn't sure how to answer her.

"And will he be coming with a group of adults and a couple of kids?"

"Eh, yeah," answered Brie confused.

"They're right behind you."

"Brieanne," said Aidan coming over and giving her a friendly hug.

"Brieanne," whispered Eric under his breath, "no one calls her that."

"I want you to meet my two good friends," said Brie turning and introducing the group to Stacy and Eric, before facing them again. "Let me get the logistics out of the way. The canopy over here has tables, chairs, and loungers if you want shade. There are also snacks on the big table, next to it are coolers: one has beer, the other sodas, and the last one, bottled water. There are chairs, loungers, out here in the sun, or you can sit on one of the decks. The upper deck has a table with liquor and wine, as well as snacks, and there are also coolers filled with beer, sodas, and water. The bathroom is through the patio doors on the left," she said pointing. "Feel free to use the pool, hot tub, the house; my place is your place."

As the group dispersed Brieanne led Aidan under the canopy, grabbed him a beer, and passed it to him, from a distance Eric and Stacy looked on.

"I'm so happy to see you," she said wanting to touch him.

"Me too, I couldn't wait to get here."

"It's going to be difficult to keep my hands off you, especially after a couple of these," she said lifting up her can of beer.

"I know, but—" Aidan stopped as he noticed three girls in small bikinis walking their way. "Do you use this white canopy for weddings?" asked Aidan pretending to be admiring it.

Brieanne was puzzled. "What?" she asked then quickly caught on as she noticed them from the corner of her eye. "Yes, and parties too."

"Brie!" screamed a voice coming inside the canopy.

"Bev!" said Brie excitedly, giving her a hug.

"You remember my friends Dawn and Helena?"

"Of course," said Brie hugging them. "Aidan, this is my cousin Bev, her friends Dawn, and Helena. Girls, my friend Aidan."

"Hello," said Aidan shyly.

"Did Brie tell you we spotted you two last week on Gulf Boulevard?" asked Bev lightheartedly, putting him on the spot. "I have a photo to prove it."

"She did," answered Aidan unfazed, "she also told me that you are quite the CSI detective?"

Bev turned to Brie "You told him?" she asked embarrassed. "Tell me you didn't?"

"Everything," said Aidan throwing Brieanne under the bus.

"Brie, how could you?" screamed Bev playfully.

"You make a fool of yourself, you play the price," said Brie matter-of-fact.

"That's unfair, I have nothing on you?" she said hopelessly.

Aidan cleared his throat. The four girls looked at him.

Bev caught on quickest. "You have something on Brie?"

"Maybe."

Brieanne looked closely at him wondering what it could be. Not the French lesson that would give them away. He had so much he could tell them, but which one, she wondered.

"Tell me!" pleaded Bev.

As Stacy and Eric joined them, Aidan started to tell them about Brieanne's Madeira Beach skill of testing a mattress.

At the end of his story, they all laughed, including Brieanne. She liked that story, and to her, it was a fun one they could share.

"People jump up and down on them, we don't lie on a bed here to test it, no, sir," repeated Bev laughing hysterically.

"I was caught off guard," Brie said in her defense, "and it was all I could come up with at the spur of the moment."

"You could have come up with another way of testing a mattress, if you know what I mean," said Stacy making the girls giggle.

Brieanne quickly glanced over at Aidan and smiled at their secret. "Okay, ladies, I need help setting up lunch."

Aidan and Eric walked into the sunshine and watched the girls heading for the house, not knowing they were talking about Aidan.

"Brie says you're vacationing here for the summer?" asked Eric.

"That's right, staying at that condo there," he said pointing to it.

"Where are you from?"

"Rochester, New York."

"Have you lived there all your life?"

"No, Syracuse, then Rochester."

"I've lived here all my life, Stacy also, and Brie," said Eric trying to make a point.

"It's a beautiful place, friendly people," responded Aidan complimentary. "I can see why you would."

"We are all friendly people here," stated Eric, "sometimes people can confuse that with something else."

"Really," said Aidan unsure, "like what?"

"Tourists like to take advantage of us friendly people," he claimed.

"How so?" asked Aidan wondering if he meant him with Brie.

Eric was too clever to be direct. "Tourists tend to want to take advantage of us friendly locals, haggling for a cheaper price, and so on."

Aidan was a little puzzled; he had a feeling he was really referring to tourists being with local girls but let it go and concentrated on him being ripped off by tourists. "What do you do for a living?"

"Fisherman," he said bluntly, "I learned to fish after I learned to walk."

"You must be pretty good?"

"Not bad," he said humbly.

"When you say fisherman, is that as in you go out on a boat with a crew for several weeks, catch fish, come back, and sell them?"

"I used to do that," he said honestly. "That's hard work and can hurt your pocketbook really quick on days when the fish don't bite."

"I can only imagine it being tough," said Aidan.

"My dad did it all his life, best there was, ever will be," he said proudly. "He taught me everything I know. Some of my fondest memories I have are with me and my dad out on the boat."

"That's amazing," said Aidan genuinely. "I take it you don't do that anymore?"

"No, I charter my boat for fishing trips: morning, afternoon, evenings, days, overnights," he explained.

"Busy?"

"Yeah, it's been a good start to the summer," he admitted. "I hope it stays that way to the end." Eric was enjoying talking to him and was actually starting to like him, but Aidan was a tourist, and he had to be on his guard, for Brie's sake. "What do you do?"

"English teacher?"

"Do you teach little kids, elementary school?"

"I can, but I currently teach high school?"

"Do you like it?"

"Yeah, I find it very rewarding."

"You must have to like kids to do that?"

"It helps," said Aidan half-joking.

"These people in your group, who are they?"

Aidan explained who they were. "You have any family, besides your dad?"

"No, he passed away years ago, just me now."

"I'm sorry I thought he was—"

"No need, you didn't know."

They talked for a while longer until Stacy returned with Brie; both had taken off their shorts and top, and were now wearing sexy, bikinis.

"What are you guys talking about?" asked Brie nervously.

"We were talking about fishing," said Eric quickly, "and family, locals, tourists."

It was those last two words that worried Brie.

"Eric was telling me how he's a fisherman and about tourists haggling with the locals for a better deal," Aidan explained. He didn't say anything about the unsettling feeling he had received from Eric's indirect displeasure of male tourists being 'friendly' with the local girls.

"That's nice," said Brie somewhat relieved. "Lunch is ready."

"Come on Eric, let's get something to eat," said Stacy grabbing his hand and walking away.

Brieanne walked inside the canopy telling everyone lunch was ready, before coming back to Aidan and waiting for them to pass. She slowly walked with him to the house. "What did you think about Eric?"

"He's a nice guy, a little rough around the edges, but that might be just an act," he summarized. "And he was candid with me. He told me how his dad taught him everything he knows about fishing, that he ran a charter boat, and how his dad passed away and has no family. So, he was quite open about that."

Brieanne was a little surprised. "He told you his dad was dead?"

"He kind of had to, Eric made it sound that his dad was still alive, so I asked him if he had any other family besides his dad. He told me his dad passed years ago and was on his own."

"I'm surprised, he doesn't usually like to talk about his dad, especially about him being deceased."

"Well, he did ask about mine, maybe he thought it was only fair to tell me about his," he suggested.

"I just think people like you," she said admiringly, "and you're easy to talk to."

"Maybe we should have tested my bed the way Stacy suggested," said Aidan cheekily.

Brieanne snickered. "Please don't start that talk, I'm horny enough as it is. This day alone is going to test my will, and I don't need your help in making it any more challenging!"

The group of thirty ate lunch around the pool, on the beach and under the canopy. Aidan met Bev's mom and dad, Cathy, and her husband, as well as friends that lived locally or worked in the restaurant.

Throughout the day Aidan and Brieanne kept close to one another but far enough away as to not raise any suspicions. When late afternoon arrived the BBQ was turned, the food cooked, and dinner was served. As the evening slowly sneaked in, the adults congregated in and around the canopy waiting for the sunset, while the children swam in the pool.

Aidan looked around for Brieanne who he thought was right behind him. Suddenly his phone beeped indicating he had a text.

Brieanne: "My bedroom bathroom, now!"

Aidan: "On my way." He slipped inside, went up to her room closing the door behind him, and into her bathroom.

Brieanne lunged at him kissing him passionately. "I couldn't take it any longer I needed to kiss you. We don't have time for anything else."

Aidan kissed her back; his hands roaming all over her body. They were both getting carried away. "We need to stop," said Aidan breathing heavily, "it won't take people long to realize we are both missing."

"I know, I know," she repeated, "one more kiss." Brieanne kissed him feverishly for a while then slowed down and gave him a quick, gentle, kiss, before pulling away and fixing her bikini. "I'll leave first," she instructed, "wait a few minutes then come out, I will save you a seat next to me."

Aidan waited several minutes before leaving, then talked to the children in the pool, before going onto the beach and sitting next to Brieanne.

"Did you bump into anyone on the way here," she whispered out of the side of her mouth.

"No, only the kids in pool," replied Aidan, overdramatically copying her, and making her laugh. "Did you?"

"No."

The group watched the sunset. At nine, the children were told to come down to watch the fireworks along the beach, they weren't disappointed. At ten the fireworks ended, everyone helped clean up, and people slowly started to leave. A small group consisting of Brieanne, Aidan, his parents, aunt, uncle, and Bella, sat on the upper deck; while Jane and Steven soaked in the hot tub watching the four children playing in the pool."

"Brieanne, I have to say that was a wonderful day," said Paul.

"It truly was, "agreed Theresa, "thank you so much for having us."

"It was my pleasure," replied Brieanne sincerely.

"To a charming, beautiful, hostess," said Bill raising his glass, "and someone whom we can call our very dear friend, Brieanne, cheers."

"Cheers," everyone replied.

Thirty minutes later, Bella and her grandchildren said goodnight, and several minutes after that Aidan's family stood and did the same. Brieanne and Aidan glanced quickly at one another unsure what to do, should Aidan stay or leave with them.

"Brieanne," said Jane. "Do you want to walk with us on the beach to our condo?" Then she glanced over at Aidan. "I'm sure Aidan will make sure you get back safe."

"I would like that," said Brieanne standing to join them.

The group strolled along the shoreline, Jane put her arm through Brieanne's, and slowed down their pace till the group was a distance away.

"How long?" asked Jane.

"How long what?" asked Brieanne, not fully understanding the question.

"How long have you been in love with my brother?" said Jane with a smile.

Brieanne thought Jane was searching. "We are only friends."

"Just 'good, close, friends…that's it'?" she probed, quoting her brother from last night.

"Yes, that's all."

Jane stopped and looked at her. "I know what you two are doing and I think it's the right thing, for now."

"You do?" she asked apprehensively. "What would that be?"

"Hiding the way you feel for one another. Keeping your emotions intact. Desperately trying to forbid physical contact with one another in front of people who you know. Worried that they may think it's too soon."

Brieanne realized the charade was up with Jane. "When did you figure it out?"

"I had my suspicions last night. The way you looked at one another, catching yourselves before touching the other's hand, your body language," she said as they began walking again. "I tried to get it out of Aidan last night, but he baited, hooked, and reeled me in; he's good at that."

"He sure is," said Brieanne in total agreement. "Do you realize you are talking using fishing terminology?"

"I am, aren't I," said Jane realizing it was true and acting shocked.

They both laughed.

"Today you were subtler, you played it well for those around you, but for me…let's just say you made it more obvious."

"Do you think anyone else noticed?"

"No," said Jane adamantly.

"Good," said Brieanne feeling more comfortable. "When did you know for certain?"

"When you came of your house before sunset, you were sitting looking over your shoulder, then I noticed Aidan come out sit next to you, and you two whispering," she explained. "I'm guessing you snuck somewhere private for a kiss and a cuddle."

Brieanne felt like a schoolgirl. "We did," she said shyly glimpsing at Jane. "You won't tell anyone?"

"No, of course not," said Jane compassionately. "The only reason I'm telling you I know is so that I can help you both out whenever I can."

"Help us out, how?"

"I got you out walking with us, didn't I?"

"You did."

"And I made sure Aidan has to walk you back, alone."

"He does," said Brieanne catching on. "How long do we have before he is considered missing, and questions start to get asked as to why he has been gone so long?"

"I will tell them that you said you had some additional cleaning up to do before you went to bed, move chairs and so on, and that I told Aidan to stay and help you out," she said glancing over at her. "At the least that buys you a good hour or two."

"Thank you," said Brieanne ecstatically. "I was worried I wouldn't be able to spend some time alone with him on this holiday night."

"It's your first Fourth of July together, it should go out like a firework."

"Like a firework?" questioned Brieanne.

Because they were close to catching up with the group Jane whispered in her ear, "with a big bang."

Brieanne burst out laughing.

They caught up to the group, who said goodnight to Brieanne, and thanked her again for a memorable evening. Brieanne gave Jane an affectionate hug before cheerfully turning for home with Aidan. On the way she told him about her conversation with Jane.

Arriving at the house Brieanne led Aidan to her room where they undressed, slipped underneath the covers, and made love to the early morning.

Chapter 22

"Uncle Aidan!" shouted Maddy jumping on the sofa bed.

"Wake up!" said Ethan joining her.

"What do you two rascals want?" he asked grabbing and tickling them.

"Can you take us to the pool?" asked Maddy.

"Please," begged Ethan.

"What time is it?"

"Almost nine," she replied.

"Okay," he replied sitting up. "Go put on your bathing suits, cereal then pool."

"Yay!" yelled the children, merrily scampering off.

Aidan's was eating cereal with the kids when his phone beeped.

Brieanne: "Text me when you wake up."

Aidan: "I'm awake, eating cereal with Maddy and Ethan."

Brieanne: "They woke you up."

Aidan: "Yeah."

Brieanne: "What are you doing this morning?"

Aidan: "Taking them to the pool. Do you want to meet us?"

Brieanne: "Okay, see you in thirty."

Brieanne showed up with Jen and Ben. "I hope you don't mind me bringing them?" she asked sitting down next to him and watching them playing in the water with Maddy and Ethan.

"No," replied Aidan, "you can bring them anytime."

"Last night was amazing," she whispered squeezing his knee.

"It was," he said moving closer.

"When did you leave?"

"Before four, the sofa bed was made when I got in."

"Jane?" asked Brieanne.

"I believe so."

Brieanne thought momentarily. "Are you still moving out tomorrow?"

"Yeah."

"When are you going to tell them?"

"Tomorrow, after I confirm I have a room."

"I was thinking that maybe you could stay at the place I just bought," she said carefully. "You already agreed to help me fix it up, it's empty, and you can let me know if there are any problems with the place. You know, be my trial renter."

Aidan looked at her hesitantly.

"You will have the whole place to yourself," she said with a pleading smile. "House, deck, balcony, view of the Gulf, access to the beach, and you can use my pool and hot tub whenever you want. What do you think?"

"And conveniently located next door to you," he added.

"That too," "she said blushing, "you will also be helping me out, and its rent free."

"You don't want me to pay you?"

"No, you're helping me fix the place up!" she replied. "You can move in tomorrow, tell you family tonight."

"Where would I sleep?"

"You can sleep on the sofa bed for a couple of nights, make your bedroom top priority, and we can have it ready for you within a couple of days."

Aidan gave her a big smile. "Okay, it's a deal."

"Yeah!" she said quietly clapping hand and catching herself from kissing him.

Twenty minutes later Jane and Steven joined them, and they all went to the beach. Around one, Aidan's parents showed up with a picnic and they ate lunch. At five, Brieanne left with Jen and Ben telling Aidan to text her after she spoke to his family.

Brieanne anxiously looked at her watch, seven thirty; she didn't want to text him especially if he was in the middle of telling them. Brieanne went back and forth, and decided to just send one, worse he would do was not reply, she thought. "Text me when you can." She waited a couple of minutes before assuming he must be busy discussing it with them.

Aidan: "How was dinner?"

Brieanne: "Good, I ate with Jen, Ben, and Bella. We're going for a walk on the beach in ten minutes. How did it go?"

Aidan: "We are going for a walk too. I'll meet you on the beach and tell you then."

Brieanne: "Okay, we will head your way…Not knowing is killing me!"

Aidan: "Prefer to tell you in person rather than long text."

Brieanne: "Fingers crossed it's good news."

Aidan: "See you in ten minutes, miss you."

Brieanne beamed, whatever the outcome was, he was still staying in Madeira Beach: "Miss you more."

Aidan's group met Brieanne's on the beach and walked with them. Brieanne purposely slowed Aidan down to the back of the pack.

"Tell me! Tell me!" she pleaded.

"I spoke with all the adults after dinner telling them I was thinking about leaving on Monday to go to Boston but have decided to stay and help you fix up your new place…That I was considering getting a hotel room, only you offered me the place we are fixing up…and that it would also be a trial run for your September renters," he explained looking at her.

"What did they say?"

"They said they felt bad because I had to sleep on the sofa bed. I told them that wasn't the reason. I said besides helping you, I also needed some space and time to think, and since I was going to be working on your place anyway, this was the perfect option."

"And?"

"Jane spoke up, said it was a great idea. That it was just down the beach, and…" said Aidan thinking.

"And what?" said Brieanne hurriedly.

Aidan chuckled. "They would all get to hang out with me for the summer, as opposed to me leaving, and being in Boston. Which I believe made the rest stop and think. It also made them realize my situation and understand the reason why I was doing what I was."

"By situation, you mean you potential moving?"

"Yes."

"And by reason, you are referring to space and time alone, to think?"

"Yeah," he confirmed.

"You have to love Jane," said Brieanne appreciating her more and more. "Are you moving in tomorrow?"

"I was planning on it" he replied. "I wasn't sure what time you wanted me there?"

"You don't have to wait for me. Walk with me to my house tonight and I will give you the spare key," she said happily. "I'm working in the morning and won't be back till one, we can have lunch together, and make out the list for the house."

The group stopped, watched the sunset, then turned around and headed back towards the condo. The children swam for a while in the pool as the adults watched on before Bella told Jen and Ben it was getting late and time to leave. Aidan told his family he would walk Brieanne, Bella, and the children home and would be back shortly. On the way Aidan played with the kids while Brieanne and Bella talked in front of them. When they arrived at the path, Brieanne called the kids to run and join her, while Bella waited for Aidan.

"Can we talk for a moment?" asked Bella.

"Sure," replied Aidan walking with her towards the shoreline.

"Brie was telling me that you are moving in next door to help her fix the place up?"

"That's right, tomorrow," he confirmed.

"Believe me I wasn't asking that as a question because I'm prying, I just wanted to let you know Brie had told me."

"I understand."

"Your mom has told me you are an English teacher, high school?"

"Yes."

"Brie has also told me, though I see it with my own eyes, you are very good with children," she said.

"Thank you," he replied, noticing her tentativeness. "Is there something you wanted to ask me?"

"There is," she replied. "Ben has been having difficulties this year with spelling and reading. The teacher told me that I should try getting him some help from a tutor over the summer to help him catch up to his fellow classmates. Otherwise, I can wait for the school year to start, where he can get some extra help on the side. Personally, I would prefer to have him receive the help in summer rather than being pulled out of class," she explained, then hesitated. "I really don't know anyone to ask, and Ben is a little shy around strangers, which doesn't help when it comes to finding a tutor. But he seems fond of you and is more his old self around you."

"Old self?" asked Aidan unsure.

"With his mom dying last year, and father six months prior, it has been very tough on him, on both of them," she said looking up towards the house at them. "Brie has been a tremendous help to me and the children, more than I can ever express. You see with Jen, she has Brie, me, you know other females to be with and to talk to. Ben also has us, but I'm afraid a boy needs a male figure, and I believe the lack of one has made him a little distant and even introvert over these last several months."

"I can understand how something like that can affect a young boy," said Aidan feeling sorry not only for Ben, but Jen also.

"Please don't take this the wrong way, I'm not asking you to be a parental figure for him or take on those responsibilities in any way. I just wanted you to know some of his background before I asked if you could help him."

"With his spelling and reading?" he reconfirmed.

"Yes," she replied. "I understand you are on vacation, have your family here, and are helping Brieanne fix the house. So, I won't be offended at all if you are busy and have to say no," she said truthfully. "I only thought, with you being here for the summer, living next door, and Ben already knowing you. You may consider it if you have the time? Before you answer, I won't have enough money to pay you fully for your lessons, but I am willing to pay you what I can," she said slightly embarrassed.

Aidan looked at her flushed face. "I will do it on one condition?"

"Okay?" she asked somewhat relieved.

"That you don't pay me," he said steadfastly.

"No, I would—"

"That's the condition. Take it or leave it?" he said giving her a lighthearted, unwavering look.

Realizing she wasn't going to change his mind, she answered, "I'll take it."

"Good," said Aidan with a smile. "Don't tell Ben we spoke," he suggested. "Instead, suggest to him that over the summer I could help him with his spelling and reading, and we will give him a couple of days to see if he mentions it to me."

"And if he doesn't?"

"Then me and you will talk again in a few days," he said reassuring her. They started for the house. "Now, how is Ben's writing?"

"It's very good, he writes interesting stories, only he misspells words that he shouldn't be."

"Does he write them the words the way he thinks they sound?"

"Yes,"

"Good," responded Aidan.

"Good?"

"Seems spelling is his only issue, not constructing sentences, or telling a story."

They met up with the other three, Bella and the children said goodnight, while Brieanne and Aidan went inside her house.

"Here is the spare key," she said handing it to him.

"Did you know what she was going to ask me?"

"I did," she said honestly. "She asked me, about asking you and what I thought you would say."

Aidan moved closer to her putting his arms around her. "What did think I would say?"

"He most definitely, will," she said looking into his eyes, "and you did."

"Yes, I did."

Brieanne kissed him softly. "That's one of the reasons I love you so much."

Aidan kissed Brieanne, and then led her upstairs to her bedroom, where he placed her duvet on the floor in front of the open balcony doors. As they slowly made love, the delicate cool breeze blew across their warm glistening bodies, while the distant sound of the waves melodiously caressing the sand whispered in their ears.

Chapter 23

Aidan unlocked the front door, placed his bags next to the sofa, before going out the patio doors and strolling to the back gate. He looked at the beach for a while then decided to sit on the deck to wait out the hour for Brieanne. As he strolled back, something caught his eyes at the side of the deck, and he went over to investigate. It was several planks of wood and a box of nails. Aidan quickly countered the planks then the damaged ones on the fence; both equaled six. He surmised the prior family either ran out of time to replace them or had just forgotten. Aidan went inside, found the toolbox and using a hammer, removed the damaged pieces then began to nail in the replacements.

"What are you doing, Aidan?" asked a young voice behind him.

"Hey, Ben," he said a little startled. "Fixing the fence, I just pulled off those broken pieces, and I'm nailing in these new ones. I have four more to go."

"Can I help?"

"Sure," said Aidan as he grabbed another plank. "Here, I will hold the wood in place while you hammer the nails in. Now we need two nails in the top and two in the bottom. We will do the top ones first," instructed Aidan holding the wood and putting the nail in place. "Now hammer directly on the head with some force," said Aidan smiling at him.

Ben started to hammer gingerly.

"You can hit it a little harder," suggested Aidan.

"I don't want to miss and hit your hand," said Ben.

"Don't worry, I'll be okay."

Brieanne could hear the hammering from inside the house, going to the patio doors she noticed them, and partially opened one. Saying nothing, she watched and listened, as they finished the fence.

"That's the last one," said Aidan standing up and taking the hammer from him.

"Thanks for letting me help," said Ben happily.

"Thank you," replied Aidan. "I'm going to be here for the next little while fixing stuff up if you want to help."

"Any more hammering?"

"No, mostly painting."

"I like painting, too."

"Well, when you have some free time drop in and you can help me. If I'm here, either the back doors will be open or you can shout up to me through those balcony doors," he said pointing up.

"Okay," he said shyly and waited momentarily. "Grandma says you are an English teacher."

"I am."

Ben looked at him apprehensively. "My teacher says I'm behind in my spelling and reading."

"That's okay, you can catch up."

"I don't like spelling and reading," he said honestly.

"Why not?"

"It's not as much fun as skateboarding?'

"You like skateboarding?" asked Aidan.

"Yeah, I like it a lot!"

"Do you know any tricks?"

"Yeah, a few."

"Spelling and reading are a lot like skateboarding," said Aidan sitting down.

"They are?" queried Ben sitting next to him.

"When you first got on a skateboard, were you good?"

"No, I fell a lot."

"How did you get better?"

"I practiced."

"When you learnt tricks, you must have practiced them?"

"I did, but some of the bigger, cooler kids helped me too," he admitted.

"Just like skateboarding, you have to practice spelling and reading to get better."

"But skateboarding is fun," he replied, "not spelling or reading."

"It is if you make it fun," suggested Aidan.

"Can you make it fun?"

"I sure can."

Ben looked at him. "Would you be like one of those, older cool kids who teach me tricks?"

"Yeah, something like that," said Aidan with a snicker. "Although probably not as cool as them."

Ben chuckled. "Yeah, those kids are pretty rad."

"Would you like me to help you?"

"I guess so," said Ben unsure.

"How about this?" said Aidan thinking. "Why don't we try it for a week, no more than an hour a day, and no weekends? If you don't want to do it anymore, or you're not having fun, you can stop."

"You won't be upset with me?"

"No, of course not," said Aidan, "it's summer. I want you to have fun."

Ben went silent.

"Why don't you take a couple of days to think about it? Maybe on Wednesday come by and let me know what you've decided?"

"Do I still get to paint?"

"Yes, whether you want to do it or not."

"Okay," said Ben grinning and standing up. "I have to go, my friends will be here soon, we are going for ice cream."

"Hold on then," said Aidan standing, reaching into his pocket, and handing him several bills, "for helping with the fence."

"Wow, thanks, Aidan!" he said excitedly running off.

Aidan watched him go, went to the patio door, and noticed Brieanne on the other side opening it. "How long have you been standing there?"

"Long enough," she said with a wild look in her eyes. Brieanne jumped on him kissing him feverishly.

"What are you doing?" he exclaimed, surprised at her unexpected behavior.

Brieanne gently shoved him towards the door leading into the washer and dryer room, opened it, pushed him inside, and closed it behind her. She kissed him intensely while rubbing his manhood hard. Then pulled down his shorts, took off her underwear lifted up her skirt, and positioned herself on top of the dryer. She kissed him avidly. "No need for any foreplay," she warned breathing heavily and shaking her head from side to side, "I'm already there, and I want you inside me, right now!" Twenty-five minutes later she gave out a loud scream as she trembled and came. Aidan came minutes later. Brieanne softly kissed his lips while he lifted her off the dryer. She wrapped her arms and legs around him and looked into his eyes. "I'm so in love with you, and with who you are."

Aidan kissed her tenderly whispering, "I'm in love with you."

After he let her down, they straightened themselves out, and walked out into the kitchen.

Brieanne looked out at the fence. "Where did you get the planks of wood from?"

"They were at the side of the house. I'm guessing they had planned to fix it before leaving, they must have run out of time or forgotten."

"That's one thing less to do," she said cheerfully. "Which reminds me, we need to do a list? Let's go over to my place, have lunch, and make one up. Then prioritize it." On the way to the front door, she noticed his bags on the living room floor and looked at him. "It doesn't make sense for you to sleep on the sofa bed when I have two extra beds at my place," she said looking at him. "You should stay at my place, at least till your room is ready?"

Aidan gave her a dubious look.

"What?" she asked innocently. "Once it's done, you can move in, sleep in a nicely painted room, on a new comfy bed," she said justifying her reasoning. "I'm thinking two nights, tops," she said with a cute smile, "and you can sleep in your very own bed."

"Two nights?" verified Aidan. "And I can sleep in my very own bed?"

"Two nights," she reconfirmed, "and your own bed."

Aidan grabbed his bags, dropped them into the same room he had slept in before, and then joined her in the kitchen for lunch. As they ate, they made a list, prioritizing what rooms needed to be done first, and what items needed to be purchased. Once finished, they showered, then went to the hardware store and picked out the paint for the bedrooms, bathroom, and hallway. Next the department store to choose a mattress and box spring. Of course, when they got there Aidan had to tease Brieanne by asking if she was going to do her Madeira Beach mattress test, to which she replied she would just stick with the Stacy test and gave him a sexy wink. They found a set they liked and arranged to have it delivered on Friday. Then they picked out a duvet, bed sheets, pillows, sheer curtains, and drapes for Aidan's room. Brieanne, still unsure what to do with the smaller room left that for now. Instead, she picked out a shower curtain and accessories for the upstairs bathroom, before getting the last two items on the list, a TV and DVD player for Aidan's room. All done, they packed up the Jeep drove to Brieanne's new house and unloaded everything into the family room.

"That was so much fun," said Brieanne flopping on the sofa. "I'm done for the night, time to relax." She looked at him as he sat beside her. "Do you want to go for a walk and grab a beer?"

"I would," he replied. "Somewhere casual, I don't feel like changing."

"Me either," she agreed. "Let's go visit Stacy, she's working tonight."

"Is it close?" asked Aidan.

"She works in John's Pass Village," she confirmed, purposely omitting where.

"Perfect," he said not wanting to walk too far.

They walked past the 'John's Pass Boardwalk' sign and stopped at the entrance of the establishment.

"Hooters?" asked Aidan reading the sign.

"This is where she works," she said trying to make him blush, but it backfired.

Aidan kissed her softly. "That's one of the reasons I love you so much."

"I said that to you last night because you agreed to help Ben and you're saying that to me now because I brought you to Hooters."

"Yep!"

Brieanne shook her head. "You filthy Scallywag!"

Aidan gave her an innocent, 'who me?' look.

"Don't give me that look, it's not fooling anyone…and eyes up here, not down here," she warned pointing from her eyes to her breasts.

"Don't worry, I will only look at your eyes."

"Every girls' eyes, or else," she said trying to be serious.

"Let me guess…or you will make me walk the plank!"

She laughed as they walked inside and sat on the bar. Stacy came over, said hello, and took their order. Aidan's phone rang; answering it he excused himself and went outside.

"How is it going with you two?" asked Stacy.

"It's going good," she replied, "we're becoming close friends," and then proceeded to tell her about him moving into her new place to help fix it up, and the items they had bought.

"And you two are only friends?" asked Stacy unconvinced.

"Yes, of course," she responded trying to sound believable. "Aidan's helping me fix it up, I'm not paying him, the least I could do was give him a place to stay. And he is going to be my trial run for the September renters."

"I can see your point," replied Stacy not sure what to think. "And he is only here for the summer, so you don't want to get too attached." Then she leaned over whispering, "but if you don't tap that before he goes, I will never talk to you again."

Brie laughed loudly. "You are bad!"

"Uh-huh," she replied.

"Sorry about that," said Aidan returning. "What did I miss?"

"Girl talk," said Brie, answering before Stacy could, who in return gave her a sly smile before leaving. Brieanne turned her attention to Aidan. "Is everything okay?"

"Yeah," he said in a low voice, "Liz was calling to remind me that tomorrow morning at nine she is contacting the clients to let them know about their refused offers."

"I'm sure everything will turn out fine," said Brieanne encouragingly, "and you will have updated offers in no time."

"I'm sure I will," said Aidan drinking his beer.

"Brie, can I borrow your Crockpot this weekend?" asked Stacy walking over to them.

"Yeah," she replied looking at her. "I can drop it off Wednesday afternoon, say around four?"

"Good," said Stacy. "Can you drop it off here? I'm working a double."

"No problem."

They had several drinks, ordered some wings, and talked with Stacy for a while. Then walked home, got ready for bed, and sat on the balcony.

"How about an early night tonight," suggested Brieanne. "I'm tired and I wouldn't mind us unwinding in bed."

"Us unwinding in bed?" queried Aidan.

"Yes, us in bed!"

"I thought I was sleeping in the other bedroom, you know, own bed?"

Brieanne stood, sat on his lap, and said tiredly, "you will be in your own bed, but I will be joining you."

Aidan shook his head and grinned at her.

"What?" she asked harmlessly, snuggling into him. "I said you can sleep in your own bed I didn't say I couldn't sleep with you."

Aidan carried Brieanne to his room. After helping her under the blankets he slipped in next to her. She sleepily cuddled into him and within minutes they were fast asleep.

Chapter 24

Aidan woke up alone, left his room, and went into Brieanne's. Hearing her in the shower, he walked over to the partially opened door, and spoke. "You're up early?"

"Not really, I'm late," she replied through the glass door. "Did you look at the time?"

"No."

"It's almost nine thirty, I woke up ten minutes ago," she confirmed sliding the door open and peeking out. "Come here."

Aidan walked over.

"Join me?" she asked reaching out her hand.

Aidan removed his pajamas, grabbed her hand, and stepped in next to her. "I thought you were late," he said as she kissed him.

"I am, but I own the place, who is going to tell me off for being—"

"Late," he said finishing her sentence.

"No, naughty," she replied kissing him again. "But it will have to be a quickie."

"Okay," he said kissing her intensely before turning her around and taking her from behind.

Thirty minutes later Aidan came downstairs, poured a coffee, and sat on the deck. Fifteen minutes later she joined him.

"I need to get going," she said quickly drinking her coffee. "I will meet you around one."

"While you are gone, I will tape the bedroom up, cover the furniture, and have it ready for us to paint this evening," he replied. "I'll meet you on the beach."

Brieanne put down the empty cup and sat on his lap as he held her. She had never been so happy in all her life. "Love you, see you later," she said kissing him, not wanting to go.

"Love you," he said watching her leave. Aidan suddenly got up, called after her, and caught up to her in the foyer.

"Everything okay?"

Aidan put his arms around her. "I want to tell you before you left how happy I am, how lucky I feel to have met you, and how much I love having you in my life."

Brieanne thought she was going to burst into tears of joy. She gave him a lovely smile and kissed him tenderly. "I feel the same way."

Brie didn't realize it but everyone she spoke to at work noticed she had a glow about her, those closest to her knew, Aidan had something to do with it. Shortly after one, she pulled into her driveway, jumped out of her Jeep, and hastily walked toward the front door. Suddenly, a white pickup truck came to a sudden stop outside her house, turning to look, she realized it was Eric.

"Brie, what's going on?" he asked walking towards her.

"What do you mean?" she asked, unsure.

"With you and tourist-boy?" he said loudly.

"That's none of your business," she snapped back.

"To hell it isn't," he said unhappily. "Stacy told me about your conversation last night, she said he is living next door, and helping you fix up the place."

"Yeah, so?" she replied.

"How long before he starts living here?" said Eric, pointing at her home.

"How dare you come on to my property, insult my character, and my close friend."

"Close friend now, is it?" said Eric. "Isn't that what you said about your last boyfriend?"

"Again, with him," she said in disbelief. "Aidan's not like him," said Brie protectively.

"He's a tourist, only here for a good time and not a long time, come the end of summer he will leave you."

"Then I have all summer to hang out with him," she said smugly.

"Yeah, and it will be me who will clean up the mess again," said Eric sternly.

"Wow, Eric!" she said fighting back the tears. "That's cruel."

Eric noticing see she was welling up, realized his tough love routine had been the wrong tactic, he softened his approach. "I just don't want to see you get hurt and go through all that again."

"Eric, my last boyfriend was a conceited, selfish, jerk, and we can both agree on that. But you don't know Aidan like I do; he's a really nice guy. Please, get to know him for my sake, and see what I see in him."

Eric shook his head with a defiant no. "I will watch out for you, you are my concern, not him."

Aidan had got changed in Brieanne's house then walked over to her new place to drop something off for tonight. For a change of scenery, he decided to walk down her street and cut through the condo. As he opened the front door, he heard Brieanne and Eric, and stood still.

"If you keep this up then you will end up losing me," she warned him.

"Brie, I love and care about you, I'm not going to stand by and do nothing."

"I love and care about you, too, but you need to tread carefully," said Brie. "Don't you think Stacy may have something to say about what you are doing? It's not right."

"Stacy isn't going to find out about this?"

"Maybe not from you," cautioned Brie, "but someone else."

Aidan slowly walked back inside and gently closed the door clicking the latch to lock it.

"Did you hear that?" asked Brie in a panic. She ran over to her new place, tried the door, then looked inside but couldn't see anyone.

"What are you doing?" asked Eric who had followed her.

"I thought I heard this door close, I must have imagined it," she said walking back with him to her driveway. "Eric, I like Aidan, he's a nice man and a good friend. I'm not going to stop being with him because he's a summer tourist."

"He may be your friend but he's not mine. To me he's just a summer tourist predator," stated Eric, "and I will be watching his every move."

"Do you know how creepy that sounds?" said Brie shaking her head.

"Yeah, it does, doesn't it?" said Eric laughing a little. "I didn't mean it like that, I meant he better treat you with respect, that's all."

"I have to go," she said having enough of Eric.

"To meet him?"

"Yeah, him, his sister, his brother-in-law, niece and nephew, on the beach," she said making a point. "Yeah, Eric, he's quite the predator."

"Bye, Brie," he said unamused with her sarcasm and started for his truck.

"Bye, Eric," she replied heading to her door. Then thought about something and turned to him. "You met him on the Fourth of July, talked to him for some time, and met his family. What did you think about him?"

Eric looked over at her; he wasn't going to tell her what his real opinion was. "I thought he was a tourist, plain and simple, and you can't deny that he isn't."

"Okay," she said walking away frustrated with him. She wondered if that is what he really thought or was he just being a jerk.

Eric got in his truck. He was sorry about the way he handled talking with her about Aidan. He knew the way he could be sometimes, and so did Brie, but what was really bothering him was that he hadn't been honest with Brie about his first impression of Aidan.

From behind the living room wall, where he had hidden, Aidan couldn't hear any more of their conversation. But once he heard the truck start, he bolted to the back door, out onto the path and quickly walked safely out of eyesight. As he slowed down, he thought about what he had heard between the two of them and wasn't sure what to make of it. He assumed it was nothing to worry about, to do with him, or any of his business. Besides, Brieanne would tell him later, especially if it was important.

As Brieanne put on her bikini she chalked up the conversation with Eric, as Eric just being Eric, and quickly forgot about it. She sauntered down the path onto the beach, spotting Jane and Steven; she went over and sat with them.

"If you are looking for the hired help," joked Jane, pointing toward the Gulf, "he's in the water with Maddy and Ethan."

Brieanne spotted him throwing Maddy up in the air, her landing with a big splash, then doing the same with Ethan before looking back at Jane. "He's been a really good help so far," she said complimenting him. "He's finished the fence and prepped the bedroom. It's ready to be painted."

"Doesn't surprise me," said Steven looking at Brieanne, "his work ethic is second to none. You should see what he did to his place. Unbelievable, it's like night and day, and most of it on his own!"

"He told me he did a lot of work on it and that it's beautiful," she replied, unsure what else to say, then changed the subject. "I'm glad to have him helping me on mine."

"I don't think you will be disappointed," said Jane, as she looked over at Aidan with the children, then back at Brieanne. "Would you like to take a walk down the beach?"

"I would," she replied, standing, and walking with Jane.

"How are things going with you and Aidan?"

"Couldn't be any better," she admitted. Then told her what they had been up to and about him helping Ben.

"Ben and Jen's parents, are deceased?"

"Yes, they are."

"Jen was telling Maddy that they spend a lot of time with you at your place, that you help them with homework, take them shopping, and so on."

"They do, and I do," said Brieanne apprehensively, thinking for a moment. "Can I share something with you?"

"Of course."

"Now, how do I say it without being rude to Bella," said Brieanne thinking out loud.

"I promise, I won't take it as you being rude," said Jane reassuringly.

"Well, with me being younger, I'm more physically and mentally capable in helping the children with their needs. Unfortunately, with Bella it's, a struggle."

"I can see that," said Jane, "and I can also see that those children love you."

"I know, and I love them, too."

Jane shook her head no. "I mean they love you, like my kids love me, like a mother."

Brieanne went silent for a moment, deciding to keep her secret to herself, a secret that only she, April, and Bella knew about. "That is very kind of you," she replied, then quickly changed the subject. "I'm taking Jen shopping tomorrow, do you and Maddy want to join us?"

"We would love to. What time are you going?" asked Jane, as they made plans on their way back to Steven.

Noticing Aidan and the kids were still in the water Brieanne excused herself and swam out to join them. They spent the afternoon swimming and playing on the beach. At five, Brieanne and Aidan said goodbye to them, then ate, changed into old clothes, and went next door to paint the bedroom.

"This room shouldn't take us too long," said Brieanne looking around.

"No," agreed Aidan as they began.

"Aidan!" shouted a voice from the yard, "Aidan!"

Aidan and Brieanne went onto the balcony.

"Hi, guys," said Aidan looking down at Ben and Jen.

"I wanted to know if you wanted some help?" asked Ben. "Jen wants to help, too?"

"Yes, both of you can, come on up."

"The door is locked," replied Jen.

"I'll get it," said Brieanne leaving then returning with the children.

"Jen, here is a brush for you, and Ben, one for you," said Aidan handing them out. "Now, smooth strokes, up and down like this," he explained showing them, and then watched them for a moment. "Perfect! You guys are good to go."

They painted for ninety minutes, only stopping for short breaks in between, and once completed, they stood back and admired their work."

"We did a great job!" said Brieanne happy with what she saw.

"I really like this color," admired Jen, "it's beautiful, and it makes the room so much prettier."

"And bigger," added Aidan.

"It does," said Brieanne standing next to him. "I guess we're done for the night, now what?"

"I'll tidy up in here," he said looking at her. Then turned to the kids covered in paint, and with a horrified look and in a ghastly voice said, "you can tidy them up!" making them laugh.

Brieanne took the kids to her place and told them to put on their bathing suits while she changed into hers. She rinsed them off under the shower on the deck before telling them they could jump in the pool. Brieanne had just finished cleaning her paint off when Aidan arrived. "I'm done, go put on your bathing suit, rinse off under here and join us," she instructed, and watched him leave before diving into the water.

Brie played with the kids and noticed Aidan had been gone for a while. She was about to get out and go inside to call for him when he walked out onto the deck over to the shower. Brieanne watched him as he cleaned his sexy body, then dive in.

"Did you get lost?" she asked ribbing him.

"I had a message from Liz and one from Joyce, I had to call them back," he whispered.

"Everything good?" she hoped.

"Yeah," he said in a low voice, "I have to go meet Joyce tomorrow morning. Liz received all four offers back and has sent them to her for me to review."

"That's great news, sounds very promising."

"Yeah, it does," he said uneasily.

"Everything will be fine," said Brieanne forgetting the children were there and about to assume her favorite pool position with him.

Aidan reacted quickly by grabbing her legs and dunking her backwoods. The kids looked on laughing.

Underwater, Brieanne realized why he had done what he did. She stood up slowly, hair over her face, whispering, "you filthy Scallywag." Then turned to the kids, "Jen, Ben, let's get him."

They children yelled, "get him!" as they swam after him.

Once caught the three of them dunked him till he surrendered. They played for a while longer, dried off, and then the children helped Brieanne make hot chocolate.

"Jen and I are picking up Jane and Maddy at nine thirty tomorrow morning," revealed Brieanne.

"Then we are going to shop, till we drop," said Jen excitedly, "I can't wait!"

"Ben here isn't interested," said Brie.

"It's boring," he replied sipping his drink.

"What do you have planned for tomorrow morning?" asked Aidan looking at him.

"I don't know, thought I'd come over here, hang out."

"I have to prepare the bathroom in the morning then go to a meeting at ten for twenty minutes or so. Do you want to come around eight thirty to help me out then come with me to the meeting?"

"Sure," he said.

"Don't worry, you won't have to sit there bored, you can play games on my phone while you wait."

"Okay," he replied liking the sound of that.

"I should get you two home," said Brie looking at the time "We will pick up your clothes from inside and take the street route."

The four of them strolled to the children's house. Aidan stood back as Brieanne went with them to the front door and dropped them off. On the way back Brieanne looked up at her new place.

"We didn't get around to preparing the bathroom this evening like we discussed," she noted.

"Ben and I will do it tomorrow for sure," promised Aidan.

"Yes, or you will have to stay at my place longer than two nights."

Aidan gave her an unconvinced look.

"What?"

"You don't think I noticed you specifically asking for the bed to be delivered on Friday, that's means I'm already staying at your place for an extra two night."

"No, it wasn't that," she said scrambling for something to say in her defense. "I didn't think we would be done upstairs by then, and I really want them to carry it right into your finished room, and I was right because we are behind on our schedule."

Aidan gave her a skeptical look. "Last chance to come clean. Did you plan it?" he asked casually looking up at the stars waiting for her answer.

Brieanne seized the opportunity and ran. Aidan didn't know she was gone until he heard her laughing in the distance and gave chase. Inside the house he saw her going up the stairs then heard her go into her bedroom. He went inside her room, noticing her hiding under the duvet he lay next to her, and removed the cover from her smiling face.

"You did plan it, didn't you?"

"Most definitely!"

"What am I going to do with you?" he sighed.

"Kiss me, hold me, and never let go."

"Okay," he replied.

"Promise?"

"I promise with all my heart," he said kissing her, holding her, and not letting go.

Chapter 25

Five Weeks Earlier: Wednesday, July 8

Brieanne got ready for the mall then went over to watch Aidan and Ben finish prepping the bathroom. Thirty minutes later they were done and went back to Brieanne's place to clean up, while Brieanne went to pick up Jen, then Jane and Maddy at the condo. Fifteen minutes later, Aidan and Ben left for his meeting.

"Hello, Aidan," said Joyce, noticing his young companion. "What's your name?"

"Ben," he replied timidly.

"Here's my phone with the games you downloaded," said Aidan, "I won't be long."

"We'll be right in there," said Joyce pointing to her office. "If you need us just come in."

"Okay," he replied transfixed on his game.

Aidan followed Joyce into the room where she left the door open so he could see them.

"That's your son?" asked Joyce, not recalling whether Aidan mentioned having children or not.

"No, that's Brieanne's neighbor, Ben. He lives with his sister Jen and their grandmother, Bella."

"April's little boy?"

"It is," replied Aidan. "Brieanne is out shopping with Jen, my sister, and my niece. Ben wasn't interested and wanted to tag along with me instead."

"That's nice," she said pleasantly, before getting down to business. "This shouldn't take too long."

For fifteen minutes they reviewed the four offers, Aidan picked the one he liked best, and they were done.

"Liz or I will contact you as soon as we hear anything," explained Joyce walking him to Ben.

"Thank you," said Aidan gratefully.

"My pleasure," she replied, walking them to the front door and saying goodbye.

"Are you hungry?" asked Aidan as they strolled down Gulf Boulevard.

"Yeah," he replied giving Aidan his phone.

"Do you want to get some breakfast?"

"Pancakes?" he asked.

"Pancakes it is."

They arrived at Lisa's Cafe, sat outside, and ordered.

"How come you aren't married?" asked Ben looking around at the couples and families eating.

"I guess it because I haven't met the right woman yet."

"How do you know when you have met the right one?"

"Well, when you meet someone that you like, you want to see them and hang out with them. If you start liking them more you want to see them more often. And if you really like them a lot, eventually you want to live with them, and see them all the time."

"Is that what they mean by falling in love and getting married?"

"Yeah," replied Aidan with a grin.

"You see a lot of Brie. You must like her a lot?"

"I do. She's a very good friend, and we get along really well, so we hang out a lot."

"Maybe one day you two will fall in love and get married."

"Maybe," said Aidan.

"When you get married, do you want to have kids?"

"I would like to have a family."

"Good," he said openly, "because I think you would make a really cool dad."

"That's kind of you to say."

"Here we go," said the server dropping off the food. "Enjoy!"

"Buttermilk pancakes, whipped cream and fresh strawberries, my favorite," said Ben licking his lips. "Yours too?" he asked looking over at Aidan.

"Mine too," he replied as they dug in.

The girls arrived at the mall and shopped in half a dozen stores before stopping for a drink and a muffin.

"I think your uncle Aidan is so much fun," said Jen sitting next to Maddy.

"I know, he makes me laugh all the time." Then she leaned over and whispered, "my mom thinks he spoils me too much."

"He does," said Jane overhearing her.

"You do, too, Mom."

"Not like he does," she replied.

"Brie spoils me rotten, too, well, that's what my grandmother says. I don't really know what that means but I like it," said Jen in a quiet voice to Maddy. "Brie's like my mom."

On hearing that Brie didn't want to make eye contact with Jane, instead, choosing to concentrate on the girls.

"Imagine if my uncle Aidan and Brie got married," stated Maddy as both girls giggled.

"Then they could adopt me and Ben."

"That would be so awesome," said Maddy, "then we would be family and hang out all the time."

Jane noticed Brieanne was getting upset. "Okay, girls enough planning let's eat up and get back to shopping."

"Do you think I can come over tomorrow and you can tutor me?" asked Ben.

"Definitely" replied Aidan. "What time were you thinking?"

"I don't know, maybe after lunch."

"That's fine," he said, thinking momentarily. "Now, there are some things I need to find out about you first, is that okay?"

"Okay," said Ben. "What do you want to know?"

"What kind of stories do you like?"

"I like stories about superheroes. Thor, he's my favorite, and Spider-Man, Superman, X-Men, Hulk, Batman, that kind of stuff."

"Do you like comics?"

"I don't know I've never read one."

"That's okay," said Aidan. "I was thinking maybe you and me could do something once a week that you would like to do. Can you think of anything?"

"I would like to go fishing, not on a boat because that's probably expensive, but from the shoreline or a pier." he explained. "All my friends, their dad's take them, and their brother's, sister's, and mom's go along, too."

"Fishing it is," he said pausing momentarily. "Did you want to invite Jen, maybe Ethan and Maddy can come along also?"

"Yes," he said excitedly, "that would be amazing. Do you think they would come?"

"I'm sure they would."

"You seemed to be getting a little upset," said Jane as they walked behind Maddy and Jen.

"Thank you, I was," she replied, managing a smile. "I shouldn't though, they're just girls with vivid imaginations."

"True," said Jane, wondering which part had upset her: not being Jen and Ben's mom or not being married to Aidan, or perhaps, both. "We'll let the girls have their fun shopping," said Jane lightening the conversation, "then we can have our fun with a glass of wine at lunch."

"A couple," suggested Brieanne.

"Of bottles," added Jane, making them giggle.

"Who do you think would be a good person to ask about fishing spots?" asked Aidan as they started for home.

"Eric!" said Ben straight away. "He's the best fisherman around here. Everyone that lives here knows that."

"That's who I was thinking of," said Aidan nodding in agreement.

As they turned onto Gulf Lane, in the distance, they could see a group of boys.

"Those are my friends waiting for me" said Ben starting to run before realizing what he was doing and stopped. "Is it okay if I go play with them?"

"Of course, just make sure you tell your grandmother where you are going."

"Will do," he said happily running off, "thanks for the pancakes."

Aidan watched him join his friends and thought about going to Brieanne's place. Instead, he decided to walk over to John's Pass Village to see if he could find Eric. Crossing over Gulf Boulevard his phone rang. "Hello."

"Hi, it's me. How did it go with Joyce?"

"It went well."

"Okay, you will have to tell me later because your sister is close by. How is Ben?"

Aidan told her about Lisa's Cafe.

"Those pancakes sound good."

"They were amazing," he confessed. "Ben ordered them for us both."

"That's so cute."

Then he told her about tutoring him and going fishing with the other kids. "I don't know any spots so I asked who he thought would know, he said Eric was the best, that's who I was thinking about, too."

"Definitely, talk to him, he can help you out."

"I'm on my way to the marina now to see if he's around."

"All right, I will let you go. After we're done shopping we're going for lunch. I should be home in a couple of hours."

"Okay, I will see you then, bye."

"Bye."

Aidan arrived at the marina, asked around, and was pointed in the direction where he would find him. "Hey, Eric."

"Aidan," he said cautiously.

"I was hoping you could help me out?"

"I'll try."

"Do you know if there are any good shoreline fishing spots close to Brieanne's place that I can walk to?"

Eric gave him a funny look. "What, I fish these waters all my life and you stroll along asking me for the prime fishing spots."

Aidan felt awkward now for asking. "I didn't mean it that way."

"Well, that's the way it came across."

"Sorry, that wasn't my intention."

"No problem," he said condescendingly.

Aidan let it go. "You wouldn't happen to know if one of these stores sold comic books or a place, I could buy some?"

"I heard of grown man reading comic books, but I never actually met one," said Eric laughing at him. "Do I look like I read them, let alone buy them? You need to go home and look that sort of stuff up on the internet. You don't want the fisherman hearing you talking about comic books and making fun of you nonstop."

"I was going to Google it," he explained feeling foolish, "instead, I came straight here."

"Okay, then," said Eric enjoying himself. "Any other questions I can help you with today?"

"There is one more thing," replied Aidan. "Can I hire you and your boat, three weeks from Friday?"

Eric was thrown off guard. "What?"

"Can I charter you and your boat?"

Eric paused; he wasn't sure if Aidan was messing with him. "How many people?"

"Sixteen."

"That's a good size party," he said. "Are you paying for everyone?"

"I am."

"Must be nice," he claimed, reaching for his phone, and dialing a number. "Hey, honey it's me. Do you have the calendar handy?" he asked then waited. "Can you check and see if I'm available three weeks Friday?" He looked at Aidan covering the phone. "For how long?"

"Morning till afternoon," said Aidan unsure of the timeslots.

"Seven till three, eight hours?"

Aidan nodded his head.

Eric removed his hand. "Seven till three," he confirmed waiting for a response. "It's available, okay, put down a party of sixteen under Rochester. Also, can you work out how much that will that be?" Eric waited. "Okay, thanks, I'll see you soon." Eric hung up telling him a higher price.

Aidan thought it was a little steep, but he was the best. "That's fine."

"I will need a nine-hundred-dollar nonrefundable deposit today, cash, to keep the reservation."

Aidan looked around for an ATM.

"Right over there," said Eric pointing. "I'll wait for you here."

Aidan came back, gave him the money, and watched Eric count it.

"Follow me and I will give you a deposit slip."

"No, I trust you," replied Aidan extending his hand, "a handshake will do me fine."

Eric was a little surprised as he shook it. "Thanks for your business," he said watching him walk away.

Aidan changed at Brieanne's house, went for a swim in the Gulf, then lay down on his towel to sunbathe. Aidan was bothered by the way Eric had spoken to him, but he was Brieanne's friend, so he decided to let it slide and tried to forget about it. An hour later he woke up to the sound of his phone ringing. "Hi, Brieanne."

"Hey, what are you doing?"

"I'm relaxing on the beach."

"We just finished lunch. I'm dropping off Jane and Maddy first, then Jen. After, I have to go see Stacy at her work and drop off the Crockpot. I will see you at the house around five, okay?"

"Okay," he said, "I'll meet you in the pool, put on your bikini, and join me."

"Will do," she said. Then whispered, "love you, bye."

"Love you."

Brieanne sensed something different about Aidan; she couldn't quite put her finger on it. She dropped Jen off, grabbed the Crockpot and headed to Hooters. Once inside she handed it to Stacy.

"Thanks, Brie, I will give it back Monday," she said taking it from her. "Do you want a quick wine?"

"Sure."

Stacy poured a glass and handed it to her. "Anything new, since we last talked?"

Brie told her about Aidan and Ben: the pancakes, tutoring, fishing, and the comics.

"That is so sweet of him," cooed Stacy. "He is a really nice guy. I've liked him since the first time I met him."

"He is," said Brie with a happy grin.

"Hey, honey," said Eric kissing Stacy. "Hey, Brie. So, what are you two talking about?"

"Girls' stuff," replied Stacy.

"Oh, let me guess?" said Eric. "Aidan the Tourist!"

"Why are you being like that?" asked Stacy, disappointed with him.

"Since the two of you are so interested in talking about him," said Eric pompously. "He came over and talked to me today, right here at the marina."

"Really," said Brie ignoring his arrogant attitude and excited to hear what they talked about. "What did he want?"

"Guys a dork!" said Eric. Then proceeded to tell them what he told Aidan about the fishing spots, grown men reading comics, and the internet. When he finished his story, he let out a boisterous laugh.

Tears streamed down Brieanne's face. "You are such a dick!" she shouted furiously and stormed out.

"What? What?" he asked looking at Stacy.

Stacy gave him an extremely upset look, and luckily for him she was at work, or he would have gotten an earful, too. Instead, she calmly told him about Ben.

"Oh shit!" said Eric nervously. "Do you think I should chase her and apologize?"

Stacy picked up the Crockpot. "You have three seconds before I split your lip with this."

Eric ran outside, looking both ways he spotted her walking towards the 'John's Pass Boardwalk' sign, and caught up to her. "Brie, I'm sorry," he said out of breath. "Brie!"

Brie turned around with tears still falling and glared at him. "How could you do that?"

"I'm sorry, you are right, I am a dick. Let me make it up to you. Let me make it right. I promise I will."

"You say you love me, care about me, then you go and do something like that to me."

"I do love you and care about you. I will make it up to you, I promise." He tried to move closer to her.

"Don't, you come near me! Don't!" she shouted moving away. "I love you, too…but right now, I don't know if I do anymore…I just feel really sorry for you, betrayed by you, and ashamed of you." Brieanne shook her head sadly then quickly walked away.

"I will make it up to you, I promise," he yelled after her.

What Brie and Eric had failed to notice, that behind Brieanne to her far left, were Theresa, Paul, Amy, and Bill. They had witnessed the whole event and heard the exchange between the two of them.

Brieanne sat in the car for a few minutes sobbing and wondering what she was going to say to Aidan. She realized the only thing she did know was that she needed to be with him and hold him. As she drove home, she decided to wait until the conversation came up and deal with it then. Brieanne wiped her eyes, put on her bikini, and went to the patio doors. She waited till Aidan swam to the other end before quickly jumping in.

"There you are beautiful," he said swimming to her. "Are you all right? Your eyes look red. Have you been crying?"

"I think it's just my makeup and the chlorine, they will be fine soon."

"Okay," he said believing her.

"Aidan, come close to me and hold me in your arms?" she asked.

Aidan held her. "Hey, are you sure you're okay?"

"I missed you, that's all," she said feeling much better with his arms around her. "Can we just hangout tonight, have a BBQ, and a bottle of wine?"

"I'd like that."

Aidan helped Brieanne cook the burgers and prepare the salad. They ate down on the lower deck, enjoying the late sun along with a glass of wine, and then took a stroll along the beach. As the sun started to set, Brieanne talked about her day and Aidan about his.

"The offer that I picked was fifteen percent over asking price and they wanted to move in immediately."

"That's great," said Brieanne "When do you think you will hear back?"

"I'm guessing Friday, latest Monday."

"Fingers crossed," she said.

Aidan smiled at her.

She knew she had to ask. "Did you meet up with Eric?"

"I did."

"How did it go?"

"Well, he said he couldn't tell me any good fishing spots and didn't know any places I could buy comics, he did he suggest I look it up on the internet, so I will."

"Okay," she said, realizing what he was doing, and let it go.

They sauntered quietly under the starry sky before heading home and stopping at the patio doors.

"Hey, do want to have a glass of wine and soak in the hot tub?" she said mischievously.

"Yeah, let's do that," said Aidan innocently going for the door.

"Where are you going?"

"To get changed."

Brieanne shook her head slowly and seductively smiled. "No bathing suit required," she whispered in his ear before gently nibbling it. "I'll get the wine and glasses, you get undressed, and in the hot tub." She turned on the hot tub jets, left for the kitchen, and when she returned Aidan was already in. She put the wine and glasses next to him and turned off all the lights except the ones in the hot tub.

Aidan watched Brieanne slowly undress, and with the moonlight shining off her perfectly shaped body, she carefully stepped into the hot tub, sat on Aidan's lap, and nestled her head on his chest as he held her. She lifted her head towards him, gave him a sensual open mouth kiss, before repositioning herself on his lap. With her back to him, she opened his legs wide, and then moved hers between them. Brieanne slowly glided her vulva back and forth over his erect manhood. Brieanne suddenly stopped, placed her labia above the tip of his manhood, and gently let it sink deeply inside her folds. She softly moaned as she moved very slowly up and down. Aidan put his arms under hers, and with his hands gently caressed and pulled on her hard nipples, making Brieanne moan loudly. He then moved his right hand down between her thighs. Brieanne moved feverishly in unison with Aidan as he massaged her yearning clitoris and pulled on her wanting nipple. Passionately he kissed her shoulder, her neck, then nibbled on her ear. She was almost there. Realizing this, Aidan moved his hands to her hips pushing them back and forth, faster, and faster over his erect manhood, allowing her clitoris to rub against his thick shaft. Brieanne lay back onto his chest; she was no longer in control. She wanted to scream and moan loudly, she knew she couldn't, which only turned her on more. Brieanne put her hands on his thighs, squeezing them tightly she let out a long, low, moan as her body quivered. Aidan, unable to hold on any longer, thrusted his manhood deep inside her and moaned as he came.

Chapter 26

Brieanne dipped her brush into the paint. "How long do you think it will take to finish the bathroom?"

"Thirty minutes tops, that includes taking off all the tape," estimated Aidan moving his brush up and down.

"Then the smaller bedroom?"

"That will take a little longer, we still have to prep," said Aidan thinking about what needed to be done. "We should be finished by noon."

"What time is your pupil arriving?" she asked with a grin.

"He said after lunch."

"Probably around one," guessed Brieanne. "Did I tell you last night was amazing, amazing, amazing?"

"Only hundred times last night, a thousand times this morning, plus three more times now," Aidan teased. "I am pretty incredible."

"You are," said Brieanne excitedly covering his face with kisses.

"Stop," said Aidan laughing, "or we will never get this done."

Brieanne went back to painting. "Party pooper," she said, pretending to pout.

"The quicker we get the painting done the more chance we have of some afternoon delight before Ben shows up."

"A quickie?" she asked suggestively.

"Yep, right here on the small bedroom floor," he said, "both of us covered in paint, naked, sweating, caressing—"

"Stop it, you're making me wet!" she said frowning.

"Well, let's concentrate on getting these walls wet with paint first," he said stroking his brush up and down then glancing over, "I can do this all day."

Brieanne unimpressed with him, turned her back, and then cutely looked over her shoulder mouthing the words, "I love you."

As soon as Brieanne ripped the last bit of tape from the bedroom wall and placed it in the garbage bag, they undressed. They stood kissing for a while before Aidan lifted her up to straddle him. Brieanne vehemently kissed his neck and earlobe as he grabbed her bum to move her up and down his shaft. A few minutes later he tenderly placed her on the floor where they continued to make love. Brieanne asked him to go on his back so she could come on top. Twenty-five minutes later they showered, dressed, and ate lunch at Brieanne's before heading back to her new place. Hearing knocking on the patio door, Brieanne walked over and unlocked it.

"Hey, Ben," they said.

"Hi, Brie, hi, Aidan."

"Are you ready?" asked Aidan.

"Yeah," said Ben a little uncertain.

"Don't be nervous, you will do fine," assured Aidan.

"I'm going to go upstairs to fix up the big bedroom and bathroom," said Brieanne leaving them.

Aidan and Ben went into the living room, sat on the sofa, as Brieanne listened in from upstairs.

"I know I said spelling and reading are fun, and they will be, but not so much at the beginning. First, I need to find out what level you are at, so we need to go through some exercises to figure that out." Aidan explained. "Okay?"

Ben nodded yes.

"Good," replied Aidan. "Let's start off simple. Can you say the alphabet for me?"

Ben did.

"Good," he said giving him a lined notebook. "What I want you to do next, is write the alphabet in lower case, and only put one letter per line. There are twenty-six lines so you can fit them all onto one page."

Ben quickly completed it.

"Great. On the next page, do the same thing, but in uppercase."

Again, he finished quickly.

"Good," said Aidan. "Now, let's go back to the first page. I'm going to say a letter and I want you to circle it as quickly as you can. I am going to time you until we have finished all twenty-six. Just remember it's more important to be correct, than fast."

"I understand," said Ben.

Aidan randomly said the letters, when Ben finished, Aidan stopped the timer on his phone and showed him.

"That's very good," said Aidan. "Here's a pencil, now right the time up here, and next to it twenty-six out of twenty-six.

Aidan did the same exercise with the uppercase. "Look," he said showing him his time.

"Five seconds quicker," said Ben, as he wrote down the time, then looked at Aidan. "All correct?"

"Yes," confirmed Aidan as he watched Ben finish writing before then taking the book from him. "This shows me a few things about you: that you know your alphabet; you can write in lower and uppercase correctly, in other words none are backward; and you can pick random letters out very quickly and correctly," he said smiling. "That was excellent."

Ben gave a big grin.

"This next exercise will further evaluate your skill level and identify areas that we have to focus on, so it will be a little more difficult. Are you ready?"

"Ready."

"These are the words that a nine-year-old should know for his age. Every word on this sheet has two boxes next to it: one you tick off if you can read the word; the other you tick for correctly spelling the word. Today we are just going to concentrate on reading the words. So, what I want you to do is go down the list and say each word out loud. If you don't know what it is, just say I don't know, and we will move on."

"Okay."

"Do you want to tick the ones you know?"

"Yeah," replied Ben enthusiastically.

Ben completed the exercise in twenty minutes.

"Perfect," said Aidan taking the sheet from him and writing down the time. "That's it for today."

"That wasn't so bad," claimed Ben.

"No, it wasn't," replied Aidan. "Tomorrow we will go through the same list of words, except this time I will say them to you, and you have to spell them out loud."

"That's seems a little tougher."

"You will be fine," said Aidan rubbing Ben's hair. "You know, if you decide you want to keep on coming, after you complete your final tests, we should celebrate. Where would you like to go?"

"Do you mean go out to eat and play games?"

"Yeah, you can bring Jen, your grandma, Brieanne, Ethan, Maddy, whoever you want?"

"I would like to go to the pizza place in John's Pass Village, then the arcade down the street," he said excitedly.

"DeLosa's Pizza and Beach Fun & Games," shouted Brieanne, giving herself away.

"Okay, pizza and arcade it is," he said to Ben. Then shouted upstairs, "thank you Ms. Nosy Pants," making Ben laugh. Aidan was about to say something else when there was a knock on the door. "I'll get it!" said Aidan calling up to Brieanne. "Eric!" he said surprised.

"Hey, Aidan, can I talk to you for a minute outside?" he asked quietly.

"Sure, what's up?" he said, going out with him.

Brieanne quickly ran to the open bathroom window and listened.

"I eh, wanted to apologize for my behavior yesterday. The way I talked to you, it was eh, rude of me," he said cumbersomely. "I wanted to let you know that it won't happen again and I'm really hoping you won't hold it against me."

"Probably having a rough morning, we all have them," said Aidan playing it off. "No need to worry, no harm done."

"That's kind of you to say it like that," he said understanding what Aidan was doing. "I'm just hoping we can get passed it?"

"Consider it in the past and already forgotten," suggested Aidan reaching out his hand.

"Thanks, that's great," he replied, shaking it. He had been worried it wouldn't go so well. Eric lifted up the bag he was holding in his other hand. "I have some comics here for you and Ben, and some things for you, Ben, and the kids," he said pointing to the wall.

Aidan looked at the fishing equipment. "Wow!" said Aidan surprised. "Come on in. Ben's inside and I think it would be nice to show him what you have for him."

"I don't know," said Eric hesitantly.

"He's just finished his exercises," explained Aidan. "Trust me he will be thrilled, and it will make his day," said Aidan convincing him.

Aidan helped Eric bring the stuff inside into the living room while Brieanne took off to the top of the stairs and sat.

"Eric!" said Ben happily.

"Hey, big guy, heard you finished your exercises today, how did you do?'

"Awesome!" he cried.

"Aidan said you were looking for some comic books, so I went and picked some up this morning," he said passing him the bag.

Ben quickly removed the comics. "Thor, Superman, Spider-Man, X-Men, Batman, Hulk, and a bunch more. These are so cool, thanks, Eric."

"I also got you, Jen, Aidan's niece, and nephew, a fishing pole each. A full tackle box and a big container full of bait."

Ben happily jumped up and down.

Eric looked at Aidan. "There are a couple of extra poles for you and Brie in case you want to fish, too. Also," he said as he pulled out a piece of folded paper from his pocket and handed it to Aidan, "I've marked several great fishing spots on this map and they're not too far from here. Typically, sunrises and sunsets are the best times to go, with kids anytime is good they'll still catch fish. If you run out of bait, stop by the marina, and I'll fill up the container for you."

"Thank you for everything," said Aidan overwhelmed and pleasantly surprised. "This is fantastic."

"I just wanted to help out and mostly make up for yesterday," he said, "and thanks for bringing me in to see Ben's reaction." Eric looked over at Ben. "Well, I have to get going."

Ben gave him a big hug before Aidan walked him to the door, shook his hand again, and said goodbye.

"When can we go fishing asked Ben?"

"I will need to talk with Brieanne first," he replied. "Why don't you drop by here later and we will let you know?"

"Okay, I will," he said energetically heading for the patio doors, "see you later Aidan."

Aidan was putting the sheets in the folder and was about to place it on the dining room table along with the map when he turned around to see Brieanne standing in front of him.

She kissed him on the lips. "You were incredible with Ben," she said softly caressing his face, before kissing him again. Then turned around to look at the items Eric had left.

"That was very thoughtful of him," said Aidan.

"It was," replied Brieanne, but in her mind it was the least Eric could do for the way he treated the man she loved.

"I should put these in the fridge," he said lifting up the container of bait and going into the kitchen. "How are you doing upstairs?"

Brieanne was silent.

Receiving no reply, he came out, and glanced over at Brieanne's guilty look on her face. "You didn't do anything, did you?" he said accusing her. "You listened in the whole time to Ben and me, then our conversation with Eric, didn't you?" continued Aidan walking slowly toward her. "That innocent look isn't going to help you this time, you have been very, very—"

"Naughty," she answered, before taking off upstairs.

Aidan caught up to her on the balcony.

Brieanne put her arms around him. "I know we need to get things done," she admitted out of breath. "Just let me hold you for a minute."

Aidan held her quietly, giving her as much time as she needed.

"Thank you," she said giving him a peck on the cheek. "Okay, let's figure out what we need to do?" she said walking inside. "In this room, we have to hang the sheer curtains and drapes. Bring up the TV and DVD player and put them on that dresser." She led Aidan into the bathroom. "In here, put the mirror back up, as well as the towel rack, the new shower curtain, and accessories. I also need to get towels from my place." Brieanne looked over at him. "I have a closet full that I've never used. I know a couple of sets that would be perfect in here and the downstairs powder room." She pulled him into the smaller bedroom. "At first, I wasn't sure about putting these blinds back up, after painting this room; I think they would look really good. What do you think?"

"I think so, and if kids will be staying in here, blinds are ideal."

"That's a good point," said Brieanne thinking for a moment. "When are we going to paint the hallway?"

"It will have to be done by tomorrow?"

Brieanne knew why he said that. "I'll be back in a minute I have to make a call," she said grinning as she left.

Aidan went into his bedroom, sat on the floor, and waited for her to return.

"Okay, that's settled."

Aidan gave her a look like 'I know what you did.'

"What? We can't have them carry the mattress and box spring up a wet, painted hallway."

Aidan shook his head at her. "Okay, what day and time are they delivering it now?"

"Tuesday morning," she answered plopping herself on his lap. "What, you don't like cuddling me in bed?" she asked in a melancholy voice.

Aidan pulled her on the floor onto her back. "I love it," he replied, kissing her quickly. "Now, can we get moving and get this stuff done?" he said tickling her till she begged him to stop.

They worked together doing Aidan's room first, next the bathroom, and finally the small bedroom. Brieanne went to her house and got the towels for both bathrooms, leaving one set downstairs in the family room, before hanging up the ones for the upstairs. With that completed, they were done.

"Wow, this is starting to look really good, and it's going to look incredible when the hallway is done, and your bed arrives. A few scenic pictures spread out throughout the rooms and hallway. Some comfy chairs and a table for the balcony," she said pleased with what she was envisioning. They headed down the stairs into the kitchen bumping into Ben and Jen who had just arrived.

"Hey, guys," said Brie. "What's up?"

"We came to ask about fishing," said Ben.

"I totally forgot," said Aidan. "Brieanne I was going to talk to you about a good time to go." He quickly looked over at the kids saying, "give us a minute," and went with Brieanne into the dining room.

"Tomorrow I have to go to work for a couple of hours in the morning."

"I'm tutoring Ben at eight."

"We want to finish the hallway tomorrow afternoon."

They looked at one another, thinking.

"How about tonight after dinner, say six thirty, till around eight?' suggested Brieanne.

"I like that plan. You tell the kids to come back then and I will call my sister and see if Maddy and Ethan want to go."

"Okay," she said leaving for the kitchen.

The three of them were standing, waiting, when Aidan walked in. "Is everything okay?"

"They wanted to wait and see if Maddy and Ethan were coming," replied Brieanne.

"They are," he confirmed.

"Yes!" said the kids in unison before taking off.

"Jane and Steven are going to come along also," said Aidan.

At six forty-five they arrived at the fishing spot. Aidan and Steven helped the kids set up the poles, put on the bait, and showed them how to cast. In no time they were pulling in several small fish and getting their pictures taken with them before Aidan and Steven took them off and released them back into the water. On the walk home, the kids counted all the fish they caught and confirmed to the adults it was sixteen. As they were saying their goodbyes Jane pulled Aidan to one side.

"Can you come to the condo pool tomorrow morning?" asked Jane. "Mom and Dad want to talk to you about something, and they don't want the kids to hear so they're taking them swimming."

"Sure, is everything okay?"

"Yeah, don't worry; they just want to have a chat with you about something," she said downplaying it. "Is ten good?"

"That works."

Jane hugged and kissed him then did the same with Brieanne. They all said their final goodnights and went their separate ways. Aidan and Brieanne dropped Jen and Ben off, before going into Brieanne's house, grabbing a beer, and sitting on the deck.

"What did Jane want?" asked Brieanne, then realized what she had done. "I'm so sorry, it's none of my business."

"It's all right, I was going to tell you the first chance we were alone," he said wanting her to her feel comfortable. "My parents want to talk to me about something tomorrow morning. They don't want to say it in front of Maddy and Ethan, so were meeting at the condo pool so the kids can swim."

"Any idea what it might be about?"

"None."

"Maybe they have decided to move here?" suggested Brieanne.

"Oh, I never thought of that," said Aidan considering that was a good possibility. "Do you think so?"

"What else could it be?" asked Brieanne.

Chapter 27

Ben arrived just after eight, and did the spelling exercise with Aidan, ticking off the ones he got correct. When he was done Aidan highlighted the ones he couldn't read or spell.

"Thirty," Aidan said counting the last highlighting word. "That's not bad, not bad at all," he said looking at Ben. "Over the weekend I will put together a plan to get you caught up, maybe even get you ahead of the other kids in your class. On Monday we will go through it, okay?"

"Okay," he replied standing up.

"Did you want to take a comic book?"

"Can I?" he asked excitedly.

"Yes, pick the one you want to read first, and just make sure you bring it back with you on Monday so we can read it together."

Ben took off, rifled through the comics to find the one he wanted. "Thor," he said showing it to Aidan before departing.

Brieanne came downstairs a few minutes later. "Where's Ben?"

"He just left."

"How did he do?"

"Fine, he's a smart kid, he will be caught up in no time," said Aidan confidently.

"That's because he has such a good teacher," said Brieanne, strolling up to him. "I wish I had an English teacher as handsome as you?"

"I lucked out, I have a gorgeous, sexy French teacher," he replied, "Whom, I may add looks extremely stunning today."

"You are quite the charmer," said Brieanne cozying up to him. "I lucked out also; I not only have a handsome English teacher but also a brilliant cunning linguist."

"Are you referring to last night?"

"What else!" she said affirmatively. "Why do you think I have this permanent smile on my face?"

Aidan held her hands as she moved in closer, kissing him affectionately.

"See you later, handsome."

"Later, Frenchy," he said watching her leave.

Aidan arrived at ten, said hello to Maddy and Ethan in the pool, who in turn pointed out where their parents were sitting. Aidan sat down next to them, noticing his parents, aunt, and uncle looked uncomfortable, while Jane and Steven seemed relaxed.

"You four look tense," said Aidan looking for a sign from his sister and getting none. "What's wrong?"

His dad spoke up. "Aidan, we don't want to get involved in your personal affairs, but something happened a couple of days ago that myself, your mother, aunt, and uncle witnessed."

Aidan looked over at Jane.

"We weren't there," she confirmed.

"What?" asked Aidan turning to his father.

"Before I tell you, we want you to know that we talked a long time about whether or not to tell you, which is why we involved Jane and Steven, to give us some youthful advice, which they did."

"Well, you all agreed to tell me, so please do," he stated.

His father told Aidan in detail the scene they witnessed between Brieanne and Eric.

Aidan sat back in his chair. "Well, I can see why you would be concerned," he said, wanting them to feel okay for telling him. "What day was this?"

"Wednesday around five?" his father replied.

Aidan thought back. "Did Brieanne have a Crockpot with her?"

"No," replied his mom, "she was upset and had one hand covering her face the other at her side, I think it was to hide her crying."

"Brieanne went to Hooters to drop off a Crockpot to Stacy, Eric's girlfriend, she must have gotten into a disagreement with Eric over something, that's all," explained Aidan making it sound harmless, although he wasn't one hundred percent sure. He also wasn't happy with Brieanne and Eric having this episode to begin with, never mind having it out in public, and especially in front of his family.

"That makes sense, we've probably caught the tail end of it," said his dad. "I hope you understand we didn't think it was right keeping it from you."

"I'm glad you did otherwise you may be still thinking the worse," said Aidan convincing them they had done the right thing.

"Good, we're going upstairs to have some breakfast," said his dad satisfied and standing.

The two older couples said goodbye and left.

"What advice did you give them?" asked Aidan looking at Jane and Steven.

"That they should tell you, be simple and straightforward, and when you will find there's nothing to be concerned about let it go," she explained leaning forward. "Aidan, the way Brieanne looks at you, there is no way that girl is even considering anyone else."

"No way," agreed Steven. "She thinks you are all that and a bag of chips!"

Aidan and Jane burst into a loud laugh.

"You and your mid-nineties slang," said Jane, wiping the tears from her eyes. "I love you," she said kissing him on the cheek.

"Steven, you know how to turn something completely awkward into something completely funny," said Aidan complimenting him.

Steven quietly took his wife's affection and Aidan's compliment.

Aidan's phone rang, he excused himself, answered it and returned to the table.

"Brieanne?" asked Jane.

Before he could answer, his phone rang again and he walked away from the table, returning several minutes later. "Brieanne," he said, "I'm supposed to be meeting her back at the house to paint the hallway." Which was the truth, the second call was from Brieanne, but the first was from Liz.

"How is it going over there?" asked Jane.

"It's coming along nicely," he stated. "We're making a lot of progress."

"Jane was talking about the painting," said Steven cleverly.

"I was talking—" said Aidan starting to answer him until he realized what Steven meant, "ha, ha, funny man," then looked back over at Jane. "The house is going well."

"We'll have to drop in and see it when it's finished."

"You should," said Aidan standing hastily. "She's waiting for me I have to go." Aidan kissed his sister goodbye on the cheek, said bye to Steven and the kids, then left.

"Are you hungry?" asked Brieanne as he entered the kitchen.

"Yeah, what are you making?"

"Nothing special," she said matter-of-fact. "Just eggs Benedict, home fries, and toast," she revealed glancing over at him.

"I woman after my own heart," he said coming behind, holding her, and kissing her cheek.

"Grab a coffee, a seat, and tell me how it went with your parents," she said eagerly.

Aidan poured his coffee slowly and took his time taking a seat, thinking about what to tell her.

"Okay, what did they say?" she asked impatiently.

"It wasn't to do with them moving here," he said.

"Oh" she said. Too bad, she thought. "Personal matter?"

"Yeah," he said casually.

Brieanne left it at that.

They finished breakfast, went to the new place, and started painting the hallway. Took a late lunch break at Brieanne's and took a quick dip in the pool. When Aidan went to his room to change, he noticed he had missed a couple of calls, one from Liz another from Joyce. He called Liz first, then Joyce, before going downstairs into the kitchen.

"I thought I'd put the dirty plates in the dishwasher before I changed," she said closing the dishwasher door.

"You look very tempting prancing around in that sexy bikini," he said putting his arms around her and squeezing her butt.

"Mr. Jones I will have you know I'm not that type of girl!" she said playfully.

"Too bad," he said with a frown.

"We have a hallway to finish," she said deliberately rubbing her breast against him as she left to change.

"Aidan," she shouted minutes later, "come up stairs and look at this!"

Dolphins, Aidan thought, as he walked into her bedroom. Brieanne was lying naked on her bed.

"See anything you like?" she asked in an innocent voice.

Aidan smiled, undressed, and made love to her.

"We really have to practice being faster with our quickies," said Aidan as they entered the new house.

"I like the sound of that," replied Brieanne cheekily.

A couple hours later they were finished, tidied up, and sat on the stairs admiring their work.

"I love this color doesn't it just make the hallway look brighter, bigger?"

"It does," replied Aidan, "the other color was darker, claustrophobic. This is really pleasing to the eye."

"Pleasing to the eye," repeated Brieanne, "I like that description."

They went back to Brieanne's place and showered together. Neither of them was in the mood to cook so they decided to go to Sculley's in John's Pass Village for dinner. Aidan was busy picking out clothes when his phone rang. Noticing it was Joyce, he picked it up and answered, then hung up and called Liz. Aidan finished getting ready and met Brieanne downstairs. They walked over to Sculley's, sat at a table outside, and ordered beers.

"This is lovely out here," said Aidan looking around.

"Yeah, it's a very popular spot."

Aidan looked over at her. "You look beautiful."

"You are being way too kind," she said, "this is casual."

"If you look this beautiful casual, I'm curious to see what you look like dressed to the nines."

"I guess you will have to wait and see," she replied smiling.

Aidan leaned over. "Guess what?"

"What?" she said leaning over thinking he was going to say something silly.

"My house sold today!" he said cheerfully.

"That is amazing!" said Brieanne getting up. "Stand up and let me give you a hug," she instructed him as she held and kissed him on the cheek. "I'm so happy for you," she whispered.

"Brie?" said a voice from the boardwalk.

She looked over, not realizing she was still holding Aidan. "Harriett, George," she said, quickly letting go of him and walking over to them. Brieanne talked to them for a few minutes then brought them over.

"Aidan you remember Harriett and George," said Brieanne.

"Of course," he said as Harriett hugged him, and George shook his hand.

That's two out of two for hugs, thought Brieanne. "Where are you off to?"

"We just left the store, and with it being Friday evening, thought we would come get a bite to eat," revealed George.

"Come join us," suggested Aidan.

"We wouldn't want to impose on you two young'uns," said Harriet, motioning no with her hand.

"You are not imposing," said Brie, "please, join us."

"Look, there's a bigger table over there, let's grab that," said Aidan picking up their drinks and commandeering it.

"What have you two been up to since we last met?" asked Harriett.

Brie gave her a summarized version intentionally leaving out Aidan living next door. She wanted to tell her mom that herself.

"You've done a lot of sightseeing," said George. "How do you like it?"

"It's beautiful here," said Aidan, "the people are friendly, and the food is great."

"Beautiful like Brie," said Harriett admiring her.

"Gorgeous," said Aidan before he could stop himself. He quickly tried to think of something else to say, instead, George did it for him.

"She's gorgeous all right," said George, "if I were a couple years younger."

"Maybe a couple of decades," jibbed Harriett. "Besides, you have tough competition with Aidan here; I fear you don't stand a chance."

"George," said another voice from the boardwalk.

George turned around. "Stan, Mildred, how are you two doing? Come on over."

"Do you know Aidan?" asked George looking up at them and introducing him.

"I do, his family lives in the Gulf Shore condos, I see him all the time, Brie too."

Harriett glanced over at Brie. Brie just smiled innocently and continued looking at Stan.

"Are you two out for dinner?" asked Harriett.

"Yes," replied Mildred. "We were just deciding where to eat."

"Join us! We just got here," stated George "we can grab a bigger table."

They moved to a large table where George purposely asked for four more empty seats.

"You never know who is going to show up next," he prophesied.

And he was right, minutes later Larry and his wife, Cindy, showed up followed by Bev's friends, Helena, and Dawn. Aidan sat in between Brieanne and George, while Brieanne was in the middle of Aidan and Helena. They all ordered food, Brieanne had the herb crusted Mahi-mahi, while Aidan had the crab stuffed flounder, both with vegetables and yellow rice.

"That was incredible," said Aidan whispering to Brieanne.

"It was delicious," she whispered back. "Do you think anyone noticed us trying one another's?"

"No," said Aidan sounding convincing.

"Really?" she asked.

"Yes, they all just happened to be looking away at those precise moments we were sampling each other's food," he kidded.

Brieanne laughed out loud making everyone look at her. "He reminded me of something funny," said Brieanne saving face.

"Can you let us in on it?" asked George elbowing Aidan.

"Yeah, tell us," said Stan.

Aidan was quickly thinking of something to say.

"Was it the mattress test?" asked Helena.

Saved by Helena, thought Aidan.

"Mattress test?" asked the older couples who hadn't heard the story.

Brieanne wanted to sink under the table and hide.

"Yes, Helena it was," confirmed Aidan as he proceeded to tell them about Brieanne's mattress test.

The group broke into a loud laughter.

Brieanne smiled, red-faced, and out of the side of her mouth whispered, "I'm going to get you for that, you filthy Scallywag!"

Doing likewise Aidan replied, "I have two words to say to you…hot tub!"

Brieanne broke into a laugh again at his silliness.

"Another story," said George as the group eagerly looked on.

"It's about a French lesson," said Aidan glancing over at Brieanne's shocked face, "but I will save that story for another day."

"Oh, too bad," said a disappointed George, I like your last one immensely, and resumed chatting.

After the group finished their drinks, the older couples went home; Helena and Dawn went to see Stacy in Hooters, while Brieanne and Aidan decided to go to The Hut Bar & Grill. They sat at a table, ordered drinks, and listened to the live music for a few minutes.

"You must be happy your house sold?" she asked.

"I am, and I'm glad it sold sooner rather than later."

"So, everything is done?"

"All done, they had the keys by five this afternoon."

"That is amazing!" she said moving in closely and quickly kissing him on the lips.

"I must admit you are getting bolder."

"I don't care," she said, which she didn't. "I'll just blame it on the beer."

"Well then drink up, ye sultry wench, drink up!" he said in a comical pirate's voice.

Brieanne laughed. She liked the way he made her feel and loved being with him. "Can I ask you a personal question?"

"Do I have a choice?"

"No, not really," she replied.

"Okay, ask away."

"Do you ever serious think about moving here?"

"I will be honest with you, no," he said bluntly then went silent.

Brieanne was shocked at first. "Nice try mister," she said giving him a friendly push, "you're teasing me."

Aidan smiled. "You're catching on to me."

"Yep," she replied proud with herself, "the more I'm around you the more I'm figuring you out."

"I have thought about moving here," he said truthfully, "actually, quite a bit."

That's good to know, thought Brieanne, and left it at that.

They had a couple more beers and listened to the live music before heading home. They got ready for bed, took off their clothes, and slipped under the sheet. Brieanne snuggled into Aidan and within minutes they were fast asleep.

Chapter 28

"That was so much fun last night," said Brieanne rolling on her side, "and meeting all those people."

"It was," agreed Aidan.

"You seemed to be especially enjoying yourself when you were telling them my mattress test story," she said pretending to be upset and putting her back to him.

Aidan tickled her naked body.

"Stop It!" she said, "I'm upset with you."

Aidan put his fingers between her moist thighs. "I should get you upset more often."

"I told you! I'm upset with you!" she said liking what he was doing.

Aidan placed a finger inside her folds, Brieanne responded by moving her bum closer to him. He moved his finger gently in and out for a while before replacing it with his manhood and continued to make love to her on their sides till, they came.

After taking a shower, they got dressed, ate, and talked about what Aidan had to buy today while Brieanne wrote a list. They drove to several different stores to purchase the items before stopping for lunch. Once home, Brieanne put the gift basket together.

"Wine, cheese, chocolates, gift certificates, and a thank you card," said Brieanne, gently caressing his face. "Joyce is going to love this."

They drove to Joyce's office, went inside, and were greeted by her in the reception area. Aidan handed her the payment first, she in return gave him his invoice, and then he gave her the thank you card along with the gift basket.

"Thank you so much Aidan, "said Joyce, "this is just beautiful, and so thoughtful."

"Thank you for all your help and advice."

"Well, congratulations on the sale of your house, and if you are ever considering moving here and buying a property, I will take excellent care of you."

"Thank you," replied Aidan, "I know you will."

Aidan and Brieanne said goodbye, jumped in the Jeep, and drove to Brieanne's where they sat on her balcony looking out at the beach.

"Do you want to go for swim in the Gulf?"

"Yeah, I would like that," said Brieanne.

"When we come back, we can shower, dress up, and go out for an exceptional dinner," suggested Aidan. "Somewhere close where we can walk or take a quick cab ride."

"Should I wear a dress?" she said excitedly.

"I was hoping you would," he replied enthusiastically.

"Yay!" she said lightly clapping her.

"Where do you want to go?" he asked.

"I know a place that is chic, modern, romantic, casual, fun, has excellent food, is close, and right on the beach."

"That's exactly what we are looking for."

Brieanne's enthusiasm had gotten the better of her, a little embarrassed, she went quiet.

"What's wrong?"

She looked at him apprehensively. "The place I'm thinking about is Vegas Francisco's."

"Brieanne—"

"No one has ever taken me on a date there and I have never been as someone's guest. I know it sounds weird because I work there."

"Actually, you own the place," corrected Aidan with a chuckle.

"And I own the place," she continued giggling with him. "You probably think I'm nuts for wanting to go there?"

"No, not at all."

She looked at him surprised. "No?"

"That's the place I wanted to take you to, I felt awkward asking you because you work there and own it, and I thought you might be disappointed with me if I did."

Brieanne's face lit up. "That's where you wanted to take me?"

"Yes, I swear."

Brieanne leapt joyfully into his arms, kissing his face all over. "I love you; I love you; I love you!"

"I love you."

She quickly jumped off. "I need to call and make a reservation."

"Let me do it."

"I would like to give the staff a heads up, I wouldn't want to catch them off guard, I couldn't do that to them."

"I understand," said Aidan getting his phone and dialing, "I'll take care of it."

Brieanne listened in.

"Good afternoon, this is Vegas Francisco's. I'm Jess, how can I help you?"

"Jess is a sweet girl," whispered Brieanne.

"Good afternoon, Jess, I would like to make a reservation for this evening, please," said Aidan.

"Great," replied Jess "How many are in your party?"

"Two," he replied."

"Two," she repeated. "What time would you like to be seated?"

Brieanne put up seven fingers. "Ask for a table by the window," she whispered.

"Seven," he said. "Are there any window tables available?"

"One moment, please."

"Yes, we do have a window table available at seven," she confirmed. "May I have the name for the reservation?"

"Aidan and Brieanne," he replied.

"Aidan and Brieanne," repeated Jess, as she was writing the second name something occurred to her. "Aidan, can I have your last name please?"

"Of course, it's Aidan Jones."

"Aidan Jones," said Jess relieved as she wrote it down.

"And Brieanne Byrne," added Aidan.

"Brieanne Byrne," repeated Jess slowly noting it, keeping her composure, and treating them like any other guests. "We look forward to seeing you this evening at seven Mr. Jones and Ms. Byrne. If you do arrive early, we have a full-service bar that also offers a picturesque view of the Gulf of Mexico."

"Thank you, Jess," said Aidan.

"You're welcome," replied Jess hoping her voice wouldn't tremble from nervousness, "we will look forward to seeing you then, goodbye."

"Goodbye," said Aidan hanging up and looking at Brieanne. "Done."

"That was spot on," said Brieanne. "I'm actually glad you called and not me. I don't think it would have felt like the same night if I had."

"Brieanne you just wanted to be kind and thoughtful and give them a heads up. That's what a good person, a good owner, does," he said as he held her. "That's what I love about you."

"Thank you," she said kissing him.

"But tonight," said Aidan, "you are my guest, not an employee or the owner."

"That's all I want to be," she said squeezing him. "I loved the way you snuck in my name, that was brilliant," she said giggling. "You could tell when you said Brieanne she was unsure if it was me or just a coincidence."

"I think she was relieved when I said Jones."

"Only until you said my last name," she said still giggling. "I'm sure Jess will handle it."

Jess hung up the phone in a daze. She looked for Cathy, grabbed her, then found Bev and said they all needed to go to the office right now.

"You look like you have seen a ghost," said Cathy.

"What's the matter, Jess?" asked Bev.

"Brie is coming here for dinner tonight!"

"What?" they asked in unison.

"Are you sure you have the right Brie?" asked Cathy.

"Oh, I'm sure, Brieanne Byrne," she confirmed, then went through the conversation she had with Aidan.

"Is she on a date?" asked Cathy.

"I don't know," said Bev wondering the same thing, "but we better treat it like she is."

"What table did you give them?" asked Cathy.

"I only had window table number one left, so I gave them that for now," replied Jess.

"Let's go look at the reservations book," said Cathy.

The three of them looked it over.

"Okay, Jess," said Bev. "This is your call, what do you think?"

Jess studied the reservation list. "The best table is eight, give them that, and move eight to seven because they only asked for a window table in the middle of the restaurant. Then move seven to one, they never specified a table preference." She looked up at them. "What do you think?"

Cathy and Bev smiled at one another.

"Why not just leave Brie at table one?" queried Cathy.

"Brie always told me if someone makes a reservation, and that person is a very special guest or a close friend of the family, to give them the best seat no matter what, even if they didn't ask for it."

"Excellent!" said Cathy.

"Great work," said Bev. "Make your changes."

Cathy and Bev left Jess and went into the office.

"I'm covering for Beth tonight and I have table eight," said Cathy. "I don't think one of her best friends serving them is ideal."

"No," agreed Bev. "We need someone who won't panic when they see Brie looking up at them."

"Who served Aidan and his family last time?" asked Cathy.

Bev thought back. "Kelly!" she said. "Kelly can serve them tonight, she has the perfect demeanor, and last time she served his family they said she was amazing and left her a huge tip which means they must have really liked her."

"Kelly it is," said Cathy, "I'll change sections with her tonight."

"Okay, I will let her know when she arrives that you two have switched."

"Are you going to tell Kelly about Brie?"

Bev thought about it. "No, after what we just put young Jess through, let's see how Kelly manages it."

Cathy nodded her head in agreement. "Do you think it's a formal date?"

"I don't know," replied Bev.

Hand in hand they walked down to the beach, swam, played in the water, and sunbathed. When they got back to the house Aidan swam in the pool while she started to get ready.

Brieanne took her time doing her hair and applying her makeup, "perfect," she said talking to herself in the bathroom mirror. Entering her bedroom, she put on a very sexy bra and panty set, and then slipped into a tight knee-length black dress and high heels. She had one final look in the mirror, happy with what she saw she smiled, and went downstairs.

"You look absolutely stunning!" said Aidan coming towards her. "Look how gorgeous you are," he said grabbing her hands and admiring her. "I am without a doubt the luckiest man in the world."

"Thank you," she said shyly. His reaction made her feel amazing, beautiful, and confident. "You look very handsome," she said, "I like that shirt it brings out your blue eyes. Turn around?" she asked as he did. "And you look very hot!" She moved closer to him whispering, "I would have to say that I am the luckiest woman in the world."

"Thank you," he replied holding her. "Tonight, is all about you and me."

Brieanne liked hearing that and was glowing with anticipation. They left the house and were dropped off at Vegas Francisco's just before seven.

"Are you ready?" asked Aidan.

"I am," replied Brieanne.

They walked in and were greeted by Jess.

"Good evening Brieanne," said Jess.

Brieanne was about to tell Jess just to call her Brie, but decided not tonight, instead she replied, "good evening, Jess."

"Good evening, Aidan," said Jess glancing over at him.

"Good evening, Jess."

"Your table is ready, please follow me." Jess was amazed how calm she was. She pulled out Brieanne's seat, Brieanne sat, and after she did Aidan took his. She handed Brieanne a menu first, then Aidan. "Your server tonight will be Kelly," she said with a pretty smile, "please, enjoy your meal," and left.

Cathy and Bev had been hiding in a spot where they wouldn't be seen. They had a clear view of Brieanne and Aidan walking in and sitting at their table.

"She looks like a movie star," whispered Cathy.

"A model," replied Bev.

"Hello, my name is Kelly," she said looking at Aidan then over at Brieanne and froze momentarily, "and I will be your server this evening."

"Hello, Kelly, I'm Aidan, I don't know if you remember serving me and my family at the Special Friday Night Dinner Event a few weeks ago?"

"I do Aidan," she said honestly. "You have a lovely family and it's wonderful to have you back."

"And you know, Brieanne," said Aidan, politely introducing her.

Kelly looked over at her. "Good evening, Brieanne," she said confidently, "may I say you look gorgeous this evening."

"Thank you, Kelly," replied Brieanne beaming.

"You are most welcome," said Kelly with a kind smile then slowly glanced back and forth between the two. "Would you like something from the bar?"

"Kelly," he said looking away from Brieanne and up at her. "Can we look at the champagne selection, please?"

"Of course, Aidan," she said pleasantly, "I will be back momentarily," and departed.

"Champagne?" asked Brieanne elatedly. "What are we celebrating?"

"You and me," he replied candidly.

"Is this a formal date?" she asked trying to contain herself as Kelly returned.

"Here you go Aidan," said Kelly handing him the list. "I will give you a few minutes to peruse our fine and extensive list."

Aidan looked over the list, decided on one, and put it down.

Kelly noticing, went over to him immediately. "Have you made your selection?"

"Dom Pérignon, please."

"Excellent choice," said Kelly, picking up the list as she left.

"Do you want it to be a formal date?" he asked.

"Do I?" she asked puzzled.

"This is your town, your family, your friends, and your employees. I want you to be comfortable," said Aidan,

"The night we met your sister we both decided that we would act as friends."

"No," said Aidan slowly shaking his head. "I asked you, what would make you most comfortable? You replied, in front of people we know, we act like friends, close friends, no physical contact, but when we are alone—"

"We can do whatever we want," she said remembering.

"Then you gave me this very erotic kiss."

"I did," she said with a grin. "You remember that one?"

"I certainly do, although the first one on the beach is still my favorite."

"Your first French lesson," she said looking into his eyes. "What were we thinking?" she asked shaking her head. "Why did we ever agree to do—?"

"Here is your champagne," said Kelly showing them the bottle, as one of the bartenders placed an ice bucket next to their table.

"Thank you," said Aidan.

Kelly put the bottle in the ice. "I will be back in a few minutes to open and pour."

Brieanne watched Kelly leave. "Why did we ever agree to do that?"

"I don't think you, we, were comfortable at that time. These are your people, this is your town, and no one knows me."

"If we hadn't agreed to that, would you have asked me out?"

"Remember the night you met my sister, we walked you home, and you were worried that they were watching us on the beach, so we didn't kiss and hugged instead."

"I do."

"I almost asked you out on a formal date then."

"Why didn't you?" she wondered.

"You were too nervous, so I didn't."

"Is that why you hesitated to ask me to dinner here because of what may be construed."

"Yes," he replied as Kelly walked towards them, "I just wanted you to be at ease."

"Would you like me to pour the champagne?" Kelly asked.

"Yes, please," said Brieanne, happily.

Kelly filled one champagne flute, then the other, put the bottle in the ice, said "enjoy," and went to another table.

"I don't want us to hide anymore, I want this to be our first formal date," she said. "Can it be?"

"Okay," replied Aidan.

"Something's the matter? What's wrong?"

"I don't know," he said awkwardly. "I never really asked you."

"You did," she said reassuring him, "I just picked the place, actually, we both did."

"I guess. I just want it to be really special and a night that you will tell everyone about."

"This is very special, and I most definitely will tell everyone."

"All right," said Aidan feeling better. He lifted up his champagne flute to her eye level as she lifted up hers.

"If I would have known we were having champagne I would have…" she looked at her champagne flute then his. "You didn't?"

"Maybe," he said with a mischievous smile.

"You did," she said ecstatically, "these are our champagne flutes, and you brought them here. How did you do that?"

"I called Larry, had him pick them up with a note to Cathy and Bev asking if they can put them on our table."

Brieanne was about to cry.

"Bev, look at this," said Cathy motioning to Brie. "Is she going to cry?"

Brieanne stood up, walked over to him, leaned down, and gave him a long, enthusiastic, French kiss. "I will never, ever, forget our first formal date," she whispered, "I love you."

"I love you," Aidan whispered back.

Brieanne sat down, picked up her glass touched Aidan's, and took a sip.

Cathy, Bev, Kelly, and Jess looked on speechless.

"Yes!" said Cathy to Bev giving her a high five.

"This is amazing, "said Bev to Cathy. "I guess that answers your question."

"Did you catch all that?" said Kelly joining them.

"We sure did," said Bev.

"They are quite the couple," said Kelly, "Brie said she loved him."

"No way?" they both said.

"What did he say?"

"He whispered he loved her," replied Kelly, as happy for them as Cathy and Bev were. "By the way," she said turning to them. "Did you guys omit telling me on purpose that I had Brie's table?"

"Who us?" said Bev and Cathy quickly walking away.

"I knew it!" she said following them.

Brieanne and Aidan drank their champagne, enjoyed their meal, ate dessert then watched the sunset. In between courses, Brieanne held his hand, and when they watched the sunset, she never let go. Aidan paid the bill, giving Kelly an extremely generous tip, and on the way out he gave an envelope to Cathy and another to Bev. When he got to the front door Jess passed him a bag, and she, too, was given an envelope.

Brieanne whispered to Aidan, "if I know Cathy and Bev, they are in waiting for me to drop in the office before I leave."

"Okay, take your time," he whispered back.

"I won't be long," she said out loud to Aidan and Jess, "I just have to get something from the office."

Brieanne went inside the office, hugged her friends who told her how happy they were for her, and came out glowing. She gave Jess a big hug then grabbed Aidan's hand and walked out of the restaurant.

Back at Brieanne's, Aidan opened up the bag, pulled out the two champagne flutes and a bottle of Dom Pérignon.

"I was wondering what Jess had given you," said Brieanne.

"Where do you want to drink this?" he asked.

"Outside under the stars," she said kissing him.

They sipped their champagne and looked up at the starry sky. Brieanne turned to him and kissed him like the first time on the beach, before resting her head on his shoulder, knowing her heart was his forever.

Chapter 29

Brieanne rushed Aidan around picking up the supplies he needed for Ben, darted through the McDonald's drive-thru, then quickly drove home.

"I don't understand why we are rushing to get back here it's just noon," said Aidan as they walked into the kitchen.

"I just wanted to get it out of the way," she said with an innocent look.

"Brieanne, I know that look, you have an ulterior motive."

Her phone rang. "We are leaving in five minutes, eat up" she told him before walking away and answering.

To go where, he wondered, as he went outside with the bag of food and sat at the patio table.

Ten minutes later she came out and sat next to him. "It was my mom. Harriett called her yesterday, told her about Sculley's, me and you hugging. Mom said Harriett couldn't stop talking about you."

"Come on, can you blame her?" asked Aidan pretending to be conceited.

"No, I can't," she said grinning at him. "But I do think my mom is a little upset."

"Why?"

"I guess because she is hearing about us through others, not witnessing it herself or hearing it from me. Although, she is looking forward to visiting, they haven't booked yet, but they're almost certain they'll be here on the twenty-seventh."

"I'm looking forward to meeting them."

"They're dying to meet you, especially my mom."

"Did you tell her about last night?"

Brieanne looked at him in astonishment. "She was going on so much about Friday night and Harriett, I got sidetracked and totally forgot," explained Brieanne taking off for fifteen minutes.

"How did it go?"

"As soon as I told her, she was shouting to my dad, telling him to come in the room. Then they put me on the speaker so they could both hear me," she said glanced over at him. "They were both extremely happy our first date was at the restaurant. I said it was a night I will never, ever, forget. Then I told them about the champagne flutes, my mom says you are very romantic, which you most definitely our, and that the service and food at the restaurant was impeccable. When I finished my mom quickly said bye and hung up."

Aidan looked puzzled.

"She's calling everyone she knows here, starting with Harriett."

"Ah," said Aidan taking another bite into his Big Mac. "It was nice to have a lie in this morning."

"You needed the rest after last night," she said taking her food out of the bag, "I guess my cute little dress and matching underwear set did the trick?"

"You were an incredibly beautiful, sexy, seductive, temptress! How could I resist?"

She smiled at him, quickly finished her food, and stood pulling him up. "Let's go."

"Where are we going in such a rush?"

"It's Sunday afternoon, John's Pass Village will be packed with locals and tourists."

"And?"

"And, I want to go show off my new handsome, amazing, boyfriend."

Brieanne happily held his hand as they walked around John's Pass Village and introduced him to everyone she knew. Harriett spotted them from inside the store walking by and ran out telling them her mom had told her the great news. She gave Brie a hug, and yes, hugged Aidan for a third time. After several hours of walking around, they sat at the bar at the Bamboo Beach Bar & Grill and had a beer.

"Can I tell you something?" she asked.

"Sure."

"I have to admit that since last night, when we agreed to—"

"Go public," interrupted Aidan.

Brieanne slapped his arm. "Okay, for the use of a better term, go public, I feel like this great weight has been lifted off my shoulders. I don't have to hide anything, watch what I say or do with you, for example," she said leaning into him and giving him a long kiss. "It's so liberating; I'm so happy."

"I know what you mean," said Aidan, jumping off his chair and doing a groovy dance that made people look at him as they walked by.

Brieanne knew he was trying to embarrass her and jumped off her chair and started to do the floss.

They stopped, laughed, and held one another.

The crowd at the bar clapped and cheered.

"Thank you," acknowledged Aidan waving while Brieanne hid her head in his chest.

"I know what you mean," he whispered, kissing her. "I feel the exact same way."

"You two are better than the live entertainment," said a voice behind them.

"Bev," said Brie letting go of Aidan to hug her.

"Come sit with us," she said pulling her, "follow me Aidan."

"You remember Dawn, Helena?" said Bev.

"Yeah," said Brie, "we all had dinner together Friday night."

"That's right, they told me, I completely forgot."

Aidan excused himself to get a round of drinks.

"He told his mattress test story again," said Dawn to Bev.

"Yes, he did, and he got in big trouble the following morning," said Brie playfully. "I didn't speak to him for at least three seconds."

"Only three seconds?" asked Bev curiously.

"That's how long it took me before I let him have make-up sex with me."

"Tell us more," said Bev leaning in as her friends did likewise.

Brie looked at them carefully. "I can't."

"Why not?" asked Helena wanting to know.

"Because if I do, you girls will be running me over, to get to him," said Brie half-joking.

"He's that good?" asked Bev as the other two also waited in anticipation for the answer.

"Amazing," she bragged, "we can't get enough of one another."

"You know the three of us hate you right now," stated Bev. "Handsome, smart, fit, loves kids, and is great under the sheets. Thanks for making us realize how pathetic and lonely our lives truly are, Brie."

"The server is going to bring the drinks over," said Aidan sitting. "What are you guys talking about?"

"Girl talk," said Brieanne. She knew what Bev had said about him was true, in local jargon; he was a hell of a fine catch. So, Brieanne kissed him because she could.

"Tell us the French Lesson story?" asked Helena.

Aidan looked at blushing Brie then at Helena. "I have a better one," he claimed. "Do you want to hear how I got the name Aidan?"

"Yes," they replied.

Aidan proceeded to tell them the story.

Arriving home, they changed into their swimsuits, and jumped into the pool. Brieanne assumed her position.

"I think those three girls have a crush on you," she said. "Do you know that?"

"No," he replied, "I've never thought about it."

"No?" she asked inquisitively.

"I have you," he said honestly, "you are all I want."

Brieanne smiled at his answer. "And I have you," she said kissing him. She put her head on his shoulder and looked up at the window of the smaller bedroom in her new house. "I still don't know what to do with that smaller room. Should I make it a bedroom for kids, a den, or an office?" Brieanne looked at Aidan. "You're a professional living there, what would you like that room to be?"

"I really can't answer," he said candidly.

"Why not?" she asked, unsure of his reason.

"I'm not living there per se," he said openly.

Brieanne had this terrible feeling come over her. "Aidan, I am so, so, sorry! I said you could live in that house, help me fix it, and it would give you your own space and time to think things through. I've totally suffocated you. You haven't even slept there yet!"

"No, it's, not like that at all, you're being too hard on yourself," he said comforting her. "You were right, I couldn't have lived there till the upstairs was done and it has taken us longer than expected to complete. And if they had delivered the mattress on Friday, it would have sat idle in the living room till the hallway dried, and Tuesday was the next day they had available."

"I know. I never realized how difficult it would be for you to live there with us fixing it up at the same time."

"Neither of us did, I've enjoyed what we have done so far, everything is good."

"Come Tuesday you will be living there?"

"I think that will be exciting, don't you?"

Brieanne wasn't sure how Aidan living there, sleeping on his own, would be exciting. "Exciting, how?"

"Once I'm next door, you can come over and visit me. I can make you dinner, we can hang out, and I can entertain you. You can do the same for me. It would be like coming to the condo, remember how much fun that was?" he said. "Or does that sound silly?"

Brieanne remembered, it was fun going to the condo, and then she thought about last night before they left for dinner. "It would have been nice if you had called on me and I answered the door all made up in my dress or when I come home from work, get ready at home, then come over to your place and have you open the door," she said kissing him. "No, it's not silly at all, in fact, I think it sounds wonderful." She thought momentarily, she loved sleeping with him and waking up next to him in the morning, would that change? "What about the end of the night would you or I go home?"

"If I am here, I will sleep with you in your bed; if you're at my place, you will sleep with me in mine. That's if you want to?"

"That's definitely what I want," said Brieanne cheerfully. But she knew, as she rested her head back on his shoulder, what she needed to do.

Chapter 30

Just before nine Brieanne left for work and a few minutes later Ben showed up.

Aidan told Ben the plan. "We will meet for forty-five minutes Monday to Friday. Every Thursday will be your spelling and reading tests: the first fifteen words the first Thursday and the second fifteen, the following Thursday. The last week would be his preparation for the final tests which would take place on third Thursday, his final day." Aidan then told him the structure of the lessons. "We will practice spelling and reading the fifteen words, then read books geared towards nine-year-old boys, as well as your comic books. How does that sound?"

"That's sounds, good," he replied, "So, it's only for a few weeks?"

"That's it," said Aidan with a smile.

They began his first lesson and Ben breezed through it.

At work Brie told Cathy everything that happened Saturday night and Sunday. Then at twelve she left to meet Jane for a quick lunch and chat before heading home.

"How did it go with Ben today?" she asked walking in.

"Excellent, I think he will do fine, he may even be done sooner than expected."

"That's' great," she said taking a container out of a bag and placing it in the microwave. "I brought lunch home for you, it's a veal sandwich and fries," she explained. "What did you do after Ben left?"

"I walked over to see Joyce, she had all the copies of my paperwork for me, and I was hot and sweaty when I got back so I jumped in the pool."

Brieanne took his food out, placed it on the counter, and watched him eat.

"How was work?"

She told him about her morning and Cathy.

"Are you ready to do the living room?"

"Actually, I've changed my mind, I want to do the kitchen and powder room next."

"Okay," he said, "it all has to be painted eventually."

Good she thought. "I'm going to get changed, after you eat, we can go pick out the paint," she said kissing him on the cheek.

They quickly picked out the paint, went to the new house, and started on the kitchen, not stopping until it was finished. They took a short coffee break then painted the powder room and were done by five. At Brieanne's place, Aidan cooked steaks on the BBQ while Brieanne prepared a salad.

"You were in high gear today," said Aidan.

"We started later than usual, and I wanted to make sure we got it all finished, after five I start faltering."

Aidan's phone rang; it was Jane. He listened to her, saying okay in between, then handed the phone to Brieanne. "Jane wants to ask you something."

Brieanne took the phone from him, spoke with her, and then hung up. "That's exciting, boys' and girls' days out."

"It is," replied Aidan cutting into his steak. "I'm glad you're spending time with them, I think it will be good for you, and for them."

"And all the guys going fishing out in the Gulf on that big boat," she said, "catching fish, drinking beer, along with fifty other people."

"Sounds absolutely terrible," joked Aidan.

"I'm sure you will survive," she said unsympathetically. "I'm just going to pop over and see Bella, they invited Jen shopping, and Ben fishing. When I come back, we'll go for a walk on the beach."

Aidan held her hand as they walked along the shoreline. "I guess I will do Ben's lesson in the morning before we leave so he can enjoy the fishing trip."

"Probably best, he will be too excited on the boat."

"Can I ask what happened to his parents? He's never brought them up to me."

"Yeah," she replied, "you never know one day he may, and it might be good for you to know." Brieanne collected her thoughts and began. "Clinton, everyone called him, Clint was in the army. One summer, April went up to the panhandle for a vacation and met him, he was stationed somewhere up there. Anyway, they fell in love, and she ended up staying there. They got married, rented a place, and over the next several years he would be called away on tours of duty: six months, nine months, sometimes, a year. During one of his leaves, she became pregnant with Jen, and wanted to move back here to raise her and be close to her parents, Bella and Dave who lived locally. Dave passed away many years ago. Clint totally supported her. He knew he was away a lot, and that April would need her parents' help. He was a good old-fashioned Southern boy and really sweet. They had both saved up quite a bit of money, bought the house where the children live, and called Madeira Beach home. Then they had Ben, and everything was going fine for them." She stopped and glanced over at him.

"Did Clint have family?"

"Clint's family was well-to-do, they didn't approve of April, and him marrying her. So, they disowned him and eventually their grandchildren."

"That's terrible."

"It was, I don't know where Clint got his sweetness from, it definitely wasn't from his parents," admitted Brieanne. "About a year ago last November he asked to be stationed locally. He had done more than his fair share of tours, explained that he had a family now, and wanted to be closer to home. Without hesitation they agreed, told him he could leave the Middle East in January, and would set him up with a position at the recruiting office in St. Petersburg. April and the children were ecstatic. They decided to keep the Christmas tree and decorations up and have a second Christmas when he came home. The kids made welcome home banners and April planned a big party for him." Brieanne paused for a moment and composed herself. "I was out on my deck when I heard this terrible, gut-wrenching scream come from the front of April's house. I ran through mine to the street, turned the corner onto her driveway, and at her front door were two army officers and the local priest. April was on the floor sobbing." Brieanne teary-eyed looked over at Aidan. "Two days before he was due to come home his unit was ambushed, a woman and an infant were in harm's way, and he went out to get them into safety. He protected them and got them behind a truck, before he made it around the corner he was shot, dying instantly."

"That is so sad," said Aidan comforting her.

"Clint had saved the woman and infant's lives and was a hero. He was in all the papers, had a military funeral, and was buried just down the road. Of course, none of that mattered to April, she never saw him as a soldier or a hero. He was Clint, her husband, the love of her life, and the father of her children. She never recovered from his death. April started hitting the bottle to take away the pain and pills to help her sleep. Bella and I helped her as best as we could. We eventually got her into counseling, but she wouldn't show up, instead, she would just get drunk at home. I ended up having to take care of the children at my place while we tried to get her better, only she never did, she only got worse. A year last June, five months to the day after Clint died, I received a call that April's car had skidded off the road into the causeway, killing her."

"Was it an accident?"

"They did a toxicology report on her and said she was clean. The sheriff, that's Stacy's dad, said there was heavy rain and strong winds that night. I also think she was probably upset and hadn't been watching the road as carefully as she should have been. So, they said it was an accident."

"Sounds like you don't believe it?"

"I do," she replied. "There were rumors that she was drunk, and because she never hurt anyone except herself, and with Clint being a war hero, some people were saying it was a cover up. Stacy's dad is a good, honest man, and he would never do that. I just thought that it was a foolish conspiracy theory." Brieanne let out a heavy sigh. "The day before she died, she had written out a will, and had it notarized," she said looking at Aidan. "I just took that as being a coincidence and nothing more. I could never see April leaving her kids purposely."

"I'm sure she wouldn't," said Aidan consoling her.

"She was my good friend, and I loved her like a sister, and I miss her." Brieanne started crying in his arms.

Aidan held her closely.

After a while Brieanne wiped her eyes and continued. "We decided that it was best for the kids to live here and not move away. They had already lost their parents. There was no need for them to lose their friends, school, and house. So, Bella moved into April's house. You see Bella's house is in Orlando, she has family there, and in Jacksonville."

"I understand," said Aidan.

"I helped Bella take care of Jen and Ben last summer. And during the school year more so me: I made their lunches, went to school activities, parent-teacher nights, helped them with homework, and bought them clothes for school."

"You have done a lot for them," said Aidan, "I see why they love you so much."

"I love them and care about them. I just want what's best for them," she said. "They deserve to be happy and have a good life."

"They do," agreed Aidan.

Chapter 31

At six forty-five Aidan walked over to Ben's house and brought him back. Ben read his words, books, and comic. Aidan went upstairs, kissed Brieanne, said goodbye, and they left. On the way, Ben practiced his spelling words and was finished by the time they got to Hubbard's Marina where they met up with Aidan's father, Uncle Bill, Steven, and Ethan. The group listened to a seminar thirty minutes before they boarded, then at eight, the boat left the dock for the Gulf of Mexico.

"Hey, guys, my name is Scott, how are you doing?" asked one of the crew.

"Good," replied Aidan.

"Hopefully we'll get you guys a lot of fish this morning."

"That would great," replied Paul. "Have you been doing this a while?"

"Yeah, I've been doing this for a few years. I'm here for the summer with my girlfriend then we're back to college in September."

"This is your summer job?" asked Steven.

"Yeah, one of them. I also do odd jobs around town building and fixing decks, landscaping, painting, whatever I can find. Summer is pretty busy; people are always looking to have something repaired or built."

"What's you major?" asked Aidan.

"Business, same as my girlfriend, we go to the same college," said Scott. "We're both locals, high school sweethearts, that sort of thing."

"That really nice," said Aidan liking him. "Where does she work?"

"She has a great job at a fantastic restaurant called Vegas Francisco's, have you heard of it?"

Aidan smiled. "Yeah, my family and I went there a few Fridays ago for the special dinner night."

"Really?" asked Scott. "She worked that night."

"What's her name?"

"Kelly."

"She was our server!" said Aidan. "She was terrific!"

"Wait a second, are you the guys from New York?"

"Yes, that's us."

"She told me about you guys, said you were great, and gave her a sizeable tip."

"Kelly deserved it having to put up with us all night," piped in Bill.

Scott looked at Aidan curiously. "Is your name Aidan?"

"Yeah."

"No way, I don't believe it!" said Scott happily. "I've been hearing your name from all sorts of different people and have never actually seen you, so I thought you were an urban legend."

"Well, I'm real," said Aidan grinning. "Where did you hear about me?"

"My sister Stacy mentioned you to me first."

"Your sister is Stacy; she's a lovely girl."

"Yeah, she is, I'm here youngest brother," he explained. "I also heard about you from Bev, Dawn, Helena, Harriett, George, I could go on and on, all good things, man." Then he whispered to Aidan, "but Kelly is definitely one of your biggest admirers, that tip Saturday night, snap! You're her number one customer, and Jess's too, she said she almost fainted when she opened her envelope."

"They deserved it! They were all under pressure that night and managed it really well," said Aidan complimenting them.

"I have to go but I will keep an eye on your group," he said shaking his hand, "Aidan, The Man, The Legend! Hold on a second. Do you mind?" asked Scott pulling out his phone. "Selfie, me and you?"

"Not at all," replied Aidan.

Scott took their picture. "I'm going to send it to all the people I just mentioned," he said cheerfully. "I'll talk to you soon."

The boat sailed for about an hour, during which there was a seminar on safety, as well as tips and tricks to catching fish. The group ate breakfast sandwiches before the boat stopped approximately ten miles out. They baited their hooks with cut up squid, dropped them to Gulf floor forty feet below, and waited. Within no time the group was hauling in gray snapper, porgies, and black sea bass. Scott, who was especially helpful along with the rest of the crew, helped them remove the fish then placed them in an allocated bin for the group. The men drank beer while the boys had juice and snacks. After three hours, the lines were reeled in, and they headed back to the marina during which time a tip jar was passed around and filled. An hour later the group received their fish and disembarked.

"Aidan," said Scott calling him over, "two groups don't want their catch, there's about forty fish. Their hotel rooms don't have kitchens. Do you want them?"

"Sure."

"This group will take them," said Scott to the people behind him.

Aidan called Ethan and Ben over saying, "grab those fish guys." The excited boys took them then waited in line with Steven to get them filleted.

"Thanks, Scott," said Aidan. "The men are heading to Hooters after this, do you want to join us?"

"I have to run to another job, I'll meet you there in an hour," he said. "Stacy is working the tables, I'm seeing her before I leave, and will tell here you are coming in."

The filleted fish were put in bags, which the boys carried. The group walked to meet Jane who was there to pick up the boys.

"Don't forget, at the condo by five," she shouted out the window before driving away.

The group of men headed to Hooters, met Stacy, and were seated for lunch. They ordered wings, nachos, and pitchers of beer. As they ate the delicious food and drank, they talked, and watched sports. An hour later Scott joined them, Aidan had held a personal whip-round for him, and handed him a very generous tip. At five, the four men walked to the condo and met the women. They men told the women about fishing and Hooters while the women talked about shopping. After dinner, they sat on the balcony, and watched the sunset. At ten, Aidan and Brieanne said goodnight and headed home with Jen and Ben.

"You guys had a good day then?" asked Brieanne.

"We did; it was a lot of fun. And you girls, too?"

"It was fantastic, I had such a great time, I'm really happy how today turned out," she said, "but I'm exhausted."

"Same here."

They dropped the kids off, arrived at Brieanne's house, and went straight to bed.

Chapter 32

Four Weeks Earlier: Wednesday, July 15

Ben arrived at nine, had his lesson, and left forty-five minutes later. Aidan went upstairs and joined Brieanne who was just stirring.

"Do you want some breakfast?"

"I would love some," she replied.

"Okay, come down when you are ready," he said giving her a kiss.

She went into the kitchen and sat at the counter as Aidan placed a cup of coffee in front of her. "When is Ben coming?"

"He's been and gone."

"Already, what time is it?"

"Ten," he said looking away from the bacon frying.

"I must have been tired," she said rubbing her sleepy eyes. "What time did you get up?"

"Just before nine," he said flipping the strips over. "What kind of eggs do you want?"

"Over easy," she replied.

"Did the mattress arrive yesterday?"

Brieanne suddenly remembered what today was and perked up. "Yes, it did, after breakfast we can go over there and make your bed."

"Okay," he replied.

Before Brieanne opened the door, she told him to close his eyes, which he did. Then lead him up the stairs into his room, and said, "you can open them now."

Aidan looked around the room. The bed was made with throw cushions on it and the end tables had night lights on them. She grabbed his hand, opened the closet door, and switched on the light. Aidan looked inside at his shirts and pants on hangers, and his shoes arranged neatly on the floor. She took him over to the chest of drawers where she pulled out the draws revealing his T-shirts and underwear neatly folded.”

“Come out to the balcony,” she said. “Two patio chairs and a small rectangular table.”

Aidan followed Brieanne into the small bedroom. There were bunk beds made up with kids’ designs on them, a matching chest of drawers with a TV and DVD on it, as well as a small desk with a chair.

“I put your laptop on the desk, underneath is a printer, and the yellow sticky on it has the password for the Wi-Fi. I thought you may want to write in here or do stuff relating to Ben’s lessons. Oh, the TV in here and in your room, both have cable and Wi-Fi access.”

Brieanne led him to the bathroom which had a matching floor mat, toilet mat, and seat cover “Here next to the sink, you have a new electric toothbrush, toothpaste, and soap. Shampoo, conditioner, and body wash are on the ledge in the shower. Extra toilet paper and tissues are under the sink. In the cabinet, basic medicines, floss, mouthwash, etcetera.”

“Brieanne—”

“No, let me finish,” she said joyfully leading him downstairs to the powder room. “Toilet paper, tissues, hand soap, towels, matching toilet mat, and seat cover.” And then took him into the last room, the kitchen. “You a have kettle, coffee maker, and toaster oven on the counter, and down here, a toaster, blender, pots, frying pans, and an electric griddle. Up here, a dish set for twelve, an assortment of different size glasses, and coffee mugs. Cutlery, steak knives are in here,” she said pointing to the drawers, before opening the fridge and freezer doors which were packed full of groceries. “In these cupboards, you have dry goods, canned goods, coffee, tea, and sugar. On the counter here, a bowl of fresh fruit, a stocked wine rack, with a few bottles of champagne,” she said excitedly. Brieanne showed him the kitchen table which had a white tablecloth and a vase containing colorful, fresh flowers.” She then took him out onto the deck. “BBQ and accessories, patio set, loungers, and a big cooler full of beer and ice." Brieanne turned and gave him a cheerful smile. "Welcome to your new place."

Aidan was speechless. He kissed her, gave her a big hug, and whispered, "thank you, this is incredible" He let go and sat down on a patio chair. "How...When…Did you do this all on your own?" he asked wondering how she managed to pull it off.

"Well, when you guys were fishing, drinking beer, eating lunch, drinking more beer, and admiring the Hooters girls. Me, Jen, and the ladies in your family, did this."

"How?"

"Your mom and aunt were responsible for the food, beer, wine, and bathroom items. Jane, Maddy, Jen and I, were responsible for the furniture and bedspreads."

"How did you get it here?"

"The bunk beds, mattresses, chest of drawers, and desk, I bought at same place as your mattress and box spring, so they delivered it all together. The patio sets, BBQ, loungers were in boxes, so we squeezed them into the Jeep and the Cadillac, which Jane drove, and we had to make a couple of trips back and forth."

"But someone had to set up the BBQ and bunk beds?"

"Scott."

"Scott?"

Brieanne realized he was trying to figure out who he was. "I will give you a hint, The Man, The Legend."

The penny dropped. "Scott, Stacy's brother!"

"One in the same," she said. "He came over and had it all done in about an hour."

"He said he had a job to do but never said here."

"Scott didn't know till after he got off the boat and met Stacy."

"That's why Scott said he was going to see her before he left and would let Stacy know we were going into Hooters." Aidan said thinking out loud. "He said nothing when he came back?"

"To him it was just another job or maybe he thought you already knew," she said unconvincingly.

"You told him not to say anything to us and ruin your surprise?"

"Yep, pretty much," she said, with a cute grin. "Besides, he's still in awe of you, 'Is he an urban legend? No, he is real because I met The Man, The Legend, The Aidan!'"

"Okay, he said something like that but not that dramatic."

"Let me show you," she said pulling out her phone and going to her text messages. Brieanne showed him the picture of him and Scott with their thumbs up on the boat and those exact words underneath. "I got this from Stacy and most of my staff has it. He sent it to everyone. He even posted it on his Facebook page where he's already received hundreds of likes. My mother even got it."

"How?"

"Bev sent it to her mom, who sent it to my mom."

Aidan leaned back in his chair with his hands on the back of his head. "Yeah, it's tough being me."

Brieanne laughed as she sat on his lap. Aidan put his arms around her.

"This is truly amazing," said Aidan, "thank you," and kissed her tenderly on the lips.

"What you said yesterday got to me. I thought about your family not being able to visit you, your niece and nephew unable to have sleepovers here, I felt sad for you; I had to make it right."

"Well, you did that and so much more," he said looking at her.

"I'm happy you like it."

"Like it, I love it," he replied, "and I love you."

"I love you," she said kissing him.

Aidan looked over at the loungers and the BBQ. "Did you pay for everything?"

"I wanted to, but I couldn't, your aunt and mom insisted on buying the food, booze, and toiletries. They wanted to buy some of the furnishings. I reminded them that it was a rental unit, so I bought those. The items in the kitchen are not top quality, if they get broken, they are easily replaceable. I think they are waiting for an invite to come over this afternoon and for dinner," she said smiling at him.

"Oh, they are, are they?"

"It will be so much fun the two of us cooking in your new kitchen for your family."

"It will be," he said taking out his phone. "What time did you tell them?"

"Three."

"Three it is. Did you want to invite Bella, Jen, and Ben?"

"Like your family, they just need a confirmation on the time, and I'll go tell them while you call your family," she said standing. "I'll be right back."

Brieanne returned. "Okay, we have three hours to kill."

As Aidan picked her up, she straddled him. "I don't think I've thanked you properly for what you did," he said carrying her inside and up to his new bedroom.

"Is this my reward?" she asked in anticipation.

"You are getting more than one reward."

"Lucky me," she whispered nibbling on his ear.

Brieanne went home and changed. She was looking forward to helping him entertain his family and showed up at two thirty holding a bag, Aidan looked at it curiously. "My overnight bag," she said, tilting her head with a grin. "I'll go put it in your closet."

Brieanne showed, Paul, Bill, and Steven the work that her and Aidan had done to date, and what the women had accomplished the previous day, before joining Aidan, the women, and children on the deck. Brieanne helped Aidan make dinner, which consisted of the grilled fish the men had caught the day prior, steak, chicken, vegetables, and a Caesar salad. And for dessert, they had hot blueberry pie with vanilla ice cream. After dinner, they officially told everyone that they were dating, which was met with smiles and congratulations. They watched the sunset on the deck, then strolled down to the shoreline, and walked towards the condo. Maddy, Ethan, Jen, and Ben caught up to Aidan and Brieanne.

"Uncle Aidan can we have a sleepover at your place tonight?" asked Maddy, the spokesperson for the children.

"Sure, as long as it's okay with your mom and dad, and grandmother."

The kids screamed as they ran back to ask their guardians, then met as a group to confer their findings, before catching up with Aidan again.

"All good," said Maddy.

The group reached the condo, said goodnight to Brieanne who left with Bella, Jen, and Ben, to help pack an overnight bag for them while Aidan went upstairs with his family to wait while Jane packed one for Maddy and Ethan. Arriving back on Aidan's deck, the girls went upstairs into Aidan's bedroom to change into their pajamas, while the boys went into the other one.

Aidan noticed Brieanne was a little distant. "Are you okay?"

"I'm happy all the kids are having a sleepover," she said, sitting on his knee. "I just wanted to sleep her tonight with you."

"You aren't?"

"Well, I thought—"

"Because the kids are here?"

"Yeah."

"They know we're dating—"

"But not sleeping together," she pointed out, as the kids came running onto the deck.

"Guys, do you want Brieanne to join us for our sleepover tonight?"

The kids went silent.

Brieanne's was embarrassed.

"What?" Aidan asked.

The spokesperson answered. "We just assumed she was," said Maddy with a surprised look on her face.

"I guess because you didn't include her in your plans when you asked me, she thought maybe didn't want her to come?"

The children ran over to her. "No, Brie, we want you to have a sleepover here with us, please, please, please!" they begged.

"Okay, okay," said Brie happily.

The children talked on the deck while Aidan and Brieanne went upstairs to put on their pajamas.

"Should I go into the other room?" she asked as she turned on the light and went inside the closet.

"No," said Aidan closing the door behind her, "you can change in there." There was no response; Aidan opened the door to see her staring at him disapprovingly.

"You think you're pretty funny, don't you, mister?" she said gradually walking toward him.

"Yeah, I think I'm pretty funny," he replied kissing her.

She fervently kissed him back to which he responded.

"Uncle Aidan," said Maddy from the bottom of the stairs "Are you going to be much longer?"

"We'll be down in two minutes," he replied, as they quickly changed. "I haven't seen that shirt on you for a while."

"I'm behind on my laundry, so I put my dirty laundry in with yours, and dropped it off at the laundromat yesterday morning. I picked it up in the afternoon. I wasn't too sure what clothes of yours were clean or dirty so had them all washed, even your cute boxers."

"Your underwear, too?"

"Heavens no, I don't want anyone seeing my unmentionables, only you," she said walking down the stairs.

"Okay, kids," said Aidan going onto the deck with Brieanne. "What do you want to do?"

"Watch a movie," Ethan replied.

"With treats," added Jen.

"Then follow me," said Aidan as he walked them upstairs into his room. "Brieanne and I are going to lie on the bed, you can lie with us, or you can lie on a bunch of blankets and pillows over here at the end of the bed in front of the TV."

The boys picked the floor while the girls chose the bed. Brieanne set up all the blankets and pillows, while Aidan put on Netflix, and searched for a family movie they all could agree on.

"Now, let's go find some treats," said Brie as they followed her downstairs to the kitchen.

They found chips and dip, popcorn, loads of candies, and juice boxes. Jen and Maddy put a bag of popcorn in the microwave as Brieanne set the timer.

"Did you go to the New York State Fair?" asked Ethan looking at her T-shirt.

"Last time I was there I was around your age?"

Ethan was puzzled. "Why is your shirt so big?"

"This is your uncle Aidan's shirt, he gave it to me so I could wear it to bed," she said then remembered that Ethan and Maddy had given it to him. "I hope you don't mind?"

"Nah, I like it on you," said Ethan. "He must really like you if he gave it to you, that's one of his favorite shirts, he wears it all the time."

Brieanne glanced over at Aidan who innocently looked away. He had never mentioned it was his favorite which now made it more special to her.

"I think it looks good on you, too," said Maddy, "makes you look sexy." The way she emphasized sexy made them all laugh.

"What's the New York State Fair?" asked Jen.

"Yeah, what is it?" said Ben.

"You guys have never been!" said Ethan excitedly. "Only the coolest place ever!"

Ethan and Maddy told them all about it.

"Llama Limbo and Leaping Llamas competitions!" said Ben imagining what it looked like.

"That place sounds awesome!" said Jen, "I want to go!"

"When we get home," continued Maddy, "we are going there at least five times. You guys should come, stay at our place, and go with us, you too, Brie."

"Can we, Brie? Can we?" pleaded Ben and Jen.

"We would have to speak with your grandmother first and see what she says," advised Brie, thinking it would be fun to take them.

The popcorn done, they went upstairs, and got settled. The boys spread out on the floor while the girls lay next to one another facing the TV. Brieanne nestled her head on Aidan's shoulder as the movie began.

"This has been a lovely evening," whispered Brieanne before kissing his cheek. Looking around at the children, she imagined them as parents, and how good they would be.

Chapter 33

"Are you ready?" asked Aidan.

"I'm ready," replied Ben."

Aidan conducted the spelling and reading test with him. "Congratulations," said Aidan, "perfect score!"

Ben jumped up for joy then took off to join the other kids messing around upstairs.

"How did he do?" asked Brieanne coming out onto the deck.

"He got a perfect score," replied Aidan.

"That's amazing," she said. "Will he be caught up before the school year begins?"

"I think he will be ahead," stated Aidan.

Brieanne and Aidan made breakfast then took the children to Brieanne's and watched them swim.

"Are your parents coming on the twenty-seventh?"

"I forgot to tell you they called yesterday and confirmed they are they've booked their flight. My mom also said they have something important to tell me."

"Do you have any idea what it could be?"

"No, she said they wanted to tell me when they get here. She says its good news."

"I'm glad they will be here for Ben's pizza party and the fishing trip."

Brieanne gave him a confused look. "Fishing trip?"

"You know, the charter?"

Brieanne shook her head mystified. "I don't know anything about any charter."

Aidan realized she didn't. "I must have forgotten," he said and told her about booking Eric for the day. "I thought it would be a great family trip. Now, I can tell them tomorrow. I've just waiting to see if your parents would be here first."

Brieanne realized something that made her heart skip. "Did you include my parents on your family trip?"

"Of course, I did, I told Eric there would be sixteen people."

She sprang onto his lap kissing him. "Tell me all about it, who are you inviting?"

"I'm inviting my family, your parents, Bella, Jen, Ben, and Stacy."

"You invited Stacy so she could be with Eric?"

"Yeah, I thought it might be nice for them to be together."

"You are so sweet doing that," she said cuddling him. "When is it?"

"It's on Friday the thirty-first, for a full day. I gave him a nonrefundable deposit to hold the reservation, so we are guaranteed a boat."

"That is going to be so much fun," she said happily. "And they could really use the money. Eric says he's been busy, but they have a lot of expenses. Poor Stacy works two jobs, she also helps her father with his self-defense classes from September to June, and that's only for a couple of days a week. Actually three, she also helps Eric out with his charter bookings, although she doesn't get paid for that."

"I'm glad I can help them both out," said Aidan kissing the top of her head. "What's the story with Eric?"

"It's kind of sad," she said, looking at him. "Some of the things I'm going to tell you can't tell anyone else, okay?"

"I won't," replied Aidan.

"Well, you already know about his dad passing away."

"Yes."

"Yeah, that's a head-scratcher," she said, wondering why Eric bothered to tell Aidan, a complete stranger who he didn't like that his dad had died, when his usual response to everyone else was none of your business.

"Why is that a head-scratcher?"

"He's doesn't talk about his dad to some of the locals never mind people he just met."

"Oh," replied Aidan.

"Eric's mother left him when he was a young boy, and with his mother, went his father's heart. On top of dealing with his wife leaving him Eric's father was now left raising Eric on his own. As Eric grew up, his dad taught him everything he knew about fishing, unfortunately he also started hitting the bottle a lot more to ease his broken heart, eventually drinking himself to death. Eric was just turning seventeen, so my father took him under his wing and treated him like family. Eric never lived with us they found him a small place of his own and many of the locals helped him out with furniture and stuff. Eric's father was well-liked, and everyone felt sorry for what had happened to him and Eric. Shortly after his death, Eric took jobs on fishing boats; you know the ones that go out for weeks, and from what my dad said it did him the world of good. After many years of doing that, Eric told my dad he wanted to be his own boss and run a fishing charter, and said he had his dad's secret fishing map. Apparently, everyone was looking for this map. Fisherman even told Eric, if he ever found it, they would pay him a bundle for it. Well, it seems that on his deathbed, Eric's dad told him where his map was, and made Eric promise not to tell anyone about it or sell it, and to use it when he had his own boat. Eric had kept his promise up until the conservation he had with my dad. He showed my dad the map and my father agreed to be his partner. My dad bought Eric a boat on the condition that he paid back half of it."

"Does he pay your dad a portion of his profits?"

"No," said Brieanne, "my father told Eric to keep his half of the profit and use my father's half towards paying off the boat. He was giving Eric a win-win situation. That's the first part that's you need to promise me on."

"I promise."

"This is the second part. When my dad bought the boat, he paid for it outright. Eric doesn't know this, he thinks my dad only paid off fifty percent, and the remaining fifty percent is his half of the debt. So once Eric makes what he believes is his final payment, my dad is going to give him twenty-five percent of that money back as a bonus. And from that point on they will have a fifty-fifty split in the profits. But knowing my dad, it will be more like twenty-five percent for him, seventy-five for Eric."

"Why wouldn't you dad loan—?"

"My dad wants Eric to work hard and have a good work ethic. There would be no incentive if my dad just loaned the boat to Eric, and he chartered it out for my father. By doing it this way, Eric had a fifty percent interest in his charter business, and has to strive to make it successful."

"That's amazing your dad doing that for him."

"It is," admitted Brieanne. "Oh, to get back to my original point, Eric has the expenses of operating the charter and paying off the boat. Its tough work, some weeks are busier than others, then there's bad weather, trips where the fish don't bite, and customer's complaining."

"Us tourists," joked Aidan.

"Yes, hunky tourists like you," said Brieanne with a cute smile. "But all joking aside, you hiring him for the day is really helping him out more than you know," she said kissing him and was just about to ask him what Eric had charged him for the day.

"We all agree," said the spokesperson leaning on the pool wall along with the three other children, "you guys should get a room."

Brieanne and Aidan chuckled.

"What was that young lady?" asked Brie, getting off Aidan's lap, and walking over to her.

Aidan quickly jumped up and pushed Brieanne into the pool.

"You filthy—" was all she got out as she splashed into the water.

The four children, coming to her defense, got out of the pool and cornered Aidan. They grabbed him and threw him in.

After lunch, the children helped Ben fill in his Pizza Party invitations, while Brieanne and Aidan made fishing trip invites on his laptop and printed them out. They took the children to play miniature golf, and then went to the Shake Shop for ice cream, before dropping them off. After dinner, Brieanne and Aidan painted the living room, soaked in the hot tub, and had an early night.

281

Chapter 34

"I will be back around five," said Brieanne kissing Aidan and grabbing her Jeep keys. "I will drop these off with Stacy on the way to work and send my parents a copy of theirs." She quickly ran into Hooters, gave them to Stacy, and by one was in her office sending a Gmail to her mom.

"What are these?" asked Eric glancing at the invitations then Stacy.

"Invites: one is to Ben's Pizza Party; the other is for the fishing trip," she explained.

"He invited us on the fishing trip," said Eric a little confused. "He's already hired me."

"I think it's mostly for me, I think Aidan and Brie want you to feel like you are part of the group, too." she said looking at him. "Don't you want the love of your life beside you?"

"You know I do."

She noticed Eric had a worried look on his face. "What?"

"Oh shit!" he said.

"Hold on a second, last time those two words came out of your mouth all hell broke loose," she said concerned. "What did you do?"

"Remember when I called you about a week and half ago, and asked you if the charter was available a few Fridays away?"

"Yes," she said feeling uneasy, "the one for Rochester."

"That was for Aidan."

"So?"

"Remember when you gave me the quote for the trip?"

"Yeah," she recalled, "it was right, and you gave me the nonrefundable five-hundred-dollar deposit for it." Still unsure what the problem was.

Eric looked at her distressed. "I charged him an extra four hundred."

Stacy glared at him. "You did what?"

"It was the same time as the comic book and fishing spot incident. I thought if I gave him an inflated price, he wouldn't bother booking it."

"And what was your plan after he paid you?" she asked in disbelief.

"I don't know, I thought maybe he would cancel, and lose his deposit," he replied looking at her nervously. "I wouldn't do that now and I shouldn't have done that then," he said regretfully.

"Eric, you have never done that to anyone, ever," she said shocked. "What's the real reason? Is this to do with Aidan?"

Eric fidgeted. "I just didn't like him messing around with Brie."

Stacy shook her head. "Eric, Brie is an adult, and can take care of herself."

"That's what everyone said last year."

"Aidan's not like her last boyfriend," said Stacy. "Can't you see that?"

"I was worried at the end of summer he is going to take off back to Rochester and we would be stuck helping Brie get over him."

"That's her choice and if that does happen, which it won't, and you have a problem helping out your friend out after the fact then maybe you aren't a friend worth having," she said upset with him. "It seems to me Eric that you believe only local boys are good enough for me, Brie, and any other girl born and raised in Madeira Beach."

"I said I wouldn't have done that today, and I shouldn't have done it then, okay, I'm sorry."

"You know if he tells Brie what you charged him, she will know straight away what you did, and I'm afraid this time she may never forgive you," said Stacy looking at him sadly. "I'm not even sure she's forgiven you completely for what you did to him last time."

"What makes you think Brie doesn't already know?" he asked simply.

Stacy looked at him in wonderment. "If she already knew, you would have heard about by now, and I doubt you would be getting any invites."

"Oh yeah," he said realizing she was right. "What should I do?"

"You need to go over and tell him the truth?"

"He won't be happy?"

"Either you deal with him unhappy or Brie," she said matter-of-fact. "And it gets worse?"

"How so?" he asked believing it couldn't.

"Brie's parents are also coming. Aidan invited them."

"Her father is going on the fishing trip?" asked Eric feeling queasy.

Stacy nodded her head. "Brie is at work till five, it's three now, and Aidan is doing work on the house. I suggest you get a move on."

Ten minutes later Eric knocked at the door. Aidan answered.

"Eric," he said, "you don't look too good, you okay?"

"Can I talk to you for a minute?"

"Yeah, come on in, no one is here."

Eric was thinking outside would be better if he had to make a run for it, but didn't want to be rude, and decided to take his chances inside. Eric told Aidan.

"You charged me four hundred more, why?" asked Aidan deeply offended.

"I have no real reason except I was being a total jerk," he said ashamed.

"That reason will do fine," replied Aidan still unhappy with him.

"I was hoping if Brie asks you, you can tell her the right price, not the price I originally gave you?"

"You want me to lie to her?"

Eric was quiet because that's exactly what he wanted Aidan to do.

"I can't do that," said Aidan, his loyalty was to Brieanne, not to him. Aidan thought about asking Eric to pay him back, from what Brieanne had told him about Eric and Stacy's financial situation, they probably didn't have the money.

"I understand," said Eric heading to the door.

"What did you do with the money?" asked Aidan curiously.

"I, eh, bought the kids fishing rods, some of the items in the tackle box, and the comics. I also took Stacy down to St. Pete, were we had dinner, drinks, and got a hotel for the night," he replied awkwardly. "We haven't been anywhere this summer," said Eric glancing up at him. "I'm really sorry. I want you to know I've never done that before, and I really am an honest guy."

"So, only tourists rip you off, right?" said Aidan remembering the Fourth of July conversation.

Eric remembered what he said and felt worse than he did before knocking on the door.

Aidan closed the door behind Eric knowing it couldn't have been easy for him to come over. But what was more unsettling than Eric trying to rip him off, was the fact that he didn't want to see him and Stacy get into serious trouble, or worse, Eric lose his livelihood, especially over four hundred dollars. Aidan opened the door and went after him. "Eric!"

"Yeah."

"Where's Stacy?"

"Working at Hooters."

"Okay, let's go over and see here."

Arriving at the bar Stacy looked uncomfortable as Aidan walked toward her.

"Two beers, please," said Aidan, passing one to Eric. "Stacy, I can't lie to Brieanne, you know that?"

"I know."

"And if I give you the four hundred, I would still have to lie to her," said Aidan not knowing what to do.

"I wouldn't take it off you anyway," said Eric, "I would rather be honest with Brie and her father."

"They may never trust you again," said Stacy, "you could lose your job, the boat, everything."

"Maybe I can pay you back overtime?" suggested Eric then realized. "You would still have to lie to Brie."

"Stacy, how would Brieanne find out?"

"I do the accounting for the charter at the end of the month then I review the numbers with Brie to make sure they are correct. After, she helps me pay our expenses, like the boat. She's much better at it than I am," Stacy explained. "Brie knows what we charge per person. If I change the amount to reflect the additional four hundred, she would review your booking, realize you were overcharged, and question us why we did that."

"I see," said Aidan realizing their predicament, "and if you don't change the books and I tell her what I paid, it won't match, and she'll know you pocketed four hundred."

Stacy nodded her head. "She may even think Eric's done this before."

As Aidan thought he looked at Stacy's worried face. "How was St. Pete?"

"It was a lot of fun," she replied. "We go to a bar that we like and stayed the night at a motel."

"What's the name of the bar?"

"Crabby Bill's."

"You're kidding me?" said Aidan.

"No, why?"

"Do you know Dee?" he asked.

"I know her really well."

"And Chuck, and Ted, the regulars?"

"Yes," said Stacy giving him a bewildered look. "How do you know them?"

"Next time you go there, ask Dee," he said.

"I will."

Then Aidan remembered something from that day. "Do you guys provide drinks and food for passengers?"

"We can," said Eric, "a lot of people tend to bring their own."

"Stacy, can you get a piece a paper and a pen?" asked Aidan.

"Okay," she said grabbing them.

"Write this down," he said looking at her. "For sixteen people, we are going to need breakfast items: doughnuts, bagels, muffins, and coffee. Lunch items: sandwiches, salads, fruit plate, vegetables, and dip. Drinks: water, juice, soda, beer, wine, vodka, rum. Snacks: chips, pretzels, and peanuts. Dessert: chocolate cake, cheesecake, pastries. Did you get all that?"

"Yes," she said.

"For each item, figure out the cost to buy them from a store," said Aidan watching. When she finished, she looked up at him. "Add on money for gas to drive there and back, and times the number of hours it will take you to buy and prepare the items by minimum wage."

"Done," she said.

"Now, add it all up."

"Around three-hundred-and-fifty dollars," she acknowledged, "but I can prepare some of these items from home for a lot less."

"To that amount add another fifty," said Aidan, "that's yours and Eric's service charge."

"Okay, four hundred."

"Now, you are going to give me two receipts: one for the charter, and one for drinks and food."

"I see," said Stacy starting to understand. "You can tell Brie the total cost of the two and it will equal what Eric quoted you."

"Exactly!" replied Aidan.

Eric may not always be on the ball, but when it came to money he was. "Who is going to pay for that?" he asked dubiously.

Aidan looked at Stacy. "She is."

Stacy gave him a blank look. "I don't have that kind of money."

"Do me a favor, get me an envelope, and another beer for Eric and me," said Aidan finishing his drink and waiting for Stacy to return. "Put your list in the envelope," he said taking it from her, "I will back in a few minutes."

"Do you know what he's up to?" asked Eric looking at her.

"Not a clue," she replied.

Aidan came back, picked up his beer, and took a sip. "Stacy, I will pay for the four beers, I have to get going."

Stacy gave him his bill then took his money.

"If you can do the food cheaper, whatever money left over is yours," said Aidan handing her the envelope back. He finished his beer, said goodbye, and left.

Stacy looked at Eric. They both realized they needed to come up with four hundred dollars before the trip. She glanced down at the envelope, noticed it was sealed, and read out loud what was written on it: "Your tip is inside, thanks, Aidan."   Stacy eagerly opened it and counted four hundred dollars. She put the envelope away, turned to her colleague and told her she was taking a quick break, and took off with Eric after Aidan. They caught up to him on the boardwalk. "Aidan," she called, he didn't hear her. "Aidan!" she shouted again, this time he turned around. Stacy gave him a big hug. "Thank you, thank you, thank you! I was so worried Eric was going to lose his job."

"Thanks, Aidan," said Eric, shaking his head genuinely. "I was really worried, too."

"Well, let's forget that it ever happened," he said with a smile. "Okay?"

"Okay," they replied.

Stacy kissed him on the cheek. "Thanks again," she said, as they watched him walk away.

"I was just looking for you," said Brieanne strolling out of her new house.

"I met with Stacy and Eric about the fishing trip," said Aidan walking toward her. "Stacy is going to buy a load of food and drinks."

"That's great," said Brieanne. "I was going to ask you yesterday, what they ended up charging you?"

Aidan told her about the amount for the charter and the amount for the drinks and food.

"That's about right," she said, "and if I know Stacy she will go overboard with the food."

Aidan laughed. "Overboard?"

"I couldn't resist," said Brieanne, laughing with him.

Chapter 35

Three Weeks Earlier: Wednesday, July 22

Brieanne wanted to have the new house completed before her parents arrived which gave them ten days. Over the next five, they finished painting the house, added furnishings, and hung pictures. With the exception of a few finishing touches, the house was done. Late Wednesday afternoon, with five days to go, they stood surveying the backyard.

"I don't know what to do with this remaining half of the yard?" she asked looking at him for answers. "It's mostly sand and grass."

"Me either," he said looking around at it.

"I don't really want to be responsible for the upkeep of a backyard like this," she confessed. "Maybe we can remove the grass and make it all sand or put down patio stones along the path to the gate and leave sand on either side…I don't know," she said unsure. "The only thing I do know is that I don't want to do nothing and let the space to go to waste."

"Yeah, leaving it as it is, isn't an option," said Aidan looking at her and thinking about her suggestions. He casually glanced over at her place. "Rather than leaving it as sand or putting down patio stones, why not build a lower deck, like you have?"

"And have steps from the upper deck lead onto the lower one."

"Yes, we can build it eight to ten inches from the ground, have it cover most of the yard, with steps leading down towards the back gate."

"We can make it a sunbathing deck, put out loungers, and a patio set. People can lie on it, kids can play on it, and young families can set up a playpen," she said excitedly. "I think that's a perfect idea! Who can we get to help us?"

Aidan thought momentarily. "Didn't Scott say he repaired and built decks?"

"You're right he does," said Brieanne. "Let's go inside and I'll call him."

Friday afternoon, Scott showed up and they explained their vision to him. The three of them calculated the dimensions and drew up the design.

"I will have to get a price for the wood and the hardware," said Scott, "and rent some equipment."

"Can you also figure out how much time it will take for you and Aidan to complete it?" asked Brie.

"Okay," he replied. "When did you want this done?"

"By lunchtime Monday," said Brie hesitantly.

"It's my weekend off, but I could use the money, and this would be fun job to do," he said looking around. "I can start tomorrow morning, and we'll have it done Sunday afternoon. It's a straightforward job," he said confidently. "Do you want me to order the wood and book the rental equipment?"

"Yes," replied Brie, "and if you can calculate the total amounts for the materials, equipment, labor, and drop it off later, I would appreciate it?"

"I can but it will have to be quick visit, I'm supposed to be meeting Kelly for a burger and a beer at Pirates Pub N Grub in a couple of hours, it's her night off."

"We could just meet you two there, say around seven, and buy you dinner?" suggested Brie. "As long as we're not intruding?"

"No, not at all, that actually works out better. We'll see you guys there," said Scott standing and leaving.

"You will like this place," said Brieanne as they strolled onto the boardwalk at John's Pass Village toward the restaurant. "It's a pirate theme, matey!" she said with a smile as they reached the entrance and walked inside.

"Welcome to the Pirates Pub N Grub," said the server as they followed her to a table.

Aidan looked approvingly at the décor. "Home at last."

"No kidding, you'll fit right in here," she admitted. "I suppose you will be ordering rum," she said jokingly.

"Can I offer you a drink from the bar?" asked the server dropping off menus.

"Pusser's Rum and Coke for me," said Aidan.

Brieanne lightheartedly shook her head at him then looked at the server. "I'll have the same, please," she replied, before turning her attention back to Aidan. "I was only teasing you."

"Never tease a Scallywag about rum," he said in a humorous pirate's voice.

"Oh please," she said giggling. "How did you even know they had that type of rum?"

"What pirate-themed bar wouldn't have a fine selection of rums?" he asked. "Especially Pusser's Rum, a rum from the home of me ancestors in the British Virgin Islands," he squawked.

"Right, how did I miss that?" she said laughing at him.

"Actually, they have a listing of rums right here," he said passing it to her.

Brieanne looked it over, hit him on top of the head with it, and then put it back. She loved his antics. "What am I going to do with you?" she asked grabbing his hand fondly.

Aidan smiled back innocently.

"Nice try," she said, as the server dropped off their drinks.

"What time do your parents arrive on Monday?"

"Around two. They will go home, unpack, get ready, and go to dinner at Vegas Francisco's. Every time they visit, the first night they arrive, they always go there for dinner," she explained. "My dad likes to see if the restaurant is still meeting his high standard of excellence."

"Is the staff ready for that?"

"They don't know."

Aidan was puzzled. "But won't the staff recognize him, like Bev and Cathy?"

"The ones who know him or have seen him before will, only they are not allowed to say anything to the ones who haven't. So the newer staff, like Jess, Kelly, won't know who he is," she explained. "The night they go, it has to be a new person seating him, serving him, and preparing his food. It's a way for him to observe the restaurant from a customer perspective besides, he likes to have a little fun with them."

"Won't their name tip them off when they book the reservation?"

Brieanne gave him a grin. "I book the reservation for them under the last name Anderson."

"Very clever," he said smiling back at her and taking another sip. "Aren't you nervous?"

Brieanne gave him an odd look and giggled. "No, the staff, service, and food will be excellent. It's what we do, day in, day out," she replied. "You've experienced that already."

"True," he admitted, "and all three times were outstanding."

"My father also gives everyone an over-the-top tip. Then the following day, we have a meeting at the restaurant, and everyone gets to meet them."

"Who will be seating him, serving him, and preparing his food?"

"Jess, and we only have a new grill chef named Antoine so my day will order something from the grill…I'm not sure about the server," said Brieanne, thinking. "I meant to look at that when I booked my parents' reservation and assigned them a table, but I got distracted. Hopefully, it's not someone who already knows him." She reached for her phone, called Bev, and quickly spoke with her. "A server named Jasmine has that section and she knows him. I will have to fix that tomorrow. I don't want to tell Bev and give her a heads up he is coming in," she said slyly.

"You're putting, not only one of your best friends, but your cousin under the bus?" asked Aidan sadly shaking his head.

"Are you kidding? She would do that to me in a heartbeat!" she replied snickering at her mischief.

"Hi, Brie, Aidan," said Kelly and Scott, joining them.

"Hi," they replied in unison.

They ordered drinks for them as Scott pulled out his calculations. "I thought we could go over this first and get it out of the way?" he said unfolding his papers.

"That's a good idea," replied Brie.

"I ordered the wood, and it's getting delivered along with the hardware at eight tomorrow morning. I booked the rental equipment and will pick that up on my way over. Scott then showed them the material and rental costs, estimated hours to do the job, as well as the dollar amount for his time; his amount was an exceptionally low number.

Brieanne and Aidan looked at one another. "This seems low," she asked pointing to his amount.

"I took total the number of hours for the two of us, divided it by two, then times my hours by minimum wage and got that number," he explained.

"Please, excuse me for one second, Scott." Brieanne whispered something to Aidan who quickly grabbed his phone, did a search, and excused himself, taking the sheets with him out onto the boardwalk.

"Kelly, how are things?" asked Brie.

"Going great," she said, "I love working at the restaurant, thank you."

"No, thank you. You are a fantastic server and did an excellent job when Aidan and I came in."

"I couldn't believe it when I looked over and saw you sitting there, I almost fainted," she said truthfully.

"You handled it very well," complimented Brie.

"Thank you," replied Kelly. "Some of the staff said you looked like a movie star, others said a model, I said you had the beauty of a model and the grace of a movie star."

"Well, thank you," said Brie blushing. "I've also seen the selfie of you and The Legend," she said teasing Scott.

"Isn't that the best," he replied. "Did you hear how many hits I got on that?"

"I heard," replied Brie. "We walked around here Sunday afternoon, and all your friends were coming up to Aidan to shake The Legend's hand."

"No way," said Scott animatedly. "How sweet is that?"

Aidan came back to the table and spoke to Brieanne in a low voice. She then grabbed Aidan's pen and wrote something on Scott's sheets. Scott looked over nervously at Kelly who was motioning to him that everything was okay.

"I asked Aidan to call around to give us an idea as to the hourly wage a contractor would charge for building a deck," she explained handing him his sheets back with his original number crossed off with a much larger number next to it. "This is what I am paying you."

Scott almost fell off his seat, showing Kelly, she gasped out loud.

"Thank you," said Scott overwhelmed. "This is amazing!"

"You're welcome," said Brie. "Now that is out of the way, let's order." She opened her menu and looked over at Aidan who was studying his. "The burgers here are incredible," she whispered.

The server came; Kelly ordered the Mushroom Swiss Burger, Scott the Philly Burger, and Aidan ordered the Pirate Burger with bacon.

"I will have the Pirate Burger with bacon, also," said Brie.

"All with fries?" she asked the group before taking their menus.

"Yes," they replied.

"I knew you would order the Pirate Burger," she said laughing.

"How can you not?" he asked indisputably. "Rum and a Pirate Burger, they go hand in hand." He then leaned towards her and whispered, "just like you and me."

Her face lit up.

"Kelly, do you like working at the restaurant?" asked Aidan.

"I was just telling Brie how much I love it there."

"I'm glad you're enjoying it," he said. "Are you working there Monday night?"

"Yes, I am," she said excitedly. "Are you two coming in?"

"No, we're not," said Brie picking up on Aidan's train of thought.

"Oh, too bad," she said disappointedly.

"While we are talking about Monday night I was going to ask, if you mind swapping sections with Jasmine?"

"That's fine," said Kelly without hesitation.

"Good, I will let Bev know tomorrow."

Their burgers came and everyone ate in silence.

"That was unbelievable," said Aidan looking down at his empty plate.

"These are the best burgers around here," said Scott finishing up, "hands down!"

"This is so tasty," said Brie taking another bite.

They waited till the girls finished then had one more drink before leaving. The young couple were going to go meet their friends but not before Scott took a selfie of the four of them with the caption: 'The Legend, Me, & our gfs, Brie & Kelly, out for dinner!' Then texted it to his friends, as well as Brie, and of course The Legend, before posting it on his Facebook page. Brieanne and Aidan said goodbye, went home for a swim, made love, and had an early night.

For the next two days Aidan and Scott built the deck, Ben hearing the hammering came over, and also helped. While inside, Brieanne and Jen did the finishing touches. Sunday afternoon, the deck was finished. Aidan helped Scott put the tools and scrap pieces of wood in his truck. Brie paid him, thanked him, and they both waved goodbye as he drove away. Then Aidan helped Brieanne put the loungers and patio set on the new deck and put his arms around her as they admired it. They took one last tour around the house, satisfied, they cleaned up, and went out to celebrate.

On Monday morning Ben arrived and sat on the deck with Aidan. So far, he had passed both his previous tests with flying colors and Aidan informed him that over the next three days he was going to help him prepare for his final spelling and reading tests: which comprised of all the words on the printout sheet, as well as the books they had read, and two comics books of his choosing. When his lesson ended Ben was about to go when he sat back down.

"Are you going to move here and buy your own place?" he asked.

Aidan looked at him. "To be honest with you I don't know. Why do you ask?"

"Well, this house is done and you're only here till the end of the summer. I was wondering if you were planning on moving here and buying your own place?"

"You're right, I guess if I do move here, I would need a place to live. Maybe I will rent this one?" he suggested.

"I would like that," said Ben. "I don't want to move from here?"

"From your house?" asked Aidan clarifying.

"I don't mind moving from my house I just don't want to move from Madeira Beach," he explained. "Neither does Jen?"

"Why would you think you would move?"

"Jen said she heard Grandma on the phone talking to our relatives in Jacksonville. She thought maybe she was asking them about us moving there."

"Did Jen hear your grandmother asking that?"

"I'm not sure, I don't think so," he said trying to remember.

Aidan didn't want to ask too many questions. "I'm sure everything will be fine, your grandma was probably calling just to say hello, that's all" said Aidan comforting him. "Where would you like to live?"

"Brie's place or here," he said looking around. "They're happy places."

"Is that because we have a lot of fun in them?" suggested Aidan.

"Yeah," replied Ben happily. "Well, I should get going, thanks, Aidan."

Aidan watched him leave and wondered if his grandmother was considering moving there with the children. In his mind, he couldn't see them moving away from Brieanne, and didn't give it a second thought.

"Everything is set up for my parents tonight: Jess will be the hostess, Kelly their server, and Antoine is the chef preparing his food," she said happily walking over and sitting next to him on the patio chair. "How was your day?"

"Good," he replied. "I did Ben's lesson with him then had a swim." He decided not to mention anything about what Ben had said, assuming if Ben or Jen wanted to tell her they would, or maybe they already had.

The following day Brieanne invited her parents over for dinner to meet Aidan. They ate in the dining room and both couples caught up on what they had been up to. Her parents, from all they had heard about Aidan, felt like they already knew him and took an immediate shining to him. After dinner, her parents wanted to share their news with Brieanne, Aidan offered to leave they insisted he stay.

"Brieanne honey," said Anne, "your father and I are moving back to Madeira Beach."

"You are!" cried Brieanne happily. "When did you decide this?"

"Several weeks ago," said Brien. "Originally, we only planned on being away for a couple of years, but my sweet loving wife was kind enough to let me stay a little while longer."

"We miss it here too much," said her mother, "and I'm tired of texts, phone calls, and pictures. I want to be here and experience it all for myself."

"I feel the same way," added Brien, "and hearing that Aidan's family is also here, we thought it would be wonderful to socialize with them."

"Oh, you will love them!" said Brieanne.

"If there as sweet as this man, then I'm sure we will," said Anne with a kind smile.

Aidan blushed.

"When are you moving?" asked Brieanne.

"We have!" replied Anne, "We are not going back. The house is up for sale."

"That is so great," said Brieanne excitedly and hugged them both.

They helped Brieanne clean off the table, sat on the deck, and watched the sunset.

"How was your meal yesterday?" asked Aidan.

"It was absolutely incredible," Brien replied. "Brie, I think you run that restaurant much better than I ever did."

"I don't know about that Dad, I think you laid down the groundwork, and I just went with it."

"She's much too modest," noted her dad.

"How was the hostess?" asked Brie.

"Jess was a sheer delight. Charming, warm, gracious, friendly; absolutely perfect."

"And the server?"

"Her name was Kelly, and she was exceptional," stated Brien. "She was informative, polite, helpful, and knowledgeable. She added tremendously to our overall dining experience."

"And the food?" questioned Brie.

"The filet mignon and lobster tail were grilled to perfection. It was impeccable, delectable, and truly a culinary delight," he described, "Antoine did an excellent job. Overall, I give it a five out of five."

Brie beamed.

"We are still meeting the staff tomorrow afternoon?"

"Yes, at four thirty. You will meet the evening staff before their shift begins, then at five thirty, the afternoon staff once theirs finishes."

"Oh, good," he replied.

"Then we are meeting Aidan's family after dinner for drinks at the Bamboo."

Chapter 36

Two Weeks Earlier: Wednesday, July 29

Brieanne and her parents were the last to arrive at the Bamboo Beach Bar & Grill and were introduced to Aidan's family. Also there was Bella, Ben, Jen, Harriett, and George.

"How did it go at the restaurant?" whispered Aidan to Brieanne.

"Really well," she said with a little chuckle, "some of the staff's faces were hilarious when they found out who the Anderson's were, especially Jess's."

"What was Kelly's face like?"

"She doesn't know yet, it was her day off," explained Brieanne. "Those people will have to meet him over the next few days."

"She won't have to wait that long?"

"She won't?" questioned Brieanne.

"Scott wanted to meet and buy us a drink. I told him we would be here. They're on their way," said Aidan, suddenly spotting them. "Here they are now."

Kelly and Scott came over to the table and sat next to Brieanne and Aidan who introduced them to the people they didn't know.

Kelly gave a surprised look. "Mr. and Mrs. Anderson," said Kelly, "how lovely to see you again."

Everyone gave her a funny look, even her boyfriend Scott, who knew Brie's parents.

Brie explained Kelly's confusion as her face went flush.

"Brie, they're your parents?" asked Kelly looking at her.

"Sorry about that," she replied. "My dad's idea."

"My dear, as I have already told Brieanne, your service was excellent!" said Brien.

"Thank you," she replied looking at him then over at Brie. "Is that why you changed my section?" she asked in a quiet voice.

"Yes," she whispered back, "first, you are one of our best servers, and second, a huge tip."

"It was an unbelievable tip," said Kelly, who glanced over at Aidan, then Brie. "Did both of you plan this?"

"You could say that," said Brie with a grin.

"Thank you," she said happily, "that tip made my night, my week!"

"I'm sure you deserved it," replied Brie.

The group drank, talked, and laughed for several hours before slowly dispersing for home.

Brieanne kept the lights off on the deck and walked with Aidan to the shallow end where she undressed and stepped into the pool. Aidan did the same. Brieanne assumed her favorite pool position and moaned as she felt his manhood slide inside her. After they made love, they dried off, and went to bed. Aidan held her closely as Brieanne cuddled into him. She thought about how flawless last night and tonight had gone. How much her parents liked Aidan and his family; and how much his liked her and her parents. As Brieanne rested her head on his chest she thought about how deeply in love she was with him and knew in her heart they would always be together, forever. She gently kissed his chest then blissfully drifted off to sleep.

Chapter 37

Ben had finished his final day of tests. Aidan told him to come back in an hour while he got all his paperwork together and put it into a binder. When he did, Aidan went through the test results with him, ending by telling him he got a perfect score, and showed him his A+ on the front page of his binder. Ben gave Aidan a hug thanking him for his help then looked at him quietly.

"What is it?" asked Aidan.

"I liked coming over and being with you," said Ben, "now I don't have a reason to."

"You don't need one." confirmed Aidan. "We still have lots of summer left to go fishing, and we can read some more comics if you like. I'm right next door."

"I know, that's what I like most," said Ben, "having you and Brie close by."

That evening they had the Pizza Party at DeLosa's to celebrate Ben's accomplishment. After the scrumptious pizza and cake, Ben read a thank you note he had written out loud. "I want to thank Aidan for helping me with my spelling and reading and taking me fishing. You are my superhero and I love you. I want to thank Eric for the comics, we had a lot of fun reading them, and for the fishing stuff we had a lot of fun catching fish. I want to thank my family for sharing this happy day with me, Love Ben xoxo."

Brieanne teary-eyed looked at Aidan whispering, "'my superhero and I love you,' how sweet is that?"

Aidan smiled at her; there was no doubt he and Ben had formed a very special bond.

Ben put his card down and opened his gifts. Brie, Jen, and Maddy gave him a special framed diploma which they had made for him, that said congratulations, along with a picture of him and a fish he caught, and a big A+. From the others, he received comic books, storybooks, gift cards, fishing accessories, money, and candies. Then it was off to the arcade at Beach Fun & Games where the adults had as much fun as the children.

Early the next morning Aidan and Brieanne walked over to the marina and met up with their group.

"This is the boat?" asked Aidan glancing up then back at Brieanne.

"This is it," she confirmed, "all forty-five feet of her."

"I knew it would be big, but I didn't know it was going to be this big," he said with a smile.

Eric took them out to the Gulf stopping at all the fishing spots he knew. With the exception of the older women, who took over from Stacy to serve food, drinks, and chat, everyone fished. At every stop, Eric was all over the boat helping the children reel in their catches and remove the gray snapper, Key West grunts, porgies, or sea bass from their lines. Some of the more experienced anglers also caught grouper and hogfish.

At lunch time, Eric took them close to the coast, and down to St. Pete were Brieanne and Aidan pointed out Crabby Bill's. Then turned around and headed north passed Madeira Beach to Sand Key Park and Clearwater where a pod of dolphins followed them. Eric pulled in close to the shore to let people swim and cool off before taking them back out to fish. He ended the trip by taking them through the causeway and back to the dock.

Once the boat was tied up, Eric, with the help of Brien and Paul, filleted all the small fish and put them into a cooler along with a few larger ones for Brieanne's dinner party. The remainder of the larger fish were left intact and divided between the couples. As they helped Eric clean up, he estimated they had caught over one hundred of the smaller, one-to-three-pound fish, and over two dozen of the larger ones. With everything done, they went back to Brieanne's.

Her dad took over the stove, where he baked, pan-seared, and deep-fried the fillets, using several of his secret sauces. Next to him Anne,

Theresa, and Amy helped make salads and rice. While outside, Brieanne and Aidan grilled fish and vegetables on the BBQ. Everything cooked; they sat outside to enjoy their culinary creations. After dinner, the group went to the beach, strolled along the shoreline, and enjoyed the sunset.

"Aidan," said Bella as she caught with him and Brie, "I wanted to tell you how grateful I am to you for helping Ben with his spelling and reading. I am very proud of what he accomplished and it's all thanks to you.

"You're welcome," replied Aidan. "Ben really worked hard and took the time out of his summer to meet with me, it's very admirable."

"It is," said Bella. "I've also seen a change in him. He's more confident, happier, and has come out of his shell. I believe the time you have all spent together has contributed to these positive changes," she explained. "I wanted to tell you all this last night at his party but there was so much going on, I thought it best I do it when we had more time to talk," she said gently squeezing his arm. "Thank you again, Aidan, from the bottom of my heart."

"It was my pleasure," replied Aidan, "he's a wonderful boy."

"He is," she said and left them to walk with Anne and Theresa.

"Ben has really taken a liking to you," said Brieanne. "That note he wrote were he said you were his superhero and that he loved you, it was very touching."

"It was," said Aidan looking over at him. "I'm glad everything turned out all right for him. I'm sure his confidence with carry on into the school year and he will do well."

"That's all because of you," she said, stopping, and running her fingers through his soft hair.

"Thank you," he said with a smile. "And what about you? You take excellent care of Jen and Ben; I can see why they both love you so dearly."

"I try," she said humbly.

Aidan gave her a frown. "I think try is a vast understatement on your part, you exceed. They couldn't have a better role model."

"That's kind of you to say," she replied. "I have to admit all the things we have done with the kids have been a lot of fun. And to me, personally, it's like having a preview of what it would be like to have our own little family. It's been incredibly special and enlightening."

"I believe you would make an excellent mother."

"And you an excellent father," she said moving close to him. "Do you want a French lesson?" she whispered.

"You know I do," he replied.

Brieanne kissed him. "I love you Aidan," she whispered, never wanting anyone as much as she wanted him.

"I love you, Brieanne," he replied, knowing his heart was all hers.

Chapter 38

Saturday afternoon Aidan had his family and Brieanne's parents over for dinner at his place. It was a chance for Brieanne to proudly show off her newly finished house.

"This looks gorgeous," said Jane, "you have really done a lot to it since we helped out."

"Come outside and see this," she said grabbing her hand and taking her down to the lower deck.

"You built a deck!" exclaimed Jane "What a brilliant idea. I love it! I love it all!"

"I wouldn't have been able to do it without this wonderful man," said Brieanne as Aidan and Steven joined them.

"I'm sure he got all his inspiration from you," said Jane admiring her.

"After seeing the before and after pictures of this place it's night and day," complimented Steven. "You did a fantastic job."

"Thank you," said Brieanne, noticing Aidan's parents, aunt, and uncle. "Time to start the next tour," she said excitedly and excused herself pulling Aidan with her.

As soon as they finished, Brieanne's parents arrived, and Brieanne along with Aidan, gave them the final tour of the afternoon before joining the group on the lower deck.

"So, tomorrow is your last full day?" asked Brieanne.

"Yes, we leave Monday before dinner," replied Jane. "You're joining us on the beach tomorrow and at pool for drinks in the evening?"

"We will be there."

"And your parents are coming tomorrow evening?"

"They are," confirmed Brieanne.

"That's wonderful," said Jane looking at her. "You should try come and visit us on Canandaigua Lake. Maddy and Ethan were telling us how you were all talking about the New York State Fair."

"We were," said Brieanne interestedly.

"Then you and Aidan should come and stay with us, if not for the week, at least for a long weekend."

"I would love that," said Brieanne feeling that her and Aidan's relationship was evolving to the next step.

"Consider it a formal invite," she said reaching for her hand and squeezing it. "I'll mention it to Aidan."

"Thank you," said Brieanne cheerfully.

Jane then looked at Brieanne inquisitively. "Maddy and Ethan also mentioned that Jen and Ben were extremely excited about the fair and were talking about how they would like them to come, also. Is that a possibility?"

"I'm not sure," she answered slowly. "I can mention it to Bella, she seems tired these days, and maybe she could do with a break."

"It's up to you. I didn't mean to put you on the spot. I told the children I would mention it to you," said Jane, thinking. "Then again, maybe you and Aidan may want to experience things as a couple first and come on your own."

"It would be lovely just the two of us going away," said Brieanne, "and at the same time, it would be fun to have the four children attend the fair."

"You have a chat with Aidan and decide what's best," said Jane.

"I will."

"Steven loves that hot tub," said Jane looking over into Brieanne's yard. "Don't believe him for a minute when he says he is just going over there to keep an eye on the children while they swim," she said with a chuckle. "Thankfully he will have his own hot tub soon enough."

"Are you guys putting in a hot tub?"

"Oh no, we are moving into my parent's place and renting out the house we currently live in," explained Jane, "and they have one there."

She suddenly realized she said too much and wondered if Brieanne had caught on.

"Oh, that's wonderful," said Brieanne. "Is it a big place?"

"It is," said Jane changing the subject. "Where is Bella today?"

"She dropped in earlier before you arrived. I gave her and the children a tour of the house then said she was going home to take it easy and have a rest."

Jane looked over at Jen and Ben in the pool. "At her age it would be much more difficult to take care of the children on her own," said Jane bluntly, "she is lucky she has you."

"She does her best," said Brieanne supportively.

"She isn't going to be able to keep doing it much longer," predicted Jane. "We have two the same age and by the end of the day Steven and I are exhausted."

"I know what you mean" agreed Brieanne. "I'm not sure what here plan is?"

"If she was smart, she would give them to you, and let you raise them," said Jane, frankly.

"Do you think so?" asked Brieanne perking up.

Jane sat up. "Those kids adore you, you obviously adore them, and you can provide for them. You're young and full of energy," summarized Jane. "In saying that, you are young, single, and dating my brother. Maybe that is more the lifestyle you want, for now, Aidan also."

"Maybe," replied Brieanne. "I love your brother dearly and I love Jen and Ben."

"Time will tell," said Jane lightening up the subject. "Everything happens for a reason."

But those reasons are yours to decide, thought Brieanne.

"That was a great evening," said Aidan.

"It was," agreed Brieanne.

"I really love this deck, it's like you, perfect," he said leaning over to kiss her.

"You say the sweetest things," she replied kissing him. "Look how clear the night sky is," she said sitting back, "the stars look so beautiful." Then suddenly remembering something she looked over at him and grabbed his hand. "Your sister invited us to visit them at the end of summer," Brieanne blurted out, trying to contain her excitement.

"I know, she mentioned it to me," Aidan said nonchalantly.

"Oh," said Brieanne unsettled by his response.

"I said, nah, we're not interested," continued Aidan straight-faced.

Brieanne glared at him. "You did what? Why?"

"If I take you there, people may think we are moving our dating to the next level."

Brieanne wasn't sure if he was serious or joking, judging by his tone he was serious. She was about to say something until he turned around and gave her a goofy face.

"You, you," she said standing, placing her hands gently around his neck.

"Filthy Scallywag," he choked out.

"Most definitely," she said removing her hands and sitting on her lap. "What did you tell her?"

"I told Jane and Steven, that we would love to visit, and that you and Jane can make all the preliminary arrangements tomorrow."

Brieanne was ecstatic. "I love you."

"Even my sense of humor."

"Eh, not so much," she replied giggling.

"I love you."

Brieanne kissed him, then snuggled into him as they watched the stars in the sky gently twinkle.

Chapter 39

Brieanne, Aidan, Jen, and Ben walked along the shoreline joining Aidan's family on the beach in front of their condo.

"Bella's not coming?" asked Theresa.

"No, she is tired," explained Brieanne. "She may come a little later or this evening for drinks by your pool."

"As long as she is okay," said Theresa, concerned for her.

"I think so," replied Brieanne, unsure.

"Come lie next to me," said Jane to Brieanne as they watched Aidan and Steven take the kids to the water. "Aidan texted me this morning saying you guys will be coming to the fair."

"Yes, we are," replied Brieanne, "he said you and I should make some preliminary plans."

"I have some information here," revealed Jane pulling out a sheet of paper. "The fair runs for thirteen days and finishes on Labor Day. You need to look at a calendar, decide when you want to come and for how long, then book a flight. You can come for the thirteen days, longer or shorter, just let us know. We can pick you up from the airport," said Jane receptively.

"I'll talk with Aidan," said Brieanne happily.

"Did you two talk about Jen and Ben coming?"

"No, we didn't. I was so happy we were coming that I forgot to bring it up," she said candidly.

"Maybe this time you may want to come just as a couple," suggested Jane.

"Maybe," replied Brieanne, deciding she would discuss the trip with him tomorrow since they had the day to themselves.

After spending the afternoon on the beach Brieanne, Aidan, Jen and Ben said bye and went back to Brieanne's for dinner. They ate and Brieanne told the children she would pick them up in an hour as she watched them run home. Aidan said he was also going to get ready and would be back in thirty minutes. Brieanne kissed him, watched him walk through his backyard, before going inside. She tidied up the kitchen for several minutes, was about to go upstairs, when suddenly there was a knock on the front door.

"Eric," she said. "Is everything okay? Is Stacy okay?"

"We're good," he said. "I'm glad I caught you in, I wanted to talk to you for a few minutes about Aidan, there is something I need to tell you."

"Come in," she said.

Eric followed her to the kitchen. "I wanted to say I'm sorry about the way I have been on your back about Aidan," he confessed. "When I first met him, I did actually like him, and I must admit the way he told the mattress story was pretty funny. But for some reason I decided if I start liking him and he turns out to be a creep then I've let you down by not protecting you from him."

Brie thought he had always liked Aidan. "You don't need to protect me from him anymore, I love and care for him deeply, and he does me," she explained.

"I know," he said, "I just don't like us not being friends."

"I know me either," said Brie as she opened the patio door and went outside to get some air.

Aidan showered, dressed, and was early, and decided to take a quick stroll to the shoreline. He was close to Brieanne's back gate when heard her and Eric walk out onto the deck.

"I just wanted to come over to let you know I am sorry," said Eric. "It was all my fault I should have been honest with you from the beginning."

"I understand," said Brie. "Does Stacy know about our conversations?"

"No, none of them, I didn't want to come across as being a total jerk."

"I understand," said Brie.

"I won't you back in my life," he pleaded, "I don't like it when you aren't, and we fight."

"I know, it's been difficult for me, too," she said sympathetically and appreciating his honesty.

"Brie, you know I love you and care about you," said Eric, "the last thing I want to do is hurt you or screw this up."

"Either do I," she said, happy they had talked.

Eric walked over to Brie, held her, and then put his arm around her as they went inside.

Aidan slowly walked to the beach; he wasn't sure what to make of what he heard and seen. Surely, they weren't having an affair, he would know, right. Then again if his past was any indication, maybe he wouldn't.

Brie closed the patio door. "If you promise me you will stop looking out for me, and protecting me, then I would like us to be friends again."

"I promise," said Eric.

"All right," said Brie walking him to the front the door. "Thanks for coming over and being honesty with me Eric."

"Thanks, Brie," he replied optimistically. "Goodnight."

"Goodnight," she said closing the door behind him. Brieanne's phone rang. "Hi, Mom."

Aidan decided to text Brieanne: "Are you ready?"

Brieanne spoke with her mom for twenty minutes, then told her she had to go, she was already late. Hanging up she noticed a text from Aidan and replied: "Sorry, was delayed, getting in the shower now."

Aidan: "Everything okay?"

Brieanne: "Yeah, come over in twenty."

Aidan sat on the beach wondering why she never mentioned Eric and what they had been doing for the last twenty minutes. He gave her the benefit of the doubt and decided to wait to see if she mentioned it tonight or maybe tomorrow when they were alone. Twenty minutes later he walked onto her deck where she met him with a happy smile and a loving kiss. They picked up the kids, who ran ahead, as they meandered to the condo.

"Bella said she may show up later," said Brieanne as she put her arm through his. "I've got this strange feeling something is up."

"Like what?"

"I don't know," she said unsure, but alarmed.

As the children swam in the pool, the adults ordered drinks and talked about Jane and Steven's time in Madeira Beach. Shortly after, Jane and Steven excused themselves and went for one last romantic walk along the beach to watch the sunset.

Brieanne moved her chair close to Aidan's and put her head on his shoulder as he put his arm around her.

"I don't think we've missed too many sunsets ourselves," she whispered.

"No, we haven't," agreed Aidan. "All of them as special as the last one."

She moved her head, looked into his eyes. "That's a nice sentiment."

Aidan kissed her softly, she kissed him back, then put her head back on his shoulder.

"We haven't missed too many sunrises either," whispered Aidan, in reference to their love making.

"No, we haven't." she whispered back, "all of those are special too." She went quiet as she thought about them making love and all the sunsets and sunrises they have shared together, and softly said, "Aidan, I will love you, till the day I die."

Aidan kissed the top of her head. "Me too," he whispered back.

Bella showed up an hour later to say goodbye to Jane, Steven, and the children, and to pick up Jen and Ben. She wasn't her usual outgoing self, leaving as abruptly as she arrived. Everyone put it down to her being tired although Brieanne sensed it was something else.

Brieanne and Aidan said their goodbyes and decided to go for a long walk on the beach. They headed north holding hands in silence, enjoying the moment, and the sound of the waves. After a while they turned around, past the condo, and up the path to her place. They went upstairs to

Brieanne's room where she changed while Aidan sat on her balcony and had a wine.

"Do you remember when we first met at the restaurant?" she said picking up her wine and sitting next to him. "I think I fell in love with you, right then and there," she admitted.

"Did you know I was checking out you bum when you were showing me to the table?" he queried.

Brieanne laughed. "Now that I think back, yeah, I do recall feeling your eyes all over my backside."

"It was a pretty sight."

"So, what you are saying is, while I fell in love with you, you fell in love with my bum."

"Pretty much," said Aidan with a mischievous grin.

"Oh please, "she said snickering and sipping her wine.

"I fell in love with you the second I met you," he said truthfully. "I was hoping you were going to be there that Friday night."

"Why didn't you ask for my number?"

"You offered me a ride to my berth I didn't want you to think it was a mutiny when I asked for your phone number, "he explained.

She looked at him laughing. "Berth? Mutiny?"

"What can I say? I'm a Scallywag at heart."

"Well, Scallywag, maybe you would like to go down on my lower deck?" she asked suggestively.

Aidan didn't need to be asked twice. Taking Brieanne into her room he lifted up her T-shirt, removed her panties then kissed his way from her toes, up to her lower deck.

Chapter 40

"Bacon, eggs, and pancakes," said Brieanne as Aidan walked into the kitchen, "orange juice and coffee."

"It looks delicious," he said sitting at the breakfast counter and waiting for her to join him.

"Well," she said eating, "we have no house to fix up, and most of the month of August is left to enjoy. I was thinking we could go sightseeing, visit historical sites, shop, go to different beaches, experience different restaurants; that sort of thing."

"I would like that," said Aidan, "and ride the trolley again."

"Yeah, for sure, that was fun."

"Maybe we could do that sunset cruise?"

"Yes, definitely," she replied cheerfully.

"With that being said, what would you like to do on this beautiful Monday morning?" asked Aidan.

"Well, I would like to talk to you about Canandaigua Lake and the New York State Fair," Brieanne replied. "Jane has given me information on it."

"Did you want to talk here? On the beach? Go somewhere?"

"Let's get ready, head to somewhere that's fun, and we can talk on the trolley on the way, like we used to."

"I like the sound of that."

They finished their breakfast. Aidan went home, changed, and met Brieanne thirty minutes later in her living room.

"Ready," she said as the doorbell rang. "Bella," she said, "come on in."

"I knocked next door at Aidan's but there was no answer," she said walking in.

"He's here," said Brie motioning towards him.

"Good," she said nervously. "I need to speak to you both."

"Let's sit in the living room. Can I get you something? Coffee?"

"No, thank you, I'm fine," Bella replied sitting.

"Okay," said Brie sitting next to her and waiting for Aidan to sit in the armchair. "Are you okay?"

"Yes," she said slowly, "I have something that I need to tell you both."

"We're listening," said Brie with a smile.

"The children and I are leaving tomorrow."

"On a vacation," said Brie. "For how long?"

"Not a vacation we're moving."

"What?" asked Brie, not sure she had heard her correctly. "Why?"

"There are a couple of reasons: school starts next week, and I need them to be there for that; and secondly, I am selling the house."

"Hold on a second," said Brie. "School, there? Where?"

"Originally, I was going to take them to live with me in Orlando, but my sister's daughter, my niece, lives in Jacksonville with her husband and two children. So, I am going to let Jen and Ben live there, with them."

"Why?" asked Brie getting upset.

"This year, especially this summer, I realized that I am too old to take care of them and give them all the attention they require. They need younger people, a younger couple, who have more energy, who can meet their needs. And since they are not going to be living in the house, I need to sell it, and put money away in a trust fund for them for college. Of course, I will also be giving a little to my niece's family to help them out initially, not much, but something. The remainder of the money I am using to pay off expenses that I have occurred since I moved here, some quite sizeable."

"If money is the problem, I will buy your house right now. You can live there rent free," said Brie getting worried.

"Brie, I know you would. My biggest concern is getting the children into a family environment. I need a couple that will take care of them and be able to keep up with them."

Brie became terribly upset. "Why wouldn't you consider me? I have known those children all their lives. I have taken care of them since April died. I dropped them off at school, tended to them when they were sick, made their lunches, bought school supplies, clothing, homework, and took them to appointments. I did that! Me! Why wouldn't you consider me?"

"Brie," said Bella in a calm voice, "you have been an immense help to the children and me, more than I can say, but you are a single woman who has her whole life in front of her. These children need a family and a stable environment. My niece can give them all that."

"Oh, so the person the children love is not good enough for them because she is single. And just forget about what I've done for them these past eighteen months, in fact, since they were born!"

"Would you deny the kids a home with a family?"

"Where was this family when April was passed out drunk on the floor, talking about killing herself? Who put those children under her roof while she tried to get April better? Me, that's who, me!" said Brie standing up now pacing.

"Let's talk about this time last summer, that boyfriend you had," said Bella. "He wasn't a nice boy. He was arrogant, selfish, and he didn't like children. If you—"

"That's all in the past," said Brie angrily.

"What happens if you meet someone like that going forward?"

Brie wasn't sure why she would say that with Aidan sitting right there. "I have Aidan."

"And he is a lovely man," she said smiling at him then looked back at Brie. "Since you brought him up, what plans do you two have for the future?"

Brie went silent momentarily. "What do you mean plans; we only started dating? We're just getting to know one another."

"So, you date and if it works out, then what?"

"I don't know, we never talked about it."

"Brie I will admit they are extremely attached to you, and over these last several weeks, Aidan also. But what happens if I give you the children and you break up months down the road? How heartbroken will they be then?"

Brie was silent.

"Let's say they continue to stay with you after that, and you meet another man, and it doesn't work out, what then? What kind of environment would that be for the children? Is that what you want for them?"

"What you want are guarantees," said Brie. "There are no guarantees that your niece's marriage won't end."

"No, but they have been married for quite some time, have two children, and our settled. That to me is far less of a risk."

"So, I'm a high risk, am I?" Brie snapped back angrily then looked at Aidan. "Say something!"

Bella looked at Aidan. "I didn't want to pull you into this. The reason I wanted you here is to let you know we are moving and to be here to comfort Brie."

"I understand," replied Aidan.

"That's it!" shouted Brieanne at him.

"Brie, this is not his fault," said Bella, "but if you feel he should be helping you out let me ask him some questions." Bella looked at Aidan and asked, "if that is okay?"

"It's okay."

"Are you planning on living here?"

"I don't know."

"Are you planning on moving here eventually?"

"I don't know."

Brieanne shook her head in disbelief. "What do you mean you don't know?"

"Bella just asked you before what our plans were. You replied what do you mean plans, we only started dating, we are just getting to know one another, and have never talked about it."

"I know what I said!" she replied angrily.

"Then how could I possibly give her a different answer. It would be a total contradiction to what you said."

Brieanne went quiet again.

"Aidan, I have a few more questions," stated Bella. "Did you know that Brie wanted to take responsibility for those two children?"

"No," he replied.

"And if I handed her the two children tomorrow and moved away, is this something you want? Are you ready for that lifestyle, that commitment, that responsibility?"

Aidan thought. "Bella, I love both those children dearly, I have to be honest it's not something I was expecting or prepared for."

"How can you say that? I told you weeks ago that I was going to promote Bev and Cathy so I would spend less time at work and be here to take care of those two children," said Brieanne shouting at Aidan before suddenly realizing she had let something slip.

"What?" asked Aidan thinking back. "You told me that you didn't want to lose Bev and Cathy, and were thinking of giving them a promotion, which would allow you to spend less time at work. You never mentioned you were doing it for the children."

Brieanne said nothing.

"In fact, now that I think about it, you told me that you had been considering promoting them before I even met me. Which means you knew all along you were doing it for the simple reason of freeing up your time to get those children."

"No, it wasn't like that," said Brieanne faltering.

Aidan looked at Bella. "Did you know about her plan on promoting Bev and Cathy?"

Bella shook her head no.

Aidan calculated in his mind when Brieanne had told him and when she had originally thought of the promotions. "Bella, in June, did you tell Brieanne that you were thinking about moving with the children?"

Bella nodded her head yes. "It was a very distant thought, and I was strongly considering leaving the children with Brie," she explained. Bella now felt awful because of the direction this had gone between Brie and Aidan.

"Well, I'm going to tell you something that neither of you know," said Brie. "The day after April died, I found her will in an envelope, it was just lying there on her dresser. I opened it up and read it. It stated that April wanted me to have the children," claimed Brie. "I put the will back inside the envelope and placed it where I had found it. A couple of days later it was gone. Bella you took that will and have never mentioned April's dying wish to me."

Aidan looked over at Bella. "Is that true?"

"That part is true," she admitted, "I hadn't realized until now Brie had read it. April did say that she wanted Brie to have the children on the one condition that I thought she was capable of providing them a solid, family environment."

"There are millions of single moms out there that are fantastic mothers, who love their children, and take care of them day after day," said Brie. "They give them a solid, family environment!"

"I'm not denying that," Bella replied standing. "All I have made clear to you is that Jen and Ben's family in Jacksonville can give them a stable family environment. "You and Aidan have no immediate plans, which is the way it should be for a couple, in love and dating. You have the rest of your lives to figure things out. Unfortunately, I don't have the luxury of time, neither do Jen and Ben," summarized Bella going to the door and opening it.

"Have you told them yet?" asked Brie in a quiet voice as she sat.

"I'm going back to the house to do just that," she said sadly, closing the door behind her.

Aidan stood up to leave.

"Why didn't you say something to her?" asked Brieanne.

"Why didn't you tell me the real reason behind your promotion plan was to free up your time to get the children and take care of them?" asked Aidan.

"You let me down," she said unhappily. "You said you would always be there for me."

"No," he said shaking his head, "I think you mean, you let us down."

"Get out!" she screamed walking over to the door and opening it. "Get out!" Brieanne watched him leave, slammed it, and then fell to the floor crying.

Aidan walked down Brieanne's driveway, saw Bella in the distance, and called out her name.

Bella turned around and waited. "Yes, Aidan?" she asked wiping her tears away.

"What time are you leaving tomorrow?"

"Around one."

"Can I come over say around twelve and say bye?"

"That's fine."

"Do you need any help loading the car?"

"I'm only taking luggage, if you could help me with that, I would appreciate it."

"No problem," said Aidan. "What about your furniture?"

"Joyce told me if I didn't need it, I would be better off leaving it in the house till it sold. She said furniture would help it sell quicker," she explained. "There are some items I want, others I don't. If the new buyers want to purchase them, I will sell them, otherwise I will have them shipped to Orlando and sell them there."

Aidan suddenly realized this is what she must have been doing on the weekend when she wasn't around. "When is Joyce putting it up for sale?"

"Friday."

Aidan looked at her. "Can I ask you one favor?"

"Of course."

"After you tell the children, can you let them go over to Brieanne's and have a sleepover with her?"

"I'm sure the children would like that," she said studying him for a long while. "You are a good man Aidan and Brie is a good woman. Don't waste too much time on plans; at the end of the day actions are what matter," she said before turning around onto her driveway and going into her house.

As he walked away, Aidan wasn't sure what she had meant by that. He went upstairs, lay on his bed, and thought of what had just happened between him and Brieanne.

Brieanne got up off the floor, went to her bedroom, and flopped on the bed. Everything was such a mess. They were supposed to be riding the trolley and talking about the New York State Fair. How happy they would be. Look at us now, she thought, and sobbed.

An hour later, Aidan heard Jen and Ben running past his backyard crying and calling out her name.

As Brie lay restless next to the sound asleep children, she realized this was the first night in a very long time that her and Aidan had slept in separate beds; she missed him terribly.

Chapter 41

The next morning Aidan heard Brieanne walking with the children to their back gate and listened to their tearful goodbyes. Bella came out to talk to Brie, from what he could tell she walked away from her. As she did, Aidan could see in Brieanne's face, she was heartbroken.

At twelve Aidan went outside onto the driveway and met Bella. The children ran to Aidan crying and hugged him tightly.

Last night the children had told Brie about saying goodbye to Aidan at lunchtime. So, she watched and listened through the street-side balcony door.

"You two take care of yourself," said Aidan, "and take care of your grandmother."

"We will," said Jan.

"Why are you letting us go?" asked Ben wiping his eyes.

"Your grandmother has plans for you to live with your relatives. They're a family and have two children around you age."

"I know where we are going," he stated. "I'm asking you, why are you letting us go?"

"Why didn't you want us to stay?" added Jen.

"I do want you to stay," said Aidan.

"Then why didn't you say that to my grandma?" asked Ben.

"Your grandma is your guardian and it's her decision to make, not mine."

"You could have said you wanted us to stay. You could have told her and tried to make her change her mind," said Ben starting to sob.

"Aidan why didn't you fight for us?" asked Jen crying.

"I…I," said Aidan looking for an answer. "It's more complicated than that."

"Brie told us she fought for us, and you just sat there and said nothing," said Jen. "She told Grandmother she would take us and that we could live with her, you said nothing."

"Because she loves us, and you don't!" said Ben. "I thought you loved us! I thought you were my superhero!"

Aidan was holding back his tears. "I do love you."

"No, you don't!" yelled Ben. "And I don't love you anymore! I hate you! I hate you!"

"Ben!" said Jen, "Don't say things you don't mean."

"I do mean it!" send Ben crying and running to his house as Jen giving chase.

Aidan wiped the tears from his eyes, quietly went over to her driveway, picked up the luggage and loaded up her car. Then looked at Bella, "are you sure you are doing the right thing for those children?"

Bella looked at him sadly. "I don't know if I am doing the right thing," she admitted, "I know I am doing the best thing."

"I understand," said Aidan giving her a hug then turning toward his front door.

Jen chased Ben into the house and found him lying on his bed. "Ben," said Jen sitting down next to him. "Ben, you don't want your last words with Aidan to be that you hate him, do you?"

"I thought me, you, Aidan, and Brie, were going to be a family. That Maddy and Ethan would be our cousins. We hardly ever see our cousins, ever," said Ben between sobs. "And I thought Aidan's parents and Brie's parents would be our grandparents, too, and we would have aunts and uncles," he said sobbing. "I thought I would have a family."

"I know," said Jen, "so did I."

"So, did Maddy and Ethan," said Ben sitting up, "remember, we talked about it all the time. About us visiting them in New York and going to the fair."

"I remember, but we have to leave now," said Jen. "You are upset, and Aidan is upset, too. Do you want to leave with him thinking that you hate him?"

"No," said Ben wiping his tears.

"Don't you think you should tell him that before you leave?" suggested Jen. "He may go if you don't hurry."

Ben jumped off the bed, ran out of the house, and passed his grandmother screaming Aidan's name.

Aidan was almost at the front door when he heard Ben calling him and turned around.

"Aidan," said Ben running into his outstretched arms. "I love you; I love you, I'm sorry I said I hated you I never meant that," he sobbed.

Jen ran and hugged Aidan. "I love you, too."

Tears streamed down Aidan's face as he kissed them both. Bella, witnessing what was happening, went onto her driveway to cry.

"Listen, I will keep in touch with you both. I'll come visit you and you can come visit me," promised Aidan.

"Do you promise?" asked Ben.

"I promise," said Aidan.

"Cross your heart and hope to die?" asked Jen.

"Cross my heart and hope to die," he repeated.

Aidan walked them to the car, gave them a hug and kiss, and watched them climb in. Then went over to Bella, hugged her, and waved goodbye as the car drove away. Aidan turned around and slowly walked up his driveway.

Brieanne could see the pain in his face and wiped the tears streaming down hers. She closed the door, went through her bedroom, and sat on her balcony.

Aidan went inside, upstairs through his bedroom, and sat on his.

They sat silently for an hour, staring out, neither of them realizing they were both looking at the same horizon.

Chapter 42

An hour later, Brieanne left the balcony, picked up her phone and texted Aidan: "We need to talk!"

Aidan: "Okay. Where? When?"

Brieanne: "My place in thirty minutes."

Aidan: "I will see you then."

Brieanne opened the front door. He followed her into the living room and sat in the armchair while she sat on the couch.

"I am so upset with you," she began, civilly. "I thought you would support me, have my back, you let me down."

Aidan suddenly realized she was blaming him for all this. "Actually Bella, the children's guardian, made a decision based on their best interests."

"Maybe if you would have stood at my side and told her that you wanted the children to stay, she may have changed her mind."

"You wanted me to tell her to leave the children here?"

"Yes."

"With you?"

"Yes."

"And what about me, you, and our relationship?"

"What do you mean?"

"We just agreed to start dating, the next minute you have two children, and you expect me to go along with it. Like I don't have a say in it."

"But you love children, you teach them," she said. "I've seen you playing with Maddy, Ethan, Jen, Ben, and the brothers at the pool. You're great with them."

"Yes, I do like children, but after I teach them at school, play with them at the pool or have sleepovers, they all have one thing in common."

"What's that?"

"They all end up going home to their parents, to their families."

"So, Ben and Jen mean nothing to you, they're just tools for you to show off your teaching skills and playfulness?"

Aidan ignored her sarcasm. "Of course, they mean something more to me than that, but they have a home with a grandmother who takes care of them. My role with Ben and Jen was to be a teacher and a friend, and to Maddy and Ethan an uncle, never anything more. Who am I to assume that Ben and Jen needed or wanted something more?"

Brieanne looked at him silently.

"Did you ever look at it from my perspective?" he asked. "Maybe I don't want to, or I'm not ready, to date a woman who has children."

"Oh, so you wouldn't date a single mother?"

"Here you go again with your single mother line," he said shaking his head. "My point is that if I met a woman who had children it would be my decision whether or not that would be something I would be okay with. Just as it would be that woman's choice to determine whether she's the type of man she wants to date and be around her children. There's a lot more to it than what you're implying," he said. "And newsflash, we are two single people dating; you're not a single mother."

"Don't talk down to me," she said, "it's not like I haven't thought this through."

"That just brings up another interesting point," he said holding back his anger. "Why didn't you tell me about the possibility of you getting the children?"

Brieanne stumbled for words. "I should have told you."

"The reason you didn't is because you preferred to lie, trick, and manipulate me!"

"No, I didn't," she said defensively.

"No," said Aidan with a sarcastic laugh. "I was going to move into a condo resort across the street, you told me to move in here. Bella told you about Ben's problem with spelling and reading, you said to ask me to help, knowing I would. You moved me right next door to Ben and Jen and used me to help you get them."

"That's not true," she said panicking, "those things just happened that way, I didn't plan that."

"You never thought that me moving in next door, teaching Ben, spending time with him and Jen, and with you, wasn't going to help you get guardianship of those children?"

"No, I didn't, but when it started going that direction, I thought maybe it would," she said upset, and then looked straight at him. "So yes, I thought it would help me, are you happy now? Is there anything wrong with me giving these kids a better happier life, a brighter future, and my love?"

"Of course not," he said staring at her. "You just don't get it!"

"Tell me then! Tell me what I don't get!" she yelled.

"Yesterday morning we talked about spending August together and going to New York to visit my family. There was no mention of children," said Aidan, calming down. "You have never included me in your plan to get those children, and I repeat, your plan, never ours. So, why not?"

She had no answer.

"If yesterday, Bella had said okay kids you can move in with Brieanne, what would have happened to us? To the life we live? Going sightseeing and spending the rest of the summer together? What about us?" Aidan was raising his voice and took a deep breath. "You never thought once to include me, you lied to me, and you used me for your own benefit…and Brieanne…you chose those children over me. If they would have moved in yesterday and I said I didn't want to have that responsibility, what would you have done? Given them back to Bella to keep me or let me go?"

"It wasn't like that…I thought everything would work itself out and we would all be together as a family."

"And in there lies the problem because it was, 'I thought'" he said emphasizing the quotation with his finger as he stood. "Never, we."

"I just didn't think it was that big of a deal me having the children. I thought you would understand, be on my side, and stand up for me."

"Be on your side?" he questioned. "How can I, when you never once let me be on it?" Aidan shook his head in disbelief. "What about me?"

"You?"

"Did you ever once think of me? That maybe I would want you to come live with me somewhere other than here?"

"You never mentioned that, ever," she stated.

"Okay, I will ask you now, would you want to come live with me?" he asked bluntly.

"I…I…I don't know," she mumbled thinking about his question.

"Let me help you with your answer…it's no, because everyone has to make sacrifices for you. I need to live here, Ben and Jen need to live here, and what are you sacrificing…nothing."

"You are being so unfair to me right now."

"Would you rather me live here?" he said looking around. "In your house, surrounded by your things, your furniture? What about my things, my furniture?"

"Everything you see here is bought from a department store, it has no sentimental value to me, of course I would let you have your things here," she said."

"Let me," he repeated.

"Please stop, you are taking everything thing I say out of context and twisting it around to make me look selfish."

"Or maybe, it's because you are just that!"

"I am not selfish!"

Aidan snickered. "I guess you're not a liar either?"

"I've never lied to you!" she said standing up to him.

"Oh really," he said mockingly. "Let me ask you this, have you been seeing Eric behind my back?"

"What? No!" she said wondering why he would even think that.

"Have you ever had conversations with just you and him in private, and in public, for that matter?"

She went quiet. Where was he going with this, she thought.

"I will take that as a yes."

"Take that as, I don't know where you are going with this."

"Let me simplify it for you," he said. "Did you and Eric have a public altercation by the 'John's Pass Boardwalk' sign? Where you said you loved one another, and he would make it up to you?"

"How do you know about that?" she whispered.

"First off it was in a public space, so not too private, more specifically my parents, aunt, and uncle, witnessed it from ten feet away."

"Jane and Steven, too?" she asked.

"No, they weren't there. My parents talked to them about it after because they wanted their advice on whether to tell me or not."

Brieanne suddenly realized something "That night when Jane said to come to the condo pool the following morning, that's when they told you?"

"Yeah," he replied. "I told them you two were probably having a disagreement and not to worry about it. They said okay, and we left it at that."

"It was just that."

"How about this one," said Aidan looking at her. "A few weeks ago, prior to you meeting me on the beach, I came outside my front door, and I heard you two talking again. This time it's about how if Eric keeps this up, he will lose you. How he loves and cares about you. How you love and care about him, too, but he needs to tread carefully. And don't you think Stacy may have something to say about what he is doing? But apparently, Stacy isn't going to find out about this…maybe not from him you say but maybe from someone else."

Brieanne sat down. "So, it wasn't my imagination, I did here the door closing," she said looking at him. "What you heard that was out of context."

"Hold on?" he asked. "There is one more."

One more, she thought, feeling unwell.

"Sunday night after dinner I was ready early and thought I would go for a walk down to the shoreline. I'm walking past your gate and once again you two are talking. Only this time he was sorry, it was his fault. You asked if Stacy knows how he feels, he says no, you say you understand. Eric says he wants you back in his life, how he doesn't like it when you aren't, and when you fight. You say something like, I know, it's been difficult for me, too. Again, he tells you how he loves and cares about you and doesn't want to hurt you or screw this up. You reply, me either…and this is the best part, he gives you a long hug, and you walk arm in arm inside your house."

Brieanne was silent.

"It gets better," he said trying to be calm. "I text you right after and you don't reply. In fact, you don't reply for twenty minutes. When you do you tell me you're just getting into the shower."

Brieanne suddenly realized what he was suggesting and stood up. "You don't think I slept with him? That I'm having an affair with him?"

"After the events of these past two days I don't think that anymore."

Brieanne walked over and slapped his face. "How dare you accuse me? I have explanations for all those conversations and everything you heard was out of context."

Aidan chuckled. "Wow," he said walking backward. "If you had heard me talking and acting that way with another woman, would you had thought any differently than I did? My family obviously thought it; why else would they have mentioned it to me."

Brieanne realized what he was saying was true, but what he thought had happened, wasn't.

"In my heart I didn't believe you would do that," he said looking at her. "What really bothers me is that you and Eric talk that way in private and in public. And what really hurts, is that you never once talked to me about what was going on between you two. You kept me in the dark, just like you did with the children…which makes you untrustworthy and a liar."

"You are a liar, too!" she yelled. "You said you would stand by my side, support me no matter what! The first chance you get to prove that to me, you fail miserably. If you loved me as much as you said you did, you would have shown me, and proved to me that you did. You could have told Bella that I would be an excellent mother to Jen and Ben. You could have said to her she was doing the wrong thing by taking the children away…you could have given me complete happiness…the four of us could have been a family," she sobbed.

Aidan didn't like the truth being thrown at him as he walked toward the door.

"Yeah, "she said looking at him, "walk away you coward!"

Aidan stopped.

"Better still run away! Just like you did in Rochester. Who leaves a house they love and a promotion they wanted? Maybe one day you will have the courage to tell me what really happened up there!"

"You want to know?"

"Yeah, coward, I do. I think I deserve to know. It may help shed some light on who you really are."

Aidan calmed down as he walked back to her then thought momentarily then told her. "My ex-girlfriend, Carly, used to like throwing dinner parties. I didn't mind them at first, but it really wasn't my thing, and I started feeling like the relationship wasn't working out. So, one Friday she had booked a dinner party for around twenty people. I told her I won't be able to make it I have to go visit my parents on Canandaigua Lake. Plus, I had essays that I wanted to mark while I was there. I go into the office to pick up the box the essays were in; she calls me out to help her get some glasses from a cabinet in the kitchen. I put the box down, helped her out, and locked the office forgetting the box of essays. I get to my parents, hang out to do some thinking, and decide when I get home, I'm going to break up with her. On Saturday evening, I realized that I left the essays at the office and get up early Sunday morning to go back to pick them up. I walk in the house, unlock the office, get the box, and carry them out. I notice on the family room coffee table, two glasses and two empty bottles of wine. I put the box down, walk over to the staircase, and littered on the stairs are articles of clothing. I ascend them and follow the trail to the bedroom door, which is ajar," he said reaching for his phone, searching then showing Brieanne a picture.

Brieanne looked at a man with his arm around a woman in bed; she didn't have to ask who she was.

"I took the picture, picked up the box, and left."

"Why didn't you say something to them?"

"I guess in my mind I was going to break up with her, so what was the point."

"Yeah, but she didn't know that."

"To me it wasn't worth it, and I had my reasons."

Brieanne still thought he should have made a scene. "What's selling the house got to do with it?"

Aidan looked extremely uncomfortable. "That Friday she asked to use my house for the dinner party. When I went in to get the essays I was going into my own home. They were in my bed and had been living in my home all weekend."

"Oh," said Brieanne feeling sorry for him.

"I left and stayed at a hotel for a couple of days before I went back. When I did, it was all cleaned up, but to me it felt weird and dirty. I threw my mattress and sheets out, slept in the spare room, and never sat in the living room again," he explained. "It was very difficult for me to live in a house that they had used to have sex in, where they had eaten my food, and drank my booze. It never felt like home again."

"When did you break up with her?"

"She called me that Sunday evening as if nothing had happened. I broke up with her a few days later and told her it wasn't working out."

"Okay, I get you wanting to move, but why did you refuse the promotion?"

"When I applied it was through the school board. The board sent me the job offer via the school. The principal called me in to meet with him and give me the written offer. I said I needed an hour to think about it. I took that hour to write up my letter of resignation and gave it to him."

"Why?"

"The guy in the picture with her, he's the principal."

"Oh no" said Brieanne quietly. "You had to see your ex and her lover every day in school?"

"Yeah, in the hallway, the staff room, at meetings. All the time they acted as if nothing was going on," explained Aidan. "Now, not only did I not want to be in my house any longer, but I also didn't want to be at my workplace either. So yeah, I ran away," he said looking at her.

"Oh," said Brieanne realizing the magnitude of his situation. "You should have said something to them at your house. You should have made them feel uncomfortable at the school. You should have done something."

"Maybe I should have, but in my mind I had all that I needed, my written offer for the department head position, which was better than any reference letter, and my resignation letter."

"Did you believe that was the first time she cheated?"

"I did, at first," he replied. "But when I think back, I'm not so sure. I would catch them talking alone and coming out of his office late at night. She would make up reasons and tell me I was jumping to conclusions." He stared at Brieanne. "That I didn't know the whole story, that what I heard or seen was taken out of context, so I believed her."

Brieanne quickly realized what he was insinuating. "Oh, so you think I'm like your slutty ex-girlfriend!"

"I don't know what to think anymore," said Aidan quietly.

"You should have told me about this. We could have talked about it and worked it out," said Brieanne.

"Oh, that's hilarious coming from you," said Aidan. "The person who kept quiet about wanting the kids and running around with Eric. When did you ever consider talking to me about those things? You weren't honest, open, or upfront with me about them…instead, you lied to me."

"Well, at least I'm not a coward," she said glaring back at him. "You should have woken those people up and thrown them bare-ass out of your house you should have stood up for me and took my side with the children. Even if Bella didn't give them to me at least we would have failed trying together," she sobbed. "Get out of my house! Get out of my house next door! Get out of my life!" she screamed.

Aidan walked out the front door and turned around. "Now you have no kids, no me, congratulations."

"Leave me alone! I hate you! I hate you! I hate you!" she yelled walking over and slamming it shut.

Chapter 43

Brieanne picked up her phone and dialed a number. "Mom, me, and Aidan had a huge fight. I kicked him out and told him I never want to see him again and that I hate him," she said crying.

"I'm on my way."

Fifteen minutes later her mom walked into the house frantically looking for her and eventually found her sobbing on her bed. Her mom lay next to her and held her till she stopped.

"Why don't you wash your face and come downstairs. I will make you a nice cup of hot tea and we can talk about it," she suggested.

Brieanne nodded okay, went into the bathroom, and looked at herself in the mirror. He was right she had no kids and no Aidan. She was about to start to cry again but contained herself, washed her face, and went downstairs.

"Here you go dear," said her mom passing her a cup of tea. "Why don't you start from the beginning?"

Brieanne told her how nice the morning started right through till she threw him out, stopping several times to cry.

"Brieanne, don't you think you should have told him about Jen and Ben sooner?"

"I do now," she replied sharply.

Her mom studied her. "Don't you think you may be asking a lot out of him in such a short period of time?"

"What do you mean?"

"Well, you said it yourself. Your plans were to go sightseeing, visit Canandaigua Lake, and go to the New York State Fair. To me, that sounds like a young couple enjoying their time together, not really planning too far in advance, and just wanting to enjoy themselves."

"That's what it was and that's what we wanted."

"Then I'm confused. Why do you want to throw children into the mix?" asked her mom inquisitively. "They are a lot of responsibility and can take up a lot of your free time."

"I don't know, I'm confused," she said looking at her mom. "I love him so much and I also want to give those kids a good life. They've been through so much and them living with strangers breaks my heart."

"They're not exactly strangers," suggested her mom, "their family, and a young couple with children who will probably love them as much as you do, don't you think?"

"Maybe,' said Brieanne.

"When I first started waitressing in Vegas, your father and I used to work together all the time, just to be with each other. After we started dating, we only ever wanted to be with one another, and children were the furthest things from our minds. Even after we got married, we knew we wanted children eventually, but there was no rush."

Brieanne was silent.

"I remember when I started selling my pies, I went in the odd shifts just to be with him, and at home during the day he would talk with me and make me laugh while I made them. When I heard about you and Aidan working together fixing up that house up, and how much fun you were having, it reminded me of your father and I."

"It did?"

"You were fixing up your new house, just the two of you talking and laughing, just like we did," said her mom with a gentle smile and playing with Brieanne's hair. "You need those days before you move to the next step."

"I know, and it was a lot of fun," she admitted, managing a grin, then thought for a moment. "I had this vision of me, Aidan, Jen, and Ben, being a family, and all living together here. It totally surprised me the way he reacted."

"Not me!" said her mom bluntly.

"What?" asked Brieanne unsure what she heard.

"It's a perfect normal reaction," she replied. "You are dating a man whom you are making plans to go sightseeing with and on a vacation, then you drop two children in front of him and say, 'oh by the way these are now mine take it or leave it.'"

"I didn't make it sound like that," she said defensively.

"I think you did, and I believe you put him in a difficult position to choose, which was very unfair of you."

"Choose between what?"

"Either you with two children or no you," she stated. "You weren't a single mother when he met you."

"Oh boy," she sighed, "that was his point."

"If you would have told him about the children and what may happen. He probably would have supported the idea, and if not, you could have decided then who was more important Aidan or the children. Now, you have no children, and no Aidan."

Brieanne burst into tears. "That's the last thing he said to me," she sobbed. "Why are you taking his side?"

Her mom held her. "There are no sides for me to take," she said, "and Brieanne, if you thought you were right, you would never have phoned me in the first place."

"I know," said Brieanne wiping her tears. "I messed up."

"Unintentionally," said her mother, "and that Eric, sometimes he can be an idiot."

"He is an idiot," confirmed Brieanne. "I should have told Aidan about Eric's issue with him straight away; I just didn't want to lose Aidan."

"I know," said her mom holding her.

"His whole family witnessed me making a scene, I'm so embarrassed."

"There, there, I'm sure they have forgotten all about that," whispered her mom, thinking momentarily. "I'm going to let you in on a parents' secret."

"What secret?" she asked curiously looking up at her.

"Well, we all hoped one day you two would be get married and have a family."

"You, Dad, and Aidan's parents, hoped that?"

"We not only hoped it, but we also thought it was just a matter of time," she said giving Brieanne a thoughtful look. "Why do you think we moved back here?'

"Really?"

"And another secret, which they were going to tell you both tomorrow, Aidan's parents are also moving here. We all thought this is where our grandchildren were going to be."

Brieanne held back her tears. "I blew it Mom!"

"No, my dear, you didn't. You thought the children were going to be here for another school year. You and Aidan would date, get engaged and married, and somewhere along the way Jen and Ben would assimilate into your lives."

"That's exactly what I thought," she stated. "I didn't expect Bella to move so soon, and with Jen and Ben."

"Life is like that, it throws a curve at you that you don't see coming, and you have to deal with it one way or another. Unfortunately, sometimes you deal with it in the wrong way."

"You mean like I did," Brieanne said sadly.

"No, honey, like you both did," she replied. "You aren't totally at fault for wanting to take those children, to raise them, and take care of them. That's the kind of person you are. Your father and I are very proud of you, and those children, would be blessed to have you in their life."

"Thanks, Mom," said Brieanne, then remembered something Aidan had said. "Do you think I'm selfish?"

"In what way dear?"

"Aidan said that I would never move from here and live with him. He claimed that everyone else had to make sacrifices for me. That him, Ben, and Jen needed to live here, while I was sacrificing nothing. I told him he never mentioned me moving away with him before, so he asked me if I would."

"And what did you say?"

"I said I didn't know and that he was being unfair putting me on the spot."

"Sounds like you were both putting each other on the spot," suggested her mother.

"We were."

"In Aidan's eyes, he may see what you did as being selfish because you never included him, and he took that as you doing what you wanted to do."

"I guess," replied Brieanne.

Her mom let go and looked at her. "You two were on a path leading to love and happiness, but now you have come to a fork in the road, and your paths are going in slightly different directions. What you need to do is find the path you both can agree on and follow it together. That's where you will find true love and happiness."

"I should have talked to him instead of yelling at him."

"That probably would have been a good idea," said her mom, "but when things in life through us off balance, we sometimes forget the simple things, like talking and listening."

"Do you think I'm not sacrificing anything, and I am asking everyone else to?"

Her mom thought for a moment. "During your life as a couple, sometimes you have to make sacrifices. The only important thing to remember is that when you do sacrifice something, the end results greatly outweigh the original sacrifice. If it does, then to me, it's not a sacrifice but a life-choice. In the event that the results do not meet or exceed the original sacrifice, then it can become a negative, a burden, and potentially strain the relationship."

"What do you do if they don't meet or exceed?"

"Then you talk about it, fix it, and move on," she said simply. "Life isn't always going to be easy, but when you both love one another, what's important is that you always find a way to get through it together."

"Do you know when you and Dad talk to me like this, you remind me of Aidan?" said Brieanne.

"That's probably one of the reasons why you like him so much."

"It is," said Brieanne thinking of him.

"Is your answer still, 'I don't know'?"

"What?" asked Brie.

"Would you move to be with him?"

"I can't see my life without him being in it, so yes, I would if that is what it takes."

"Okay," said her mom. "Now, what are you going to do about all of this mess, as you put it?"

"Going to do about it?" she asked bewildered. "Mom, I told him I hated him and kicked him out, not only from here, but next door, too."

Her mom held her hands. "Close your eyes and look into your heart, honey," she said softly.

Brieanne did.

"What do you want most in your life?"

"I want Aidan," she said immediately, smiling as she thought of him.

"What about Jen and Ben?"

"They will be fine, they have a loving family," she replied. "Aidan comes first."

"Then I will ask you again. What are you going to do about it?"

Brieanne opened her eyes. "I need to find him and talk to him."

"It's as simple as that."

"What happens if he doesn't want to talk to me?"

"Brieanne, you love Aidan with all your heart, and he loves you with all of his. Trust me, he will want to speak to you as well, and once you start talking, you both will figure everything out."

"He's probably at his parents," she said thinking out loud. "Should I go over there now, maybe tonight?"

"Why don't you give him some time to talk with them, maybe drop by there tomorrow?"

"Do you think he is telling them everything?"

"I'm sure he is, you told me everything," she pointed out, "and knowing them, I'm sure they are telling him the person he needs to talk to is you."

"I'll wait till tomorrow morning," said Brieanne with a smile. "Thanks, Mom."

"That's what moms are for," she said holding her. "Now, you go get a shower, I will make us a lovely dinner, and we can talk about happier things."

Brieanne left, jumped in the shower, and got dressed. She was happy knowing she was going to talk with Aidan tomorrow. He needed to know what she wanted most in this world was him, that he was the man who had her heart, the man she wanted to spend the rest of her life with, and the man she would move anywhere for.

Chapter 44

Aidan left Brieanne's house walked over to his place, packed his bags, and left. Twenty minutes later he knocked on the condo door.

"Aidan," said his mother surprised to see him as she watched him pick up his bags and walk inside. "What's wrong? What's happened?"

Aidan said nothing and walked into his bedroom, placed the bags on the floor, and sat on the edge of the bed with his head in his hands.

"Is everything okay, son?" asked his father standing in the doorway.

Aidan shook his head.

"Do you want to talk about it?"

"I'll be out in a few minutes," replied Aidan.

Five minutes later Aidan went into the living room where his parents, aunt, and uncle, were sitting chatting. They stopped when he entered the room. Aidan sat with them and told them what had happened.

"Surely, you don't believe she is having an affair with Eric?" asked his mom.

"No, I don't, I just don't like the secrecy."

"Maybe she was doing that to protect you," continued his mom.

"What do you mean?"

"Sometimes people hide things from the ones they love to protect them. Maybe she thought it may hurt you or jeopardize your relationship with her. You said it yourself, when you first met Eric, he wasn't too fond of local girls dating tourists. And with what happened with her last boyfriend, maybe he thought he was helping Brieanne out by trying to persuade her to stay away from you. Obviously, Brieanne didn't to listen to him or want to get you involved in it, so she protected you from that nonsense."

"Maybe," said Aidan seeing his mom's point.

"Seems to me that you two spent a lot of time together talking and getting to know one another," said his dad. "Yet, when something like this happens, you go after one another rather than talking it through."

"I guess it was sprung on us, and our emotions took over, and everything we were hiding surfaced," said Aidan.

"By the way, I think she was right," said his dad. "You should have, as she put it, 'thrown them bare-ass out of your house.'"

"I told you, I wanted to get the offer first, and I didn't want me making a scene to affect that in any way."

"I understand that part," explained his father, "and I didn't necessarily mean the day you caught them together. I was referring to sometime after you got your offer and before you boarded the plane to come here. You should have dealt with that, instead, you ran away from it."

Aidan didn't like hearing the truth. "You're right, I should have said something before I left." Then he thought about something else Brieanne said. "Do you think I'm running away now?"

"Depends?" said his father.

"On what?"

"On why you are leaving," replied his dad. "Do you love her?"

"Yes."

"Is there anyone else you could see yourself with?"

"No."

"Well, then yes, you are running away," stated his dad.

"You are not going to solve these problems sitting here talking to us," said his mom. "You two need to talk, tell one another what you want, and how you feel. Find some common ground, work through it, and move forward."

"I know," agreed Aidan, "it's just that the children and her not telling me."

"Is it the children, or her not telling you?" asked his mother.

"I guess both."

"Maybe she should have told you," said his mom, "but she didn't know Bella was going to move with the children so suddenly. It obviously forced Brieanne to open up and reveal what she was thinking and wanted much sooner. If they weren't moving, she would have had a whole school year to let you know what was on her mind, and may have even told you a lot sooner, probably before she promoted Bev and Cathy."

"I guess," said Aidan.

"You two have only been together for a short period of time, did you really expect her to come straight out and tell you?"

"I guess not."

"And do you really think she tricked you into moving into her new place and tutoring Ben?" asked his mother.

"No."

"Why did you think she wanted you next door?"

Aidan was silent.

"Brieanne wanted you and her to be as close to one another as possible."

"I know."

"And look how well that worked out for you. You both fixed up her house together, you helped a young child with his spelling and reading, and most importantly you fell in love." His mom squeezed his hand. "Aidan, you must know this girl is deeply in love with you."

"The way she looks at you, talks with you, and acts around you. Her affection for you is second to none," added Amy. "The last thing Brieanne would ever want to do is intentionally hurt you in anyway."

Aidan was starting to feel very uneasy about the way he had acted and talked to her.

"If you had met Brieanne and those two children were hers, would you love her any less than you do today?" asked his mom.

Aidan shook his head no.

"Then, the question you need to ask yourself is, whether you are going to walk away from her forever or support and stand by her? And if comes down to it, Jen, and Ben, also?" asked his mom.

Aidan was quiet.

"Son, it's easy for us to see things clearly sitting over her. We know when you met Brieanne, you were two single people enjoying each other's company, and wanting to spend as much time together as possible. All couples want that, and they take that time to get to know one another and grow. Only, sometimes life isn't so straight and narrow. It thrusts things upon us that define who we are and who we want to be. For you this is one of those times," said his dad sitting up. "You need to decide if you want Brieanne, and possibly Jen and Ben, because Bella may change her mind and ask Brieanne to take them, or do you want to move on and find someone else?"

"I want Brieanne, I love her," replied Aidan, "without her I'll be miserable."

"Then, what are you going to do about it?" asked his father.

Aidan knew. "I need to go over to her place and talk with her."

"You do," agreed his dad.

"Why don't you wait till the morning? Give you both sometime to simmer down," suggested his mom.

"I will," replied Aidan looking at them, "thanks," and was about to stand up.

"Hold on," said his dad. "We need to tell you something and now will probably be as good a time as any."

"Okay," said Aidan relaxing.

"This condo," began his father, "your mother and I, Amy, and Bill, bought it together. We didn't want to say anything to you and Jane at the time because we had only been thinking about moving here. We were unsure about leaving you and Jane, but with you thinking about moving, and Jane needing a bigger place, we've decided that we are."

"That's great news," said Aidan happy for them. "When?"

"Jane is going to rent her place and start living in our house in September. She is also going to oversee renting out Bill and Amy's house. We gave her a list of things we wanted packed and shipped; mostly clothes, family pictures, and such."

"So, you're not going home, you're just staying here?"

"We will probably need to go back end of August to take care of some financially and personal things that will be more like a vacation."

Aidan noticed that his mom was getting upset. "What's the matter?"

His mom wiped the tears from her eyes and looked over at him. "We all thought you would be moving here, too. Settle down with Brieanne, maybe have grandchildren, and only be a short walk away," his mother confessed. "We even talked about it with Brieanne's parents. Do you know that was one of the main reasons they moved back?"

"No, I didn't," said Aidan.

"Not to put any additional pressure on you and Brieanne," his uncle joked.

Aidan gave him a smile.

"Aidan, it was only one of the reasons why we, and her parents, were moving here," reiterated his mom. "There is no pressure on you two whatsoever. You two decide what's best for the both of you, not us."

"We will," said Aidan walking over and giving her a hug, then went to his room and lay on his bed. He knew what he had to do and would tell her tomorrow.

After her mom left Brieanne went upstairs and got her clothes ready for the morning. She remembered she had bought lipstick and tried it on. Liking what she saw in the mirror she decided to wear it for Aidan tomorrow. Brieanne suddenly heard someone knocking at the front door. Aidan thought excitedly, and quickly ran downstairs and opened it. "Eric!"

Chapter 45

One Week Earlier: Wednesday, August 5

Aidan placed his bags against the wall and knocked on Brieanne's door.

"Hold on," said a male voice inside. The door unlocked and opened. "Aidan, come in," said Eric wearing boxers.

Aidan followed Eric into the living room and stopped.

Eric turned around. "I'm putting on a pot of coffee. Do you want a cup?"

Aidan looked at the coffee table. It had two wine glasses, an empty wine bottle, and several empty cans of beer.

Eric followed his gaze. "We had a few drinks last night and had a little bit of a party," he explained.

Aidan looked over at a pair of small black panties on the floor next to the couch.

"Oops, sorry about that!" he said walking over and picking them up. "We got a little carried away."

Aidan was silent.

"Brie just stepped into the shower, she should be down soon," he said. "Do you want that coffee?"

"Eh, no thanks," he replied in shock.

"Are you feeling okay?" asked Eric. "You look a little pale."

"Yeah, I'm fine," he replied. "I just came by to drop off these keys. I'll leave them on the table," he said going over to one in the foyer and placing them on it. "I have to go."

"Okay, dude," said Eric, "later."

Aidan closed the door behind him, picked up his bags, and walked onto the sidewalk out of sight.

Brieanne came down the stairs forty-five minutes later and went out onto the deck.

"I hope you don't mind me swimming my boxers?" asked Eric.

"No," said Brie in a hurry, "I have to go, I will be back soon." She went back inside, she heard Eric calling after her, ignored him and left.

Theresa opened the door. "Brieanne!" she said surprised. "Come in."

Brieanne stepped inside. "Can you let Aidan know I am here?"

Theresa looked at her oddly. "He's not here, he left about an hour ago to go talk with you, and he had his bags with him," she said confused. "Maybe he went for a walk first or to your new house to drop off his bags?"

"Maybe," said Brieanne, "I should go, he may be looking for me." Brieanne left knocked on the door to her new place there was no answer. She decided to check to see if his bags were inside and went home to get the spare keys. When she opened the door, she noticed Aidan's set on the table. Brieanne picked them up and headed for the kitchen.

"Brie is that you?" asked Eric meeting her by the stairs.

She lifted up the keys. "These were on the table."

Eric looked at them. "Yeah, Aidan dropped them off."

"While I was gone?"

"No, while you were showering."

"What did he say?"

"Not much, just that he was dropping the keys off and had to go."

"Did you say something to him?" she asked in a loud voice.

"No," he replied. "Wait, I did. I asked him if he wanted a coffee, he refused."

"What's going on?" asked Stacy coming down the stairs and rubbing her eyes.

"That's what I am trying to find out," said Brie turning away from Stacy and looking at Eric. "Did you answer the door in your boxers?"

"Yeah," said Eric not understanding what the big deal was.

"Okay," said Brie calming down. "Tell me what happened and what was said word for word."

Eric told her.

"Did you mention Stacy's name at all? That they were here panties?"

"No." said Eric still not catching on.

"You, big dummy," said Stacy coming down the stairs and shoving him against the wall.

"What?" exclaimed Eric.

"Aidan thinks you partied with Brie last night. That they were her panties you picked up off the floor, that you slept with her, and that she was upstairs cleaning herself off in the shower."

"Oh shit!" said Eric.

Stacy was going to give him an earful, but when she heard Brie weeping on the couch she went over and held her instead. "Why don't you try call him, tell him to come back, we can explain everything to him."

Brie called his number twice. "It says his phone is no longer in service," she said with a confused look.

"Maybe he's next door?" suggested Stacy.

Brie stood to go check.

"He's not there," confirmed Eric, "after I put the coffee on. I was cleaning off the table. I heard a car outside and looked through the window, it was Larry's taxi. Aidan threw his bags in the trunk, got in, and they drove away."

Brie picked up her phone and called Larry.

"Larry the Taximan, how can I help?"

"Larry, it's Brie."

"Hey, Brie, do you need a ride?"

"No," she said quickly. "Is Aidan with you?"

"No, I dropped him off at the airport about thirty minutes ago."

"Did he say where he was going?"

"No, but we talked about Boston a lot, asked me if I have ever been there and I said—"

"Okay, thanks," she said hanging up and standing. "I need to go speak to his parents." She went into the powder wiped her eyes and came out. "Make yourself breakfast, I will be back later."

Theresa opened the door and let Brieanne in.

"Have you heard from Aidan?" she asked.

"He called us about twenty minutes ago from the airport," said Theresa upset. "He said he was getting on a plane."

"Did he say where he was going?"

"No, and we can't contact him. He said he was throwing out his phone's SIM card and getting a new phone number."

"That would explain the no service message when I called."

"Aidan said he wanted some time alone and would contact us soon with his new number," said Theresa worried. "What happened?"

"What's going on?" asked Paul looking at their distraught faces. "Let's not stand in the foyer, come into the living room, and have a seat."

Brieanne told them what her and her mom had spoken about, then Theresa and Paul revealed their conversation with Aidan. Brieanne explained to them what happened last night at her place with Eric and Stacy, and this morning with Aidan.

"Oh dear!" said Theresa looking at Paul.

"It's obviously a misunderstanding on his part," said Paul comforting Brieanne.

"I know, but now he thinks I have been lying to him about Eric, just like his ex-girlfriend did. And even if that isn't the case, I'm sure he thinks I was having a good time drinking and partying with Eric," she said getting upset. "I wish I would have told him about Eric, about Jen and Ben, all of it."

"Dear," said Theresa, "you can't beat yourself up about that. You did what you thought was right at the time."

"When we make decisions in the past and look back at them wishing we had done something differently, they're called mistakes. We all make them," said Paul. "Realizing both of you made a mistake is the first step, rectifying them is the second, and not making them again is the third.

Aidan and you both are at the rectifying stage. And the fact that you love one another means that you will both forgive, forget, and move on," said Paul reassuring her.

"How can we rectify them if I don't even know where he is?"

"Be patient and have faith," said Theresa holding her hand. "He knows you can't find him, he will have to find you, and he will."

"Do you think so?" she asked unsure.

"You have his heart," said Theresa, "He'll be back."

As she slowly walked home Brieanne had a terrible feeling in the pit of her stomach that she was never going to see Aidan again. She wondered where he was and how much he was hurting. Entering the house, she quietly went upstairs, and lay on the bed. Stacy came into the room, lay next to her, and asked what was going on. Brie told her as Stacy held her and listened. She knew Brie had probably heard enough advice over these last two days and didn't need anymore. When Brie woke up, she was alone.

Stacy came out of the bathroom. "Did I wake you when I got up?"

"I don't think so," she replied.

"I have to go to work and Eric has a charter this afternoon," she said. "Bev is on her way over, the only thing I said to her is that you and Aidan had a fight, and you were upset," she explained, sitting on the edge of the bed.

"Thanks."

"Eric feels awful."

"What happened this morning is not entirely his fault," said Brie sympathetically. "Let him know, okay?"

"I will," she said. "Besides, I already gave him an earful after you left. He's been warned to stay out of your life, or me and you, will be out of his forever."

Brie gave her a half smile.

Hearing them leave Brie went downstairs. She was making a sandwich when Bev showed up and made one for her. They ate in silence, then went into the family room, where Brie brought her up to speed.

"What are you going to do?" asked Bev.

"What can I do?"

"Can you ask his parents for his Gmail?"

"No, he told them he needed time and would contact them when he was ready. I don't want to put them in an awkward position."

"What about Facebook?"

"He doesn't have a page because he's a teacher and he doesn't want students looking it up."

"Makes sense," said Bev. "So, what then?"

"There's nothing I can do," she said starting to cry. "I messed it up for me and him. It's all my fault."

"It's no one's fault," said Bev, "just a misfortunate serious of events."

Bev kept Brie distracted for the afternoon, when she left, Cathy showed up with dinner. As they ate, she told her what had happened. After, they watched several movies in Brie's room, before they both fell asleep.

Aidan landed at the Greater Rochester International Airport, rented a car, and booked a room downtown. He made two calls then went out for one drink. When he came back, he phoned Jane, and the following day drove to his parents' place where his sister and her family were staying.

"Hello," he called out as he walked into the house.

"Uncle Aidan," shouted Ethan and Maddy as they hugged him.

"Aidan," said Steven, shaking his hand. "Jane is out on a girls' lunch date. She called and said she will be home in a few minutes…Oh, here she is now," he said hearing the door opening.

"Aidan," said Jane hugging and kissing him, "I'm sorry I'm late."

"You're not, I just arrived," he replied.

"I am going to take these two to the park, then get some ice cream," said Steven, giving them time alone.

They said goodbye then Aidan followed Jane into the kitchen where she made him some lunch and poured them each a glass of wine. After they finished eating, he told her everything.

"Do you honestly believe that after you two argued, she invited Eric over, partied with him then slept with him?"

"It's a stretch I know."

"There's more to that story than you know," she surmised. "Why didn't you stick around and ask her?"

"I don't know. I was planning on leaving anyway. I guess I just didn't want to deal with that and the lies."

"So, you think she is lying to you about Eric?"

"I don't know," he said confused, "Probably not. I just don't appreciate bumping into him all the time and having to look for answers to what I see."

"I can understand how that can be annoying, she really has to put a stop to that, but you still have to ask her the questions and hear her answers, there's no getting around it. Unless you want to continue making up your own answers, like you are now, that aren't true."

"You don't believe she would?"

"Are you really asking me that question!" said Kate offended. "Of course not. If I know Brieanne she has been sobbing uncontrollably, gone over to the condo looking for you, and called you nonstop." Kate stopped and looked at him. "She has called you?"

Aidan felt ashamed.

"What?" asked Jane sensing he had done something she wasn't going to like.

"I threw away the SIM card for my phone, bought another one, and got a new phone number."

"Aidan," she said disappointedly, "that poor girl!"

"I know, I know. I was upset, hurt, and I reacted."

"I understand," she said sympathetically. "You don't think she slept with him?"

"No."

"And you believe she needs to put an end to this secrecy, right?"

"Yes."

"So, why are you here talking to me? It sounds like you need to be talking with her."

"I know," he said hesitantly.

"There's something else," said his sister. "What is it?"

"I just don't know if I'm ready to be a dad."

"Ready or want to be one?"

"Ready to be one."

"You don't have a problem being one?"

"With Bella everything was happening so fast my head was spinning. After speaking with Mom and Dad, and having time to think about it, I don't."

"No couple is ever ready to be a mom or dad. You're in hospital, giving birth, and a few days later the three of you are at home figuring it all out for the first time. If you have good parents, like we do, then you can get some sound advice. But the child is always your responsibility, twenty-four seven," she explained. "In a nutshell Aidan, you will never be ready. Although I do believe you and Brieanne would be excellent parents."

"We both thought that," said Aidan recalling their conversation on the beach and the kiss she gave him.

"Jen and Ben think the world of you two, so do Maddy and Ethan," she said, then thought for a second. "I am going to tell you something that may help you out."

"Okay," said Aidan sipping his wine.

"When we were away and heard about Jen and Ben's parents both being deceased. Steven and I got to talking about what we would want for Maddy and Ethan if the same thing happened to us. We both agreed straight away on the one person we wanted to be their guardian, and raise them, that person was you."

Aidan smiled at her.

"Out of common courtesy we were planning on asking you first before we wrote our wills out. So, I am going to ask you now. Would you be Maddy and Ethan's guardian, their dad, if something were to happen to Steven and me?"

"Of course," said Aidan without hesitation.

Jane gave him a long look. "Say you are in Madeira Beach, prior to Bella moving, and you find out we had died. Maddy and Ethan would be moving down and living with you after the funeral. Would that be okay with you?"

"Yes," he said, "of course."

"What about Brieanne?" she asked.

He smiled at his sister. "You are very clever Jane," he said shaking his head. "What you are really asking me, is if she would embrace those children, support me, by at my side, and help me raise them, or take off?"

"Well?" she said proud of herself.

Aidan felt awful. "She would be there at my side without hesitation."

"Without a doubt she would be!" said Jane bluntly. "If you were married to Brieanne, Steven and I would be blessed, knowing that both of you would be taking care of our children."

"I messed up," said Aidan slowly, "it's all my fault."

"It's no one's fault," said Jane as she sipped her wine. "You two need to talk it through."

Aidan looked at her glass as she put it down and noticed the lipstick mark on the rim then looked at his.

"What is it?" she asked as he stared at her.

Aidan told her.

Chapter 46

The following morning Cathy left when Brieanne's mom arrived.

"How did you find out?" asked Brieanne.

"Theresa called and invited us over last night; she told us everything that happened. How are doing?"

"Not good, Mom," she said crying in her arms.

"There, there, "she said stroking her hair, "everything will be fine." She waited for her to calm down then led her into the kitchen.

"What's in the bags?"

"I thought we could bake some apple and blueberry pies," she said.

"Blueberry is Aidan's favorite," said Brieanne unpacking them, "and mine."

"I know that's why we will keep most of them here."

"Mom he is not coming back," she said disheartened.

"You need to give things time, dear," she said helping her set things up.

"Why hasn't he called me?"

"He probably has his reasons," she said looking over at her. "Besides, when you two do talk, don't you think it needs to be face to face?"

"It does. I just know he's hurting," she said feeling helpless, "and I want to hold him."

"I'm sure he feels the same way, too, Brieanne," she said reassuring her. "Now, let's not talk about that anymore and do some baking."

Brieanne and her mom baked all afternoon, stopping only once for lunch. Her dad came over with dinner, and they ate at the kitchen table. Afterwards they went for a walk along the beach. He told Brieanne when she was a little girl she used to run around and chase the birds and write her name in the sand. His stories were a good distraction for Brieanne, but when the sun started to set, she asked if they could go home to watch a movie. They stayed over and left after an early breakfast to give her some space and time alone.

Brieanne watched them drive away and suddenly realized this was the first time she had been on her own since he had left that morning in the taxi. She went into her bedroom, closed the curtains, put on his T-shirt, and slid under the sheets. An hour later she woke up to the sound of men on her street, peering outside she noticed a moving truck outside Jen and Ben's house. She got dressed and went outside to investigate.

"Hi, there," she said.

"Good morning Ms.," said one of the movers.

"Are you moving someone in or out?"

"We are moving someone out," he replied. "The previous owner gave us a list of items she wanted packed and delivered to her."

"Previous owner?"

"Yes, Ms., the house is sold. We need to have this stuff out by this afternoon so the new owners can move in."

Brieanne went back into the house and phoned Joyce.

"Hi, Brie," said Joyce. "How are you doing?"

"Fine," she replied. "Did you know the house two doors down for me sold?"

"Yes, I do," she replied. "I sold it."

"Why didn't you let me know it was on the market?"

"Dear, I thought you did know?"

"Why would you think that?"

"Because Bella said that she got my name from you."

Brie thought back, and then remembered when she was giving Bella and the kids a tour of her new house, Bella asking who the real estate person was that she used. "How come you didn't call me? I would have outbid whoever bought it?"

"Actually, the house wasn't supposed to go on the market till today. Someone called yesterday and made an offer, I contacted Bella, and she accepted," said Joyce. "It was an incredible offer, and she was extremely happy knowing that a family will be living there."

"Okay, thanks," said Brie hanging up and phoning Bella.

"Hello, Bella, this is Brie," she said trying to stay calm.

"Hello, Brie, how are you?"

"Why didn't you tell me when you were selling the house or call me so I could have put an offer on it, too?" she asked omitting the small talk.

"I think by me selling it to another person, I did what I thought was best for you, Jen, and Ben."

"What does that even mean?" asked Brie with attitude.

"It means that when the children come to visit you, you won't be telling them that you bought their place and dangle it over their heads. The person I sold it to have the best intentions for that place and said that a family will be living there," she explained.

"I would never do that," said Brie, "dangle it over their heads."

"Like I said, what I have done is what's best for you, Jen and Ben," she repeated.

"Will you stop saying that? You know nothing about what's best for me and those children!" yelled Brie. "You stupid, old hag!" and hung up.

Brieanne cried going up the stairs, putting on his T-shirt, and sliding under the sheets. She got up at dinner time, made a bowl of cereal, and ate it in bed while watching a romantic love story. Brieanne wasn't sure if she could get through one, but she did, and liking the happy ending she watched another, then another, till she fell asleep.

The next day around lunchtime she was getting ice cream, was about to go upstairs, when she heard men again out on her street again. She looked out her window, witnessed a different moving truck, changed, and went outside.

"Someone moving in?" she asked,

"Well, the furniture is," replied the mover.

"Do you know who they are?"

"No, ma'am," he replied.

"Do you know where they are from?"

"No, ma'am," he replied, "although the truck driver sounded like he was from North Carolina."

North Carolina, she thought. "Okay, thanks."

Brieanne went up the stairs, put on his T-shirt, and slid under the sheet. She got up at dinner time, made a bowl of cereal and ate in bed, while watching romantic movies with happy endings till she eventually fell asleep.

For the next two days, wearing only his T-shirt and with the curtains drawn, Brieanne did the same routine: ice cream for lunch, cereal for dinner in bed, while watching romantic movies with happy endings. She refused to see anyone, talk to anyone on the phone, go to work, or even watch the sunset; she was heartbroken.

Chapter 47

Present Day: Tuesday, August 11th

By the third day Brieanne was going stir crazy. She had tried her best not to give up hope, be patient, and have faith he would come back to her. Only each day felt like an eternity, and it was one day more he was away, and less likely to return. There were too many memories of him and her in this house, and for her own sanity, she needed to escape from them. After dinner she took a shower, put on shorts, and a top. Then grabbed her beach bag and placed a bottle of wine, a plastic cup, beach blanket, and towel inside it before heading to the beach. She set up her blanket, poured some wine, waited for the sunset, and thought about Aidan.

She knew she had lost him forever and the only person she could blame was herself. He was never coming back, and deep down she couldn't blame him; it was all her fault. The facts of what had happened, she would have to live with for the rest of her sad and lonely life, and the reasons why, would haunt her forever. It had been seven days since he had walked out of her life, and to this very second, sitting alone, waiting, her hope was quickly fading.

Since she could remember she loved coming down to the beach, almost every day around the same time, never once believing it could get any better than the day before. Until she met him, Aidan, how happy he made her feel; she had never smiled and laughed so much in her life. And how handsome, strong, gentle, and kind he was, her list could go on and on, if it wasn't for the pain of her heart slowly breaking apart, piece by piece; and the tormenting reality that he was the only person who could ever put it back together. Even the wine she sipped couldn't numb the aching she felt deep in her chest; instead, it only allowed tears of hopelessness, despair, and regret to fill her eyes, and slowly roll down her lonely face. Suddenly, the laughter of a young family sitting close by disrupted her harrowing thoughts. A most welcome distraction she hoped, as she listened to them talk about their sandcastle.

"This is Mom and Dad's room here," said the young girl, "and mine is right down the hall from them with my own bathroom."

"My room is over here," said the boy, "right next to the drawbridge so I can keep guard."

"This can be our family room," said the father pointing to it.

"And this is our dining room," added the mother, "and here, the kitchen."

Brieanne observed the family placing colorful seashells around its perimeter and couldn't help but notice the big smiles on the young girl and boy's faces; how happy they were. She thought about Jen and Ben in Jacksonville, and wondered if they were also happy and smiling, deep down she hoped so, and needed to believe they were.

All this was too much for her heart to take; she broke down letting the tears stream down her face as she whispered over and over again, "What have I done? What have I done?" But she found no comfort in asking that question, because she knew exactly what she had done, and had very little hope of being able to redeem herself.

Brieanne watched as the family eventually left their solitary sandcastle to the fate of the wind, and sadly looked beyond it to the sun slowly setting in the distance. And she knew, just as sure as the sun would set this evening, Aidan was never coming back to her.

"I have a theory about a sandcastle in the wind," said a voice standing behind her.

She recognized it immediately, it was Aidan's.

"Would you like to hear it?"

Brieanne wiped the tears from her eyes and nodded her head yes.

"May I sit next to you?"

Yes, she nodded again, as she watched him from the corner of her eye sit on the blanket. "What is your theory?" she asked keeping her eyes forward as her heart raced.

"I believe the most important ingredient of a sandcastle, is the mixture of the sand. It needs to be strong, cohesive, and supportive."

"I see," she replied.

"And I would have to strongly disagree with someone's argument that the sandcastle gets built only once then gets stronger as the weeks, months, and years pass."

"Sounds like a viable hypothesis to me," she suggested.

"It is viable," he agreed, "but I feel it has vast room for improvement."

"Vast room for improvement," she said playfully. "Please, do tell."

"I believe every morning when the couple wakes up the sandcastle starts to build itself, one grain at a time. Eventually these grains start to make rooms of all different shapes and sizes within the sandcastle. Each of these rooms makes up one positive attribute of a relationship: love, affection, caring, trust, honesty and so on. That evening, when the couple falls asleep in each other's arms, the sandcastle disintegrates. The following morning when they wake, it starts to build itself again. Only this time, it remembers what rooms were built from the previous day and builds them slightly quicker. As every new morning passes, it builds these rooms faster and faster. Till it reaches the point, that as soon as the couple awakes, the structure of their sandcastle is already built. And as the days go by, only the rooms inside that sandcastle change in shape and size, and sometimes new ones are added."

"So what you are saying, is when the next morning starts the sandcastle is built based on the previous night, before it disintegrated?"

"I am."

"And each morning is the start of a brand-new day for the couple?"

"Yes."

"And each and every day, the positive attributes within the sandcastle continue to develop and grow, and new ones can be added over time?"

"Yes."

"So, in summation, they should live every day like it's their first; but continue to build on the previous one," she whispered.

"Yes," he whispered back.

"Then what is the wind?" she asked.

"The wind is life," he said.

"Life," she repeated, liking that thought.

"Life can change your sandcastle at any time. It can make it stronger, make it weaker, and sometimes blow it away. But more importantly, life can thrust things upon you that you weren't expecting and build negative rooms inside the sandcastle."

"Negative rooms," she repeated. "Are those the things that can hurt, ruin, or end a relationship?"

"They are."

"How do you get rid of those rooms?" she asked.

"The couple needs to remove them from the sandcastle," he replied.

"Is that why you are here now, because you want to help remove them out of our sandcastle, out of our relationship?"

"Yes," he said softly, "and I believe we can only accomplish that if we talk and listen, to one another."

She looked at him for the first time. "Are the talking and listening rooms still in our sandcastle?"

He sadly shook his head. "They used to be," he said honestly. "Unfortunately, we both got rid of them when we fought."

"Would you like to go find them and bring them back?" she asked.

"I would," he replied. "Do you?"

"I do," said Brieanne putting down her wine and standing. "Let's go for a walk on the beach, where we can talk and listen."

Aidan stood beside her.

As they strolled towards the shoreline, Brieanne glanced over at him, he needed to know. "I need to tell you about what you saw that morning with Eric, it wasn't what you thought. Eric and Stacy showed up at my place to return my Crockpot. I invited them in and had one glass of wine with Stacy then went to bed. The panties were Stacy's; she apparently flung them at Eric when she was going up the stairs to bed. I didn't sleep with him or party with them. I went to bed early because I wanted to come over see you in the morning, to talk."

"I know," he said, then corrected himself. "Well, I guessed that's what happened."

"You did?" she said wondering how.

"When I was visiting my sister, we were drinking a glass of wine, and I noticed her rim had lipstick on it and mine didn't. That morning at your place, both wine glasses had lipstick on them, I surmised Stacy was there, too…unless Eric has started to wear lipstick?" he joked.

Brieanne laughed for the first time in a long while and it felt good. "Your sister's?" she asked curiously. "Where did you go? Where have you been?"

"That morning I came to your house, I came to talk to you, and tell you about me leaving."

"You were planning on leaving me?" she said sadly.

"No, not leaving you," he said quickly noticing the change in her voice. "I needed to go to Rochester for a few days. I was hoping we could clear things up before I left and was planning on coming back."

"What did you go to Rochester for?"

"To do what I should have done before I arrived here," he confessed. "When I got there, I rented a car and got a hotel for the night. I called Carly up first, then her lover, and had them meet me at a bar downtown. Neither of them knew the other was going to be there. They were awkward and tried to play it off like they were surprised to see each other. I showed them the picture, told them when I took it, and watched them squirm in their chairs. Carly tried to explain to me what happened, I told her I wasn't interested, and was planning on breaking up with her anyway. Then I stood up and walked out with a big smile on my face."

"What made you go back and do that?"

"You," he said. "You were right. I should have confronted them long before I arrived here. So, taking your advice, that's what I did. Now I have closure and I'm much better off for it."

"I'm sorry I called you a coward," she said remorsefully.

"I'm glad you did it made me realize I couldn't run and hide from my past."

"When you were gone and I was in my house, everywhere I looked reminded me of you and all the great, fun memories we made. The bedroom, balcony, pool, hot tub, kitchen, my whole house, reminded me of you and of us," she explained. "It made me realize how much I missed you and how awful it must have been for you to be living in your home with those dreadful images of the two of them together. It couldn't have been easy?"

"It wasn't," he admitted. "Maybe coward was a harsh word," he said teasing her, "but it did get your point across and look what it made me do."

They walked quietly for a minute before Aidan stopped and turned to her.

"I'm sorry I didn't stand by you and support you when we spoke with Bella. I should have. I always said I would be at your side, hold you, and never let go. I let you and myself down."

"I'm sorry for not telling you about the children," she said glancing up at him, "and when Bella sprang that on us, I should have handled it much better. I should have just listened to what she had to say, not confronted her, and when she left discussed it in private with."

"I think we can both agree we handled that badly," suggested Aidan.

"I'm also sorry about not telling you about Eric, I should have. That day on the boardwalk, when he told me how he had spoken to you, I was furious, upset, and left the bar. He followed me out and we had words, unfortunately, in front of your family. The time outside my house, he was trying to tell me to tread lightly with you. My last boyfriend was a jerk, and Stacy and Eric were two of my friends who helped me get over it, and Eric didn't want to see me like that again. The last time, on the deck, he came over to apologize, and admit he was wrong about you," she said looking into his eyes. "I was protecting you, us, from his tourists dating locals' stance. I should have told you from the get-go what was going on, and we could have dealt with it together."

"I understand," said Aidan, "he was just watching out for you, and he didn't want to see you get hurt."

"Which are what friends do, but to a point," she clarified. "Me, and now Stacy, have told him in no uncertain terms, to stay out of my affairs."

"Oh, I'm just an affair?" kidded Aidan.

"No," said Brieanne giggling, "you know what I mean." She looked deep into his blue eyes. "What I'm sorriest about most, was saying I hated you, and telling you to leave," she confessed starting to get upset.

"We both said things we didn't mean," he said putting his arms around her.

Brieanne thought she would never see him again and here he was holding her closely. She wept on his shoulder and Aidan held till she stopped then wiped her eyes.

"I'm sorry for everything, I will never let you down again," promised Aidan. "I love you, Brieanne."

"I'm sorry, too, Aidan," replied Brieanne, "You are my life, my love, my soulmate." Brieanne needed to kiss him, and did, the way he liked to be kissed then gently pulled away. "I want to move with you to Boston and live there with you."

"What about Jen and Ben?" he asked.

"They will be fine and are with a family who will love and take care of them. They can always visit us, and we can visit them. You are my first and only priority. Without you, there can be no us."

Aidan smiled at her, gently caressed her face, and softly kissed her on the lips. "If you move to Boston, you will be living there on your own," he said matter-of-fact.

Brieanne pulled away, giving him a puzzled look.

"I'm moving here," he said.

"You are!" she said excitedly with a big smile. "When?"

"I already have," he replied.

"Yay!" she yelled quietly clapping her hands.

"But I will only stay here, on one condition?"

"Name it!" she said eagerly.

As the sunset on the horizon, Aidan dropped down on one knee asking, "Brieanne Byrne will you do me the honor of being my wife?" he asked, opening up the ring box.

Brieanne looked down at the 'Sunset for Two Lovers' ring. Then looked at him with tears of joy rolling down her cheeks, saying, "yes, yes, forever, yes!" as Aidan placed the ring on her finger then stood Brieanne kissed him passionately.

Then, arm in arm, the two lovers watched the sunset.

Chapter 48

Brieanne looked at the ring. "How on earth did you manage to get this from Harriett?"

"On Saturday, I contacted my parents, then yours and invited them to their condo that afternoon. I told them what I had been up to, said that I was going to ask you to marry me, and wanted to surprise you with this ring but wasn't sure how to go about asking Harriett. Your mother called Harriett and George, and they came over for dinner. I told them about me asking for your hand in marriage and asked if there was any way she would sell me the ring. Then her, and your mom, told me this story about the ring—"

"Wait, what story?" asked Brieanne looking at him.

"Well, we know the story up until that lady from New York wanted to buy it and she refused her because she didn't appreciate?"

"Yes," she replied quickly wanting him to continue.

"Well, when other people came in and told Harriett what they saw in the ring, it always paled in comparison to what you did. Every time your mom saw Harriett, she would tell her how much you talked about that ring and how much you loved it. Harriett finally realized the reason she couldn't sell the ring was because it could only belong to you, the person who truly saw it for what it was. So, Harriett and your mom made a secret agreement that the ring would only be sold to the right man; the man who wanted it to ask you for your hand in marriage."

"I thought Harriett loved that ring and would never sell it?" asked Brieanne.

"No, Harriett and your mom kept that ring safe for you, for this day. That's the reason she stopped letting people touch it, and only put it on display for a couple of hours, to protect it and keep it safe for you. That evening, Harriett had brought the ring with her. I bought it from her right there and then and hid it in a safe place."

"Harriett and my mom kept that ring all these years for me, for this day?"

"Yes."

"That makes it so much more special," she cooed. "And it was given to me by the man of my dreams," she said with a happy smile.

"Now it is safely on your finger, where it will stay forever."

"Forever," Brieanne repeated, "I like the sound of that." As she looked back at her ring then Aidan. "When are we going to get married?" she asked arriving at her blanket.

"I think you should decide."

As she packed the items into her bag, she glanced up, giving him a shy look.

"What?" he asked, "I know that look."

She stood up, strolled over to him saying, "I want to get married sooner than later."

"Me too."

"I want to get married this Saturday," Brieanne whispered.

Aidan looked at her beautiful smile and into her loving eyes. "Saturday it is," he said softly.

"Yay!" she yelled kissing him on the cheek. "That's only four days away, well five, including today."

As they started to walk back to her house, she spoke about the wedding day in great detail. She had been so busy talking; she hadn't noticed that they had walked off the beach onto her street and had just passed her home. "How does that sound?"

"That sounds perfect."

"We should make a list when we get in the house," she said noticing they had walked too far. "I guess I was talking too much," she stated with a giggle and turned around, while Aidan stood still, and stared at Jen and Ben's old house. Brieanne suddenly realizing he wasn't next to her came back and stood beside him. "Bella sold it to some family in North Carolina.

If I would have known I would have bought it and fixed it, like we did the last one," she said disappointed.

"Did you like doing that?" asked Aidan.

"I loved it," she said cheerfully. "We had so much fun."

Aidan smiled at her. Then held her hand, led her to the doorway, and gave her a key.

Brieanne took it from him. "No, you didn't!" she said anxiously putting it in, turning it, and unlocking the door.

"Consider it an engagement present," he said as they walked in.

"This is ours!" she said excitedly. "This furniture is yours?"

"Mine and whatever Bella left me."

"This your dining room set, it's beautiful," she said quickly looking around, knowing which pieces were his, and which ones Bella had left, "and this table?"

Aidan nodded yes. "I thought we could start working on it after our honeymoon."

Our honeymoon, thought Brieanne, as she strolled over and kissed him vehemently. She suddenly stopped and looked around. "How did you manage to get this place?"

"Last Thursday afternoon, I called Joyce telling her I wanted to put an offer in on the house. I gave her the specifics of the offer then asked her to contact Bella with the details. Bella agreed, we signed ownership over on Friday, and the house was mine by four."

"How did you know to call Joyce?"

"The day Bella left your place; I was talking to her on her driveway. She confirmed she was using Joyce and was putting it up for sale on Friday."

"Why didn't Bella tell me it was you that bought it when I called her on Friday morning?"

"I can only guess she wanted to wait till it was official."

"That makes sense," said Brieanne, and then looked over at Aidan embarrassed. "I called her a stupid old hag and hung up on her."

"Ouch!" said Aidan, "I guess I got off easy with just being called a coward."

"Oh, will you please stop it!" she said chuckling and shoving him lightheartedly. Brieanne happily realized they were quickly returning to the way they were before the fight. "The mover said the driver was from North Carolina, I assumed that's where the family was moving from?" she asked locking the door and starting for her place.

"The New York driver can't drive nonstop," explained Aidan, "so they had to change drivers in Raleigh, North Carolina to get it here on time."

"Oh," said Brieanne thinking. "Joyce and Bella also said a family was moving in?"

"Well, hopefully after we fix it up, we will rent it to a family on vacation," replied Aidan.

"You are something else," she said shaking her head. "Does that mean we are we going to live here?" asked Brieanne standing in front of her place.

"Do you want to?" he asked.

"Only if you do?"

"I do," he replied, "but after the wedding."

"Deal, and a lot of the furniture you have, I want to put in her," she said. "And what we take from this house we will put in our new place."

"I like the sound of that," said Aidan.

Brieanne went to unlock her door. "That's odd it's unlocked?"

"I knocked and no one answered so I used the spare key under the rock," he explained. "I came into your house, then out to the backyard, and spotted you on the beach."

"I guess I should find a new spot for that," she joked.

"Don't worry, I kept it," he replied with a grin.

"You did? That's very naughty," Brieanne whispered, moving close, and kissing him seductively. "I will have to discipline you when we get inside."

"Hey, not in front of the kids," he said opening the door.

"You're not a kid," she said laughing at him as she walked inside. "What made you…say…that?" asked Brieanne stopping in her tracks. "Jen! Ben!" she shouted looking at them standing in her living room.

"Brie," they gleefully shouted running towards her, hugging, and kissing her.

"What are you two doing here?"

They both walked Brie into the living room where another person was waiting around the corner.

"Bella!" said Brie surprised. "You too? What is going on?"

Bella pulled out a document from an envelope and handed it to her. "This document makes you the legal guardian of Jen and Ben, effective immediately."

"I don't believe it!" said Brie looking over at Aidan then down at the children's delighted faces and kissed them both. She was teary-eyed and speechless as she sat on the couch with Bella and the children. Aidan excused himself to give them some time alone.

"When I left here," started Bella, "I was unsure about Jen and Ben and if I was doing the right thing. I needed to sell the house, not only to make sure they were looked after financially, but to help me with my dire financial situation. I also knew that it was becoming more and more difficult for me to take care of them and maybe the children could live with my niece in Jacksonville. Only once we left, I saw how upset the children were, and how much they missed you. I decided to stay in Orlando to think through it for a while longer; I was at a loss. I was strongly considering not selling at all and coming back," she explained. "Then I received a call from Joyce with Aidan's offer and his request for me to contact him, which I did. He told me he would buy my house, help me put the money into trust funds for the children's education, and that I could keep the remainder to see me live a wonderfully comfortable life through to my dying days. He was extremely generous," she said holding back her tears. "Aidan then said he was moving back here, was going to ask to marry you, and if I would consider giving you guardianship of the children. He told me that Jen and Ben would never go without, as long as they had you, and that you were not only the best option for the children but the right one, whether you accepted his marriage proposal or not."

"You're saying, me getting the children was not solely based on us getting married?"

"No, not at all, it was based purely on you," Bella said. "I'm assuming you said yes."

"I did," said Brie, showing her and the children the ring.

"That is so beautiful," sighed Jen.

"That it is!" said Bella examining it. "It's truly magnificent."

"When are you getting married?" asked Jen.

"Saturday," said Brie.

"I can't wait!" said Ben merrily.

"Me neither," added Jen. "Are Ben, you, Aidan and I, all going to live here after?"

"Yes, we are."

"Yeah," shouted both of the children hugging and kissing her. Then agreed they needed to do the same to Aidan and went looking for him.

Smiling as she watched the children run off Brie turned to Bella. "So, what happened after the phone call with Aidan?" she asked, wanting to know the whole story. "Aidan flew to Orlando Friday lunchtime, picked us up, and we drove here. When we arrived, we signed the documents for the house, and then went to my lawyers to have him start writing up your guardianship papers. After, Aidan took us to the Madeira Bay Resort and got us a two-bedroom condo suite. Saturday morning, we went grocery shopping. Then he went to his parents, came back Sunday for lunch, and took Jen and Ben shopping for school supplies—"

"You reregistered them at their school?" asked Brie.

"I never told the school they were moving they were still enrolled," she explained.

Brie wondered why she hadn't but didn't concern herself too much about it; she was too overjoyed thinking about being their mom. "They went to school today?" she asked.

"Yes, Aidan dropped them off," she replied. "Later, we went back to the lawyers, picked up the document, then the children. We went to McDonald's, back to the resort to change, and then we all came here," explained Bella. "Aidan came into your place first. He called us saying you were down on the beach, and after he spoke with you, would bring you through the front door and for us to wait inside. We heard you outside, I told the children to be very quiet, and then you came in."

Brie looked at her reflectively. "When I called asking about your place selling, and you said you were doing what was best for me, Jen and Ben, you meant this?" said Brie holding up the papers.

"I did," she revealed joyfully. "Aidan had asked me not to tell you. He wanted it all to be a lovely surprise for you and I think he did a wonderful job."

"He definitely did," said Brie tearing up. "It's a surprise beyond my wildest dreams."

"I'm just so happy the way it all turned out Brie," said Bella, "I truly am."

Brie started to cry a little. "I feel so bad."

"Bad, about what, dear?" asked Bella.

"Because I called you a stupid, old hag."

"Oh, don't you be getting yourself all worked up over that. You were going through a tough time, and I know you didn't mean it," she said comforting her.

"Thank you," she said wiping her eyes, "I am so very sorry."

"I know you are," said Bella reassuring her. "It could have been worse?"

"How so?" asked Brie wondering.

"You could have called me a coward," said Bella straight-faced.

Brie gave her an, 'are you kidding me,' look. "Aidan told you to say that didn't he?"

"Yes, he did," said Bella with a laugh, "He said you would get a kick out of that; he's quite a funny guy."

"He's something all right," said Brie laughing at his sense of humor.

"Now, let's go find your future husband, and your children," said Bella putting her arm through Brie's.

Future husband, thought Brieanne, and children.

They went onto the deck, sat with him, and watched the children swimming. Brieanne glanced down and admired her ring. How beautiful it looked, how perfect it sat on her finger, and how perfect was the man who gave it to her. She looked over at Aidan and smiled at him.

"Where is my little angel?" shouted Brie's dad coming down the hallway followed by her mom, Aidan's parents, aunt, uncle, Harriett, and Gorge.

"Last surprise," said Aidan, "I invited them all over to celebrate."

"I love you!" she said adoringly. "And I thought our first formal date would be hard to beat!"

"We still have our wedding day!" he said reminding her.

"And our wedding night," she said giving him a suggestive wink.

Brieanne went inside, where they each took a turn hugging and congratulating her. Aidan came in after her, where their attention turned to him. Noticing the bottles of champagne on the counter Brieanne suddenly remembered something, slipped away, and came back holding their champagne flutes. "We can't forget these," she whispered to Aidan, kissing his cheek.

The champagne was poured and Brieanne's father made a toast to them. They sat outside where Aidan called his sister to tell her the good news after which Brieanne told them about their plans for their wedding. The group gave suggestions, and talked about things that needed to be done, which Brieanne happily wrote them down. Satisfied, she put the pencil and pad away. Then stood up, telling the children to say goodnight, before taking them upstairs to bed. After tucking them in, she told them she loved them, and kissed them both on the cheek before returning to the party. At midnight they all departed and Brieanne and Aidan walked out onto the deck where she sat on his lap and cuddled into him.

"Do you think Bella planned this?" she asked.

"How do you mean?"

"Well, she left abruptly, kept the children in Orlando, and never called the school to say they were leaving," she explained. "Do you think she was hoping that this would happen between us, and with Jen and Ben?"

"When you put it that way, I guess she may have given us a little push," said Aidan thinking about it some more. "What would she have done if this didn't happen?"

"Bella said she was thinking about not selling and coming back because she saw how upset the children were and how much they missed me. She also said she had decided to stay in Orlando to think it through because she was at a loss."

"Maybe it was more the financial issues that were worrying here?"

"I know that had a lot to do with it, she's a proud woman," said Brieanne, "and wouldn't take money. She would look at that as a handout."

"Now that you mention it, and I think back," he said. "I believe when she came over to talk to us, she expected us both to tell her to leave the children here with you, and that we would help her sell or even buy her place and come up with some financial arrangement with her."

"Like she did with you?" asked Brieanne.

"Exactly," said Aidan, then he remembered something Bella had said to him. "That day on her driveway, after she left your place, Bella said to me 'don't waste too much time on plans; at the end of the day actions are what matter.'"

"She wanted you us do something!" said Brieanne.

"Yes," replied Aidan now convinced. "Bella didn't want to go back to tell the children they were moving to Jacksonville. She wanted to go back and tell Jen and Ben they were moving in here."

"I believe that too!" said Brieanne looking at him. "When we had our…meltdown. She must have been in a panic because it had backfired on her. That's why she was at a loss."

"If I had just stood by you," said Aidan.

"No, if I had only told you, "said Brieanne.

"You're right," teased Aidan, "it's all your fault."

"Hey," she said snickering at his antics. "You are, and always will be, a filthy Scallywag," she said kissing him. "But you will always be my filthy Scallywag." She tenderly caressed his hair and face, whispering "take me upstairs and make love to me."

Brieanne straddled Aidan as he picked her up. He carried her into the bedroom, placed her on the bed, and gently lay on top of her. They passionately kissed, undressed, and took their time enjoying every sensational moment of their love making. As he held her, Brieanne snuggled into him, and for the first time in a week she slept soundly.

Chapter 49

The following morning Aidan came over, helped Brieanne make breakfast, and get the kids ready. They walked them into school then went to the office where Brieanne updated their address and guardian information. Then they spent the remainder of the week, with the help of family and friends, organizing their wedding day. With Brieanne's main focus being the wedding day and reception, while Aidan's was the wedding night and honeymoon.

The night before the wedding Jen and Maddy stayed with Brieanne, while Ben and Ethan stayed with Aidan. On the wedding day the girls went to the spa for a manicure, pedicure, and then the salon. While the boys swam, played PlayStation, showered, and got ready.

Thirty minutes before sunset, Aidan, wearing cotton pants and an open button shirt, and the boys wearing the same, went onto the beach and waited along with the fifty guests. Several minutes later, Jen and Maddy walked out of Brieanne's house wearing matching lilac summer dresses, followed by Brieanne, who was wearing a white, tight-fitting summer wedding dress. She was holding a white Calla Lily bouquet in one hand, and the other, was wrapped inside her father's arm. They slowly walked down the upper deck down onto the lower one, then onto the path, and down the beach. As they walked between the sitting guests, Brieanne and Aidan looked at one another, and smiled. She stopped next to him, her dad kissed her on the cheek, shook Aidan's hand, and the ceremony began. Twenty minutes later they were married.

The couple posed as the photographer and guests took photos of them along the shoreline. The last photo was of Brieanne and Aidan with the sun setting behind them, the same one they would frame and hang up on their living room wall.

Vegas Francisco's was closed for their reception. They had a three-course meal with wine, followed by champagne, toasts, and the cutting of the cake. Then everyone went down to the patio and circled Brieanne and Aidan as they danced to the first song they ever danced to together, 'Love Me Tender," by Elvis. After it ended the crowd clapped and cheered. The party started, and everyone danced the night away under the starry sky.

At midnight, Brieanne and Aidan said goodbye, and left for their wedding night. They arrived at the Treasure Island Beach Resort, checked in, and went up to their one-bedroom Gulf Front Suite. Aidan placed their bags on the floor, pulled out a bottle of champagne from one of them, and followed Brieanne out on the balcony.

"Look at this view, it's magnificent," she said.

"Breathtaking, just like you," he replied giving her a kiss.

As Aidan opened the champagne Brieanne quickly ran inside. "I almost forgot these at the reception," she said holding out the champagne flutes as Aidan poured.

"To my beautiful wife, Mrs. Brieanne Jones."

"To my handsome husband, Mr. Aidan Jones."

They kissed, touched glasses, and sipped their champagne.

"You remembered," Brieanne said.

"I did," he replied.

"So, my dream came true, I am here with my Princess Charming," she said thrilled, and realizing it wasn't so corny.

They finished the champagne, made love, and the following morning ordered breakfast to their suite and ate it in bed.

For the next three mornings they ordered delectable room service, swam in a pool surrounded by palm trees, then lay on light blue loungers under pretty matching umbrellas ordering specialty drinks and delightful lunches, before hitting the afternoon happy hour. In the evening, they dressed up and went down to the BRGR Kitchen & Bar and ate mouthwatering dinners inside the chic restaurant or outside on the picturesque terrace. After dinner, they sat on Adirondack chairs, beside the poolside fire pit, to watch the sunset and the stars appear one by one. When they returned to their suite they would go out onto their balcony, drink a glass of champagne, before going inside to make love.

Wednesday, after an early breakfast, they left the resort driving to The Don CeSar. There, they had a one-bedroom Gulf View King Suite with another spectacular view and spent the next four days regaling in room service, swimming in both pools, and ordering drinks and food from The Beachcomber Bar & Grill. They also had specialty drinks at The Rowe Bar, ate delicious meals at the Sea Porch Café, and exquisite dinners at the Maritana Grille before finishing the night off with a nightcap and live music in the Lobby Bar. And like every other evening, they would end their night with a glass of champagne and making love.

Saturday afternoon they left the hotel, drove to the Port of Tampa, and boarded the Carnival Paradise where they had a Grand Vista Suite with floor-to-ceiling windows and a large balcony. They departed Tampa for their five-day Western Caribbean cruise. On Sunday they had a fun day at sea, Monday they disembarked for the Grand Cayman, the next day they debarked at Cozumel, and Wednesday they had another fun day at sea before docking at the Port of Tampa on Thursday morning.

From there, they drove their car to the Tampa International Airport to pick up Jen and Ben from Aidan's parents. When they arrived, not only were his parents there, but his aunt, uncle, and Brieanne's parents, who informed them they were all coming with them on their twelve-day trip. They flew into Greater Rochester International Airport then drove to Canandaigua Lake. Brieanne, Aidan, Jen, Ben stayed with Jane and her family, while Brieanne and Aidan's parents stayed with Amy and Bill. Almost every day they went to the New York State Fair, and Jen and Ben finally got to see the Llama Limbo and Leaping Llamas competitions. While there, Brieanne and Aidan bought the four kids New York State Fair T-shirts, who turned around and bought them one.

On Labor Day afternoon they landed in Tampa, jumped in their car, and headed home. Within the hour they pulled into their driveway, unpacked their luggage, and put it in the foyer. Aidan turned around and noticed them standing outside, looking at a package by the front door, and went out to join them.

"There's a note on it for you Aidan," said Jen passing it to him.

Aidan opened it and read it out loud, "I put two hooks above the door, tested it, and it looks great. Congratulations, love, George and Harriett."

"What is it?" asked Brieanne.

"It's a present for all of us," he said. "Go ahead, rip off the brown wrapping," he said to the kids.

The kids ripped it off in no time and handed the item to Aidan.

"It's a burnt wood sign that I asked George to make to name our home," he explained as he reached above the doorway and hung it up.

"Sandcastle In The Wind," read Jen. "What does that mean?"

"Yeah, what does that mean?" asked Ben.

Brieanne crouched down close to them. "It means that the Sandcastle is us: our family, our love, and our support for one another. And the Wind, no matter how hard it blows, will never be strong enough to blow our Sandcastle away," she explained kissing each of them on the top of the head as she rose.

"I like that," said Jen.

"Me too," said Ben.

"Me three," said Aidan putting his arm around her. "Okay, Jen, Ben, grab that wrapping put it in the garbage, then go upstairs and put your swimsuits on."

Brieanne watched as they happily crumpled it up and ran inside. She turned to Aidan whispering, "I have a secret."

"You do," he said curiously.

Brieanne reached for his hand, placed it on her tummy, saying, "we are going to have a baby."

Aidan jumped for joy, put his arms around her, and kissed her. "When did you find out? How far along are you?"

"I took a test a few days ago. I wanted to wait till we got home, and tell you first, alone," she said beaming. "I'm somewhere between two to three weeks. If I had to guess, I would say somewhere between our wedding night and the first week of our honeymoon."

"That is amazing," he said with a big smile.

"You know that if it is a girl, I get to name it," she said, "and if it's a boy, you do."

"Okay," said Aidan, "Since you've had time to think, I'm guessing you already have a girl's name picked out?"

"I do," Brieanne said. "Sunset Jones!"

"Wow, I really like that name!" said Aidan.

"I know, isn't it great," she said excitedly. "Now, your turn, a boy's name."

Aidan thought for a few moments. "I got it!" he said smiling happily. "I'm afraid it may be better than yours."

"Okay," said Brieanne in anticipation. "What is it?"

"Scallywag Jones!"

Brieanne burst out laughing, as did Aidan.

"What?" he said. "I think that's a great name!"

"It is," she said smiling at him. "I love you Aidan Jones."

"I love you Brieanne Jones," he said, kissing her, and holding her in his arms.

"Maybe you should write a story about us?" she suggested.

"Maybe I will," replied Aidan lifting her up as she straddled him. Brieanne kissed him as he carried her inside their, 'Sandcastle In The Wind.'

About the Author

Kevin McGann lives in

the small, friendly town of Aurora,

Ontario, Canada.

You can contact him on his website:

www.kevinmcgannauthor.com

Or on Facebook:

Kevin McGann – Author

www.ingramcontent.com/pod-product-compliance
Lightning Source LLC
Chambersburg PA
CBHW020912110726
47900CB00001B/119